"This here's Liz Jo̶̶̶̶̶̶̶̶̶̶̶̶̶̶̶̶, the cameraman. "New reporter. She wants to do a stand-up in front of the house. She'll need the facts on the guy, you know, the regular stuff."

Liz flipped out her notebook, grateful to Eddie for pointing her in the right direction. "Maybe you could tell me his name, Detective Mason."

"No names, honey. Guy could blow himself away; then we'd have to hold his handle until the relatives were notified."

"But you . . . know . . . who he is?"

"Yeah. Some nut case, flipped for real this time. He took the woman and kids at eleven A.M from an apartment on East Horton. Now he's hunkered down in this ole house here with a couple rifles and lots of ammo. That's about it."

Liz nodded and scanned her illegible notes, trying desperately to work the chaotic facts into a sensible sentence or two. Why did everything she came up with sound like an excerpt from a 1930s *Police Gazette*? There was no time to polish it; Mason was positioning her against the fender of a police car, a hand on her shoulder, and enjoying it, and Fast Eddie was living up to his name, crouched, camera ready on his shoulder, waiting for Liz to begin . . .

THE EXCLUSIVE

Also by Carole Nelson Douglas
Published by Ballantine Books:

EXILES OF THE RYNTH

SIX OF SWORDS

THE EXCLUSIVE

Carole Nelson Douglas

BALLANTINE BOOKS • NEW YORK

Library of Congress Catalog Card Number: 85-91210

ISBN 0-345-31993-1

Manufactured in the United States of America

First Edition: March 1986

For Elaine Knox-Wagner,
who always knew
only the brave are free,
and for all the newswomen, past, present, and future,
who must fight for their rightful places
in broadcast journalism.

DOROTHY = ZACK JORDAN
B 1912 D. 1951 B. 1908 D. 1986

LIZ JORDAN
B. 1950 -

Special thanks and gratitude to veteran broadcast journalist Marcia Fluer of WCCO-TV in Minneapolis, Minnesota, for sharing the routine of her busy workday life and for insight into the professional pressure cooker of television news reporting, and to WCCO-TV assistant news director David Nimmer.

Part I

Margaret, are you grieving
Over Goldengrove unleaving?
Leaves, like the things of man, you
With your fresh thoughts care for, can you?
Ah! as the heart grows older
It will come to such sights colder
By and by, nor spare a sigh
Though worlds of wanwood leafmeal lie;
And yet you will weep and know why.

—GERARD MANLEY HOPKINS

— *Chapter 1* —

The men made ready to lower the remains of Zachariah Jordan into the hard, overturned November earth. The casket was oaken and had been chosen by some miracle of delicately unspoken mutual deferral by Jordan's surviving wife and his only daughter. The Reverend Walker's words—first in the small Episcopal church and now here at the bleak cemetery, where the fierce fall wind drove them back down his throat—were pure, rolling King James.

Zachariah Jordan would have scoffed as the entire population, seemingly, of Turtle Bend strained to hear the funeral oratory. He hadn't held with funerals.

Liz Jordan stood beside her stepmother, Myrtle, feeling as wooden as the waxed and gleaming coffin, letting the sound, the surrounding silence, the wind and the words, roll indifferently off her own slickly impervious façade. Her presence caused a constant, explanatory buzz that tainted the funeral's solemnity. It wasn't her fault, but inquisitive youngsters had to be hissingly informed that, yes, the woman in navy by the casket was *the* Liz Jordan— hadn't they known that her father was *their* Mr. Jordan?

Only three days before, Zach Jordan had been seventy-eight and still on his aching feet, white shirt-sleeves rolled up, green eyeshade pulled down, emanating an aroma of ink and an aura of hayseed, even though ink had evaporated years before from weekly newspaper life and Zach Jordan had been no nearer a haystack in his life than he could help.

The newspaper. That's what they talked about in this tiny town tucked into rolling Wisconsin backcountry. Zach's newspaper. Thanks to fifty-two years of Zach Jordan's blood, sweat, and invective, the *Turtle Bend Sentinel* was an obscurely famous journalistic icon. Even sophisticated big-city dailies subscribed, almost reverentially. People like Ben Bradlee of the *Washington Post* and Watergate fame hailed the *Sentinel* as the standard of one-man editorship, small-town gadfly journalism, and writing as short, simple, and sharp as a watchdog's bark.

Liz had ultimately found that assessment patronizing, but Turtle Bend still busted its buttons at this notoriety, and her father had long before learned to live up to his own legend. Now he had

3

died, and the legend and the man had been consigned to cold type and black-bordered obituaries on editorial pages the country over.

The high-sounding words ended at last, leaving the whistling wind with the final melancholy say. It whipped sere, rasping leaves across the dead grass as strangers filed by, clasping Myrtle's hands, leaning too close to voice comforting clichés. Few addressed Liz, though the eyes of all acknowledged her. They knew who she was.

I wish to hell I did, Liz thought wryly. It was sobering to lose your only remaining kin, especially if he was the energetic father you had adored since you were old enough to recognize him. Now, standing by his coffin as the last mourners straggled back to their parked cars strung along the long, straight cemetery road, Liz wondered what they'd think if they knew where her rather public life was heading.

She had meant to tell her father what she was planning to do, but then Myrtle had called, and it was too late to tell Zach Jordan anything. Even good-bye.

Liz was the last to leave. She rarely had the luxury of attending a funeral in full. Usually, as the minister's last words were being intoned, she stood in front of the departed and the departing, a tiny metal boutonniere of microphone discreetly clipped to a lapel, face sober, voice steady as she described the life and death of— well, there had been Bill Stewart, the network TV reporter slain in Nicaragua in the seventies, her first. Later, when assigned to Washington, Liz had played electronic Greek chorus at the deaths of a half-dozen contemporary heroes; her assignment editors said she was particularly sensitive to death, whatever the hell that meant. But they were always men, those whose funerals merited lights, action, and network camera, it occurred to her now as she stood a mere silent witness at her own father's interment. Not even Golda Meir had received full media honors.

Now, though, Liz could have her own, private last word. She stared at the shiny coffin, never having anticipated this moment. Her father had seemed immortal—always there, always would be. There were so many ways to sum up a life, and he had been a giant in his small, lifelong community. Liz searched for a last word, distressed that tears weren't storming her eyelashes, that her throat was calm and open. She could have done a beautifully modulated one-minute stand-up in a single take, perfectly professional.

How to sum up? She had known what Zach Jordan had been to Turtle Bend, and a wider world. But what had he been to her?

Liz studied the polished wood, seeing the murky reflection of her respectfully dark-clad figure, seeing beneath it to her father's waxen face frozen into a tinted Byzantine icon of itself by the undertaker's icy art.

She shook her head, bewildered. The word that came to her mind surprised her, and shamed her a bit, but it was there, whistling through her mind like the wind, soft and insistent.

It was simply—daddy. Daddy.

— *Chapter 2* —

"Hold the presses, Lloyd!"

Z. J. Jordan stormed into the second-floor composing room, loops of oatmeal-colored copy paper flapping in his hand.

"I've got a blistering editorial on the Soviet invasion of Hungary to replace the one on Halloween pranks." He stopped in his tracks, an effect akin to a steam engine halting on a dime. "Say, what's the termite doing here?"

Lizzie's dark, serious eyes peeked over the composing table rim. She'd never seen her father like this. She'd always known he was big, a towering, white-shirted force that intervened at critical moments of her life—like holding her hand when she stood in line outside the redbrick schoolhouse to begin first grade. But now, in motion, bellowing, he was truly awesome. She couldn't have answered her father's question to save her six-year-old soul. What was she doing here? Something awfully wrong, maybe.

Lloyd, a gray-haired printer whose heart was pure melting Milky Way inside the crisp outer wrapper, as Lizzie had seen that afternoon, was not afraid to answer.

"It's an awful long walk home alone for a six-year-old, Zach. This was closer. And cool down; I'll get your damn editorial in as soon as I finish something important for Lizzie."

Lloyd clenched his teeth on the soggy cigar that functioned like an always-present irreverent tongue, circled it disdainfully in Z.J.'s direction, then looked down at Lizzie and winked.

In a minute he had pressed a big proof sheet over the tray of leaded type. "There we are." Lloyd squatted down. "How d'you like it?"

"It looks nice. I'm going to learn to read in school; Miss Mather said so. And to write my name. Read it to me, Lloyd, please!"

"Let's see. It says: 'by Elizabeth Jordan.'"

"In seventy-two-point type?" Z.J. had come to peer down at

the new proof of yesterday's front page with Lizzie's name in inch-high type replacing the regular headline. "Ain't that a little over-important, Lloyd?" he joked.

"Who's to say what's more important: you writing an editorial on some commie tomfoolery over in Hungary or Lizzie here learning what her name looks like in print." Lloyd stood with a crotchety creak of his knees. "All right. Give me your blamed sermonizing, Zach. I'll get it set, though why you think the folks of Turtle Bend give a toot what you think of Hungary is beyond me."

Lizzie giggled. She'd never heard anyone talk back to her father before, and basked in secondhand courage.

Z.J. caught and tweaked one of her brown shoulder-length braids, woven each morning by the neighbor lady. "What're you laughing at, sprout? If you give me any trouble, I'll throw you to the Linotype machine."

"Oh, Daddy . . ."

But her eyes widened as she followed him to the machine in question. The Linotype machine had fascinated Lizzie since her first toddler's visit to her father's newspaper. It was a giant version of the typewriter Z.J. kept at home, a big black, hunkering metal monster that rattled and howled like the five-o'clock freight train, loud enough to wake the dead. Z.J. called it the newsman's pipe organ, and Lloyd's gnarled, ink-stained hands pounding the over-size keys did look like the church organist's as they moved rhythmically, punching Z.J.'s words into type just as they had banged out Lizzie's name only minutes before. E-liz-a-beth Jordan. Lizzie stared over Lloyd's shoulder, ignoring the rank cigar smoke, the clamor, watching with Z.J. until the story was set.

As Lloyd spun away from the Linotype, finished, Lizzie's observant eyes fastened on the plastic apron that covered his clothes.

"I thought only ladies wore aprons," she said.

Lloyd and Z.J. exchanged an amused glance.

"This is a *man's* apron, Lizzie. There's a difference," said Lloyd.

"What?"

Z.J.'s laugh was more a wheeze as he waited for Lloyd to answer.

"Mine's, uh, tougher. This is really tough plastic, kid." Lloyd was stomping away, and even Lizzie had sense enough to let the matter lie.

Z.J.'s hand, as big and ink-smudged as Lloyd's, descended to her slender shoulder.

"All right, sprout. What're you doing here? You're supposed to go home to Mrs. Swenson's."

"That's not home, Daddy. And, and . . . I'm not sure I know the way. Yet."

He led her up the narrow backstairs to his third-floor office. Turtle Bend wasn't a large town and the *Sentinel* wasn't a high-circulation paper, but Zachariah Jordan figured an editor and publisher wasn't worth his title unless he had an office at the top.

"You can't come here, honey. I'm working. It's important stuff, and I can't be worrying about where you are after school. Don't you like Mrs. Swenson anymore?"

Lizzie perched on the golden oak armchair, her dangling legs as narrow as the spindles that fenced in the chair's back. Her face had already lost its babyish curves, and early maturity staked its claim in her sharp, restless eyes, relentlessly curious upturned nose, and serious chin. She put a braid tip in her mouth, then jerked it away as she remembered the habit was discouraged. There was so much she couldn't do, it seemed, since she had started first grade.

Lizzie sighed gustily. "Oh, I don't know, Daddy. It seems like such a long time before you come home. And Mrs. Swenson is no fun. All she ever tells me to do is make Mr. Potato Head. I'm too old for that."

"But not old enough to find your way home after school." Z.J. sighed in his turn, a muted, half-denied adult sigh. He studied his young daughter. He was a widower in his late forties who found himself perpetually perplexed by the bright but oddly alien workings of the little mind behind the big dark eyes. "You look like your mother," he said abruptly. "Like you're always expecting something."

"I do?" Z.J. seldom mentioned her mother, who had died soon after Lizzie's birth. It made Lizzie feel guilty. And curious. Mostly curious. "What did she look like, Daddy? Tell me, please!"

"I'll do better than that." Z.J. was standing, rolling down his white shirt-sleeves, donning his suitcoat. He leaned cajolingly nearer. "I'll show you a picture; how'd you like that?"

"Oh, yes." Lizzie was standing, too, prancing from foot to foot.

"But first we go over to Mrs. Swenson's like we're supposed to."

"Oh, Daddy . . ."

She ran to his side to take his hand, something Z.J. felt uncomfortable doing. His little Lizzie seemed so fragile, so small and quick. He feared something would break.

Father and daughter walked down the three flights of stairs to the street. Turtle Bend was beginning to bustle with late-afternoon foot traffic, but the October sunshine felt warm and welcome enough to encourage pausing.

"Afternoon, Mr. Jordan. My, your little girl's growing. Lizzie, is it? Such a well-behaved child."

Lizzie fidgeted, anxious to get home now. But her hand remained wrapped in his, she squirming from the end of it like a minnow out of water while they talked, talked, talked. She wondered if grownups knew how boring it was to wait and listen while everybody talked above your head.

At last they left the downtown area, with its magical rows of three-story-high brick buildings, some of them turreted, and were climbing the Main Street hill to the residential sections above. Z.J. walked to work. The automobile was the curse of the walking class, he used to say, although he kept a snazzy red-and-gray Nash in the garage for state occasions like parades and rare trips to bigger cities downriver. Lizzie liked walking, and promised herself never to step on a sidewalk crack the whole way home, a genuine challenge, given the age and condition of Turtle Bend's sidewalk squares.

Z.J. glanced at his daughter's intent, downcast head and breathed secret relief. He could talk about any international political situation, but carrying on a conversation with his six-year-old daughter seemed a dangerous and uneasy occupation.

Their street was a line of neat, 1940s bungalows, all painted white with black or green trim. Had an owner produced shutters of another color, the house would have stood out sorely, which was why nobody did. Nobody wanted to stand out in small towns, not in 1956.

Mrs. Swenson was waiting at her green screen door. She lived alone, had grown children somewhere far away, and cooked dinner for the two of them every night. She wore flowered aprons and lace-up shoes and had curly white hair and glasses. Lizzie thought it would be appropriate for her father and Mrs. Swenson to marry someday, but apparently nobody else did.

"Oh, there she is! I called the *Sentinel*, but you'd gone. I was so worried, Mr. Jordan."

Everybody except Lloyd called her father "Mr. Jordan." Lizzie guessed that was because he was an important man.

"The sprout just took a detour home, Mrs. Swenson." Z.J. swung his hand loose.

"Now you go play," Mrs. Swenson told her. Lizzie obediently went into the front bedroom that nobody slept in and pulled out the box with her dress-up doll. Through the open door she could hear the grownups talking on. About her. About why she hadn't come straight to Mrs. Swenson's as arranged.

"You are bad," she told the small, dark-haired doll. "Naughty, naughty. No supper tonight."

Beyond the door, the voices lowered. Lizzie listened harder.

". . . not much to occupy her, Mr. Jordan. She's a smart little girl. . . . Maybe—well, she has no brother or sister, and there aren't that many young ones in the neighborhood right now. Maybe you should try . . ."

The voices sank even lower, as they always did at the good parts. Lizzie gave up eavesdropping and concentrated on working a pink organdy apron over her doll's pink-and-black checked taffeta dress. When grownups didn't want you to hear something, they were generally smart enough to make sure you didn't. Someday, Lizzie promised herself and the doll, she would learn to write her name—and to hear everything.

Mrs. Swenson took Lizzie around for Halloween that year. Lizzie went as a witch and got to wear the green lipstick that Mrs. Swenson had found at Dexter's Drug Store down on Main Street and a pointed hat stuffed with cotton batting.

Nineteen fifty-six was a banner goodies year: carameled apples, corn candy, jawbreakers by the dozen, Tootsie Rolls, and even some cookies, which crumbled by the time Lizzie and her bulging pillowcase got home. Everywhere they went, Lizzie was asked into strange living rooms lit by warm circles of lamplight and quizzed. "Whose little girl are you? Oh, Zachariah Jordan's daughter. My, you've gotten big. How'd you like a nice juicy carameled apple?" Come, bite! Lizzie thought. She'd seen Snow White. "You're very welcome. Such a polite little girl. Have fun, now." Lizzie could never understand how people could have fun on command.

Of course, the candy was taken away from her and parceled out piece by piece, but that didn't matter. Her real treat that Halloween wasn't the candy, but the photograph of her mother that her father had managed to find.

"Well, here it is." He awkwardly elevated a dull golden frame. "She had it taken a few months before you were born. I don't know what got into her; hadn't had a picture taken for years. Oh, snapshots, of course, around here somewhere, but nothing formal."

Z.J. finally gave it to Lizzie, who sat on the sofa with the photograph covering her lap like a TV tray. Her mother's hair was funny, all puffy on top, and she was wearing big round earrings. She looked happy.

"What do you think?" Z.J. sounded like he really wanted to know.

Lizzie bit her lip, another bad habit, she'd been told. She didn't know how to say what she thought, didn't know what she thought yet.

"Can we . . . can we put it up?" She held it out, looking toward the mantelpiece opposite them, where Christmas cards thronged annually and where Z.J. kept a roll of Life Savers that only he was tall enough to dole out as special treats.

He frowned. His hair had grayed at the temples; his stomach had long since given up the ghost of youthful leanness. He felt silly confronting an image from a past long gone. Lizzie sensed his hesitation, and waited. Then he took the frame and turned his back on her as he carried it to the mantel.

When he stepped away, the photograph was propped there on its cardboard support. Z.J. waited for Lizzie's reaction.

"That's nice, Daddy. Just right."

That Christmas Z.J. and Mrs. Swenson went to extra lengths getting the house decorated. The Christmas tree was moved nearer the front door than the fireplace. That was because, Mrs. Swenson said, Santa had written to say that he had a special present for Lizzie that year, and it would take a lot of room.

She hoped for a bike, a real two-wheeled bike like the big kids rode, even though she knew she was too young for one yet. Mrs. Swenson and her father didn't seem to believe that she was getting too old for Miss Frances and *Ding Dong School* on the television set—and tricycles. But Lizzie just knew she was getting a bike and hardly slept all Christmas Eve night. At least she'd get up first and find out what Santa had left her.

But she didn't. Z.J. was up first anyway, as he was every Christmas, and so was Mrs. Swenson. The tree was surrounded by gaily wrapped packages, most of them for Lizzie. They didn't have a lot of relatives, for some reason. Among the presents was a big basket; her father and Mrs. Swenson kept looking at it and trying not to smile, so Lizzie went to it first.

The basket barked. Lizzie jumped backward and the grownups finally let themselves laugh.

"Open it, honey. Come on."

A bright-eyed, foxy face popped out, black nose snuffling noisily. The rest of the dog followed—brown-spotted, short-haired white body, spindly legs, and a pointed tail that was beating so hard it hit Lizzie over and over on the leg.

"Is it . . . mine?"

"Sure is."

"My puppy?" It was beginning to dawn on her.

"Well, not exactly a puppy." Z.J. was beaming down on Lizzie and the dog, watching it bathe her amazed face with an equally amazing length of pink tongue. "It'd be kind of hard for us to housebreak a puppy. But he's only a year old, and smart, they said. Whatcha gonna call him?"

"Oh . . . oh—" The dog darted off her lap and began trotting around the room, sniffing the perimeters. He spun and ran for the forest of wooden chair legs under the dining room table. "Whizzy!" she decided. "He's fast! His name is Whizzy."

Mrs. Swenson rolled her eyes. "I hope not, at least not on the rug. That was the whole idea of getting a grown one."

"Whizzy and Lizzie, huh?" Her father chuckled. "Sounds, er, good to me. Sounds like quite a team."

"Oh, yes. Thank you, Daddy, thank you!" She hurled herself to his lap.

Z.J. glanced at Mrs. Swenson. "Thank Santa, honey."

"Well . . ." Lizzie sighed and rolled a braid around her fingertip. "I hate to tell you, Daddy, but I don't really believe in Santa anymore. I just pretend to 'cuz you like it."

"Not believe in Santa? Where'd you get such an idea?"

"At school. None of the kids do. Only little kids do. Babies and stuff."

"I see," said her father, patting her on the back. "Maybe you should let Whizzy out. He's pretty excited. Then we'll see if we have something to feed him, and you can open the rest of your presents."

Whizzy was eager to go out, and etched mad circles in the snow while Lizzie stood behind the glass storm door, watching. He was a fox terrier, Mrs. Swenson had said, and had a pedigree. Lizzie didn't know what a pedigree was. She just knew that she got an important, warm feeling watching him run, that she was proud of him and pleased with herself for being a girl whose daddy would get her such a nice dog. He must love her very much, she thought, and she would love him back just as much, forever.

— *Chapter 3* —

"When did this one die, the one with the lamb?"

"Geez, I don't know."

The childish voices whispered, because they really weren't supposed to be here, in the small graveyard behind St. Clement's Episcopal Church, among the headstones. But they were fourth-graders; they often were where they weren't supposed to be and proud of it.

"I don't know. 'Born September twelfth, 1898. Died May thirty-first, 1901.' Get Lizzie Jordan; she's good with numbers."

"She's down by the river with Whizzy."

"Dumb dog. Dumb name. Call her anyway."

Lizzie came, a little breathless, Whizzy making circles around her legs. He had never grown in the three years she'd had him, and never slowed down. She, however, had grown taller, and thinner, and even more serious.

"Three years old," Lizzie said immediately when asked to read the headstone. "Can't you subtract at all, Larry Schultz?"

"That eighteen-hundred stuff threw me. Besides, at least I don't have a dumb dog named 'Whizzy.'"

"I bet even Whizzy could figure out that date," Lizzie retorted, flushing. She knew now that "Whizzy" was an embarrassing name, but felt it unfair to change it on him after all this time.

It was spring, with school soon to close, and youngsters were restless and trouble-prone. They loved to trespass on the church-yard, passing through the lych-gate, a small roofed stone structure just large enough to shelter a bier for a body about to be interred. In its vaguely medieval shape they saw a forbidden playhouse equally at home in the imagination as a wishing well or a castle turret.

In the cemetery itself elaborate headstones held all the veiled mystery for nine-year-olds that Easter Island figures offered archaeologists.

The monuments were magical—white marble angels atop plinths; sprawling pink-gray marble headstones stepped like pyramids about to erupt into a volcanic overflow of fanciful carving; simple old tombstones bespeaking a poorer, frontier population, with oval inset photographs of the dead gazing in calm sepia-tone

12

resignation on the curious children; plain half-overgrown head-stones illustrated with lambs, marking the deaths of those uncomfortably like themselves—children.

"Where's your mother's grave, Lizzie?" one of the children demanded. Lizzie was the only one in her class without a mother, and it bestowed a certain doleful glamour. She led them to the spot easily, to a waist-high slab of gray marble that read "Jordan" at the top and "Dorothy Marie" below it.

"How old was she, Lizzie? Read the dates."

"She knows already," Larry Schultz objected.

But Lizzie didn't; somehow she'd always ignored the dates.

"September third, 1912, to May twenty-eighth, 1951. She was . . . thirty-nine."

"Wow. That's old." The other children chimed awed agreement to Larry's pronouncement.

Thirty-nine. A whole thirty years older than Lizzie. Why did grownups always get so hushed and sad when talking about her mother and say she had died young? The other kids were rambling past other headstones, laughing at funny names, arguing loudly whether the markers were at the foot or the head of the bodies beneath, sinking into the soft spring turf and pretending that the hands of the dead were yearning upward to grab them by the ankles. . . .

Lizzie whistled to Whizzy and they angled away from the others, across the cemetery and over the low, ornamental wrought-iron fence—the dog slipped through it—and back down to the nearby riverbank, to the bend where turtles sunned on midflow rocks, a place that had inspired the town's name.

She sat on the warm bank and threw stones to the waterline for Whizzy to retrieve. The dog was always lively, coming back with the wet stones in his perpetually smiling mouth, his eyes eager. Lizzie brushed back the straight dark hair that framed her small, intelligent face. Her eyes were as dark and eager as the dog's, but shadowed with contemplation. It was a look that disconcerted her father and various teachers.

But Lizzie knew she was different from the other kids, partly by the facts of her mother being dead, of being an only child, of having a locally famous father, the editor of the town's only news-paper. There was another reason, but Lizzie hadn't figured it out yet.

"What do you suppose it is, Whizzy?" she asked the small dog as he sat before her, panting amiably. "I think Daddy knows; he knows everything. Maybe he'll tell me someday."

Someday was not that evening, when Z.J. got home for Mrs. Swenson's Saturday-night supper of pancakes with apple butter and syrup. Mrs. Swenson's dinners were timed to Z.J.'s work schedule, which included Saturdays. Often on weeknights he didn't come home until six or seven o'clock, and Lizzie's homework couldn't occupy all that free time after school. But she had Whizzy, she would tell herself when she felt lonely.

"Daddy?" Lizzie asked after downing the first four pancakes.

"Hmmm?" Her father was reading the fine print of a foreign journal that came every Friday.

"Is there anything else of my mother's in the house besides the photograph?"

Z.J. looked up, his eyes startled over the metal frames of his bifocals. His hair was mostly white now, but Lizzie knew he'd never marry Mrs. Swenson, even if their hair matched. She was too old for him, over sixty; anyone could see that. He'd never marry anyone, she told herself, because he mourned her mother and was devoted to her memory and rearing Lizzie.

"Let's see now," Z.J. began, trying hard, though he didn't know why. "The china in the cabinet here. And the blue glass vase, I guess. And some pillowcases and such in the linen closet. We got married a long time ago, honey. It's hard to remember. What do you want to know for?"

"I don't know. Just wondered."

Lizzie did a lot of "wondering" lately. Z.J. shifted in his chair, which creaked under the burden of his slowly increasing girth.

"I know! The little rag rug in your bedroom. She made that for you, before you were born."

"The rug by my bed, the one that Whizzy sleeps on, really?" Liz jumped up and ran to look at it, Whizzy at her heels.

It was a humble rug, faded from washings but now suddenly bright with importance. Lizzie studied the shape of a lamb and a duck worked into the multicolored circus of fabrics.

"My mother made that," she mused to the dog. "And now you sleep on it. You're a lucky dog, Whizzy, to sleep on something handmade." The dog's tail beat the rug in happy agreement, his head cocked to hear every word.

"Maybe someday I'll make a rug, too. It must be hard, harder than geography." Lizzie looked to the small blond desk in the corner with its pole lamp standing alongside it like a pike. It was Saturday and she didn't have to do homework, but her daddy liked her to get good grades. Maybe her mother was watching from somewhere and was proud, too. She'd have to study hard for her mother and daddy, she told herself, and she'd have to work hard to make it up to Daddy that her mother was under the gray stone in the graveyard and not at home with Z.J. and Lizzie and Whizzy like she belonged.

* * *

"I don't understand it, Lizzie. I've never gotten a whisper of complaint about your behavior before."

Liz pulled up her knee-highs and twisted her feet together with studied twelve-year-old nonchalance, intently studying the bright copper coins decorating her scuffed penny loafers.

She sat on the dusty rose bouclé sofa in the living room. Above her father's shoulder her mother's portrait beamed overoptimistically.

"What were you and Candy Turner doing on Mrs. Nightwine's property anyway? She was very upset. You're too old for childish pranks like this."

"But not old enough to come home for lunch alone from school!" she put in, bringing up an old argument.

Z.J. paced; it was how he thought out column ideas in his *Sentinel* office, ranging back and forth like a big white polar bear. But he wasn't at work now, and he wasn't trying to phrase a column on the Bay of Pigs or Jackie Kennedy's wardrobe. He was trying to make sense of the first negative call he'd ever had about his twelve-year-old daughter.

"We're not talking about your lunch plans," he responded. "We're talking about Mrs. Nightwine calling to say that you and another girl were lurking in her lilacs after dark, trying to peek in her windows! Now, what were you two up to?"

"Nothing."

Z.J.'s eyebrows, which had grown bushier as they grew whiter, lowered ominously.

Liz sighed. "It sounds silly, but we were trying to get a story."

"A *story*?"

"About the strange house in the woods on the hill and Mrs. Nightwine. You know hardly anybody ever sees her, Dad, and that's a real big old house. We thought we'd do a . . . a feature on it to give people an idea of what it's like inside. But when we knocked and asked nicely, she . . . sent us away."

"A story? For what?"

"For . . . the *Turtle Bend Dispatch*. It's this little, uh, newspaper I wanted to mimeograph and give out. We . . . I thought Mrs. Nightwine would be a good story. And she is! Did you know there are stone *lions* at the end of the driveway near her house? And it's a real pretty house, Dad, with these diamond windowpanes and white pillars on either side of the front door. All the kids go to the woods around her house all the time, especially the boys. I don't see why Candy and I can't be there to get a story."

Z.J. sat down on his brand-new green vinyl La-Z-Boy that commanded a full quarter of the doll-size living room. As his girth expanded from age and sedentary living, so did his urge to put his feet up.

"Paper, huh? What is this paper?"

Liz ran to her bedroom. Whizzy, who'd sat with ears lowered throughout the conversation, followed her with the quick click of nails over the hall's hardwood floor. They were both back in a jiffy, Liz opening a red folder for her father's perusal.

"See, Dad? There's the masthead, and this is the front-page layout. I thought I'd lead off with a story on the new pizza place coming to Laurel Street. It's for kids at school, about things kids would want to know. Grade-schoolers don't have a school paper. And Mrs. Nightwine is something kids have always wanted to know about."

Z.J. studied the pages. "How're you gonna print it?"

"Type it, and mimeograph it."

He grunted. "And distribute it?"

"Candy and I will do it in the lunchroom."

"Well, it looks . . . good, Elizabeth." He'd taken to calling her Elizabeth lately, although at school she was known as Liz exclusively now. "But Mrs. Nightwine's privacy must be respected; you know that. You'll have to confine yourself to covering willing subjects in the future."

"But you said that investigative reporting was the noblest form of journalism. I know you did!"

"In the real world, Elizabeth. Not in some twelve-year-old's imagination."

Liz's eyes dropped to the folder in her father's lap. Putting the little 8½-by-11-inch paper together had been a lot of work, and now suddenly it seemed useless. She felt foolish, as she sometimes did when she called Whizzy by the silly name she'd given him as a dumb six-year-old. She'd thought she was smarter now.

Her father shut the red folder and studied her. "If you're so eager to get into journalism, why don't you come down to the *Sentinel* and lend a hand there?"

Liz's eyes grew round as black olives. "Really, Daddy?"

Z.J. nodded. She had fast little feet, and an eagerness to prove she could do things. Three sets of stairs were no longer something a man pushing sixty could negotiate with a whistle and a shrug. He could find lots of little chores to keep her busy and give Lizzie the sense of importance she craved. And around the house . . .

"So you want to come home at noon and fix lunch for yourself?" he asked. "I guess you can open a can of soup, but what's wrong with the school lunchroom?"

"The boys blow straw wrappers all over and squirt milk cartons at the girls and, and—besides, that's for kids who don't have anyplace to go at noon. If I came home, I could let Whizzy out for a run and, and—do some housecleaning! I could even make dinner, Dad. You always come home so late I'd have plenty of time. You wouldn't have to pay Mrs. Swenson to do that anymore."

Ever since Liz had discovered two years earlier that their neighbor lady was paid to watch Liz and cook meals, she'd lost her fondness for Mrs. Swenson. Liz didn't like the idea of people being paid to deal with her.

Her father picked up his pipe from the large glass ashtray on the side table and played with it, as grownups will.

"Maybe it's time you learned some domestic duties," he conceded. "I can't teach you; that's for sure. But you do want to do this, Elizabeth, take on responsibility at your age? You're growing up fast. Pretty soon there'll be boys 'n' cars 'n' soda fountain dates."

"Oh, Dad . . ." Liz was mortified. The faster girls in seventh grade were cinching their waists and wearing their blouses tighter to flaunt budding breasts, but Liz was blessedly flat yet, and the monthly "visitor" Mrs. Swenson had warned her about had not yet made an appearance. "Kids don't go to soda fountains on dates anymore," she muttered.

"Umm." Her father's noise had a dire accent. "Drive-ins, more like it. Well, you're too young for all that, but if you want to play housekeeper, be my guest. I'm sure not cut out for it."

Her dark eyes sparkled. Responsibility was hard to come by in Turtle Bend. At school, chores were apportioned by age, and seventh graders were still considered unreliable. The public library on Hill Street had books that no one under thirteen could check out, and you could only find out which they were by taking them up to the desk, where the librarian would spot some secret notation and order the book taken back. Liz had been humiliated too often lately by having to replace some book or other while everybody watched her march back to the shelves.

I wish I were grown-up, Liz thought as she returned the red folder to her room. It would be so much easier. She couldn't wait until she moved to the big old high school building on the hill, where there was a school paper to work on and mysterious clubs for various activities and basketball games to be a cheerleader at. Of course, she couldn't be a cheerleader without the "mountains" the boys in her class teased the girls about developing. If Liz could be a cheerleader with a ponytail and a pom-pon, it'd even be worth getting her monthly visitor.

* * *

Z.J. stared at the mess on his plate, the red willow plates they used for company eating, on which Liz had proudly presented her first home-cooked meal.

"When you go looking for a husband, he'd better be blind, Elizabeth," Z.J. joked. "What is this stuff?"

"Be serious, Dad. What do you think it is?" Her face was flushed with effort and worry. There was a speck of mustard on her straight little nose. Her dark hair, which had never responded to rags or pin curls or rollers since toddlerhood, hung in curly tendrils from Liz's minutes of poised inspection over an ajar oven door.

Z.J. wasn't a journalist for lack of descriptive powers.

"Well . . . I'd say it's a sliver off a football, burned black and oozing yellow stuffing, wrapped inside a toasted bun."

"You're not even close," Liz crowed. "It's Pigs in a Blanket. I got the recipe out of my *Betty Crocker Junior Cookbook*, which Mrs. Swenson gave me for Christmas."

"Dead pigs, I presume." Z.J. overturned one with a fork.

Liz giggled. "Daddy, don't play with your food. It's wieners stuffed with Velveeta and baked in a hot dog bun. With mustard on top. How do you like it?"

"Not as bad as it looks."

He was actually sampling the mess, she marveled, but then her father had never been a fussy eater. Liz wriggled contentedly on the chair and cut her Pig in a Blanket into bite-sized pieces. It tasted pretty good if you like charred hot dogs with gunk on them, and Liz did.

"You do like it?" she asked with one last wave of anxiety.

"Sure." He helped himself to the store-bought rolls she'd put on the table as an afterthought. "I get a good lunch downtown, so I don't much care what I get at night as long as it's hot and ready when I get home."

Faint praise for a maiden culinary effort, but enough to bring a brighter flush to Liz's cheeks. She sneaked a piece of frankfurter to Whizzy at her feet.

"Don't you worry, Dad," she told her father. "I'll have dinner ready every night. I'll take care of you."

He chuckled and scooped up loose pieces of meat and cheese with his roll.

"I'll take care of you forever," she promised.

"That's real nice, honey," said her father. "Pass the rolls again, would you, Elizabeth?"

— *Chapter 4* —

The slip was pale periwinkle blue, lavishly laced at the bodice and hem. It lay across Candy Turner's chenille bedspread like a bit of rare fairy gossamer draping a dishrag.

"It's gorgeous," Liz breathed. "But *nine* dollars . . ."

"It's my money for working at Dexter's afternoons and weekends." Candy tossed her head, her ash-brown bubble cut shimmying like silk. Her eyes were too close together for classic beauty but were ringed meticulously with drawn-on lashes, like Barbara Streisand's in *Vogue* magazine. Her lips' youthful color was paled with white lipstick. Everything about her whispered exquisite and fashionable femininity.

Liz sat on the bed while the old hi-fi in the corner played "Cherish" by The Association and absorbed it all, an impressed but singularly unenvious audience of one.

It was why they had remained friends since grade school, she and Candy. They had absolutely nothing in common. Their friendship had even weathered eighth grade, when the terrible Mrs. Felix had divided her students into "smart," "medium," and "dumb" rows; Liz had been the first one claimed for the smart side of the classroom, Candy the last for the "dumb" side.

Liz excelled scholastically; no one could miss that—assistant editor of the school paper, a coup for a junior; president of the Latin Club; a star debater and the only girl on the debating team. Liz was what teachers casually labeled "college material"—everyone knew that—though in 1965 not everyone in Turtle Bend went to college. It was a luxury a farming community could seldom afford except for well-to-do businessmen's sons and a pampered daughter or two whose parents hoped she could attract a rich city boy if given a wider field of flirtation.

Liz Jordan wasn't going to college for the right wrong reasons; she was going to college because she was too smart not to.

And Candy—Candy watched and nodded pleasantly at Liz's achievements and concentrated on enjoying being a girl. That was one area where Liz was marooned on the sidelines. She didn't seem to have what it took—oh, she was okay-looking, and her clothes were all right, if not smashing. But she just didn't seem to be doing something right. So she watched Candy assemble the feminine armaments around herself—lacquered nails in palest pink, soft angora sweaters, new shoes, fancy underwear—and admired her friend and still couldn't seem to decode the difference between them. The trouble was, Liz didn't really want what Candy's self-absorption was drawing to her like bees to rather stagnant honey.

"Isn't it a little short?" Liz asked as Candy whisked the slip back into a drawerful of similar exotica, delicately reswaddling it in pale pink tissue paper.

"Hems are going even higher, silly. Every fashion mag says so. You should really take yours up." Candy eyed Liz's hem-hidden knees critically.

"I just took this up three months ago! I don't have time to keep rehemming things. Besides, how high can they go?"

"You'd be surprised." Candy plopped down on the bedspread and knifed the heel of her hand across mid-thigh. "You watch."

Watch, yes, Liz thought ruefully. Care, no.

The two girls were quiet for a moment. There wasn't much to do on a Turtle Bend Sunday afternoon—not for Liz, who had her homework finished by Saturday night; not for Candy, whose homework was immaterial. A girl's bedroom was still the only place she could entertain privately, where girlfriends could giggle over small school scandals or redo each other's hair when the mood took them. Or discuss boys.

"I think Jeff Mayfield is kinda cute," began Candy.

"Jeff *Mayfield*? He doesn't pay attention to junior girls."

"Oh, yeah? Well, I have my eye on him, and you just watch."

Liz smiled silently. Candy was as canny as a Carthaginian general at getting boys to notice her. She just made up her mind and eventually they did exactly what she wanted. Liz had just translated the journals of Carthaginian generals and had won awards from the state Latin society.

Candy jumped up, her abrupt departure leaving Liz bouncing on the bedsprings. "Let's go out for a walk." At the mirror, she lightly combed each curl in the encircling tiers. "Did you bring a sweater?"

The two girls exited the house as if they were cat burglars, pausing only to explain their plans as briefly as possible to Candy's parents, who were still barricaded behind sections of the *Turtle Bend Sentinel*. Teenagers had a superstitious instinct that the less their parents saw of them, the less they'd meddle with vital but unexplainable rituals.

"Going out for a walk" on a spring, summer, or fall Sunday afternoon was the most sacred ritual of all. This Sunday was a fall one, early in the girls' junior year, but important in terms of the two spring proms looming in their social futures.

Liz and Candy strolled, their gaits calculatedly nonchalant, down the shadier side streets of the town. They talked. They complained that there was nothing to do, that Turtle Bend was too impossibly small, too unremittingly dull, that winter was too inevitably coming, even though only a few yellowed leaves rustled in the elmtops above them.

Occasionally, their paths would cross that of another pair—or trio, or quartet—of girls, never more than four. Somehow they were always walking in opposite directions on opposite sides of the street—that was a key nuance of the ritual—and they waved amiably at one another, but never stopped to talk. The other trick was never to stop.

Then, at first far and faint, like the five-o'clock freight, it came. The Sound. The throb or purr or rattle of a nearing internal combustion engine. Sometimes the car would pass them, a splash of Ford or Volkswagen or rusted-out Chevy truck. Or it would idle alongside the strollers in muted, lazy gear, and they could turn blank faces to study the real objects of their walks. Boys in cars.

Liz and Candy heard nothing but the remote sound of cruising cars on other streets, the voices of other girls talking to invisible knights of the small-town roads.

"This is dumb!" Liz exploded suddenly.

"Shhh!" Candy was looking a block over, where a flash of pink moved like a gaudy metal leviathan between the clapboard houses. "Look! That must be Herb Boyle's Olds 88." Candy knew cars like a used-car salesman. "Really sharp. So out it's in." It hadn't occurred to Candy that Herb Boyle drove an eight-year-old car because he couldn't afford the newer used cars the other boys had, Liz thought.

"Herb Boyle isn't our speed, Candy," Liz reminded her friend. He was a loner and a bit wild, a boy the teachers enjoyed blaming everything on.

Candy shrugged. "Jeff Mayfield has a 'sixty-two Ford Falcon. I thought I saw it on the next block over. I bet he's looking for us."

"Us" was a euphemism, Liz knew from other outings like this. Candy was the only one of them who played the mating game. But her instincts were rarely wrong.

Soon their quiet street hummed with the approach of an automotive presence. The girls' pace remained placid, their backs indifferent to the nearing car.

"Hey, there! Nice day, huh?" Jeff Mayfield was at the wheel of the Falcon, leaning across the long bench seat to hail them out the passenger side's rolled-down window. "You girls walkin' somewhere special?"

On Liz's arm, Candy's hand tightened in triumph. "Nowhere special," she drawled back, slowing enough to study the car and its passengers—a boy in the back seat and the girl he'd obviously plucked from another Turtle Bend street minutes before.

Jeff's car pulled closer and stopped. Candy and Liz did, too. He leaned even closer and finally the car door swung open, revealing a shaded, temptingly forbidden interior. Getting into a car was an act of daring, not that the girls risked anything other than their reputations, a public commitment that all Turtle Bend High School would buzz about on Monday.

Jeff grinned confidently. "Want a ride, girls?"

They consulted each other by glance first, although Liz was exquisitely certain of Candy's wishes. Jeff Mayfield was exactly what she wanted.

"I might go home," Liz said softly. She could go along, of course, as a third or fifth wheel.

"You don't have to go home, Liz. Come on," Candy urged under her breath, suddenly desperate for the endorsement of an accomplice. "We might pick up another guy."

Liz didn't want "another guy."

"No, really. I have to get home," she said more loudly, so the entire carload of kids could hear. "Nice seeing you." Liz waved and walked on, hearing the car door slam shut a moment later.

A full load now, the car's engine accelerated. Jeff and Candy and Phil and Mary Beth whizzed by, bound for a too-fast turn onto the state highway or to an informal beer-drinking session in Lilac Lane outside of town, where the boys would talk and quaff their six-packs of Budweiser and the girls would watch. Liz wasn't a good watcher.

She walked along, enjoying the light riffle of wind, ignoring the ongoing thrum of cruising cars, feeling a blessed sense of relief that she could never explain to Candy, and could hardly explain to herself.

By the time she turned onto her block, she was looking for Whizzy at his post in the front window, feeling sorry she'd deserted the dog so long, for so little reason. Lingerie bored her, and hemlines were a pain. Boys were unpredictable beings—prone to roughhousing like ten-year-olds one minute and acting tough and crude the next. Who needed them?

She opened the front door, letting Whizzy zoom past her feet into the fall sunshine, and walked on, in the direction of the unkempt town park that bordered the river. If there was any answer to teen-age rites of passage, the river knew.

* * *

"Debating match?" Z.J.'s shaggy eyebrows rose in concert. "I thought you were going to come down to the *Sentinel* office all this week and help me with the election edition."

"I'd love to, Dad, but the team's up against Glenn River tonight. I promised I'd make it." Liz pawed through the freezer compartment of the refrigerator. "Here, fried fish and peas all right?" She hefted a TV dinner for his inspection.

"I suppose so. I sure miss your creative cooking, though."

"Dad! Cream cheese and red onion sandwiches are hardly as nutritionally balanced as Swanson's. And no dishes to do. You won't miss me at all. Look, I'll put it in and put on the timer, but then I gotta run. Mike Peham's picking me up."

"Ahhh. Boyfriend, huh?"

Liz *tsk*ed her disgust. "Daddy, don't be silly. He just lives closest. We can't all take separate cars."

"You can't snag boyfriends with TV dinners, girl," her father sang after her.

Liz grabbed a sweater and her purse. "'Bye," she yelled pointedly from the hall, watching for Mike's poison-green Volkswagen out the porch windows.

"Or with debates!" her father bellowed after her.

But Liz was already out the door, running for the car. Mike Peham was a five-foot-five math whiz as aggressive as a mongoose on the debating team. But he wasn't boyfriend material by any stretch of the most fevered imagination, not even Zachariah Jordan's.

Turtle Bend High won the debate that night, as it won most of them. The team celebrated by stopping at the town pizza palace, Lucretio's, where they ordered two large pizzas with everything on it.

Liz was the only girl in the group, but that didn't bother her or the boys. They performed a lively autopsy on the fine points of the debate, laughed, and downed pizza and Pepsi as if Judgment Day were overdue.

The green VW chugged up to Liz's front door at eleven. She could hear Whizzy's sharp little nails raking the inside of the front door while she stood outside of it and dredged for her keys. Mike waited until the door opened and a shaft of lamplight warmed the front porch darkness. Liz waved and the VW churned away.

Inside, Whizzy spun into his agile greeting ritual of leaps, turns, and jumps. But the house was oddly quiet, and Liz finally discovered the reason for it in a note from her father, scrawled in his bold, oversize handwriting.

> *"The Knoxes needed an emergency fourth for bridge
> and called on me. I should be home by 10. LOCK THE
> DOOR after you come in!"*

It wasn't signed, partly because Z.J. didn't feel he had to state the obvious, partly because, Liz suspected, he didn't feel comfortable calling himself "Dad" or "Daddy."

"Ten o'clock," Liz mused to the cavorting dog. Her eyes checked the kitchen wall clock with adult disapproval—11:15. It was Liz who had engagements and extracurricular activities and basketball games and stayed out late. She was the teenager, for heaven's sake, and, despite the absence of a boyfriend, managed to lead a busy social life. Z.J. stayed home and read newspapers and listened to the ten-o'clock news and sat up waiting for *her*.

Feeling oddly disquieted, Liz threw his note in the kitchen waste can, atop the crumpled tin remains of the Swanson's TV dinner.

— *Chapter 5* —

Z.J. had won his own match the night of the Glenn River debate.

He got home at midnight, chuckling about his strategy. "Playing bridge is like riding a bicycle," he pronounced at breakfast the next morning. "You never forget how. Myrtle's a pretty good player, but it works better if she ends up dummy hand and I play the cards."

"Myrtle?" Liz asked.

"Ethel Knox's cousin from St. Cloud. That's why they needed a fourth. Myrtle's in town for a few weeks."

"A few weeks? What's there to do in Turtle Bend for a few weeks?"

"You seem to find plenty to do," her father answered, downing his Wheaties with milk and bananas and a reproving look.

"That's different."

"Now, Elizabeth, I know you're a young lady and busy with things that occupy young ladies. One of them'll be college in not too long a time. You've got to realize that your old man needs to find some new hobbies now that you're launched on your own life."

"Of course," Liz said indignantly. She was such a frequent advocate of individual freedom on her own behalf that it hardly became her to deny it to her father. "I'll do the dishes when I get home, after the school paper meeting at four. See you." She was dashing out of the house again, she noticed guiltily as Whizzy's ears lowered at her exit. And it had been weeks since she'd gone to the *Sentinel* office, ever since she'd gotten really active on the school paper.

Busy as Liz was, she noticed that the bridge games continued. Dining with the Knoxes and Myrtle beforehand soon became routine. It only meant Liz didn't have to feed her father on Wednesday nights, so she took the reprieve at face value. She got so busy sometimes she could hardly remind herself to eat, much less feed someone else.

She introduced Z.J. to take-out pizza that spring and found him a delighted advocate. The kitchen wastebasket overflowed with empty food cartons and notes from one of them to the other announcing changes in schedule and late evenings out. The mysterious Myrtle became a fixture in Z.J.'s conversation, but Liz paid her no more heed than she would expect her father to give Tom, Dick, or Harry—or Mike, Jeff, or Herb.

Then, one quiet winter Sunday afternoon at home, her father lowered his brows and his pipe in concert. Liz was doing her homework on the living room coffee table, sitting on the floor with her textbooks splayed around her.

"Elizabeth," he interrupted. She looked up, seeing—as she always did when she looked to the fireplace side of the room—her mother's portrait still and pervasive against the mantel.

"Yes?"

"Myrtle's coming over for dinner Wednesday night, instead of us playing bridge with the Knoxes—"

"For dinner? Here? Oh, Daddy, you didn't give me enough warning. I've got a million things to do for school; I can't—"

"Now don't fret yourself, honey." Z.J. beamed like a rascally old magician producing a rabbit. "That's the whole point. Myrtle's gonna make dinner for *us*. She gets to worrying about our nutrition, us being as busy as we are."

"Our nutrition's fine."

"Sure, sure. But Myrtle wants to do us a favor. I figure we ought to let her."

"And I can cook," Liz answered, but her father's eyes had returned to the fine print of his paper.

That Wednesday night Liz wore her best wool dress, a Rudi Gernreich knockoff, and pearl button earrings. Myrtle came, loaded down with a brown grocery bag that Z.J. made a Sir Walter Raleigh fuss about taking from her the instant she set foot in the door.

"Myrtle Fickett," Z.J. introduced her, "my daughter, Elizabeth."

Liz felt so flabbergasted she could hardly talk. Myrtle was a tall, rawboned woman of fifty five, about as shapely as a bowling pin. She stood stiffly surveying the small living room until Z.J. returned.

"How about a highball?" he asked jovially.

Myrtle nodded yes and sat primly on the sofa edge.

"Elizabeth?" he offered.

Her . . . *drink*? "Um, yes," Liz said, dazed.

Her father brought out the fat-bottomed crystal glasses from the dining room cabinet, each bearing an effervescent blend of whiskey, ginger ale, and ice. Liz sipped hers, the alien taste of alcohol and the uniqueness of the occasion sending a thrill through her virgin veins. Hard liquor. At home at her father's invitation. She'd bet some of the boys in school hadn't done as much yet. But she was almost a senior, for heavens sake, and mature for her age: everybody said so. . . . Liz sipped the stinging beverage and sat quietly beside Myrtle on the sofa, wondering what would come next.

"You did put those groceries away, Z.J.?" Myrtle inquired, only relaxing back into the couch after his eager affirmation.

Liz was astounded. Her father had never lifted a finger around the house since she'd known him.

The adults finished their drinks long before Liz; she had to leave her half-full glass on the coffee table when Myrtle rose to suggest that "we women see what we can rustle up in the kitchen."

In the pint-size room, they edged awkwardly around each other, Myrtle yanking open cupboards and scanning the contents with noncommittal "hmmms." The freezer compartment dismayed her.

"Tater Tots, Elizabeth? My, all this convenience food . . . I realize you're just a young girl and can get by on this junk, but your father needs something more substantial."

Out came the pink butcher paper–wrapped pork chops; out came potatoes and gravy stock; out came a premade cherry cheesecake. Myrtle bustled around the kitchen, relentlessly at home, giving orders that kept Liz running from one place to another, setting the table, fetching seasonings, mashing potatoes. . . .

They finally sat down at the dining room table, Z.J. waxing eloquent over Myrtle's imported bounty.

"Surely that dog isn't going to remain in the dining room?" Myrtle eyed Whizzy as if he were unsanitary. Liz glanced rapidly to her father.

"Of course not, Myrtle, if he bothers you. Lizzie—" he said, and her eyes rebelled—"The dog doesn't have to be at the table; send him away."

It took several sharp commands before Whizzy slunk off, brown eyes reproachful under sad, wrinkled brows. He settled in the hall where he could see the table, sank his head upon his paws, and watched.

Whizzy's exiled vigil didn't inhibit the adults. Z.J. began his grace with a flourish Liz usually witnessed only on state occasions.

"We thank you, Lord, for the fine food that burdens our table and the fine generosity that brought it to us in the person of Myrtle Fickett."

Liz could have choked, and almost did on the gravy-smothered pork chops, the butter-rich mashed potatoes. Resentment stewed in her innards. Myrtle was being catered to like a queen, this plain, stiff woman whom Liz couldn't stand already. If she'd been a substitute teacher, the kids at school would have crucified her. What was Z.J. doing? What did he see in her? If he wanted a lady friend, at his age, he deserved at least someone unique, Liz thought, someone like . . . like Arlene Francis or something.

By the time dessert came around, Liz couldn't stomach it.

"I have to study," she said, excusing herself.

"Lizzie must be in love," joked Z.J. "She usually cleans her plate, and this is sure great chow, Myrtle."

Liz retreated to her bedroom, but couldn't escape Myrtle's overhearable comment.

"Teen-age years," she hissed helpfully to Z.J. as Liz left. "Hormones. They all go through it."

Whizzy padded close behind Liz to her bedroom. When she turned to shut the door she was surprised to see him there, though she shouldn't have been; he always was. Liz crouched down to hug the dog's narrow shoulders.

"Oh, Whizzy, you're a *good* dog." She collapsed to the floor beside him, her high-heeled feet askew, and picked at the lamb design in the worn rag rug. Whizzy curled up beside her.

"She's a pill," Liz whispered to the dog. "Why would he do it, ask her over like this?" Tears oiled her eyes, making it easier for more to well in their wake. "She just came in and walked all over us, Whizzy. And Z.J. jumping like a court fool to do this for her and that for her. Highballs! Men are so dumb about women. But we don't have to like her. He can bring her home, but we don't have to like her."

Somehow the dog's mute comforting presence had lost its magic. Liz had seen Whizzy banished from the table by a stranger, a stranger who was able to walk in cold and question years of fond custom. Liz pretended to do her homework for as long as she could, until Z.J. hailed her to come out and say good-bye to Myrtle.

Liz did, quite politely, wishing all the while she believed the ritual farewells were final.

1956 That spring Liz's teachers started handing her college bulletins to take home. Next year she'd be a senior, they said; it wasn't too early to think of where she wanted to go. She showed the booklets to Z.J., who showed a peculiar lack of interest in them.

"Fine, fine, Elizabeth. Wherever you want. The money's there. I believe in higher education. You're a smart girl; you do what you want."

What she wanted she couldn't have. She wanted Sundays without Myrtle at the house; holiday dinners without Myrtle coming in to cook them, without Whizzy being sent outside thinking he'd been a bad dog when he'd merely been a dog and there.

"My land, we never let animals in the house on the farm," Myrtle would cluck whenever she came to visit and Whizzy was in sight. "They do fine outside."

Whizzy's ears lowered at the sight of her after a while, at the very sound of her thick-heeled shoes. Myrtle would tuck a tight permanent ringlet inside the hairnet she wore and purse her mouth and stare at Whizzy like Elvira Gulch at Dorothy's Toto. "You never know what diseases they might dig up."

There was no rainbow for Liz and Whizzy to escape over in Turtle Bend, only the river. That spring they walked by the river a lot—or, rather, Liz walked. Whizzy always ran, as wound up with energy as he had been a decade before.

One magnificent May Sunday when her father had been out with Myrtle, Liz and the dog came home to find him sitting on the back steps waiting for them. He was smoking his pipe and looking . . . worried wasn't the word. Maybe sheepish was.

"Sit a minute, Elizabeth." He patted the weatherworn wood beside him.

Liz sat down, watching Whizzy race around the corner of the house after some irresistible spring smell.

"Myrtle and me—we're going to get married this summer, Elizabeth."

"Married?"

"Don't sound so shocked. You'll probably be doing it yourself someday." Liz shook her head wildly, mainly to shake loose the tears before they could cascade down her cheeks and make her look like a child, a baby.

"Yes, you will. Heck, the only reason I haven't remarried, I suppose, is I was so busy raising you. But you're almost grown now, and will be going off to college—I've seen those bulletins from Chicago and Milwaukee and even the East. A man needs a companion as he gets older, Lizzie. Someday you'll understand that. For now, I hope you'll welcome Myrtle, do all you can to make her at home."

"When?" Liz's voice was choked, but her father didn't seem to notice.

"July. Nothing fancy, you know, street clothes and a small reception at the VFW hall."

Liz nodded. He patted her shoulder. "You'll get to like her. She's a hard worker, that Myrtle, and she knows small-town life."

There was silence for a while. Liz could hear the returned robins chirping. One dove to the still-yellowed grass and tugged mightily for a worm.

"And Elizabeth . . ."

Something made her heart stop beating. Her father looked as he always did to her—big and white-capped, like a mountain or a wave—something you didn't argue with. But she detected the careful tone in his voice now with a teenager's raw hypersensitivity.

"Myrtle simply can't tolerate a dog indoors. She just can't. And it would be unfair to the dog to ask it to become an outside dog after all these years. It'll have to go before Myrtle comes, that's all."

All she could think—over and over—was that she was sixteen years old and had grown up without a mother and was too old to cry.

"It's like Myrtle's allergic to dogs; don't you see, Elizabeth? If you put it that way, you understand it. You can't argue with an allergy; isn't that right?" he prodded.

"Yes, Daddy." The dog came charging around the house to throw himself at her feet, panting, seeking acknowledgment.

Z.J. sighed. "Good. I'm glad you understand. Myrtle just couldn't . . . tolerate . . . Whizzy in the house."

Why did he have to say the name? Liz looked then, where she had been trying to avoid looking, to the small short-haired dog at her feet, sitting as he always sat, bright brown eyes expectant, short curved tail brushing the grass, grinning in a dumb canine way that was quite magical. It was a good thing he was only a dog and couldn't understand things, as Liz could.

"The dog is almost ten years old, Elizabeth. He doesn't have that much time left, anyway." Nails digging, tearing into the flesh of her palms. "Myrtle knows these folks that have a fine farm where he can run and chase all day. You don't have much time for chasing these days, now you're almost grown-up." Grown-up, grown-up, grown-up. Oh, God . . . I'm not grown-up! "Myrtle's going to be a new member of the family," her father was saying. "We have to consider her wishes; isn't that right?"

"Yes . . ." No, no, no!

"Myrtle was farm-raised, you know? A farm's a great place for animals—room to run. We're lucky these friends of Myrtle's want a good, friendly dog on their place. You don't have to be there when they get the dog. Whizzy'll understand. It'll be a better place for him."

Liz stood, turned, and went to her bedroom. Whizzy might have followed, but this time she shut the door without waiting for him.

They came Monday sometime, while Liz was at school. It had all been arranged. There was no time to say good-bye, no time to rage and storm and run away from home. He was gone, as swiftly and suddenly as Myrtle had come.

Her father tried once that summer, before the wedding, to report on how Whizzy was doing on the farm. He got as far as chuckling over reports of the dog chasing the barnyard ducks before Liz said politely, "Oh, really," and left the room. After that he never mentioned the dog again.

And neither did Liz.

— Chapter 6 —

The noodles had been boiled to a limp white lump. Now they swam sluggishly in a yellow melted-butter river, sliding off the serving spoon and back into the dish. Liz thought she could use that as an excuse for not eating many of them.

"Have some more noodles, Elizabeth. Honestly, you girls peck at your food like birds nowadays."

Under Myrtle's orders, and because it was easier to obey than to fight that inflexible bundle of biases tied up into the semblance of a woman, Liz desultorily spooned more noodles onto her plate, where they squirmed in a slick, dispirited mass. She wished Myrtle hadn't mentioned birds; white worms writhed in her overimaginative mind.

Z.J. heaped the stuff on his plate. Liz finally understood how indiscriminately he ate. "Hot and handy" was all he required.

"I'm going over to Candy Turner's to study tonight," Liz mumbled to a forkful of noodles. Neither Z.J. nor Myrtle questioned her intent, though why anyone—especially brainy Liz Jordan—would consider studying with Candy Turner an academic advantage was mystifying.

Liz did the dishes alone, as always, and left quickly. The house was empty without Whizzy. She sometimes caught herself complaining mentally to the dog, and now walked faster to busy her mind with the task of wading through the January drifts to Candy's house. Despite his small size, Whizzy had never paused at snowdrifts, but had sprung through them, leaving tracks not much bigger than pipe cleaners. Liz churned leadenly forward, wrapping her wool scarf over her nose against the wind. It wouldn't do to get weepy; tears would only freeze in the subzero winter temperatures.

Liz made the usual obligatory greetings to Candy's parents, ensconced for the evening in front of the living room Motorola, and escaped upstairs to Candy's bedroom. She threw her textbooks on the bed and collapsed beside them, unwinding her swaddling winterwear.

"Hi, what's new?" Liz asked eagerly.

"Nothing much." Candy stopped filing her nails to frown at the books. "Are you really going to study that stuff?"

"No. Who cares about College Boards? I just wanted to get out of the house."

Candy's sympathetic nod was balm. Liz heaped her jacket, scarf, mittens, and boots by the warm radiator at the door while Candy, at her dainty white wrought-iron dressing table, lit a long Benson and Hedges cigarette and inhaled delicately.

"Aren't your folks gonna kill you?" Liz was incredulous.

"Not really." Candy smiled the smirk of the smug. "As long as I keep it to my room in the house, they don't care."

"Myrtle doesn't even let Dad smoke, except his pipe, and only in his chair."

"Myrtle is too much. I wonder why he married her."

"I can't imagine—I mean, it can't be sex appeal."

Candy giggled. "Imagine that. At least they're too old to get 'in trouble,' like Margie Benson."

"Is she? Is she really?"

"That's what I hear. Too far gone to make graduation."

Both girls silently mulled the one small-town scandal that touched their peers and conferred a relieved "there but for the grace of God go I" feeling. Of course, Candy didn't understand what Liz knew only too well—that disorganized, bright Margie Benson had envisioned life beyond Turtle Bend High. She'd wanted to go to the university and maybe even med school. It was a bizarre ambition for a Turtle Bend girl in 1966. Now nature and Margie's boyfriend had ended ambition and reputation in one stroke.

Liz ran her fingernail between the bedspread's wavy rows of sheared chenille fuzz. "I wonder when we'll..."

"Not until I've hooked one," Candy promised. "I may be dumb around the edges, but I know that much. Getting PG is the pits." She stalked to the window, sweeping aside the Priscillas to stare at the dark evening sentried by bare elm branches. "But I can see why Margie let it happen. Winter is awful. There's nothing to do but stay inside and go crazy."

"You should be at *my* house nowadays," Liz said glumly.

"That's too bad. Maybe you need to try something new."

"What? I'm on every after-school committee there is, but I can't stay away from home forever. Oh, I can't wait for college to start." Liz hugged a round throw pillow embroidered with a rhinestone-eyed poodle by Candy's mother long ago, and rolled onto her stomach, facing the pink-stippled wall.

"Hey, Liz, maybe you can! They're having tryouts this week for the senior class play. Why don't you audition?"

"I'm not drama." Liz had never taken any of drama coach Arnold Cooper's classes.

"Well, maybe there's a chance. There'd be a lot of rehearsal nights between now and May.... Then there'd just be summer to get through, and that'd be a snap."

Liz sat up, unconsciously stroking a silky gray poodle ear. "That's true. Who cares if I get a part? Maybe I could be a stage manager or something. Out every night. Bliss! It'd be better than a boyfriend."

"Nothing's better than that," Candy demurred, curling herself around another of the throw pillows. "*Who* do you think passed me a note in senior English today?"

"No! Who?"

And they were off on another—and for Liz, vicarious—tour of Candy's remarkable social life.

Liz got home at ten, as late as she dared stay out without having to answer for it.

"Did you have a good study?" Z.J. asked dutifully from behind his paper. Smoke puffed ceilingward from his La-Z-Boy corner, the only area of the house still a free-nicotine zone. Yet the same oversize gold-flecked pink-and-aqua ceramic ashtrays that Liz remembered from toddlerhood decorated tabletops throughout the house. Apparently Myrtle liked their dubious cosmetic value despite forbidding their use.

Now Myrtle's hand rose from the sewing in her aproned lap to fan the air pointedly. "Whew. Has that girlfriend of yours taken up smoking, Elizabeth? I can smell it on your clothes. You haven't started, I hope, because I won't tolerate it in the house or the car. Your father's bad enough; he's too old to change. You're a different story."

Z.J. remained silent, as he often was at home these days. Liz kept waiting for him to say something, do something, just as she kept looking for Whizzy out of the corner of her eye.

"No, it's not me," Liz explained wearily. "Lots of the kids at school smoke now. I can't help it if I pick it up from being around them."

"Well, keep them out of the house if they're going to have such filthy habits. And after the surgeon general's report came out, too." Myrtle looked in Z.J.'s direction for fatherly reinforcements, but he remained hidden by his newspapers.

"You don't have to worry about me smoking, Myrtle," Liz promised confidently. "It's the very last thing in the world I would do."

The second last thing in the world Liz ever thought she would do was to audition for the school play. But she paused by the bulletin board near the principal's office the next day, books cradled in her arms, and studied the notice for a play called *The Rainmaker*. Would-be thespians had checked all copies out of the school and public libraries, Liz learned when she tried to do the same.

So she went to the tryouts cold, reminding herself that she was a veteran debater, which was harder, because she had to make up her lines as she went, and that she really didn't care if she got a part or not. It turned out that there was only one female part anyway, the lead.

"And you got it!" Candy Turner had a practiced squeal, which she let loose in the school lunchroom ten days later.

"Why not? She's an old maid—and her name is Lizzie. Typecasting, obviously. Mr. Cooper told me this morning."

"You don't sound happy about it."

"It's set on a farm. There are six men's roles, and mine. Being stuck as the only girl in a cast of six boys is no picnic, let me tell you. But Cooper loves this play. He says with the cast he's got it'll be his best production." Liz rolled her eyes and plucked the mayonnaise slathered baloney out of Myrtle's baloney-cheese sandwich. "Why couldn't he have done *The Fantasticks* or something?"

"At least you'll get out of the house." Candy thought for a minute. "You and six guys. Who else?"

"The cast list is supposed to go up this afternoon."

"Let's look. Maybe there's somebody cute you can fix me up with."

Liz smiled and collected her purse from the floor. Trust Candy to cast a girl who couldn't even dig up a date to the senior prom for herself as a matchmaker.

The world hadn't hit the school grapevine yet, for Liz and Candy were the only ones studying the bulletin board. On lined yellow legal paper, Candy read Liz's fate.

"Lizzie Curry/Elizabeth Jordan. Noah Curry/Jeff Mayfield . . ." Candy stopped reading aloud. "Who's Noah?"

"My brother."

"Oh, what a scream." Candy and Jeff had long since broken up. "Who do you play opposite?"

"Starbuck, I guess."

"Any love scenes?"

Candy's first thought was Liz's last. "Oh my God, I hope not! I haven't got a script yet. All right, read it to me. Who's the lucky man?" Liz shut her eyes. There was a pause even longer than Candy's primitive reading skills should require.

"This can't be right." Her friend sounded puzzled.

Liz gripped Candy's arm and kept her eyes shut. "All right, who?"

"Liz, it's . . . Herb Boyle. That's ridiculous! He couldn't act his way out of . . . out of shop class. He's the toughest guy in school. The stories I've heard— How'd *he* get the part? At least you shouldn't have any trouble if there *are* love scenes."

Liz had heard about Herb. He was one of the boys—the leader, even—who raced their 1950's model cars directly from the drive-in at Prairie Centre to a secretly notorious grove outside Turtle Bend. There the circled cars would purr in idle while pints of whiskey made the rounds and pairs of "fast" Turtle Bend teenagers necked voraciously. Every Monday the school halls hummed with report cards on the town's most notorious makeout artists. Herb Boyle had no trouble maintaining an A+ in that subject, according to rumor.

Liz finally expressed herself, and in suitably dramatic fashion. She wailed.

WORSE choice possible even in 1947.

The Rainmaker, when Liz's small yellow-jacketed script from Samuel French, Inc., arrived, was subtitled *A Romantic Comedy in Three Acts*. She groaned inwardly and riffled through, scanning the italicized stage directions for the dreaded love scenes. Having found at least two, she read the whole script in study hall, the slim booklet sandwiched in her physics textbook.

"Candy Turner, I should kill you!" Liz was only half kidding as they walked each other home that afternoon. *"The Rainmaker* is all about a plain old maid named Lizzie. Do you know what this part will do to my image?"

Candy was unperturbed. "It'll get you out of the house evenings."

Rehearsals were the hell Liz had anticipated. While Arnold Cooper, a lean, ugly man with a sardonic wit, hollered at his rambunctious male cast and tried to bully farmboys into docile thespians, the boys themselves concentrated on smirking over the play's romantic message. They read, with leaden earnestness, the lines labeling Lizzie plain and called Liz "Lizzie" offstage, a habit all her classmates assimilated somehow. Liz gritted her teeth and did the best she could with her thankless part—after all, Katharine Hepburn hadn't been too proud to do it.

Herb Boyle, ironically, turned out to be the least of her problems. He acted as uneasy with his role as Lizzie with hers. In early rehearsals, he hunched over his diminutive playbook in the classic posture of the slow reader, eyes doggedly bent to the page only inches before them, his engineer-booted feet taking seven-league clumps across the stage when directed to move. Herb intoned Starbuck's inspired dreamer's lines as heavily as a sentence of death.

Arnold Cooper, once excited by his leads' potential, openly paced and snarled in the semidark auditorium, trying to browbeat excellence out of his young cast. After every rehearsal, he'd rip long sheets of yellow notes off his ever-present legal pad and hand them scornfully to Liz and Herb. Herb added insult to injury by not only by refusing to read his lines with any feeling but by seeming incapable of committing them to memory.

When opening night was only three weeks away, Liz's misgivings were further borne out. The boy who had the small part of Sheriff Thomas, cast apparently for his short stature and prematurely middle-aged girth, sidled up to Liz backstage and invited her to the senior prom in front of the whole cast.

There was nothing to do but accept. The other boys' sly eyes showed they knew she'd been trapped.

"All right, boys and girl." Mr. Cooper talked with a constant edge in his voice these days. "We're going to rehearse Saturdays and Sundays until opening, and until you get it right." Mass groans. "Herb, for God's sake, learn those lines; then maybe you can stop moving like an ox! Starbuck is young, fast on his feet; he's got charisma! And Liz, you're doing okay, but I don't believe deep in my soul that you feel Lizzie, Lizzie's fear of being an old maid. Think about it. You're smart enough to figure it out. All right, troops, go!"

They separated as they left the auditorium, boys hooting and pounding down the hall, Liz bound for her own errands. Among them were writing application letters to colleges, homework, and desultory Sunday-afternoon strolls with Candy.

"How's the play going?" Candy inquired on one of these outings, expertly licking a Dexter's double-decker peppermint bonbon ice cream cone.

"Don't ask," Liz answered. "We rehearse again tonight, and I just *know* Cooper is going to want us to do the love scenes for real. Ick! Course, Herb will be lucky if he knows his lines by next year, much less in three weeks."

"I can hardly wait to see it," Candy said disloyally.

Moments later a car cruised up behind them, and Candy once again negotiated a ride with the latest of her rotating beaux. By now all rides ended in necking sessions in Lilac Lane—they were seniors, after all. Liz would be stuck with whatever leftover boy there was, and eagerly used homework as a cop-out.

The car spurted down the spring street without her, under a bridal arch of tender elm buds. Liz despised tawdry teen-age mating rituals, those dangerous games of kiss and tell, but sometimes wished she rejected them out of knowledge rather than uninvited ignorance. Mr. Cooper was wrong. She knew Lizzie Curry's old maid fears too well: that's why she rebelled at showing them. Liz contemplated the senior prom again, and her unwelcome escort. Only duds aspired to smart girls. She'd seen that pattern before— guys who knew a girl like her would never go out with them unless they had no choice, but also knew that "cool" guys would avoid girls whose IQ's exceeded their chest measurements.

Liz turned a corner, oblivious to a nearing motorized purr, a sound that overtook her softly, then paced her.

She stopped abruptly, intensely aware then of the presence of The Car. "Ask not for whom the car throbs; it throbs for thee" went through her mind like a nonsense verse. She whirled.

A tank-size hunk of chrome-decked baby-pink automobile pulsed beside her. Herb Boyle was hunched over the steering wheel and, even as Liz stared in surprise, leaned to swing the passenger-side door open.

"Get in."

Liz bridled. "Why?"

Herb shrugged. "I thought we could, uh, go for a ride." He flourished his worn yellow playbook before placing it on the dashboard. "I thought we might work on memorizing our lines."

"*Your* lines," Liz said severely. "Mine are memorized."

Herb suddenly grinned. "Yeah, *my* lines. You sounded like Lizzie Curry there for a minute."

Liz studied him. "And you looked like Starbuck for a second when you smiled," she conceded suspiciously.

Herb patted the once-white vinyl seat beside him with the playbook. "Come on, Lizzie Jordan. Get in; I won't bite."

She climbed into the car. "Where are we going?"

"Somewhere private," Herb promised glumly. "I'm getting tired of being a fool in public."

The threat of privacy left Liz oddly on edge, but Herb's honesty relieved an inchoate tension. Liz sighed agreement. "Me, too."

Liz was the last Turtle Bend girl to have been picked up. No one lingered on the streets to see the amazing new twosome roll out of town and down country roads. Herb finally pulled to the side of a shady graveled lane.

"Old McGuillacuddy's apple orchard," he explained. "Nobody comes here but scarecrows."

Liz clumped awkwardly through the grassy drainage ditch and over the split-rail fence. She wasn't dressed for that, or for climbing to a seat in the low, gnarled apple tree that Herb scaled with ease. He pulled her up and waited while she struggled to arrange her skirt and brace her feet on the knotted tree fork ahead of her.

"Where'll we start?" Liz asked as Herb handed her the playbook.

"How about the beginning? If you don't mind reading the other parts."

"Anything for my art," Liz declaimed theatrically, settling into the embrace of old wood while meadowlarks trilled over the fields and sunshine dappled warmly through the young apple leaves.

Herb had obviously been working on his lines; he delivered them intently through the first act, even becoming carried away enough to exude some of the born huckster's razzle-dazzle as the self-proclaimed rainmaker Starbuck bullied and cajoled Lizzie and her family of drought-squeezed menfolk into paying him one hundred dollars to "make rain."

Herb's sullenly handsome face, mouthing the madcap words of Starbuck, radiated the same untutored, raw force that Liz saw in photos of the young Elvis Presley. There were always young men who looked like that; it was why teen-age girls screamed and swooned and their parents raged. It was natural as rain, and could be as overwhelming in enough quantity. Liz began to see why Mr. Cooper had cast Herb Boyle as the rainmaker.

"I'll give you better reasons, Lizzie-girl!" Herb was delivering his Act One final speech with something like the glorious conviction Darren McGavin must have used on Broadway in 1954, when the play debuted and they both were toddlers. "You gotta take my deal," Herb urged, "because once in your life you gotta take a chance on a con man! You gotta take my deal because . . . because . . ." Herb's growing enthusiasm hit the roadblock of his memory head-on and crashed. He found himself staring soulfully into Liz's waiting eyes with nothing to say.

"Oh . . . shit!" Herb hurled himself out of the tree and turned his back on it.

Liz sat silent, surprised. Nobody had said "shit" in front of her in her life, although Lloyd the typesetter had come close a couple of times.

Herb's hands were jammed in his jean pockets, his head hung low. It would have been funny to see the leader of the pack brought down, except that a good part of Liz's self-respect dangled on their joint dramatic commitment.

A thick-hided engineer boot savagely kicked the greening turf. "Maybe I'll quit school."

"Oh, great! And leave the rest of us in the lurch." Liz contemplatively rolled Herb's limp yellow playbook against the direction it had been habitually curled. She sighed and studied the open page, with all of Starbuck's lines painstakingly underlined in wavy dull pencil. "Why'd you try out, then?"

"Cooper asked me to. And then the guys dared me to do it. I didn't know I'd have to spout all those phony lines, all that crap about believin' in yourself, and, and . . . mush and stuff. . . ." Herb's choked emotions dribbled to a stop.

Liz leaned back against the rough bark, which scratched her back pleasantly. Her eyes narrowed. "Why, Herbert Boyle. You're *scared*!"

He whirled to face her, fists knotted in his pockets, sullen man-boy's face flaring into defiance. "It's all a bunch of baloney. Starbuck's a fool."

"No he isn't. That's the whole point of the play. He's a dreamer. He changes everybody and everything. But if you don't believe in Starbuck, if you don't believe in dreams, you *will* look like a fool onstage." Herb's face whitened, and he turned away again.

Liz waited before speaking again, before being able to say what she had to say next. "Has it ever occurred to you that *I* might feel like a fool, too? That the part of plain Lizzie Curry who wants a beau but doesn't dare believe she's beautiful isn't exactly ego-building?"

Herb's karate chop of dismissal sliced the air at his side; he didn't even turn to watch her. "That's different," he said. "Everybody knows you're smart. They *know* you're not a fool. Nothin' can hurt you if you're smart."

"If you believe that, Herb Boyle, you're not only a fool; you're the biggest fool that ever walked!"

Herb turned. "Hey, that sounded . . . sounded—like what Cooper's always harping on—it sounded 'in character.'"

"You got me mad," Liz admitted. "Look, it's true. Your lines are always about a paragraph long. I know that's hard for someone who's not used to reading or acting. But let's face it; you're the romantic lead in the thing. So what's to complain about? At least you're not cast as a classic dud."

"But *that's* the point of the play," he suddenly argued back. "Lizzie *isn't* a dud; she just thinks she is." He thought a moment, visibly. "Why'd *you* try out?"

Liz pulled a young green apple off its stem and gouged her thumbnail into the skin. "Wanted an excuse to stay away from home nights."

"Oh, yeah?" Herb boosted himself back into the tree next to her. "That bad, huh?"

"Not really, I guess . . . but . . ."

The wind whispered through the miniature spring leaves. Liz jabbed her thumbnail into the tiny apple as she turned it, then passed it to Herb.

He frowned at the etched surface, turning the apple. "T—R—Y . . ." She handed him another message-bearing fruit. "A-G-A-I-N." He grinned and plucked his own nearby apple. When he handed it to Liz, its message was succinct. "O-K."

"If you believe in Starbuck, I'll try not to be too chicken to believe in Lizzie," she promised with a smile. "Maybe if we do it right, neither of us will be fools."

They went on into Act Two, Herb's memorization improving with his new commitment to what he was doing, Liz saying her own lines opposite him with full-strength feeling instead of a rote regularity.

Cooper would have turned cartwheels, she thought as she heard Starbuck edge over more forcefully into Herb's voice and physical presence. And the more he became Starbuck, the more she dared to become Lizzie. The dreaded mushy "barn scene" at the end of Act Two crept toward them line by inevitable line, but it no longer seemed threatening—too romantic for Herb, too sexual for Liz. They were meeting somewhere in the middle. When Starbuck told Lizzie that if she *thought* she was beautiful she would be beautiful, when he told her to take down her hair and "think pretty," Herb's hand reached out to Liz's already free hair. When Starbuck told her to close her eyes and say she was pretty, Liz did, exactly as the script called for.

And just when Lizzie Curry cried out with belief, "I'm pretty, I'm pretty, I'm pretty!" and the italicized stage directions said "*He kisses her. A long kiss and she clings to him passionately*," Herb did, and Liz did, and the soft spring afternoon webbed them in its seductive shimmer.

Liz felt a sense of wonder. *Sweet sixteen and never been kissed* no longer applied. She'd always been a year ahead in school, because she was smart, and yet felt so dumb and more than a year behind in other ways. Herb's kiss was long but unexpectedly tender. Their lips trembled apart.

The script called for Lizzie Curry to sob and carry on and demand, "Why did you do that?"

"Why did you do that?" Liz asked softly.

Herb looked shamefaced and abandoned his lines. "It seemed right. You've never been kissed before." He stated as obvious what Starbuck had asked Lizzie in the play.

Liz nodded her head and hoped the heat in her face didn't mean she was blushing. She was too smart to blush.

Herb looked pleased with himself. "Now you don't have to feel embarrassed when old man Cooper makes us do it in rehearsal. It's over, see. Nothing to it. This acting's a piece of cake. Let's finish the scene."

Liz nodded.

"Only..." Herb paused. "Only maybe we should backtrack and do it again, so we get it in sequence."

Liz looked down. "Take it from 'It'll never happen'?" she asked.

"Right. Take it from the top."

"All right, children." Cooper sounded martyred, and like he enjoyed sounding martyred. "We're going to run the second act straight through, God help us. But first, the rest of you can take a break; Herb and Liz stay."

Of course they didn't go, eight lusty, grinning seventeen-year-old boys. They hunkered down in a row in the darkened seats, huge feet disrespectfully propped on the seatbacks in front of them, and watched while Cooper talked quietly with his two leads on the big, empty stage.

"I want you to play this scene for real from now on," he told them in careful tones. "Don't worry about how it looks; I'll block you into it."

He positioned them sitting on the feed sacks that the prop crew had finally produced. He iterated their lines and on each line told them what to do, how to do it.

"Then you've got your left arm behind her right shoulder, Herb. Liz, put your right arm on Herb's left shoulder. When he kisses her, Herb, put your left arm around her waist. Liz, you tilt your head right on the kiss; Herb, you left. Then you won't bump noses or anything. Got it?"

They nodded in disbelieving mortification as derisive wolf whistles screeched from the audience. Cooper turned. "No nonsense," he bellowed into the dimly lit house.

But from the moment the Act Two run-through began with Starbuck and Lizzie's father and brothers playing cards, everyone in the cast seemed aimed as tautly as an arrow at the love scene that concluded it. For the onlookers, the interest was both prurient and wistful. Herb and Liz understood that now only too well, and understood their symbolic part in it.

When the last scene with Lizzie and Starbuck came, the two settled into their vignette at stage right on the humble feed sacks. Herb said his lines with conviction; ever since the private rehearsal in the apple orchard, he'd lost his fear of Starbuck's emotionalism. Liz answered him with Lizzie's deeper, stranger brand of repressed dreaming. There was no "right arm, left arm; tilt right, tilt left" to their kiss when it came.

They played it for real and for an audience, as straight from their hearts as their abilities could make it. Herb's hand in her hair was tenderly urging. With Starbuck behind him now, his lips were bolder on hers. She responded more desperately, and yet more freely. They ended the scene with the embrace the script called for, and held it, waiting for the director's voice to release them from their frozen gesture.

But only silence echoed in the lofty auditorium. Not a seat squeaked. The rustle of their clothes sounded deafening as they separated and turned anxious faces to the dark beyond the stage lights.

The other guys in the cast still sat there in their self-appointed peanut gallery, ready to jeer but not doing it for some reason. Mr. Cooper stood in an aisle, motionless until he belatedly intoned "Curtain!" and walked back to the stage.

"That was great, kids." Mr. Cooper sounded shaken. "Just keep the magic until opening night."

The Rainmaker opened, ran three nights, and was judged one of the best Mr. Cooper had mounted. Everybody said Liz and Herb were "wonderful." The end of Act Two always left audiences hushed and stunned until they burst into gratified applause.

"There's one thing that's hard to believe," Z.J. said when he attended the final performance with Myrtle and they came to Liz's dressing room after the curtain call. He'd missed the opening night because of some city hall meeting he'd had to cover. "Nobody'd believe my Lizzie is plain, even with a bun on her head."

Myrtle eyed the open jars of greasepaint and blue eye shadow and the facing walls of well-lit mirrors. Through the walls, the boy's dressing room banged and hooted with postperformance exuberance.

"I don't know if all that smooching was necessary in a high school play," Myrtle said distastefully.

Z.J. grinned. "Can't blame a boy for wanting to kiss my Lizzie."

"Honestly, Dad! The cast party'll be late. I'll get a ride home with one of the guys."

Myrtle sniffed, but Z.J. beamed. It had been a big day for Liz. A letter from the University of Milwaukee journalism school had appeared in the mailbox that afternoon, formally accepting Elizabeth Jordan as a freshman for the fall of 1966.

"Don't keep the boys up too late, pumpkin," her father said.

But the cast party returned Liz to her preplay status. All the boys brought their steady girls. Ernest Lutz, the boy who'd cornered her into attending the prom with him, hung around until Liz finally escaped by darting into the kitchen, where empty potato chip bags strewed the countertops. The party was at Jeff Mayfield's house, because his parents always went to bed and stayed there.

Herb was in the kitchen. He started as Liz caught him spiking his Coke with the contents of a small, clear pint bottle of rum. All the senior boys did it. Liz tried to look nonchalant, although it bothered her for some odd reason.

"Celebrating our triumph." Herb hoisted his glass toastlike. He was flushed and looked a little wild, like he used to. Liz felt suddenly sad. He drank a sip, then looked around the littered kitchen. "Dumb party."

"Yeah."

"Want to split?"

His eyes dared her, and at the same time seemed braced for something.

She nodded, her throat suddenly swelling shut with excitement. The play was over, why would . . .

"I'll get the car and pick you up in five minutes around the corner."

Liz returned to the crowded living room, the noise and clutter seeming remote. The boys were rowdy now, thanks to their pint-bottle high spirits. Couples made out in the room's darker corners; girls sipped the boys' adulterated drinks and giggled. Liz felt icy sober. There was nothing here for her, and never had been. There was nothing for her in the front seat of a pink Oldsmobile, either, except the magic of the dark, the strange comfort of Herb's discontent, and the simple sexual excitement that coursed through her body and made it throb like a powerful car engine. If she went with Herb now, it wouldn't be for rehearsal, and she couldn't imagine why she'd do it, when it was so bound to come to nothing— except that she was curious and in a crazy way trusted him and she hated it so much at home now . . .

She walked into the warm evening unnoticed, her sweater swinging from her shoulders, her purse dangling self-importantly from her hand. There would be parties at college, she knew, and young men. Now the dark, purring hulk of Herb's car called her. Liz got in and pulled the massive door shut. It made a loud slam in the quiet midnight air.

"Why?" she asked Herb's profile in the dark.

His fingers brushed her cheek. "You're special, Liz; I've never had anything special in my whole life."

Sometimes Liz fantasized what would happen if her father found out she was dating terrible Herb Boyle, if he knew that her long senior year summer evenings "at Candy's" were really spent in Herb's car. Zachariah Jordan's precious, grade-point-average girl Lizzie, and wild Herb Boyle.

You couldn't really call it dating. They did nothing but park in secluded lanes and talk and kiss themselves delirious. Sometimes Liz felt she was cheating Herb in some way she couldn't quite name, or that she was cheating herself.

But she couldn't stop, and the reason went beyond sheer carnal curiosity. Herb had a sensitive streak no one had ever seen, except perhaps his mother long ago. He unfurled it now, as if knowing that Liz would never blackmail him for it, that she'd never be around long enough to be a threat, that it was his last chance. He talked about dreams that he already knew were doomed. Maybe he'd enlist in the Marines, he'd say, go to Vietnam. Liz showed appropriate shock at the manly danger of the idea. They both knew Herb was destined for the farm, his father's farm.

Mostly, though, they made almost-love—slow, emotional, cinematic fake-love. A shimmer of Romeo-Juliet unreality veiled their kisses, their touches. Nothing that happened between them resembled the crudely joked about makeout sessions Liz had heard other girls whisper of so often. Liz knew in some unexplainable way she was lucky, and she didn't know why.

One hot August night they parked in Lilac Lane while other Turtle Bend teen-age lovers were still overheating the inside of their cars at the Prairie Centre drive-in.

The crickets screamed against the closed car windows, and it had finally happened; touch had led to touch, clothes had shifted aside, and Herb's big, gentle hand pressed between her legs like a steam iron on silk. It just pressed there, nothing more. Liz was athrob for what was "next," no matter what, whatever if felt like, whatever it risked.

"I always carry a pack of Sheiks," Herb muttered against her neck, as if thinking about it for the first time. His voice was different than ever before, out of control. . . .

Liz recognized the brand of condoms only from the rude jokes the boys were always making in the halls between classes. She resolved she wouldn't be the kind of a girl who teases and says no, if he wanted—

"But . . ." His hand withdrew its tantalizing warmth. "You're going to college," Herb said, kissing her as innocently and sweetly as the first time in the apple orchard over his dog-eared copy of *The Rainmaker*.

Liz smarted from the withdrawal. Her body churned unheeded, her mind resented the way Herb had sounded—for the first time in his life—so mature and superior just then. It made her feel she had been in the wrong.

They met only a couple more times, but the magic was gone. Then Liz left on the train that stopped once a day at neighboring Prairie Centre. She was going to college. It was what her father had said for as long as she had ears and English. She'd never expected a boy, a would-be lover, to say it in that final, farewell way.

— Chapter 7 —

"Hey, Jordan! I thought you were going to read this crap."

"I had statistics finals. Besides, how come I still get all the freshmen articles to edit around here?"

Roy Carpenter set a stack of typed stories down on a desk that had already run the paper chase and lost. The room was small, jammed with desks smothered in paperwork. It served as the very model of a "modern" newspaper office, Professor Random often joked when he visited the campus newspaper's headquarters.

But it had been home away from home for Liz for almost four years. She was a college senior now and assistant editor of the University of Milwaukee student newspaper. Roy Carpenter was editor, for reasons that Liz didn't like to contemplate.

"Well, somebody has to do it," Roy said.

"Why not somebody other than the only woman on staff?" Liz shot back.

Roy sat, using his heels to roll the old office chair over to hers, too close; their knees nearly touched. Liz eased her own chair back.

"Don't give me that women's lib crap," Roy said. "Work's work."

"Unless men do it, and then it's a profession." Liz turned away to edit her own copy.

1970

Roy hung there a moment, trying to figure out what to say next. He was short, smart, cocky—every female was game for his self-esteem. That made it tough for Liz, being one of the few women active on the paper staff, being the only one to stick at it long enough to inherit a title.

Hank Mangione came in. She glanced up and smiled, recognizing too late that Roy would notice and harbor yet another grudge against her. But she couldn't help it: Hank was the nicest guy in J-school.

"Hi. We all set for our editorial board meeting tomorrow night?" Hank threw down a knapsack of books and perched on the edge of Liz's desk as Roy propelled his chair back to his own desk with a sour smirk.

"One more issue to go," Liz noted nostalgically. "What're we gonna put in it? The year's almost over. We graduate. Wow."

She leaned back, stretching desk-cramped legs. Her miniskirt made itself even scarcer. Hank didn't notice, not with his Coke-bottle-bottom glasses, but Roy did. Liz shifted, pulling her skirt down. She didn't like to wear jeans to class, and she was carrying a heavy senior year program.

"Not much to write about," Roy said. "All the guys are worried about going to 'Nam and all the girls are worried about not getting married. Hey, Jordan, you could do a light feature on it."

"Funny," she responded sardonically. "I'm getting out of here, getting some fresh spring air." Liz avoided sharing the office with only Roy, and Hank didn't look like he was staying.

"I'll walk you back to the dorm," Hank offered, jumping up to grab his books and open the door in a gentlemanly fashion. Liz sailed through. She wouldn't let Roy open doors for her. It burned him that she liked Hank, acne and all, better than him.

Outside the campus was ablush with spring blooms and awash with strolling students. Liz studied it, already feeling nostalgia sweeping in to crowd out the small gnawing fear in her gut. Graduation. Then what?

"Got any bites on your job applications?" Hank asked.

Liz shook her head. Journalism jobs were getting tight. "Maybe I'll just go back to Turtle Bend and work for my father."

"Roy may make fun of it, but Professor Random considers your dad's paper the pinnacle of small-town journalism. You could do worse."

"I don't know." Liz stopped. "I'd like to try something different."

"You mean after four years of hearing the Milwaukee hotshot back there call your dad's paper the *Turtle Bend Trumpet*, you're tired of it," said Hank. "Don't give him the satisfaction; he's just an ass."

"He's a lot worse than that. It burns me to see him getting all the glory. You've worked as hard on the paper as he has."

"And you. Harder."

"Oh, hell, Hank. Let's drop it. I'm tired of my father's paper and Roy Carpenter and *studying*! Let's go for a pizza."

"Roy'll be pissed you didn't ask him."

"Good!"

Late the next afternoon, Liz dropped by the campus newspaper office early for the editorial board meeting. It was empty. The latest *Milwaukee Observer* lay across Roy's desk. Under the masthead and the date—May 5, 1970—ran a picture more gripping than any Liz had ever seen printed.

"Holy cow!" Liz sank into Roy's empty chair to read the front-page story through its numerous jumps. But it was the photo that riveted her; that, and the enormity of the event, its implications for them all as students, as journalists.

The others came in, one by one, already aware of the story, morose and quiet. Roy Carpenter was last, and—as usual—loudest.

"This is a travesty. I can't believe it! This goddamn country's going to hell. First Cambodia; now this. Then they want to draft us." Roy looked Liz's way. "Except for Liz, of course."

"That doesn't mean I don't worry about the draft," Liz answered. "I think women *should* be drafted, just like men."

"Never happen." Roy turned his back.

The guys sat around, talking big and thinking worried. They talked about a campus demonstration in protest, about what they'd do if someone tried to arrest them, about freedom of speech and democratic ideals and the fucking Nazis in control. Look at Chicago '68, they said, and the "democratic" convention. The country's going down the toilet, and it's trying to take us with it. . . .

Liz swiveled her chair to face the old manual Royal centered on a battered typing pad. Everything in the office was hand-me-down, but nobody seemed to care. Coping was the number-one journalistic virtue. Liz coped with the dismal news her way: she rolled some limp oatmeal copy paper into the platen and began writing.

The striking of the keys sounded like Poe's Raven "knock, knock, knocking" at someone's chamber door. It was a common news office sound. The guys, circled around Roy like indignant doomsayers, ignored it.

After a half hour, Liz yanked out the last sheet with a shrill spin of the platen. That they noticed. Hank's eyebrows rose above the rims of his granny glasses; he ambled over.

"What's this?"

Liz handed it to him silently. He read. Then he walked over to the gathered young men. He tugged on a sleeve and Mike Haidukovich turned, saw the sheaf of papers, and started reading. The piece made the circle, one by one, until it reached Roy, who was busy being the centerpiece and hadn't noticed the perimeter stirrings. Hank handed the pages to him.

"Take a look at this."

Roy read, then studied their faces. He read their reactions even better. He finally rose and walked to Liz, alone at the typewriter on the other side of the room.

"We'll run it as an unsigned editorial," he said. Behind him, the young men nodded wordlessly. Roy tapped the papers' edge on the typewriter top. "Good piece."

Liz smiled wryly.

We won't be running it," Roy told the staff two days later. This time everybody was present, including the sophomore girl who did theater reviews and the freshman interns.

An aghast murmur stirred the room.

"What can I say?" Roy looked not unpleased. "Professor Random says it's too 'controversial' to run, and he's our adviser."

Boos and hisses.

"I thought this was a *newspaper*, not an administration mouthpiece," Hank said.

"We've been ordered not to run it."

"I know that, Roy, but we won't be here that much longer. What can we lose?"

"A lot! Jobs, for one thing. Okay, okay." Roy took a dramatic turn around the room. He looked at Liz, who was staying out of it. "If you guys think it's up to our journalistic honor to run the thing, well, let's do it anyway."

"How?"

Roy thought, all eyes except Liz's on him. "We'll put in a

dummy editorial to proof and show Random. I'll get the printer to slip this one in at the last minute. Then the paper'll be out, and what can they do?"

"All right! Right on! I like it!" Approbation exploded from everyone at once.

Roy turned to Liz. "What do you think, Jordan? It's your piece."

She shrugged. "It's your paper, Roy. You're the editor."

Liz had never been asked to write an editorial for the paper in four years, although the boys had divvied up the privilege among themselves regularly. She hadn't been asked this time, either. But when a fresh stack of papers, still reeking of ink, hit the student union lunchroom, Liz grabbed one and sat down to read what she had written, headlined "A Fable for Historians."

It began; "Once upon a time there was a country. . . ."

It looked good in print, Liz thought as she scanned the final paragraphs.

> The soldiers were very sorry and couldn't seem to explain how it all had happened, how a State that thought so highly of freedom of speech had come to shooting its citizens for disagreeing with it.
>
> No one else in the world was surprised. A corrupt government will always revert to slaughtering its citizens, said sages elsewhere, marking down the name of the State as one to be remembered in infamy for the events of May 4, 1970.
>
> But this is only a history lesson, and easily forgotten.
>
> What will not be forgotten is the name of the State.
>
> Kent State.

Later, in the newspaper office, Liz swiped some copies from a bound pile of fresh papers and paused again to study the *Milwaukee Observer* front-page photo of the Kent State student sprawled dead on the ground with the girl kneeling above him, her eyes and arms wide in frozen disbelief. *was not a student.*

No one who had been a student in 1970 would ever forget Kent State. For the first time since she had left Turtle Bend, Liz felt satisfied with something she had done.

"You don't have to tell them you wrote it. Hell, it was Roy's idea to sneak it in, and we all agreed it should run."

Hank Mangione was leaning over Liz's desk, trying to convince her.

"I know that, Hank. That's why editorials are unsigned."

She wore her best girl-graduate suit of light gray wool with a rose silk blouse. Her dark chin-length hair gleamed, as did her mouth, lipstick adorned for the first time in two years. She was checking the contents of her purse as if looking for something that wasn't there. Her hands were cold, and Hank's reassurances rolled away like rain down a distant window.

"Ready?" Roy was standing there, cocky in his jeans and T-shirt, always playing the campus rebel. Mr. Liberal.

They met in the brick administration building, in a conference room paneled eight feet up with cherrywood and furnished with an oval mahogany table surrounded by claw-footed leather chairs.

The university regents, a collection of civic leaders, mostly male, mostly past middle age, nodded frostily as the two students entered.

Liz found the chair they invited her to take catching on the thick carpeting. She wrestled it away from the table and sat, Roy lounging next to her. It was an "investigative" meeting to discover the why, how, and who of the Kent State editorial, which had offended regents and private citizens from one end of Milwaukee to the other. Roy as editor and Liz as assistant editor were literally being called on the royal red carpet.

"We're talking simple freedom of speech here," Roy said when asked to defend himself.

"Such issues are never simple, young man," rejoined a snowy-haired eminence.

"Well, it is for some of us. Either the university student newspaper is a vehicle for free speech or it isn't."

"It's not so much what was said as the fact that a piece that had been recommended to be dropped was kept in surreptitiously," the dean of students said slowly. "Although the condemnatory tenor of the editorial in question bespoke all the immature earmarks of a knee-jerk liberal mentality, we're not saying such drivel can't be written, simply not printed without permission. I hope I don't need to point out that disciplinary action can and will be taken to reinforce the point of the university's responsibility to the community at large."

Roy squirmed and tucked his Jefferson Airplane T-shirt in his jeans. "Look. Maybe the piece was immature; I felt it was in bad taste. I can't say it was my idea to put it in. But we did it and it's yesterday's news. Most of the paper staffers are about to graduate. There's no sense in punishing them, and maybe the underclassmen learned a lesson."

The regents considered this tacit apology while Liz felt her carotid artery indignantly knocking on the high-buttoned collar of her blouse.

"What about you, Miss Jordan?" asked the dean. "As assistant editor, do you concur with Mr. Carpenter's assessment that running the editorial was ill-judged? Of course, we realize that you're not as responsible as the actual editor," he added soothingly.

"Yes, I am, Dean Smythe. I wrote the editorial; I'm a poor person to ask to abjure it."

A sensation. Dull gray business suits rasped with their wearers' uneasy motions. Men all around the table leaned inward to peer more closely at Liz.

"Shit, you could have kept your mouth shut," Roy hissed.

"*You* wrote that editorial?"

"Sometimes women *are* allowed to write for the campus newspaper."

The silence this time lasted longer. Throats cleared. Two regents leaned toward each other to whisper. Liz thought she heard her father's name.

"Well." Dean Smythe removed his eyeglasses. "It was not our purpose to act as inquisitors and unearth the authorship of the article in question, but to examine the process of a student-run newspaper in the long term. Your . . . admission . . . puts us in a difficult position, Miss Jordan. We can't ignore it—"

"And I can't believe I did anything culpable. I saw a wrong and I responded to it. My peers agreed with what I said and wanted to print it. The issue has nothing to do with how one university student newspaper is run; it has to do with how all newspapers are run—in Washington, Paris, Belgrade, Moscow, and even Milwaukee. I thought that's what we were here to learn—responsibility. I can't retract what I wrote; I can't be sorry it saw print. I don't know if I would have gone against Professor Ransom's instructions to kill the editorial—that wasn't my responsibility." Beside her, Roy fidgeted helplessly. "But I wrote what I wrote, it was damn effective, and I won't apologize for it."

She waited for them to answer her, her whole body trembling with anger—and fear. God, so close to graduation. If only the odious Roy hadn't played Peter with such sickening alacrity—all freedom of the press one minute and "I didn't have anything to do with it" the next.

"We'll have to consider this." The dean replaced his glasses. "You're both excused."

Roy dawdled until Liz left, apparently unwilling to be seen leaving with her, but he caught up in the foyer.

"Showboater," Roy sneered under his breath, coming up behind her.

"Don't you wish," Liz returned. "You were fast enough to torpedo the First Amendment."

"You could be expelled two weeks before graduation, you know that?" He was openly angry now. "Stuck-up broad. Who do you think you are, Zachariah Jordan's daughter? If I get one demerit on my record because of this, I'll—"

Liz spurted ahead of him down the long white marble steps from the administration building.

She walked briskly across campus, her unaccustomed high heels rapping the sidewalks like a drumroll. She was angry, indignant, disgusted by Roy and the regents, and scared silly about what would happen to her, to her academic career, her future.

She found out two days later. The dean of students called her to his office, where he told her she was forbidden to write for the paper the rest of the school year—which was a very few weeks—and was no longer assistant editor. In view of the controversial nature of her actions, he told her, she should be forewarned that her opportunities for finding employment were severely handicapped.

"I didn't want to take it," Hank Mangione swore when she found out he was the new assistant editor until graduation.

"That's all right. Who wants to be an assistant to a rattlesnake anyway? Carpenter is the sleaziest, slipperiest, sickest bastard that ever slithered. You should have seen him evading the blame and pointing fingers at the regents' meeting."

"Well, cheer up." Hank pulled a triangle of pizza off the tin between them and wound the cheese tails onto his finger. He'd taken her to Mama Angelica's for a combined celebration and commiseratory pig-out. "The excitement's bound to die down in a day or two."

Liz sighed and pulled a piece of curled pepperoni off her side of the super-duper giant Mama A's special pizza. "I'm afraid it won't, Hank. The *Milwaukee Observer* called. They want to interview me about academic freedom of the press."

"And you're doing it? Mama mia!"

Liz shrugged and finally took her first slice of pizza. "What else have I got to lose?"

"Oh, Liz, I'm so glad you can do this."

Candy Turner's face seemed to light up the cramped, underilluminated dressing room. A rainbow of floor-length gowns hung from a single, too-short hook. Candy's lacquered nails paged among the rustling skirts.

"I don't know which color . . . the lilac would be lovely on you, but then the blue, too—Try it on."

Liz stripped off her jeans and blouse, feeling silly cramming heels on her bare feet and slipping a long, fussy bridesmaid's gown over nothing more than a flimsy Gernreich bra and bikini panties. It didn't seem real, but then neither did Candy's getting married in June.

"I thought the dope would never ask!" Candy complained when Liz had expressed surprise at her long-distance call. "Three years of going steady. I mean, really."

He was a Turtle Bend boy—Liz still thought of her high school classmates as "girls" and "boys," inhabitants of a Wisconsin Brigadoon cut off from the growing pains of the outside world.

"Oh, that's lovely on you, Liz." Candy's cold fingers pulled up the back zipper. Liz saw herself besleeved and beskirted and beruffled in the mirror, looking surprisingly pretty. "Do you like it?" Candy inquired anxiously.

"I'm only the maid of honor; you're the bride. You choose."

"Linda's my matron of honor and she's got reddish hair, so I guess . . . this style! But in lilac, if that's okay."

"Okay, okay!" Liz laughed and shrugged the voluminous gown over her shoulders. "You're wearing the whole schmear—white gown, train, veil . . . ?"

"Of course." Candy leaned inward and giggled. "And of course, I really shouldn't be."

Liz caught the reference but desired to know no more about it. Turtle Bend carnal knowledge didn't hold the attractions it once had. She couldn't help weighing herself and Candy in the mirror. Her father would say Liz was better-looking, and maybe she was, but she certainly couldn't boast that it did her much good, the only virgin in her best friend's wedding party.

"Is there someone special in your life?" Candy was asking.

"No, just friends." Liz smiled. She'd considered sleeping with Hank just to get it over with, but retreated before the thought should sire any unrescindable action. Despite the vaunted "sexual revolution," the girls at the dorm still had to sneak off to Planned Parenthood to get the Pill, and even then pretended they were engaged.

"Speaking of friends . . ." Candy folded the lilac gown over her arm and perched on the tiny built-in bench provided. "I guess you won't be seeing much of Turtle Bend anymore."

Liz zipped up her jeans and stuck her hands in her back pockets.

"I'll come home to visit. But I'm staying on in Milwaukee. I got a job offer after a brouhaha over some editorial I wrote for the university paper." It never did any good to explore the nuances of larger issues with Candy. "The *Milwaukee Observer* managing editor offered me a job after graduation. Can you believe it? The guys, needless to say, are all green."

"You don't want guys jealous of you, Liz; you want them white with lust!"

Liz laughed into Candy's saucer-wide, close-set blue eyes. "I can't help it. I inspire envy, not lust. Maybe that's not so bad. Anyway, the university regents are also miffed. They threw me off the roof and I landed on my feet."

Liz took the gown from her friend and leaned against the mirror. "You know, Candy, we've been friends for a long time, through some pretty crazy stunts. We've written each other while I was at college, and I'm going to be in your wedding now ... but it's different. It won't be the same, even if I do visit Turtle Bend. There's a time for things, and sometimes that time passes people by. If there's someone else you should have in your wedding party, someone from Turtle Bend, you don't have to ask me for old times' sake."

Candy ran her hands through the hanging dresses again, her face turned away.

"I know, Liz. I'm not as dumb as Mrs. Felix thought. You're not really part of Turtle Bend anymore. Maybe you never were." She turned back. "But you have to come back now and then to see your father, so why not be part of a wedding when you do it?" Tears blurred the blue of her eyes.

Liz sometimes felt she was on a train, a big, grinding, rolling train that was surging through alien countryside, leaving everyone she knew small, fading figures beside some distant track.

"It was a beautiful wedding!" Myrtle wore a flowered hat and a string of mother-of-pearl beads. She beamed as they stood in the churchyard watching Candy and her new husband cram sixteen yards of bridal train into a Ford Maverick.

Liz's lilac skirt billowed gracefully against her legs, but her arches ached from hours of standing on high-heeled shoes.

"Well, now you've got your B.A., apparently by the skin of your teeth, from my what friend Judge Abernathy the regent tells me," Z.J. said, beaming Liz's way. He always beamed at public ceremonies, even funerals. "When are you going to work on your M.R.S.?"

"I've got to work on the *Milwaukee Observer* first," Liz hedged lightly.

"Men work there, too," Z.J. said, grinning. He looked at the disappearing car with its cacophony of trailing tin cans and honking horns. Pieces of crepe paper streamers buffeted down the road. "You know, Elizabeth, things can happen. People get suddenly sick . . . die. It's good to have someone in this world, someone to be there when things go wrong. And right."

"I know, Dad." She shielded her eyes to stare into the distance as the rear of Candy's car shrank into a red dot.

"That's what blasted institutions are for, like weddings. They were here long before institutions like newspapers."

"I know, Dad." She did know what he was trying to say; she just didn't want either of them to have to say it. "Maybe I'll never get married," Liz said suddenly. Myrtle turned, disbelieving. "Maybe I'm like Lizzie in the play, or Katharine Hepburn. Maybe I'll be a career woman."

Myrtle sniffed and walked away.

"Maybe I'll come back to Turtle Bend and be an old maid newspaper editor."

Her father's hand, big and rough, closed on her arm. He hadn't touched her in years, not since she was a child. Time had polished apples of age onto his cheeks; his snow-white hair was as long as an old-time lawyer's or snake oil salesman's.

"You don't want to do that, Lizzie. You've got your own life to live. Besides, after that editorial . . . A right sharp bit of opinionizing, all right, but too much sass for Turtle Bend. You go to Milwaukee, Elizabeth, and pretty soon you'll get tired of type and long hours. You'll find some nice-looking young man and start thinking of houses and kids—"

"I haven't yet," she interrupted, sounding defiant and feeling betrayed.

Her father stared into her eyes with the same piercing look he gave her when she was five and he thought she was lying, although she almost never had.

"You just haven't met the right man, Elizabeth." Z.J. patted her arm as he released it. "But you will."

It almost sounded like a threat.

— Chapter 8 —

There were only two ways to leave Turtle Bend: west to the nearby Minnesota/Wisconsin border and the Twin Cities of Minneapolis and St. Paul—or east to Milwaukee.

Liz had driven east the last two years of college in the used Ford Pinto her father had found at Big Bob Bailey's in Prairie

Centre. Now she pointed its snub red nose in the same direction, but with a watershed change of purpose: she was leaving home to go to her first job in the big city.

Milwaukee wasn't the nation's largest metropolis, and the *Observer* wasn't Milwaukee's biggest daily paper. Yet they both overwhelmed Liz at first, compared to her father's one-man operation and a one-train town like Turtle Bend.

Elwood Hopkins, the bold managing editor who'd hired her over the phone on the basis of her Kent State editorial notoriety and her résumé, turned out to be a plump, balding man as brusquely pungent as the cigar perpetually cocked in his teeth.

"You found a nice place to live?" he inquired avuncularly, sitting her down in the tiny open-ceilinged interview cubicle off the paper's labor-intensive newsroom.

"I think so." Liz smiled confidently, picturing her boxy beige one-bedroom apartment with nothing in it but a bed, card table, and TV. But it had potential, she told herself. And so did she.

"Now . . . I assume, of course, that you plan to stay with us awhile."

Liz was surprised into silence. Why else would anyone apply for a job?

"A pretty girl like you has boyfriends, I know. But no marriage plans and babies imminent?" Hopkins grinned widely.

"Oh, no, Mr. Hopkins. I plan to make journalism a career. Even if I did . . . do that, I'd still work."

Hopkins' quick, quirky smile silently rebutted her words. "But for the next year or so, you'll be here?" he prodded.

"Of course."

"Just checking." He arranged a wide, white smile around the emphatic, tobacco-brown exclamation point of his cigar. "We don't want to hand you a slot someone else would take seriously only to have you drop out in a few months."

"Nobody'd take my job more seriously than I," Liz insisted, her hands wrapped tightly around her purse frame.

Hopkins grinned. "Fine, fine." He shuffled some papers. "I'm putting you in the Affinities section. You'll do general assignment reporting, feature writing, whatever comes up." *better than OBITS*

"Sounds great." Liz loved writing features, despite the fact that "soft" news about people earned less peer respect than "hard" news, which Liz tagged "the three Bs"—bureaucrats, bodies, and bombings.

The Affinities section turned out to be a small, open room crammed with desks and the mad chatter of manual typewriters.

"Madge O'Toole," Hopkins barked as he stopped at the first desk. "She's section editor and your boss."

"Have a seat," said a woman of thirty-some whose raw country-red face bloomed under an impeccably teased hairdo. She indicated a newspaper-heaped side chair. Liz lifted the stack, sat, and balanced the papers on her lap; there was nowhere else to put them.

"Everyone pretty much has set assignments," Madge added as Liz studied the office. "You'll be our fill-in person. That's Edith Maxwell, who does the social column." A dated beehive across the room nodded regally in Liz's direction. "And Gloria Hobbs is fashion." A horsey woman with a blond bun glanced over her half glasses. "Melissa Ripley's food." There came a cold, assessing stare from a fat, fair-skinned woman consumed by an op art—pattern dress that looked homesewn. "You'll be general assignment."

Madge escorted Liz to an empty desk facing a second door from the office. Liz welcomed the idea of air flow and quick egress—or escape.

"Get settled. I want you to do an interview at two in Minneapolis. Here's the background stuff."

"Thank you." Liz set her purse at her feet and looked up to find Edith Maxwell silently shaking her frosted and teased head. Liz raised her eyebrows questioningly. Edith pointed down and mouthed "the drawer."

After Liz's purse was secured in her bottom desk drawer, she scanned the materials before her. The cover letter's blue letterhead trumpeted the women's auxiliary of a veterans' organization. Their national president was addressing local members at a luncheon that day. Liz was to interview her afterward. She read copies of previous interviews with the president, complete with canned head shot. The photo made Madam President look like Eleanor Roosevelt on a bad day, the quintessential clubwoman—hatted head, brooch-studded bosom, and the dated look of a matron from a Marx Brothers movie.

Oh, Lord, thought Liz as the typewriters around her banged away in ill-assorted rhythms, what have I got myself into?

"The women's department."

"What?"

"I said, are you the new gal in the women's department?"

"I'm Liz Jordan," she returned with dignity, "and I work in the Affinities section."

"Same difference. Burt Sampson. I'm one of the photographers. You'll probably get me for some assignment."

Liz returned to studying the newsroom bulletin board, a giant cork message center outside the supervisory offices that indiscriminately mingled company memos and internecine newsroom notes.

"I wish I'd had you yesterday, Burt," Liz said ruefully. "The photographer never did show up to shoot the VFW auxiliary president like he was assigned to. We had to go with a fuzzy head shot this morning."

Burt's big shoes shuffled guiltily. "Yeah, well, sometimes breaking news cancels out feature stuff. That's the way it is."

Liz sighed as he left her alone with the board and its mass of official memos about health insurance rates and expense account policy. Staff members had posted clippings from the *Observer* and rival papers, all heavily marked to castigate writing and headline style, criticizing one another's work with anonymous relish. Liz regarded newspeople, despite a tradition of claims to the contrary, as among the most opinionated on earth.

A familiar type style snagged her attention; Liz found herself rereading her father's column on fishing as a philosophical pursuit from the previous week's *Turtle Bend Sentinel*. Bold handwriting in the margin proclaimed, "This guy can write; we should take lessons."

Another unseen presence loomed behind her; apparently the bulletin board functioned as a free zone and anyone idling away time reading it as fair game for conversation.

"You're the one who got into trouble over that editorial in the university paper."

This guy was younger than Burt. He didn't ask questions; he declared facts. He was also decent-looking, so Liz decided to get off on a better, more feminine foot.

"Yes. Liz Jordan. Hi." Her smile, she was sure, would have made an alligator green with envy.

"Jim Kennedy. I'm general assignment off the city desk. How'd you end up in the Bunny Hutch?"

"The *what*?"

Jim's auburn head jerked toward the distant Affinities section. "Bunny Hutch. Don't look at me; Della Olson christened it that." This time he nodded toward a middle-aged woman at the copy desk.

"It's still sexist! Just because everyone in Affinities is female . . ."

Jim's smile engorged into a grin. "I thought you looked like a women's libber."

"I didn't know we advertised."

His eyes dropped to her bell-bottomed purple polyester pants. "Any woman around here wearing a pantsuit can expect a ribbing. You mean you hadn't noticed that your officemates are all women?

The front office just changed the section name a few months ago, but the content's the same: food, duds, yakety-yak, and crapola."

"Give me a day or two," Liz said grimly. "Maybe I'll like it."

Jim Kennedy squinted hazel-green Irish eyes at her. "Yeah." He nodded dubiously. "Maybe pigs wear toe shoes."

Some stories were people-related; some were event-related. Liz came to call her Affinities assignments "good works—related." There was the Red Cross ball committee chairman interview, the United Way women's division chairwoman interview, the mayor's volunteering wife interview, the governor's cleaning lady interview, and of course, the "Mother of the Year" interview, which became one of Liz's more exciting stories when a irate reader called after it ran and tagged the revoltingly selfless mother of nine Liz had dutifully profiled "a sewer rat."

"I wish I *had* interviewed a sewer rat!" Liz exploded on her first dinner date with Jim Kennedy. "It would have been a hell of a lot more interesting."

Jim chuckled mildly, which Liz hoped meant sympathy. She couldn't be sure. Most newspapermen, she had observed already, were not as idiocentric as Z.J., although they were fully as egocentric. They exuded pleasant, bland self-satisfaction like trendier men oozed musk after-shave lotion.

"Just imagine," Liz went on. "We could do a special Sunday section on it. Edith could outline the social climb of Mrs. Rat and offspring, Melissa could offer a holiday menu of stewed sewer rat, and Gloria could devise ratty little wardrobes. I, of course, would handle the human-interest angle. Rat bites!" Liz bit savagely into her steak.

Ice rattled as Jim set down his water goblet. "You could ask for a transfer to city desk."

"I have," Liz confessed. "Hopkins said no."

The following Monday, Liz approached Madge O'Toole, who ran Affinities with laissez-faire routine. She held a woman's magazine in her hand and hoped her face looked suitably humble.

"Did you see this article on latchkey children?" Of course Madge hadn't. "It's really quite . . . interesting. I thought I could do something like that for the section." Madge's face was depressingly blank. "You know, interview working mothers who have to leave kids to their own devices. It's a growing problem and I know something about it—I was a latchkey kid myself."

That last revelation intrigued Madge. "Oh, were you? Well, I suppose, if you have time between your regular assignments to fit in a long-range article like that . . . It would have to be well documented," she warned severely.

"Of course." Liz hopped up before Madge could change her slow-moving mind. What Madge knew about documentation Liz could put in the dot on an eight-point-high letter *i*.

It wasn't going to be easy, Liz thought as she settled at her desk. She wasn't the only journalism-trained woman on the staff, but she was the youngest and most progressive. The others long ago had become accustomed to whiling away their workdays on voluminous amounts of pap: Edith typed with two ladylike fingers, handkerchief tucked into her right palm, detailing the weddings, charity balls, and antique sales of Milwaukee's finer families; Gloria pushed high heels one week and low heels the next, whatever whimsical trend the fashion industry fed her through the never-ending flow of New York press releases; Melissa's food sense was as tasteless as her clothes sense. She churned canned recipes into her typewriter each day, considering her efforts well rewarded if the food manufacturers kept a continuous and copious supply of edible and drinkable "payola" coming to her home address—if they goofed and sent the goody boxes to her at work, she had to share with her officemates, which always made her grumpy for a day or so afterward.

But the latchkey idea was sufficiently nonthreatening for Madge to okay. Over the next few weeks, Liz interviewed teachers and sociologists, parents and kids, gleaning enough material for a series. The next step was to sell it, which she did by writing it first and presenting a hopelessly long story—a literal ladder of pasted-together copy paper—to her editor.

Madge read and unraveled, her brow wrinkling. "This is so long, Liz!"

"But the material's great."

"Yes, but . . ." Madge didn't like decisions that might give the front office opportunity to question her judgment. She also hated to tell anyone bad news. "Perhaps if we divided it into parts—"

"That's a wonderful idea," Liz chirped. "I know just how to do it! Here, I'll take it. Thank you, Madge!"

Madge was left blinking.

The latchkey series was followed by Liz's big Sunday front-page story on single women not waiting for Prince Charming to come by, but going ahead and buying houses themselves, forcing real estate and banking professionals to revamp institutional prejudices against taking women's wages seriously.

Next Liz investigated the trend to use midwives so women could have home births instead of regimented hospital lie-ins. That one brought ardent letters to the editor from indignant nurses who questioned the safety factors.

But the triumphs rang in Liz's awareness alone; despite adulatory letters from women real estate agents and the La Leche League, nobody seemed to notice the new tenor in Affinities' subject matter until Liz entered the annual Wisconsin newspaper competition and walked away with first place in the "women's" division. Until then, male city desk reporters who dabbled in a "soft news" story now and again had won it.

Yet every significant story came at the cost of dozens of insignificant stories. Liz worked harder, and faster, to get routine assignments out of the way, still rescheduling interviews for the long-term ones embarrassingly often.

By the end of her first year at the *Observer*, she had talked Madge into letting her investigate male vasectomies. Finding the men to interview was even harder. Liz cajoled them over the phone, using all her charm and intelligence.

"It's really a public service," she told a reluctant high school football coach. "A lot of men still have a foolish idea that surgical sterilization will affect their masculinity." The coach laughed nervously. "I really need to interview people—men—who've had the procedure. Anything you want to be off the record . . . you will? Wonderful! Uh, sure, this afternoon's fine. The sooner the better. Okay, I'll be out at three." Liz's triumphal shout as she hung up was choked off when Madge's worried eyes met hers.

Madge glanced to Melissa's unoccupied but messy desk. Everyone in the office knew that Melissa was at Milwaukee's finest hostelry being extravagantly wined and dined by the California Vineyards Association. A heavy holiday box of assorted wines would undoubtedly bless the Ripley doorstep that Christmas. Melissa relished everything about her job but the ethics of it.

Madge was coming Liz's way, a sheet of paper that screamed "instant assignment" all over it.

"Madge, I can't! I'm doing the first vasectomy interview today. You don't know what I went through to get this guy to talk."

"Liz . . ." Madge sighed and straightened. "You have to go. The state Home Economics Association is meeting in town and I've scheduled a piece for tomorrow. Your interview isn't urgent."

"Oh yes, it is. To a man, talking about a vasectomy is the next worse thing to *getting* one. Why can't Melissa do it? Food's her beat."

Madge looked away. "Melissa's . . . out. Apparently she forgot the assignment."

Fat chance, Liz thought. "What is it?"

"A talk on . . . how to safely stuff a turkey. For the holidays."

"I don't cook anything more complicated than an omelet!" Liz exploded. "You want *me* to tell people how to avoid food poisoning? That's like assigning Lucrezia Borgia the story. Madge, please..."

"It's got to be done. You can see your man some other time."

Liz sighed and picked up the phone to reschedule her precious interview. "If you want a first-class demonstration in how to stuff a turkey," she grumbled over her shoulder, "you should send a reporter and photographer to the freebie wine growers spread at the Sheraton."

Later, Liz hotfooted it over icy November sidewalks to the Civic Center several blocks away. She arrived in mid-lecture, took assiduous notes, and rushed back to write a how-to on turkey stuffing. It turned out to be a complex and arcane process. She struggled to translate complicated terminology into something the average cook could master, cursing internally all the while. It was probably the most dangerous story Liz had done, she thought, given her abysmal ignorance of culinary matters. Visions of salmonella-succumbing toddlers danced in her night brain until a week after the story had run and no accusing phone calls had come in.

"You're getting a reputation around here," Jim told her one day soon after, materializing behind her while she studied the bulletin board to see who played target for that week's peer invective.

Liz whirled. "About us?" They still dated intermittently, but Jim was too Irish to push beyond the casual stage. He kept all women except his mother at an amicable distance.

"No," he said, oddly pleased. "Your stories. I hear you got Hopkins to okay an exclusive on 'The Big V.'"

"Yeah," Liz said, glowering, "if I can ever get to it. Boy, they sure love my father's stuff around here." She pointed out another one of his columns, clipped and starred, on the board.

Jim looked, and then his face fell. "Oh."

"What?" Liz glanced under her father's clipping. Her story on turkey stuffing had been neatly razored out and pinned up. "A chick off the old cock" was penned in large, vindictive ballpoint over the headline, with the "Jordan" in her byline circled.

"Those, those turkeys!" Liz pulled her clipping down. Her face flamed. It was so unfair to compare an assignment like that with her father's glorious self-assigned journal. It belittled her, home economics, and women everywhere.

She marched back into the Affinities office. "Look at this! It was on the board under a column from my father's paper."

Madge O'Toole pursed her lips. "They really shouldn't use

obscenities on the board, but they always do. Hopkins' secretary takes them down if she sees them first."

"What's obscene is the way the men around here put down women, and this department. My God, how far can they go?"

Madge just looked troubled, as if, by pointing out the problem, Liz had created it.

"Forget it," she urged. "These things come and go. It's just some coward who's afraid to sign his name."

"With a lot of men who should know better standing silently behind him—smirking," Liz raged. "They're scared! They're scared of us because women are working and taking ourselves and our jobs seriously and buying houses and living alone. They can't fight fair; they're afraid they might lose."

"Just do your stories and forget about it, Liz. My goodness, you're privileged. You've gotten to do far more than any other woman at the paper."

Liz stared into Madge's hardening brown eyes. It wasn't only the men who were threatened.

She took the clipping home to her new apartment, with its framed dance posters on the wall, and taped it to a kitchen cupboard. Z.J., Madge O'Toole, and the vast anonymous mass of men out there—somehow they forged an unholy trinity in Liz's mind. She didn't understand why, but she did understand that her mere existence put her at odds with something big and hidden and pervasive. Maybe it was called "life."

"This is 1972, not the Stone Age! If I could get condom-dispensing machines in every gas station in the state, it would decimate VD, unwanted pregnancies, teen-age maternity. . . ."

Liz scribbled it all down in her cryptic note-taking style, a cross between shorthand and hen scratches. Her "good quote" antennae were tingling. Her good sense stood silent behind her, saying that such a radical proposal would never fly in a whole-milk-and-family-picnic state like Wisconsin.

But her interviewee was young, overeducated, enlightened, progressive, and from out-of-state. He was also the new head of the Wisconsin Planned Parenthood.

Condoms in gas stations? As if people who shouldn't be having sex—the young, the unmarried—actually were out there *doing* it? Heaven and every social and civic institution forbid!

"If we could send educational representatives into the schools . . . Ignorance, not knowledge, is responsible for the country's poor infant mortality rate; too many young, unmarried mothers not getting proper prenatal care. . . ."

On went her fat, eraserless yellow pencil, standard newsroom issue, capturing every word or jumping ahead to the current one if it had fallen behind. Her brain went faster. Such ideas were seldom expressed in Milwaukee, a blue-collar, beer-drinking-and-brewing town steeped in religious tradition. Liz seldom got her pencil and teeth into such meaty issues. She couldn't believe she was hearing this; she couldn't believe it when he mentioned the forbidden word. So she took it all down and reported it for the next morning's paper.

"Abortion!" Hopkins's cigar end glowed cherry-red as his face slowly heated up to match. "That's a touchy issue in this town." His forefinger tapped the morning paper, folded back to reveal the Affinities section front. "How'd you get into a topic like that?"

Madge O'Toole and Liz looked at each other. It was Madge's place to respond, but Liz had proposed interviewing the new Planned Parenthood director.

"It may be a touchy topic, but it's vital to about half our readership," Liz answered. "And that half is pretty vital to the other half of our readership."

"Don't quote readership at me, young woman." Hopkins glowered over his glasses. "We've done reader surveys. Most people in this community consider abortion an abomination."

"Yet it happens, right here in our back alleys. It may not be a pretty story, but it's true."

"It's also true that I've had twenty irate calls this morning about your so-called story, saying it was one-sided, biased, and downright immoral." Hopkins tossed the paper at her. "We've never had that kind of problem before. Cover the other side, fast, and stick to tea parties and toiletries after this."

They were dismissed.

"'The other side,'" Liz fumed to Madge as they left Hopkins's office. "The other side is *not* covering the contraceptive and pro-abortion movement. That's what newspapers have always done, ignored the issue."

Back at her desk, Madge handed Liz a list of names and phone numbers. "These are some of the calls *I've* gotten this morning. You can start with them. We'll run the rebuttal Sunday."

Liz returned to her desk. Heads all around the room were carefully lowered as her coworkers tried to read her face surreptitiously. They never got into trouble with the front office; Melissa could take PR firm payola to the tune of hundreds of dollars a year and no one would blow the whistle. Touch a controversial subject, like abortion, and the entire newspaper writhed like a worm stranded on concrete.

* * *

"And so they made me write a follow-up, just because a few calls and letters had come in." Liz waxed indignant at Sunday dinner in Turtle Bend.

"How did you do it?" her father inquired, pushing his glasses against his forehead.

"I went to all the patented antiabortion spokeswomen in town; there are a half dozen groups, even though they all say the same thing. Anyway, they're very sincere, but they want to make everybody else think like them."

"You seem to have taken on some liberal ideas in Milwaukee, Elizabeth," Z.J. went on. "Were you fair to these other people?"

"Of course I was fair!" Liz said, bypassing Myrtle's butter-drenched lima beans despite her stepmother's intimidating surveillance. "I presented their side of the question as sympathetically as I could. And I bet there'll be fifty calls and letters from pro-abortion advocates saying my latest story was unfair or that the other side got too much ink. It's an emotional issue, and you can't really win by covering it. But I was educated to believe that *not* covering community controversy is no way to run a newspaper! What's your position on reproductive issues, Dad?"

Myrtle snorted and Z.J. smiled.

"We called it 'sin' in my day, Elizabeth; not a very fancy word, but it seemed sufficient."

"It's not that simple, Dad. Things have changed. Women are dying; their lives are being changed—"

"Well, I'm just old-fashioned then, Elizabeth. Don't ask me." Lima beans slid in a yellow-green flood to his plate. "Good spread, Myrtle. I'm sure glad I'm too old for all these newfangled social ideas. It was simpler in my day—you either sinned or you didn't."

"Maybe sin has gotten subtler," Liz argued, but the fire had gone out of the discussion. Politically her father was progressive; socially he was a dinosaur. "Maybe sins of omission are worse than sins of commission," she said into the silence.

Liz stubbornly kept the reproductive freedom beat, learning more of contraceptive methods than she had any use for. She and Jim remained "friends," platonic to the point of slight mutual boredom.

Most of the men Liz met in her work were married, so newspaper parties were close-knit but staid affairs where Liz was left to chat with her coworkers' mousy homemaker wives. She had no women friends. The few women on the city desk looked down on her as a "bunny hutcher," no matter how many groundbreaking stories she did, and she had zero affinity with her self-absorbed Affinities coworkers.

That spring when the annual statewide journalism competition came, the rules had been changed. Editors, not reporters, entered stories. Liz happened to spot a pile of contest clippings on Madge's desk. The office was momentarily empty, so with an odd sense of precognition, Liz flipped through them. None of her stories were among the pallid array of ill-written, good-girl drivel readied for submission. Submission was the word, Liz told herself, trying not to feel hurt.

Once again newsmen won the women's-interest category, one with a lewd lowdown on the life of a stripper, another with a sentimental tribute to a self-sacrificing mother.

"No wonder newsmen are so behind the times," Liz complained to Jim, who was at least a bachelor. "The women in their lives are models of demure submission."

"You sound like a radical feminist."

"I'm not," Liz said quickly, then slowed down to think. "Or maybe I am. You see how you men have made even the appearance of being concerned with women's issues a crime! It's not easy doing that abortion beat, you know. First from that side, then that. I walk a narrower line than the city hall reporter."

Jim's dark beer swirled in the frosty mug as he tipped it consideringly. They were in one of Milwaukee's dark Irish pubs, a crowded, casual place.

"You'll never win at a newspaper, you know. It's too easy to bury someone like you in the Affinities section."

"Why did Hopkins hire me?" Liz demanded. "My God, he knew from the Kent State piece I wasn't bunny meat."

"Window dressing, Liz. Same reason he's hunting high and low for a black worth hiring. A black here, a woman there, and he can answer charges of no women and minorities on staff. And your father isn't exactly a lightweight name in Wisconsin . . . but don't expect him to take you seriously."

"But I do. That's just it; I expect people to take me seriously." Liz sipped her own brew, a Black and Tan, a coward's combination of light and dark ale that sat easier on the bland American palate.

Jim's smile was tolerant. "You'll get over that. In the meantime, you might want to look for another job."

Liz's eyebrows hit the ceiling as Jim shrugged modestly. Journalists were inveterate rumormongers and liked those pertaining to themselves and their profession best of all.

He leaned confidentially forward. "I hear a big chain is about to snap up the *Observer*. You know what kind of shake-up that'll be. Maybe you better look somewhere else, like Chicago. Or the TV stations. At least there you'd be visible; you'd get more credit for what you did. But the *Observer* . . . bail out, hard times coming. Kennedy predicts."

"A chain? Maybe a chain will be progressive; maybe I'll do better."

"Maybe crows will wear top hats," Jim answered, burping contentedly.

By the fall of 1972 the rumor was fait accompli. An out-of-state newspaper conglomerate had made the *Observer* the newest weak link in its chain. The changeover was stealthy, merely a slight shift in tone in company memos. Teamwork was encouraged, company spirit and good writing, as if merely paying lip service to these virtues ensured their practice.

Liz watched hopefully for a meatier Affinities assignment list, but none came. Instead there were daily adjurements to find and promulgate "news you can use." How to put on your storm windows. How to shop for food, a car, a new job. How to bore an inquisitive, hardworking reporter to death with niggling story assignments.

Liz doggedly kept her unpopular beats, hoping it would pay off. Even on the abortion issue, her mail from both sides now praised her fairness. It had been a long, bitter struggle to win that concession. Nobody noticed but Liz, but somehow that was enough.

The first sign of the chain's influence was the demotion of a veteran city editor. In his place came a man from the South, a man with close-cut hair that was kissing kin to a crew cut, and a slushy southern accent that sweetened the criticism he uttered about as much as maple syrup would dull an ax blade.

"Mason is his name. Would you believe it, honey chile?" Edith Maxwell loved gossip and had a gift for mimicry. "Mason Devers, I do declare. Sheer steel under all that corn pone. He cut the ground right out from under the old assistant city editor, and assigned Jim Kennedy back to the cop shop."

Liz winced. The police beat was boring and unrewarding, novice stuff. So the prophet had been one of the first victims of his foresight.

"Maybe," Liz told Edith, "Devers won't get around to a section as lowly as Affinities."

Edith's knowing eyes rolled. "Just you wait, honey chile."

But nothing happened, despite a newsroom-wide nervousness that Devers seemed to enjoy taking personal credit for. Liz kept her eyes open for a bailout anyway, carefully querying fellow members of the Wisconsin Journalism Society at their monthly dinner meetings for job openings.

"It's closing down bad," said a tall blond woman who wrote

features at the *Milwaukee Journal*. "Nobody's hiring at most of the papers. Unless you're black," she added in lowered tones. "It's really embarrassing how few black reporters there are—and how few even qualified to be hired."

"Sorry, I don't qualify. Don't they want to increase the number of women?"

"They've already got a few of us." The woman drained her Scotch and water and looked toward the body-packed bar. "And all those underpaid clerks and secretaries. If you walk into a newsroom, you see plenty of women."

"Tell me about it," Liz said, grimacing. "Our features section opens onto the main entry hall, so there's always some pompous man sticking his head in when you're halfway through a story, demanding to be shown to the city editor. They all assume we're a secretarial pool!"

"Well, you type, don't you?" The woman, whose name was Julie, smiled wearily. "I'm getting out of this rat race." She wiggled her left hand, on which Liz observed an impressive diamond gleam. "Suburbs, two cars, three bathrooms, and four kids."

"Congratulations, I guess."

"Thanks." She sounded a bit guilty. "Say . . . the TV stations are looking for women. NOW is giving them a hard time. At a newspaper office you can't tell if the women you see are slaveys or actual reporters. On TV, if women's faces aren't right out there, everybody knows. You ever think of that?"

"I'm not an actress—well, I did have the lead in the school play. . . ." Liz added modestly.

Julie shrugged and eyed the bar again. "I'd better get back there before the souses drain the bottles. You might think about it, Liz," she said in friendly tones. "The local station approached me, and if it hadn't been for Mr. Wonderful . . ." Her ring finger waggled demonstratively. "Oh, well, so much for my budding electronic journalism career. At least you're in plain, public view on TV. You're a lot harder to control."

Julie drifted off, leaving Liz standing alone to nurse her glass of Chablis. Liz studied the room, filled with her "peers," mostly middle-aged men who did supremely well without acknowledging her existence unless they were a little high at an occasion like this and wanted to come over to ogle some pretty young thing. Liz never thought of herself that way until the men edged puckishly near, eyes dropping to the dress-up elements of her clothes, compliments suddenly oozing forth on gin-scented breaths. She put down her half-empty wine glass and left.

* * *

"Liz Jordan?"

"Yes?" Liz kept typing on her poster child story, the phone cradled on her tilted shoulder. She was on deadline and prepared to be curt with any inconvenient caller.

"Larry Westin. At Planned Parenthood."

"Oh, yes." She stopped typing, despite an eye on the second hand of the big round wall clock. Sources required cordial treatment no matter the deadline.

"I've, uh, got a story for you—" he went on.

"I don't know if I can get right to it," Liz began. She had been leery of reproduction-oriented stories ever since the arrival of Devers. Keep your head down and punt.

"It's a news story." There was something odd about Westin's voice, some ragged tension in it that made Liz sit up straighter. "It has to be done right away. It just might be your ticket to a Pulitzer." Now Liz recognized Westin's underlying emotion: grim anger. "The Planned Parenthood office has just been bombed. There are flyers all over from some antiabortion group."

"Much damage?" Liz was rolling her half-done feature out of her platen, spinning fresh sheets of copy paper and a carbon in.

"Maybe a couple hundred thousand, that's all," he said bitterly.

"Anyone hurt?"

"No . . . not this time."

"When did this happen?"

Already it was forming in her mind, the bald, flat power of a news-style story. *A bomb ripped through the Planned Parenthood offices late this morning, causing extensive damage. . . .*

Liz continued her curt inquisition. Westin was obviously dazed, scared, outraged. She'd have to get a police statement, of course. Her eyes flicked to the clock—11:10 A.M. Twenty minutes at most to hear Westin's story, check the facts, write the story, and race it to the city editor. She didn't think about the piece originally in her typewriter, which needed to be done by two. She'd skip lunch, skimp on the damn feature, get it done somehow.

This one would be harder. Could she do it? A check of the clock again. Had to. Her fingers flew across the stiff keys. Twelve minutes. Time to hang up. A bomb. What a bombshell. Nobody had bombed so much as a bank in Milwaukee, not even at the height of the 1960s internal terrorism wave. A bomb that could have killed. That *was* a story; Westin had been right. Maybe not a Pulitzer, but then again . . . Liz dialed the police department, which she knew would offer only vague comments at this early date. While she waited for someone to answer, her fingers began tapping out her lead.

* * *

"Front page." The Affinities women gathered around the first copies of the evening edition a couple of hours later. A woman's byline almost never showed up on the front page. An Affinities reporter's byline never had until now.

"By Elizabeth Jordan," Melissa noted with disapproval in her voice. "'Elizabeth,' huh? You've always gone by 'Liz' in here."

"I didn't think," Liz admitted. "I'm lucky the darn thing got done in time to get in."

"What did Devers say? You did have to deal with the city editor?" Gloria Hobbs, for all that she towered over him, was girlishly afraid of the new guy.

"What could he say? He needed the story. He took it and ran, that's all."

"Liz." The women burst apart. Madge stood nervously in the door to the office. "You're wanted in Hopkins' office."

Eyebrows raised as Liz left quickly. Hopkins had as little to do as possible with the women of Affinities, except for Madge, after he hired them.

Excitement surged in Liz's stomach, wreaking havoc on her digestion of the cheese and raisin bread sandwich she'd found in one of the company lunchroom machines. A pat on the back, maybe. She'd been right, after all. That dreary, dogged coverage of an unpopular cause had resulted in first crack at a major news story.

But Hopkins wasn't in his office; Devers was, dwarfed by the big slab of desktop, but seemingly unaware of it. His white shirt-sleeves were rolled up past his elbows, which were braced on Hopkins's paperwork.

"Sit down," he urged cordially in full drawl. Liz visualized a promotion, a new assignment, a bonus, although the last was unheard of around the *Observer*.

"Good story." Devers studied the city edition front page. "Thanks for getting it. From now on, I'll have one of the city desk guys take it."

"But it's been my beat—"

"And a pretty unpopular one, am I right?" Devers oozed frank appraisal. "I'd been meanin' to speak to Madge about all that rabble-rousin' you been doin' with those stories on birth control and teen-age pregnancy and even abortion. Shoot, Liz honey, nobody wants to read on and on about that stuff. People want news you can use, things that apply to their everyday livin'. Now, don't worry about it." A raised hand held her silent. "I don't blame you. You're young; it's easy to get led astray. But that stuff is gonna have to stop. It's not what this paper is interested in.

"Now this . . ." He tapped the bombing story, his forefinger spearing her byline. "This is news. We gotta report this. And we got a whole big city desk full of newsmen to do it."

"Newsmen haven't had a good track record at reporting news that's important to women," Liz slipped in pointedly.

Devers's silence was nerve-racking. "All right." His manner remained bland, soothing, condescending. "But we know now how impo'tant these issues are. You've shown us the light. We'll do right by them. But you are not a news reporter; you are a feature reporter, and you will write features. It doesn't mean we don't appreciate your helping us out on a tight deadline like this. But next time, let me know before you run off and write the story yourself."

"What makes you think there'll be a next time?" asked Liz. If she didn't do groundwork features, she'd have no sources who trusted her enough to give her the big exclusives that built a reporter's reputation.

"There might be." He stood now, draped a friendly hand over her shoulder—nothing he wouldn't have done with a male reporter he was chatting with—and eased her to the closed door. "Who knows what you'll turn up? Don't take it too hard, honey. You're young yet. You'll learn. You might even be a good reporter someday.

"But you know . . ." His voice dropped. The great man was about to make a personal confidence to a lowly underling. "It might be where I was raised, or my age, but I just can't accept this abortion thing. Or unwanted pregnancies. Shocking."

Devers was almost whispering now, and smiling at himself, at her. "Not, you understand, that in my younger days I didn't do all I could to see that I *got* the girls that way." He shook his snow-white, closely cropped head at the rogue he had been. "But *I* never got caught!"

Devers's rich laugh ushered Liz out into the city room, where eyes automatically rose to see who had come out of the ME's office even as typewriters clattered unabatedly on deadline. Liz walked like a zombie back to Affinities, back to her desk, where she had a poster child story to finish and not much time to do it in. But it didn't matter anymore how much thought or time or effort she poured into this story or any other. It didn't matter at all.

"A TV station? Elizabeth Jordan, I don't believe you've turned traitor. What's wrong with the *Observer*? It's a damn good paper, not a major leaguer, but respectable. And to leave it for a TV job? In Minneapolis? Why, girl, that's as good as *treason. . . .*"

Z.J. could have been a southern colonel, all florid face and cotton-white hair, blustering to his troops. Instead, he merely had an only daughter's allegiance to command. Myrtle was exempt. Her reign was total, the household her undisputed territory. About this, Myrtle kept silent. Journalism was Z.J.'s bailiwick.

So Myrtle and Liz sat silently, together for once on the pink bouclé sofa, while Z.J. raged and cajoled.

"There's no union for TV reporters, I hear. The pay's low. You don't want to be some face on the blasted TV tube that everyone owns, do you, Lizzie? It's not real journalism; it's acting. It's haircuts and teeth. You're making a big mistake."

"Maybe," she conceded. "But I've made it already. WBGO has hired me. I didn't want to tell anyone until it was done. I can always go back to print journalism."

"Not after this." Her father shuddered dramatically.

Liz finally laughed. "Dad, it's not that bad. I'm not a fallen woman or something. It may not be what you hoped for me, but it's new; it's what happening."

Z.J. paced, unconvinced. Liz watched the blank space over his shoulder, where her mother's picture had sat since she was six. It had been missing ever since she'd left for college, after Myrtle had come and Whizzy had gone.

". . . so far from Turtle Bend," her father was saying.

"The Twin Cities are only a couple hundred miles away," Liz consoled him. "I'll come back to visit, more often than you'd like."

Her father froze and looked at her, suddenly forgiving. "Well, girls will be girls." He grinned slyly. "Maybe you'll find one of those slick city fellers to be a son-in-law; some guy with a hairdo out to here like a TV evangelist—"

"Dad!" For the first time in her life, Liz managed to sound as prim, shocked, and admonishing as Myrtle.

Go west, young woman, Liz told herself as she pointed the red Pinto toward the Minnesota border. The car radio buzzed with reaction to the Supreme Court decision upholding the right to abortion. Liz's lips quirked as she thought how one landmark ruling had ended in one day a controversy she had covered for bitter, frustrating months. No one quarreled with the news-worthiness of the story now. The *Milwaukee Observer*'s front page screamed the word in seventy-two-point type, but Liz's byline wasn't on it. Liz wouldn't have a byline now, just a flash of identifying letters across her image and a verbal sign-off. "Good-bye, Milwaukee," she mouthed, letting the words drift behind her like the miles. She was en route to a new beginning, maybe the only real fresh start she'd ever known.

It was January of 1973, and Liz was just twenty-three. She was aware of her limitations, among them that she'd never slept with a man and never flown in an airplane. She didn't know which omission was worse.

But she knew how to drive, and she knew how to write. The state border was the cold silver width of the St. Croix River, traversed by a steel bridge painted morning glory blue. In summer it became a cheery reflection of the sky and water. In January it seemed sullen, a pointless blue banner flown into the face of icy-gray indifference on all sides.

Liz wasn't indifferent to anything, especially the future. Maybe she wasn't a TV star. Not with a voice as flat as a Minnesota prairie and baby fat still rounding her arms and chin. But she was smart; they'd always told her so, and they needed a token woman at WBGO. Smart might just be enough to make a journalistic impact on the brave, newly respectable medium of television news, even if her father didn't think so.

Maybe Someone Special was waiting Out There for her. Twenty-three and a virgin. Liz cringed, although it wasn't an unheard-of condition for most unmarried small-town girls even now, she knew. Old Doc Dupree hardly handed out birth control pills to married women, much less single girls. Maybe he'd changed. Maybe Liz would change. She couldn't be a small-town girl forever. Maybe someday she'd grow up into a big-city woman.

— Chapter 9 —

Liz Jordan stood, feet braced on the slick, snow-packed tundra of a Minneapolis street, a mike clutched like a metal bouquet to her chest, her back to the decrepit house where the mad gunman hid.

He had to be mad. He'd kidnapped his common-law wife and their three children, all under five, led the police on a wild half-hour car chase to this tawdry spot, and settled down to hold off the entire Minneapolis PD tactical squad.

Liz and cameraman Fast Eddie Andersen had been returning to the station after covering the January hothouse flower show at the State Fairgrounds in St. Paul when the police calls began crackling over the car radio.

Fast Eddie immediately had turned up the "squelch" dial to

listen. "Hey, look," he said. "I'll drop you off now and you can take a cab back to the station. This sounds like good footage."

"What is it? I can't make out a word they're saying."

Eddie cocked his head, one hand on the radio installed beneath the dashboard, one hand on the wheel, and half an eye on the road. "Some kook's gone bananas. Could even be a few dead-body shots here. I'll drop you."

"You've got my film in your camera. I can't do anything anyway. Why don't I come along? You'll need a reporter."

Eddie's small skeptical eyes rolled. "Look, lady. I got orders to go on any police stuff that comes down—accidents or bank robberies; anything with good action footage. These hostage things don't need reporters. The guy either surrenders or blows the folks and himself away, and you can get those facts from one call to the cop shop. Don't worry. I won't film over your precious posies."

Liz was scared silly, and didn't have the vaguest notion what she would *say* about those gorgeous flowers that Eddie had filmed so interminably in the moist, overheated air of the horticultural building, but she knew a breaking news story when she heard it happening.

"I'm going. So forget driving downtown to dump me. You can go straight out to—589 Phoenix Street." She parroted the squawking two-way radio, proud to have at last deciphered something.

"That's the *near North Side*."

"I don't care."

"It's not safe for a lady," Eddie grumbled, but he was shooting the car back toward the freeway at a steady ten miles an hour above the speed limit.

Liz sighed relief and thought a minute. "Maybe I'm not a lady," she offered tentatively, appalled at her heresy.

Eddie snorted disbelief and snapped his gum derisively. Everything Fast Eddie did was derisive, at least when it involved her, Liz thought glumly. She'd gotten him on every assignment since starting her job yesterday—three so far—and had decided he hated her.

But he knew where he was going. As soon as Liz saw the decaying urban landscape assemble around her, saw the increasing preponderance of male black faces, she began to reconsider whether she ought not to squeak "lady" and stay in the car. With the doors locked.

Still, when Eddie parked the station's Ford behind a cluster of police black-and-whites and got out, he seemed reconciled to Liz's company. He even introduced her to the detective in charge of the scene, a man as short and sloppily fat as Eddie was lank and lean.

"You're new," Mason the detective said, an arrogantly open

summation in his eyes. There was a lot of talk about women's liberation in 1973, but you couldn't censor a look, or a whole phalanx of them, for that matter. Liz surveyed the gathered police-men, who were already looking her over pretty thoroughly.

"This here's Liz Jordan," said Fast Eddie, turning chivalrous. "New reporter. She wants to do a stand-up in front of the house. She'll need the facts on the guy, you know, the regular stuff."

Liz flipped out her notebook, grateful to Eddie for pointing her in the right direction. "Maybe you could tell me his name, Detec-tive Mason?"

"No names, honey. Guy could blow himself away; then we'd have to hold his handle until the relatives are notified."

"But you . . . know . . . who he is?"

"Yeah. Some nut case, flipped for real this time. Got some old debts and a girlfriend with a new boyfriend. He took the woman and kids at eleven A.M. from an apartment on East Horton. We've been behind him all the way. Now he's hunkered down in this ole house here with a couple rifles and lots of ammo. That's about it."

"When do you expect to control the situation?"

Mason guffawed, exchanging winks with Andersen. "You're a sharp one. Control the situation, huh? Well, we may have to tear gas 'im out or rush the place. We've got a call out for his minister. Baptist fellow. But all the action's not going down until much later. Much too late to make your six-o'clock news, honey, so you'll have to settle for a stand-up."

Liz nodded. "Okay. A stand-up, then." At least she knew what a stand-up was now—not a comedian, though she felt like one who was bombing, but the segment on a TV news story where the reporter stands in front of the camera and sums up the story face-to-face with the viewer. Liz scanned her illegible notes, trying desperately to work the chaotic facts into a sensible sentence or two. *This address on Phoenix Street became a house of fear this afternoon when a deranged*—too strongly stated—*disturbed gun-man held his wife and two*—no, three!—*three children hostage*. Not right; maybe . . . *After a harrowing half-hour police chase, an unidentified gunman holed up in this unassuming frame house on Minneapolis's near North Side*. . . .

Why did everying she came up with sound like an excerpt from a 1930s *Police Gazette?* There was no time to polish it. Mason was positioning her against the fender of a police car, a hand on her shoulder, and enjoying it; Fast Eddie was living up to his name, crouched, camera ready on his shoulder, waiting for Liz to begin.

"Give me a level," he barked. Level. Right. A voice reading.

"Um, testing—one, two, three, four, five—"

"That's enough. Ready to roll."

Liz patted her wind-riffled hair, licked her lips. Detective Mason hadn't moved out of camera range and was watching her nervous primping with lecherous contempt.

"You understand," he said, "that the police department isn't responsible for your safety when you're filming within our lines." Liz's eyes narrowed in puzzlement. "What I mean, little lady, is that the guy in there might get a sudden notion to up and snipe at us. I mean, you got your back to the house—it's only fifty yards away." Liz turned to regard the dilapidated building over her shoulder. It seemed to have crept closer. "You should know it's dangerous to do this. You reporters can take what risks you want as long as it doesn't endanger bystanders or the police. I just want you to know the danger, seeing you're new. Be too bad if such a pretty girl ended up dead meat," he finished, leaning confidentially close.

Liz's shoulders straightened. "Then you'd better move out of camera range and let me get this over with, Detective Mason. An ugly man would be just as dead as me," she added as he backed away. "If anything happened." She wished Fast Eddie had filmed the look on Mason's face.

"Okay, Lizzie. Let's roll." Fast Eddie's face was hidden behind the black metal mask of his camera, but Liz thought she detected a smirk.

She tried to recall the lurid sentences that now seemed the epitome of cool, unimpassioned summary. They had gone with her courage. Behind her. A loaded, lethal gun. Pointed now? Her way? Damn red coat; why had she thought the color *cheery* for the winter? Perfect for target practice more likely! She could be even now hoofing her way back to the station, dumped like a worthless burden, but alive anyway.

"Come *on*, Jordan. Say something."

"Okay." Liz tightened her grasp on the microphone stem to something resembling felonious assault. Then the words started coming, seeming to bypass her brain and go directly for her mouth. "Minneapolis police keep a dangerous vigil at this modest house on the city's near North Side, where an unnamed gunman holds his wife and three children hostage. Police pursued the heavily armed man and victims in a car chase from East Horton to this Phoenix Street address, where they waited this afternoon in hopes that the man's minister could talk him into surrendering before the authorities had to resort to tear gas or gunfire to drive him out." Liz took a deep breath, unsure what she'd say next. "This is Liz Jordan, Channel 8 News," she babbled in confusion.

"Watch out!" A blow on the back of her shoulder knocked the hoarded breath right out of her. The snow-packed street was rushing toward her and she hit it like a cherry-red tomato—*splat*—heels of her hands scraping icy terrain, microphone flying, knees playing painful brakes to her fall. A massive, unmoving weight kept her from struggling up. Mason.

His fleshy, new-moon face grinned. "Sorry, Liz honey, but I saw a rifle barrel at the window. Had to do my duty."

They were all grinning, the policemen gathered around. Fast Eddie's camera was whirring relentlessly.

Liz tried to wriggle away, but Mason wasn't helping any. "Not bad duty, Mason," Fast Eddie chuckled.

"Cut that out, Eddie." Liz scrambled to her undignified knees, not daring to rise until she was sure the threat hadn't been real. "I hope you got the first part of the stand-up, too."

"I got it. Got it all." He grinned and patted the camera's bulky black body as if it were a pet.

The men had stepped back, leaving Liz to lurch up on her own power. None of them were ducking. She guessed that their position was safely out of range and always had been. Liz brushed the snow off her coat hem, felt the beginning throb of abrasions on her palms despite her gloves, and her knees, protected only by panty hose. The sting of deliberate humiliation hurt worse. She wanted to lash out at the sexist bullies, but that would only cater to their sense of fun.

"Well." She dusted off her burning palms. "I'm glad to see Minneapolis's finest are on the job protecting the citizenry. I'll make sure to put it in my report." And she marched back to the camera car, trying not to limp.

Fast Eddie followed after filming the area, whistling as he stowed his camera in the back seat, and took the wheel. Neither talked on the drive back to the station, a boxy, four-story building in downtown Minneapolis that initially had struck Liz as having no glamour. Now it looked even less inspiring, despite the sign atop it that proclaimed "WBGO-TV" in tomato-red neon every night.

There was no time for Liz to feel sorry for herself. It was midafternoon and she had two stories to submit by four o'clock; she'd learned enough in two days to know that speed and savvy were the only attributes that would help her meet the deadline. The hostage story was, ironically, easier to do. The anchorman's introduction could update the facts, if needed. Liz hoped her stand-up had been vague enough to remain relevant in the face of later developments; perhaps even now Mason was blowing away the poor bastard inside the house.

The hostage film was dull, not really Fast Eddie's fault. Even in color, the bland, dirty white winter landscape looked tawdry, indifferent. A little blood would have livened things up. Liz blanched when her stand-up appeared on the small viewing screen; her red coat took the place of the missing gore. She winced. Oh, Lord, she sounded so pretentious, like a narrator on *You Are There*, the 1950s historical documentary show she watched as a kid in Turtle Bend. Ladies and gentlemen of the viewing audience, see reporter take stance; see reporter intone heavy words; see reporter— God, there it was—fall flat on face, both literally and figuratively.

Liz understood the true depth of Fast Eddie's vileness when she saw the cinema verité cuts of herself being pushed down, flailing, and dragging herself up. It had never been meant for broadcast, but the film editor would see the segment, too, and probably mention the "green" reporter in the "red" coat. Fast Eddie would mouth the joke among the camera crew, who seemed to be the same egocentric, generally surly lot as newspaper photographers. Perhaps they'd even sponsor "showings" for station personnel when Liz was out on assignment. She'd have debuted as a laughingstock. "This is Liz Jordan, WBGO-TV court fool. . . ." Liz sighed gustily and checked her watch. No time for self-pity.

She rewound the film to survey the flower footage. What a difference. For once Fast Eddie had lingered, his camera dwelling on the lush Technicolor undulations of the blooming flowers, indulging in caressing close-ups until an almost sensual silent message wafted from the still blooms. Wow. What to say about that? Liz marked down the numbers of particularly effective shots and raced back to her desk, which was no larger and no more isolated from newsroom bustle than it had been at the *Observer*. Management in every form of media seemed to think the frontline staff functioned better against odds, which meant a no-frills work environment.

Rolling one of the station's confusing story forms into the platen of her old manual typewriter, Liz dialed the police station for the latest dope on the hostage situation—still a stalemate. It was rotten to rejoice in bad news persisting, but Liz breathed relief that her damn stand-up would hold up. So far. She arbitrarily typed a lead-in sentence for the anchor, hoping he'd find that the structure fitted his style. If not, he'd insist on rewriting it and Liz would feel newer and more incompetent than ever. She indicated the points in the film that looked most interesting and typed in the text of her improvised stand-up. At least she'd remembered to sign off with her name and the station channel number—and said them both right. Crack reporting, right, Jordan? Count on this girl to know where she is.

Racing to turn in the carbons of her script, Liz surreptitiously studied the people on phones or bent over typewriters at desks she passed. Some of the faces might be familiar on-camera sights in Minneapolis and St. Paul, but Liz wasn't a native and they were all foreign to her. WBGO didn't believe in alotting much time for orientation or introduction. Liz had been flung out on the street with a cameraman at ten in the morning her first day. She even needed directions to the rest rooms, and every time she had to inquire about some alien new process—like winding film, marking visuals, or figuring out the story forms with their separate columns for voice track, visual track, and editing instructions . . . well, she felt her father had been right: TV was no place for a self-respecting journalist. Never had been, never would be.

"That's poppycock," Liz growled to herself, trying to cheerlead her flagging morale back to the field of victory. Several faces glanced up at her, and she flushed. Talking to herself already. But then, no one else had been friendly enough to talk to her first.

Angry, Liz typed some flowery jabberwocky into the long, narrow space left for narration on the story form. That was easy. Print reporters learned to stretch nothing stories to fill space if necessary. Liz could rhapsodize about January geraniums for three graphs if she had to, and luckily, TV news narration was a matter of mere sentences, terse ones at that. Then she had to distribute carbons to the six P.M. producer and the editor, who would splice Liz's deathless narration track with the film Eddie Anderson had made that morning. The producer, a dapper man in a bow tie to whom nobody had introduced her, called her back after a few minutes to okay the copy.

"Not bad," he said, grimacing approval. Liz couldn't tell if the comment was professional or personal. Great—now she was getting paranoid.

She dropped the script into the "Unedited" basket in the receiving room. There raw film and script came together before they went to the row of editing rooms, where busy editors were splicing together stories for the six-o'clock news. Liz dug up an editor willing to tape her flower narration. Her first voice over.

Alone in the recording room with a microphone, Liz found herself strangling the stand as she declaimed the paltry string of words trailing down the page. It was hard for her eye to move back and forth on text only three inches wide, for her voice to smoothly convey meaning when she felt she was reading staccato bits of prose. Bite-size pieces. TV reporters called the spoken part of a story taped from news sources, which newspaper reporters referred to as "quotes," "sound bites." So much was different, though essentially the same. At the *Milwaukee Observer*, by now she'd have both stories written and ready to leave her hands for good. At a TV station, coming back with the facts was just the beginning of the process.

The editor, a black woman with not much small talk in her, came in to help rewind the tape and bore it away. Liz felt like her child was being whisked from her for surgery. What if the words and pictures got mixed up? What if the editor left the wrong thing in—or the right thing out? What if *Liz* emerged from the operation looking like a fool?

It was four o'clock. Liz felt like it was eight, and wished it was. Then the whole damn thing'd be over. A heck of a way to feel about her brave new career. Relax, she told herself. Someday you'll look back on all this and be amazed you ever found it hard or unfamiliar. Remember your first day at the *Observer*, even with years of Z.J.'s ink-stained overseeing under your belt?

At least she'd located the station cafeteria, a vastly unappetizing space sandwiched between a hard vinyl tile floor and a lowered acoustical ceiling seasoned with fluorescent-lit plastic rectangles. Its sparse tables and molded chairs were uniformly unwelcoming. Except for a row of food- and drink-dispensing machines and a sink nook where a giant coffee pot dribbled hot water on command for beverages and soups, that was it. Even the damn pot was empty.

Liz fished for a quarter in her change purse, then walked over to Vendomatic Row and jammed it down the coffee machine's stainless steel throat. It slid right through to the coin return. "Great." The coin connected on its second trip down the metal gullet. Triumphant, Liz watched her paper cup wobble into position and fill with the tannish liquid that passed for coffee with cream. She felt suddenly cold and proceeded to remedy that by spilling boiling hot coffee over her already abused hands. "Shit!"

She looked up, horrified. The room was empty except for a blond man she hadn't noticed before, who was setting aside his copy of the *Minneapolis Star*, getting up, coming her way. Wonderful, Jordan, she thought. He was probably the station owner, whom she hadn't met, coming to can the foulmouthed broad he'd made the mistake of hiring away from a wonderful, slow-paced easygoing, visually anonymous career doing Women's Section club president profiles for the prestigious *Milwaukee Observer*.

"Here, let me take that," the man offered when he arrived. "There're some paper towels near the sink. That stupid machine's been overfilling cups all week." He set the cup on a nearby table while Liz returned from running her scalded hands under cold water and drying them with a paper towel.

"Thanks." She sat gingerly, expecting her purse to topple next and send personal sundries skidding across the vinyl tile. The man sat, too, and they glanced simultaneously to her steaming cup of coffee. Overfilling, hell. Her hands had been shaking, that's all. She looked at the first gallant—maybe that was sexist—the first *tactful* man she'd seen that day.

Blond, in a quiet Scandinavian way that seemed trustworthy rather than devastating. Late twenties; late-1960s mustache; tweed jacket. Someday, he might teach college and smoke a pipe. For now he wore blue jeans.

"At least you can't say you didn't get your money's worth." He pointed to the coffee, which she elevated and gratefully drank. "I'm Steve Harmon. You must be the new reporter they hired out of Wisconsin." Liz nodded and offered her name. "Nice to meet you, Liz. I do general reporting, and host an A.M. talk show."

"A talk show? Really?" Liz hadn't meant to sound impressed, but talk show hosts—well, that was Merv Griffin or somebody much more glamorous than a mere reporter.

"Look, I also do a midnight ski scene show, too, so don't get overcome. I'm the jack-of-all-trades around here."

"You like to ski?"

He grinned. "Right. Nobody watches the ski show, but it sure gets me treated well at various local resorts. And the 'more creative' cameramen get to do some nice slo-mo shots of *schuss*ing downhillers and spraying powder, so the cameramen are happy. Plus the station rakes in those ski equipment ads and has a nice little package to wrap them around."

"That's . . . practically corrupt." But Liz's tone was teasing.

"You came from a newspaper, right? And you're talking corruption?!"

"Okay, nobody's suitable for sainthood. We had a few freebie-suckers on our staff, too. It's just that—"

"—just that it's a bit more visible at a TV station. Look, it's an advertising medium, always has been. TV never had the tradition of wrapping itself in its virtue like the newspapers. It's all up front. What you see is what you get."

Liz finished the coffee. "I hope I haven't made a mistake."

"Miss the roar of the printing presses already?"

She shook her head. "Not yet. But I do take my work seriously. I want to report things that matter. So far, I've been assigned the midwinter flower show and a couple of pretty routine civic press conferences. Do they have something against giving women interesting work around here?"

"'WBGO is an equal opportunity employer,'" Steve parroted. "Even the men don't get interesting work."

"You sound like you got it made—your own talk show, ski

show . . ." Liz suddenly understood the figured sweater under his sport coat.

Steve shrugged. "Hey, I like challenge, too. It's a fight, that's all. Mediocrity is the natural condition of institutions."

"Well, at least I got to go on that hostage call this afternoon, even though Easy Eddie or whatever they call him fought it tooth and nail. Wanted to dump me downtown first."

"Hostage thing? You mean out on the North Side? You went on that?"

"Why not? I not only went on it and did a brilliant stand-up cold in more ways than one, but I had to take the indignity of some creepy cop named Mason pushing me down 'for my own protection' and Easy Eddie filming the whole scene."

"Don't get riled." Steve absently moved her empty cup on the table, not looking at her. His mouth folded consideringly shut under the pale mustache. "You know, Liz, we don't usually send reporters on breaking police cases. All we need is film. And an update. I doubt they'll run it tonight."

"They won't run it? I stood there with those . . . those goons looking on—and I don't mean the criminal in the house—and risked my brand-new winter coat back to a bullet, and they won't even run it? No. Eddie would have said—"

"He did want to dump you downtown."

Liz sat violently back. "Shit," she said succinctly for the second time.

Steve looked surprised, then noncommital, then he laughed. "You do get to the point; should do well in television. Look, Fast Eddie's notorious for pulling stuff. And the cops wouldn't have let you stand there if it wasn't safe. Just consider it initiation and forget it."

"I nearly broke my neck the last two hours getting out two stories, and now you say one will never air."

"It can even happen on a story they *intend* to run. You get preempted. That's the wonderful world of television. Didn't the paper ever pull one of your stories?"

"Yeah, but they ran it later."

Steve's head shook soberly. "Not TV. Instant on, instant off. We do news on a day-to-day basis. If it doesn't make it, it's not news the next day."

"Hmmm." Liz crushed her cup. "So there go a new pair of Christian Dior panty hose for nothing." She thrust out her legs in demonstration, bracing them on her boot heels.

Steve leaned to look at the bridge of leg between her skirt hem and her boot tops. He whistled, not in approval but awe. "I haven't seen ladders like that since I covered the volunteer fire department drills last summer." He frowned. "You've got a nasty scrape or two; better clean it off. It must hurt."

Liz followed him desultorily to the coffee nook and leaned against the sink. "I hadn't had time to notice, I guess." She reached for the paper towel he'd dampened with warm water.

"Better let me. You'll have a tough time seeing the damage. You ever notice knees are one of the hardest pieces of your anatomy to see properly?"

"Not particularly—ouch!"

"Good thing you're not on a talk show; these knees'd look like sunsets. On a talk show set, there's nothing to hide behind—no desk, no camera shot from the waist up only."

"I guess I made my own talk show this afternoon at 589 Phoenix Street. All show and no talk. Are you *sure* they won't run it? The six P.M. producer didn't say anything—"

"Weatherby?" Liz shrugged in uncertainty. "Little dude with a crew cut and bow tie?" She nodded vigorously, biting her lip as Steve gently patted her abraded knee. "He wouldn't make a peep if he were going to pull film of the first landing on Mars and replace it with the six A.M. farm report live from Dubuque. He's too scared."

"Of whom?"

"The station manager, the news director. You. But maybe... well, watch the news tonight and see."

"Thanks." Liz flipped her skirt over her knees and limped back to the table. She turned to watch Steve clean up the sink area. "You know, you're the first decent person I've met around here."

He looked pleased but grinned fiendishly. "You just don't know me yet."

— Chapter 10 —

Liz curled up on her apartment sofa that night, her Bactine-anointed knees discreetly covered with matching Band-Aids, her icy feet jammed into warm, fuzzy slippers, and waited breathlessly for the ten o'clock news. She'd left the station just late enough to miss the six o'clock version, and, unlike newspapers, TV news didn't wait around to be caught up with later.

The portable TV sat across the apartment's small living room on its inexpensive wheeled stand. Liz hated TV stands, but her furniture—a collection of college dorm castoffs, donations from home, and her own impulse purchases—was scanty, and pride goeth before a budget. Her salary was only $11,000 a year and she hadn't seen the first installment yet. TV reporters weren't unionized, either. He ex-colleagues at the *Observer* could count on annual raises. Liz couldn't rely on anything but a fine-print contract that seemed to spell out everything from sneezing to overtime and ask her to commit her life, fortune, and sacred honor to the management of WBGO-TV.

Liz Jordan, television reporter and rising star, she announced to herself, since the TV seemed unlikely to trumpet any mention of her status or new employ. The nightly news introductory graphics unwound. A series of familiar Twin Cities scenes, more Minneapolis than St. Paul and more summer than winter, cut quickly into one another to the tune of some chipper, anonymous Muzak.

The anchorman's face came into focus. Jeff Stone. Dark-haired, suave, a bit pompous, like Ted Baxter on the *Mary Tyler Moore Show*. Liz sat up. God, she was a living MTM! Young single woman in TV in the big city. At least Liz had an on-air job; poor Mary was forever handling crises for Mr. Grant behind the camera cables. Liz's ears perked as Jeff mentioned the hostage story up top and promised the viewers film. Maybe...

She tensed when Jeff began intoning familiar words—*her* words, the introduction she'd written for him that afternoon. They hadn't cut or changed *that*. Then recognizable footage of that afternoon's sordid scene replaced Jeff's blandly authoritative face. Now. Cut to—our gal Liz, saying...no cut. Just Jeff's voice intoning over the film that the gunman had surrendered that evening and been taken into custody. No shots fired, except for the story's last shots, those Eddie Andersen had taken of the overall scene before coming back to the car. That was it. Cut and dried. Liz had wasted her breath demanding to go on the story. On the scene or not, they hadn't needed her.

She hung in for her flower show segment, which came at the newscast's tail, just before the weather. "It's June in January at the Minnesota State Fairgrounds this weekend," said a woman with a deeper voice than Liz had ever heard herself use, "and a rainbow of color is pointing to a pot of gold." Here the camera lingered over an array of yellow daffodils. "Lovers of midwinter tulips and tiger lilies, of pansies in the snow and posies on ice, should trek right over from ten to five Saturday and Sunday to see spring"—overall shot of banks of flowers—"under glass." Shot of high arched greenhouse roof. "This is Liz Jordan, Channel Eight News, in bloom at the horticulture building." Tight close-up of a dark-haired woman's face surrounded by a blurred bonnet of background flowers.

That was it. Debut. It was her face—and nicely filmed by Fast Eddie, bless his black little heart—but her voice! She didn't sound at all like Liz Jordan, Turtle Bend valedictorian. She sounded hollow and deep-voiced, like a teenybopper Tallulah Bankhead. Why hadn't anybody told her? What a mistake. No one critiqued the sound of Woodward and Bernstein's voices. Show biz. For the first time in her headstrong journalistic odyssey from Turtle Bend High and the *Sentinel* to college to the *Milwaukee Observer* to WBGO it occurred to Liz that her father might be right. TV was no place for a journalist, and certainly it was no place for a lady.

She would have to become less of one without becoming less of the other. Liz just didn't know which vocation would lose out to which.

By morning, Liz had convinced herself that the horticulture piece hadn't been so bad. Anyone would look like a fool babbling sweet nothings about flowers, and maybe the viewers needed a break from the usual Minnesota winter of their discontent. She shivered in her wool coat and scarf at the bus stop. She'd worn an old midiskirt to cover her bandaged knees, but the hem protruded a foot from the coat and flapped around her calves, sending shafts of icy air directly up her body. Of course, her faithful secondhand Ford had decided to have a mechanical breakdown soon after her arrival in Minneapolis.

She was late for work, but the assignment editor pounced as soon as she arrived.

"Keep your coat on. I want you to cover a ten A.M. press conference at the capitol in St. Paul. You'll go with Andersen."

"Andersen again?" Liz hadn't managed to keep dismay out of her voice.

The assignment editor, a short, brusque man who'd been recently "hired away" from the *Minneapolis Tribune* with some fanfare, eyed her with cold indifference. "Don't you want to know what the conference is about?"

Liz pulled her big shoulderbag from the floor to her desk and jammed her notebook inside. "What press conferences are always all about. Gobbledygook."

"This one's about a new program the state's initiating for drug offenders. Halfway houses. I thought you were bitching about not getting to do important stuff already. Drugs should do it."

"Great." Liz brightened. She'd done a gut-wrenching piece on wives of drug addicts for the *Observer*. "But isn't there another way to cover it? Personal interviews at a halfway house—"

"No time. Maybe you can even get back in time to get a tease on the noon news. The producers want the big shot to run at six and a recap at ten."

"How much?" Liz used to get story length in inches; now, she got it in gulps of mere seconds.

"A minute-ten at six. Hell, even a one-thirty if you get enough. WBGO's committed to community issues, right?" The assignment editor winked, stuck his ballpoint into his ink-stained white shirt pocket, and rushed off. Mike Somebody. She would have to get these names down....

"Hi there." A blond woman two desks over was looking Liz's way. "So you got the governor's latest PR circus. Good luck."

Liz edged over. When Fast Eddie was ready to go, he'd find her. She'd already learned not to rush the temperamental cameramen, who, like newspaper photographers, took macho pride in refusing to be at the reporters' beck and call, especially if the reporters were women. "Liz Jordan. I started Monday, and I've had almost nothing but these dull press conferences ever since." Liz had mentally laundered the "damn" dull out of her description; this woman might be offended by plain speaking.

"Stephanie Lynch. I'm a reporter, too." A large, rawboned hand extended, then Stephanie stood up. Holy cow, was there no end to her? Liz, a compact five-foot-four, watched Stephanie uncoil to her full five-ten or -eleven. In high school one would pity any female born to tower over men, but Liz supposed it didn't matter on television. Viewers only saw your top half, and nobody looked terribly tall sitting down or bisected—like a magician's assistant—into a permanent waist-up presence by the camera.

"Been here long?" Liz asked, hoping Stephanie could become a guide and a pal.

"Yeah. Six months. You'll find that those dull press conferences are the meatiest things you ever get to cover. That flower show thing was yours?"

"You mean you didn't recognize me?"

"We all look unlike ourselves on camera; you'll get used to it. The first time I saw myself—! Then I learned I was considered *photogenic*! Suicide city! Anyway, nice writing on the flowers, very poetic. You came from a newspaper, didn't you?"

"Yeah. Didn't you?"

Stephanie's blond head shook, turning her hair into a supple, shoulder-length Clairol shimmer. Liz felt a little less sorry for her. "*The*-a-tuh, my deah. I tried some Equity work at the little theaters around here, but got tired of finding that the only part directors considered me for was Mary Queen of Scots." Liz looked only a bit less blank than she felt, and Stephanie leaned down to speak in a stage whisper. "She was *six feet tall*. Then I modeled some, but that's such a hassle.... So, here I am. At least the pay's regular." Stephanie straightened and took a mock Shakespearean stance. "But thy coachman awaiteth, Cinderella. I fear he's only a rat, but good luck, anyway."

Liz checked her rear, both relieved and disappointed to see Fast Eddie lounging against the exit wall.

"Cut the gabbing!" He hailed her halfway across the room, making it look as if Liz had been dawdling instead of killing time while waiting for him to make an appearance. "Let's go." He thrust a tripod into her ungloved hands and brushed his way out to the station parking lot.

Liz trailed him angrily, eyeing the warm gloves thrust into the outer purse flap and watching her fingers go white around fistfuls of aluminum tripod and leather purse strap as the outside air took full liberties with her exposed hands. But Fast Eddie was loping now, straining like a hound at the leash, living up to his name. She stood behind him while he threw his equipment into the car, then she hoisted up the heavy tripod, glad at last to get rid of it.

"Oooh!" Something on the tripod telescoped. The metal had sliced down on a good pinch of her forefinger.

"Watch out; you got to handle this equipment right. Hurt yourself?"

"No, your tripod did it for me. It's okay." Liz shook her hand—luckily it was her left—and watched a dark maroon blood blister form. Eddie shrugged and went around to the driver's side while Liz squeezed herself onto the cold, vinyl-upholstered bench seat decorated with fast-food wrappers. At her feet, the familiar police radio squawked fitfully.

"I always feel like a Mexican lady on a bus when we go on assignment," Liz commented, pulling her purse closer as the overflow of Eddie's equipment claimed her part of the front seat. "Down to the chicken." She eyed the cackling radio that forced her feet sideways.

"Huh? I don't get it."

"Never mind." Liz finally pulled her gloves over chilled hands and watched the winter-dulled city streets roll by. Soon they were on the interstate freeway between Minneapolis and St. Paul, but Liz couldn't see much anymore—a constant spray of dirty gray slush thrown up by the wheels of passing cars hissed onto her window. Liz stared out the window anyway, in no mood to converse with Fast Eddie Andersen. She fit the perfect definition of an explorer from the old joke: She didn't know where she was going, she didn't know where she was when she got there (or what she was going to do), and somebody else paid for it.

But Eddie knew. He slipped the Ford compact into a side-street parking spot and handed Liz the heavy tripod as soon as she got out. The state capitol building was a snowy marble edifice that crowned an impressive hill. Liz would never forget that, because she hiked up the entire steep approach to that governmental eminence that cold January day in Fast Eddie Andersen's slushy wake. The sun shone, turning distant snow banks to carved alabaster and making the sculpture of four gilded horses above the capitol entrance sparkle like eighteen-karat coursers.

Liz, shamelessly a tourist, pointed. "What's that?"

"That? Some gingerbread. You want a shot of it to set locale? That's old hat; I can get the steps and entrance when we leave."

"I didn't say shoot it; I said, what is it?"

Fast Eddie stopped and looked significantly down on her. "'Four Horsemen of the Apocalypse,'" he intoned direly.

Liz gestured with the leaden tripod. "You ought to know. Let's get on with it."

Naturally Eddie led her up the long, formal flight of exterior stairs, Liz suspecting all the while there must be an easier, ground-level entrance somewhere. The press conference was held in an ornate, highly gilded receiving room. Reporters' and cameramen's boots dripped dirty water on the heavy fringed carpets covering the marble floors.

Already a veteran, Liz sprinted for the diminishing pile of press releases at one end of the long, carved conference table, leaving Eddie to shoulder his way into frontline position next to TV cameramen from every station in town—WCCO, KMSP, KSTP, and WTCN. Liz glanced to the print reporters at the back of the room as she scooted a folding chair over the thick rug next to the table where the announcements would emanate from. Once she, too, had craned her neck to see over the backs of the possessive TV types, loathing them. Lowly print reporters always had to give way to the vital camera placements. Now Liz was a member of the privileged camp, a true media princess, and came by her royally front-row seat by unspoken if not unresented custom.

She scanned the three-page, mimeographed press release—the usual overwritten governmentalese spewing statistics and giant figures. Working her gloves off, she became aware of some sticky substance in her hand. She looked—blood. The damn tripod wound had bled into her gloves. Liz sucked discreetly at her gashed finger, but it was a painless, shallow wound that bled shamelessly. With her good hand, she felt in her purse for a tissue. The oversize bag seemed as deep as Carlsbad Caverns as she explored it and came up empty. There was nothing to do but to keep sucking her finger and making notes.

The assembled bigwigs were sitting at the table now. Liz copied their names from the signs in front of them. Later she'd know the officials by sight; now they were strangers and she had to get the spellings right and connect the faces with the right names.

"'Scuse me. I just need to peek around . . ." she beseeched the broad, ungiving back in front of her.

The KSTP cameraman was a burly guy in a down jacket only slightly smaller than the Goodyear blimp. He frowned and managed a small, semiobliging weight shift before resuming his posture directly in front of the governor. But Liz had glimpsed and memorized the needed name already and was jotting it down.

The sound of a prematurely whirring camera buzzed nearby. She glanced up to see Fast Eddie, who had twisted the unit on its damned tripod to face her.

"Must you do that?" she hissed.

Eddie's downturned mouth made an indifferent, slightly sour moue. He shrugged. "It was a good time to catch you. You'll need footage to show we were here, and I can't exactly film myself."

Liz brushed back a straggling bang with her bleeding hand. "I feel so strange about putting a clip of *myself* in a piece. It just doesn't feel . . . right."

"Look, lady. Mike'll tell you all the reasons. The main thing is that on the tube, we gotta show the people that this film we're unreeling didn't get sent in by dogsled or somethin', that a real live reporter was on the spot. I gotta get it. So if you'll just stop jumpin' every time I focus my lens on you, I'll do my job and you can use the film of yourself for Christmas ribbon, for all I care." Eddie hefted the camera onto his shoulder and leaned nearer, whirring, whirring all the while.

Liz sighed and pretended to take notes she didn't need until he moved away again. It seemed unprofessional to intrude her own image into the story she was covering, but Eddie had a point. She'd just have to learn not to flinch every time he got a notion to turn the lens her way.

The cameramen made a last-minute rush inward to adjust their microphones, then the event was under way. First the governor read the statement Liz already held a copy of, while the cameras recorded every deathless throat-clearing and Liz drew asterisks at the paragraphs she thought read well enough or the governor had declaimed well enough or that actually *said* something important enough to use in the final report.

Then came the introduction of assorted solons who had helped pass the trailblazing legislation to allow the state to help support halfway houses for drug addicts. And statements from the law-makers. This is all wrong, Liz thought. Where are the drug addicts, or the halfway house managers? Some of those people have real charisma on camera. Where are the neighbors who are worried about having a halfway house for drug offenders on their block? She decided to ask.

The press conference had already been opened to questions and her more oriented colleagues had jumped in. Liz pressed her left thumb tightly down on her bleeding forefinger, poised her pencil, and concentrated on catching the governor's eye. It wasn't too hard; she was wearing her (now authentically) blood-red coat.

"Yes, ah . . . the young lady from Channel 8."

"Governor, I'm wondering if the idea of implementing in-com-munity halfway houses has run into any neighborhood resistance yet. Or do you anticipate any?"

The governor was an overweight Democrat who wore baggy suits and clear plastic—framed glasses. He smiled. "That's a good question," he began, meaning "You've got a lot of nerve asking that publicly." He answered the congregation as a whole, ignoring Liz. "We've, uh, anticipated that a full program of neighborhood education may be necessary. Research shows there's little danger to the community at large, and much chance for improvement. I'm sure you all know the high level of crime committed by those needing funds for illegal drugs. If we can obtain a higher non-addiction rate . . ."

Cameramen were focusing furiously and reporters' notepads were receiving copious notes. Ask an unpleasant question and watch all the other jackals snap up the answer while you get left with the bones and the ill will of the state's chief executive, Liz thought grimly. Now another reporter was following up on her question. Oh, well, at least she'd stirred up the natives. She glanced down at her notepad and saw her left hand resting on top, smudging a red trail across the pale green paper. Fast Eddie chose that moment to record her reportorial persona. Liz didn't even stiffen; she just lifted her right hand to hide her left and managed to look intently interested.

— Chapter 11 —

"Got a minute, Liz?"

The news director had paused to perch upon Liz's already overladen little desk. She pulled the smudgy story form carbons away from his vicinity and sat back, wondering what had caused this visitation on the first-week anniversary of her first day. His name was Mike Roth, she'd learned, and his cramped office served as unofficial hub of the whole news operation. He seldom left it, expecting newsroom Mohammeds to come to him.

"What's up, Mike?"

Roth snapped his gum, a habit that served as introduction or punctuation and sometimes even sat in for a firm "no." "That piece on the drug addicts' halfway house legislation last week—"

"Anything wrong?" Like most reporters, Liz lived in subliminal terror of charges of inaccuracy, unfairness, or—the Big Lawsuit.

"Not a thing. But I liked that opening stand-up you did in the drugstore. How'd that come about?"

Liz laughed. "Oh, that. I browbeat Eddie into stopping at a Rexall on the way back to the station. I wanted to give the problem some context. I don't know. . . ."

Mike nodded. "It worked." He tapped a nearby pile of papers with the ever-constant sheaf in his left hand. "We want that out-there, doing-something look to our news reports—if it doesn't eat up too much time."

"It only took seven minutes or so."

Mike smiled and gum-snapped simultaneously. "Keep it up."

Liz sat still after he'd left, mentally reviewing the film segment he'd complimented. She'd merely done her opening stand-up against an array of over-the-counter drugs, pointing out that for most people the vast number of legal drugs are a vital help and cause no problems, but for some, drug dependence quickly can drive them out of the law-abiding mainstream. Then had come the stock news conference footage, outlining the problem and proposed solution.

"What brought Mike the Shrike to your stand?" Steve Harmon hovered over her desk now.

"He liked my halfway house introduction in the drugstore. You know, it's funny, but I just took what would have been my written lead-in and made it visual. Maybe that's the secret."

"The secret is making any effort at all to do more than the routine," Steve answered. "That's great; compliments are pretty rare around here."

"So are you, apparently. I haven't seen you since you administered first aid in the cafeteria."

"Haven't needed first aid again, either, right? That cafeteria's a health hazard. No, I'm either stuck in the studio with my show or out filming, like you. Sometimes you don't see a coworker for weeks around here; schedules are just out of sync. Or somebody's got the ax," he joked.

Liz lowered her voice so Steve had to lean closer, not a bad idea. She picked up a subtle whiff of aftershave and the golden glints in his gray eyes. "Speaking of coworkers, who's the woman over there? Don't look! She's been watching me since Mike came over. About forty-five, hair teased like a Brillo pad—"

"Looks like a rat terrier?"

"Tenacious, yes."

Steve nodded, his back still to the object of their speculation. "Caralee Koeppers," he whispered, leaning even nearer. "Grande dame of local TV talk shows since the fifties. Hosted a thing for KSTP until they flushed her and got an up-to-date man/woman duo. Terry and Tammie, otherwise known as Ken and Barbie. Anyway, good old WBGO can never resist a bargain and snapped up Caralee. She does whatever. I'm sure she'd love to get her mitts on *Mid-Morning*, but I'm too possessive."

"You don't like competition," Liz charged. She'd been teasing, but passing judgment on Steve's likes and dislikes suddenly seemed overpersonal, as if Liz was wondering how she ranked among them.

"Neither does Caralee. I bet by lunchtime she'll have the word spread stationwide that the new reporter from Wisconsin is a vamp who lures all the men to her desk."

Liz sat back indignantly. "I do not! Just get out of here, then. Shoo! *I* have work to do." Indignation was as good a pretext as any for inserting some needed space between herself and Steve Harmon. Like all men who made their livings on the electronic media, he possessed an innate ability to make his presence intensely felt—call it charisma, social skill, or just plain charm. Liz was too observant to be immune.

So she rearranged her always overpopulating papers after Steve left, watching Caralee Koeppers pretend not to watch her. Liz had heard the name and now had a face to go with it. Caralee was older than the other women and dressed in exquisitely tailored suits, while the sprouts Liz's age wore casual shirts and sometimes even blue jeans on assignment. And Caralee's distant figure flashed a commanding Morse code of expensive jewelry, just as her over-coiffed and permed hair telegraphed her middle age. She didn't look so bad, just not with it. In the fifties, she'd probably been the cat's pajamas—and bedroom slippers.

Liz sighed and starely blankly at her desk. That was another aspect of her whimsical career change she'd never considered. Now she'd become a commodity that was perceived to sour with age, like an airline hostess. Feminists were challenging and chang-ing the attractiveness requirement for those overworked waitresses of the air, but the same physical expectations remained in force in more ground-bound professions. There was an unwritten weight requirement at WBGO, too.

Liz, always slim and naturally attractive enough to avoid the adolescent self-hate stage, usually didn't think about looks unless she was dressing up to go out. But she'd seen nothing but nice-looking, slender people at the TV station, except for Gene Malone the weatherman—none of the shrewd but overweight slobs the newspaper industry was fond of producing and venerating. And after seeing Stephanie on film, Liz had been struck dumb to see the gangly, underweight woman she'd met transformed into a sleek on-air swan. Liz herself had been forced, for the first time in her life, to regard her own image critically. She concluded she was a bit . . . well, plump on camera. That's why a cottage cheese and pear lunch awaited in a brown bag in the small refrigerator under the cafeteria sink.

A check of her watch showed it was only eleven. Her stomach was already protesting. Think Twiggy, she admonished herself, reaching back to a high school idol. Knobby knees are erotic; look at how her knees had attracted Steve Harmon the other day. She cringed again, thinking of her ignominious push to the street. That cop ought to be arrested—chauvinist bully. Liz headed for the hall, newly outraged.

She was still mentally telling off some sympathetic police authority figure who couldn't take his eyes off her newly bony, Twiggy-ized knees, cameras rolling all the while, when the door to the women's room swung open on her.

"Oh. Hi." Liz was startled to find the object of her recent speculation a neighboring image in the mirror. Caralee Koeppers didn't look surprised at all. "They sure don't give you much of a makeup shelf around here," Liz complained as her blusher slid into the sink. "I thought they wanted us to look nice on camera."

"They're getting a new makeup room in a month or so," Caralee told her own image, dabbing her short lashes with another layer of mascara. "You're Liz Jordan." She still didn't glance Liz's way.

"Yes, and I guess you're—"

"Caralee Koeppers. I do the museum and Guthrie Theater openings, and all the fashion."

"I didn't know we had a fashion beat," Liz said innocently.

Caralee's professionally taut features tightened more. "Not enough of it," she snapped. "This management is way behind the times."

"Maybe it's because they're all men," Liz slipped in.

"Women can get off on the wrong track, too." Caralee finally shot a look Liz's way. "This women's lib stuff is ridiculous. No makeup, no clothes, no style. And tough . . . Nobody likes a tough woman." Caralee ran two expertly arched ribbons of red lipstick across her top lip and folded her mouth tightly shut, showing vertical hairline wrinkles all along her upper lip. When her mouth unpursed, a mirror image of red covered the lower lip.

"That's funny." Liz stopped her own modest primping to turn and regard the woman with a smile. "I'd say you were pretty tough yourself."

Caralee curled her left hand to study her long, enameled fingernails. She had an aquiline profile, Liz saw, and tanned skin the color and texture of an alligator bag. If it weren't for the elaborate grooming, Caralee Koeppers would be instantly recognizable as a homely woman. The woman's hand curled tighter into a fist, and Liz winced to think of those talons driving home into the sensitive palm.

Caralee unfolded her hand and watched her nail imprints fade. "Tough enough so that nobody interferes with me." She dropped her makeup bag into her purse and scraped it off the metal shelf. Good purse; little metal feet to stand on. Everything about Caralee was first-class in a stiff, old-fashioned way, and it still didn't guarantee success. No wonder she felt threatened.

Liz watched her inflexible helmet of lacquered hair march out the door—from the rear the woman looked impervious. Apparently she wasn't. Liz swept her loosely curled hair atop her head, wondering if it would slim her face. No, no better. Condemned to cottage cheese for the rest of her natural life. If only she looked angular and harsh and—tough—like Caralee.

The next day Steve Harmon was perched on Liz's desk again. It was a pity Caralee wasn't at her desk to see it.

"You've been sticking to the job too much. How about we take a lunch hour together? There's a great pizza place up the street. Something wrong?"

"Pizza? Wrong? No. Love it. Um, I guess I can go."

"You haven't got an assignment until two." Liz looked surprised as Steve shrugged disarmingly. "I checked Roth's assignment roster. You think I'd risk a turndown? Male broadcasters have the fragilest egos in the business; surveys prove it."

"Male *disc jockeys*. I've seen the same surveys. But we go dutch, right?"

"Fine, anything to get out of this asylum for a while."

Steve left to get his coat while Liz bundled up in her red number and went to the station entrance to meet him. No sense stirring up newsroom gossip. If TV stations were half as rumor-prone as newspapers, the grapevine would have her and Steve in bed by tonight. . . . The thought made her uneasy. For the first time in her life, Liz had her own apartment, and could entertain King Kong if she so desired. Scary. It gave her ideas, opportunities, choices she'd never had before. For heaven's sake, it was just a stupid pizza lunch date. Pizza. Maybe three days of cottage cheese had atoned in advance.

Steve joined her at the door and they slipped out onto the icy sidewalks, negotiating the who-walks-on-the-street-side question with unspoken readings of each other's body language. He got the curbside. In social situations, Liz was content to concede to custom, but at work her philosophy was different, and had to be: Fast Eddie, for example, just set off down the street with reporter in tow, and Liz usually had to run around to the street side to avoid the camera equipment swinging at his right hip.

"Freddie's?" Liz studied the narrow storefront with a snow-topped red-and-green awning.

"Great pizza. In summer they put little metal tables along the sidewalk." Steve took her arm as they ducked inside the dark sliver of restaurant, exhibiting evidence of either a gentlemanly rearing or lust. Liz decided neither motive would be unwelcome.

They settled in a dark corner—the entire place was dark—and ordered a large half-pepperoni, half-green pepper pizza.

"Wine or beer?" asked the waitress.

"Just, ah, water," Liz said. Steve elevated his eyebrows. "Working, you know."

"I'm having a beer; try some wine. Come on, your assignment isn't until two, and it's only—eleven-thirty."

"Okay, um, red, I guess." The waitress was off, there being no need to inquire as to variety or brand.

In a sense, having an initial lunch over pizza was a bad idea. There was that long wait with nothing to do but talk—and look at each other. And newspeople were supposed to be so glib.

"I don't know if you want to talk about it . . ." began Steve, moving the dimpled red glass candle container necklaced in plastic flowers to the side. Liz tensed. "But you must have a lot of insight on your dad's work."

"My dad? You're interested in my dad?"

"Not intensely, but I've read some of his columns. They assign his stuff in J-schools, and I started out there before switching to the 'new' communications major at college. Does it bug you, to be the great man's daughter?"

Her dad. Somehow he always came up. Bother her? "No . . . at least, not until I got out into the wider world of journalism. I guess I never knew what a celebrity he was, in a minor way. And how many people would use . . . what he was, is . . . against me somehow."

Steve winced. "Oops, I did pick a great opening topic. Maybe we should go back to something safe." His face sobered to news anchor deadpan. "How're your knees?"

"Pretty scabby." Liz laughed and took a sip from the plain wineglass the waitress had deposited in front of her. "And you say you run an interview show? Mr. Tact."

"You should sit in sometime. Better yet, I'll get you on as a guest—to talk about your famous father."

"Thanks a bunch. But why were you curious about my father?"

"I like people. I like characters. He strikes me as being made from a mold sort of rare these days. You know, Clarence Darrow. Rabble-rousing in the grand old style." Liz nodded. "I imagine—" Steve's eyes caught hers before they could slide away. "I imagine he would be kind of hard to live with."

"Let's just say he was kind of hard to live *without*."

"A pervasive personality, huh? Were you the only daughter?"

"The only *child*, period. My mother died soon after I was born. So it was just Dad and me. Until Myrtle—that's my stepmother— finally came along. But I was nearly out of high school then, and went away to college, so—"

"So you broke the parental yoke. And now you're stretching it even farther by going into a new form of journalism in a new state."

"I never . . . thought of it in those terms."

Steve sipped from his mug of beer. "Don't mind me. Amateur psychoanalyst. You get involved with the people you work with in this business. With our hours, there's not much time for normal socializing. Now, some of the news consultant outfits are talking about putting reporters on live on the six and ten someday. Can you imagine that. *No* nights off."

"I can't imagine being on *live*. I don't know how you do it every day."

"I look at each day as a new opportunity to make a fool of myself. It's kind of fun."

"You're right; I'll have to sit in and watch you in action. If I can do a little psychoanalysis of my own, I'd say you must have masochistic tendencies, Mr. Harmon."

Liz was joking, but Steve became suddenly serious. "I'd say you could say that about anybody working at WBGO and you'd be right."

"You don't . . . like . . . the station?"

Steve's eyes rolled. "Oh, Liz. I didn't want to crush your illusions on our first date—" Her eyebrows rose and he grinned. "But in case you haven't noticed it—and what does a greenhorn from Wisconsin know?—WBGO-TV is hardly the apex of local broadcast journalism. WCCO is the class act in town. KSTP is hungry—like ABC nationally—and aspires to some couth, so at least it's trying something new. But you, my naive one, have had the ill luck to land at the Twin Cities' sorriest excuse for a TV station."

"And what's your excuse?"

"Me, I'm trying to get out. That's what anyone with any brains would do. But it's hard. We've all signed these exclusive contracts swearing not to work for any other station in the same market for a *year* after quitting, so even if the competition were interested in hiring away someone local, there's that hitch."

"Are they?"

Steve hesitated. "How reliable are you on off-the-record confidences?"

Liz raised her hand. "Scout's honor."

He sighed. "'CCO was interested in me for some new concept. It wouldn't be a talk show per se, more of an in-depth reporting position. But there's that damn contract. . . ."

"And they wouldn't let you out of it?"

"Would they let Rudolph Hess out of Spandau Prison? It sets a bad example."

Liz thought a moment. "But he's the *last* old Nazi in there."

"Exactly. And I'd be the *first* WBGOer to beat my contract. Either way, there's no way in hell the system can permit an exception."

"So what are you going to do?"

"The best job I can and hope I find an out-of-state job, maybe in a major market, even. They can't stop me from sending out film. But talk-show hosts are a dime a dozen, and if I only get routine guests, it's hard to stand out. And I don't want to do talk shows forever. I'm interested in issues. News. Maybe even a public affairs show format. Except this station's idea of public affairs is Liz Taylor's love life."

"She doesn't have affairs," Liz objected primly.

"What?"

"She always marries them first. What kind of newsman are you? Don't you read the *National Enquirer*?"

"Not enough, I can see. But what about you? What are your plans—besides getting as far away from WBGO as possible now that you know the ugly truth?"

A pinwheel of pizza levitated down to the table between them, the cheese still bubbling.

"I'm gonna devour this thing. That's my major plan. I am starved. This was a great idea, Steve."

"I'm not going to let you off the hook. You've heard my sad story; you owe one back. You must have ambitions."

So, between mouthfuls of pizza she shouldn't have been eating, Liz told him of plans—she began to formulate plans on the spot— she shouldn't have had. Things that mattered. That's what she wanted to cover. "I even did a *living together* story for the *bridal* edition last year," Liz bragged. "Boy, the ME hit the roof, but it was in print already."

"ME is managing—"

"Managing editor, right. Sort of like the news director, seldom seen but often felt, usually via memo."

"You were a feisty little employee, weren't you?" Steve's look was flatteringly admiring.

"Was is right. Then, The Change came. New management. And suddenly we women reporters were back in the fifties—food and fashion and how-to crapola. Don't laugh; it was! So I left."

Steve sat back and lit a cigarette. "If you've come to WBGO looking for substance, you're in the wrong place."

Liz sighed and ate one last piece of pizza, which was five more than she should have had. It was humiliating to have lunch with a man and outeat your . . . date. Steve's low-key blond looks seemed very attractive against the garish quasi-Italian background, quiet and stable. He even smoked his cigarette slowly, unaddictively. And he understood her career frustration, her race to outrun the long shadow of her father.

"If it's the wrong place," suggested Liz, "maybe we can change it."

"I don't know about that." Steve leaned conspiratorially toward the center of the table to match Liz's intensity. "But it'd be fun to try—together."

Their eyes locked over the decimated pizza tin. They were

young and ambitious, they were determined, they were of the same mind and the opposite sex. They both knew—and their eyes silently affirmed it—that they had more in common than a mere lunch could explore.

— *Chapter 12* —

Changing WBGO was a bigger job than Liz had imagined. After a few more press conferences gave her a chance to chat with reporters from other stations, she learned that WBGO was indeed as poorly regarded as Steve had said it was.

"Blood, Guts, and Orgasms" was how the initiated interpreted its call letters. Steve complained frequently about the number of "sex book hucksters" the *Mid-Morning* producer kept booking on Steve's interview show.

"I'm the most *vicariously* sexually sophisticated male in the Twin Cities," he'd exploded once after a twelve-minute interview with the candid lady author of *How to Hold Your Man—and Where: An Intimate Guide.* Steve waved the hardcover tome in question at Liz, who accepted the challenge and skimmed it.

"How-to *and* sex—now there's a marriage made on Madison Avenue. This photo makes the author look like her last job was at Maggie's Midnight Sauna on Hennepin Avenue."

Steve snatched back the book. "No, on second thought, don't look at it. Fighting pollution begins at home."

"I might learn something," Liz objected. "Besides, if you leave it in the usual dump site for unwanted books, Gene the Weatherman'll probably get a hold of it, and that would be corrupting the innocent."

Steve smiled at the idea. Gene the Weatherman was WBGO's version of Mr. Rogers—as unassuming and innocent a media figure as you could find on television these days, to whom local viewers turned for the weather forecast with the same childlike trust with which they'd watched *Mr. Wizard* in the days of their, and TV programming's, youth. No one with a haircut as bad as Gene the Weatherman's would lie to them.

Steve tossed the book aside and changed the subject. "Hey, listen, Liz. You think you'll be off early on Friday night? That new Reynolds movie is out, *The Man Who Loved Cat Dancing.* Like to see it?"

"Sure," she said, as she always did to Steve.

Next to Liz, who broke her back trying to inject creative visuals into her reports and whose writing was naturally lively and concise, Steve was the only other outstanding reporter at WBGO. With the dearth of talent around them, they gravitated together like matched cockatoos in a cageful of wrens. Steve's spot as *Mid-Morning* host gave him a certain superiority, yet put him on a different footing from Liz, so they weren't in direct competition. They could sympathize with each other, bitch to each other, dream of separate but equal achievement together. Even plot to escape together.

Liz sometimes would slip into the studio, the only witness except for three cameramen and the floor director, as Steve conducted his interviews with a parade of passing-through celebrities, product spokespeople, and local pushers of causes both good and transparently self-serving.

Smooth, he was so smooth, Liz often thought as she perched on one of the guest chairs set around the sprawling roadmap of cables crossing the studio floor, intending to stay a minute and making it ten. She didn't think less of him for it. That's what live television demanded, cucumber-cool supermen and superwomen who could keep one eye on the floor director's timekeeping fingers, one eye on the camera, and all their attention on the interview subject.

Steve was always well informed; his questions were astute. If he interviewed a local Girl Scout about the forthcoming cookie drive, he could charm her preadolescent gawkiness into a semblance of self-possession, or at least ease her terror and somehow make the obligatory segment seem newsworthy. If he had a politician sitting opposite him on the cornily ordinary couch that served as a set, Steve could turn incisive and surprise a few frank answers out of the legislator. Occasionally, an off-the-cuff response on *Mid-Morning* merited follow-up in the daily newspapers: "Congressman X revealed his likely key vote on milk-support legislation during a television interview Monday...." Newspapers seldom credited TV sources by name, rank, and serial number—TV news operations too often used rehashed newspaper stories without any attribution—but Steve knew when his program had "broken" a news topic. Now Liz knew, too, and could share the pride. It was hard throwing good work into the heart of a whirlwind day after day. Television journalism was written on the airwaves, and yesterday's triumphal report was today's ghostly afterimage.

"At least at the *Observer* I could keep my story clips," Liz complained once, when Steve had praised her piece on no-smoking legislation for restaurants. "What do I have to show for my work here? How do I apply for a job somewhere else? What do I show them? Air?"

"You've got script copies."

Liz snorted and Steve smiled. Scripts were skeletons on which filmed reports were hung. They looked pretty unimposing until fleshed out by creative camera work and editing.

"Besides, you don't have to show them anything. They *see* you."

"Who's gonna watch WBGO?"

"Don't depress me. Look. I think if you do good work long enough, you build up something. Maybe it's not tangible, but people *hear* about you. *Mid-Morning* may not be a world-class talk show, but a lot of influential people come through town and end up on it. Who knows what might happen? That's why I keep doing it, Peter Promoter and Sylvia Sexologist notwithstanding. Besides, Liz, you're getting valuable experience here, and a good look at what *not* to do. Take Caralee Koeppers—"

"No thank you; you don't have to descend to the gruesome. . . ."

Mike Roth passed just then, giving Steve and Liz a hard look. They were leaning side by side on Steve's desk, feet braced, heels of hands pressed on the desk edge, enjoying a casual talk.

Liz straightened and moved away from the desk. "Must be having too much fun; that was definitely the management fish-eye."

"Yeah." Steve didn't budge, but folded his arms across his chest. "All we're allowed to do around WBGO is *work*, and God knows thinking and talking have nothing to do with that. Why don't we go out to dinner Friday night?" he said, abruptly changing the subject. "Someplace tony for a change. Get the station out of our hair. No shoptalk."

"No station. Heavens, what would we talk about?" she joked uneasily.

Steve's light gray eyes scintillated with gentle mischief. "Maybe it's time we found out."

The Radisson Flame Room was the haunt of the fur-stole set. The menu prices were high, the lights low, and the ambience distinctly a middle-brow notion of elegance. The real drawing card was not food but music, romantic music dished out by candlelight and the assiduous efforts of the Golden Strings, a complement of violinists who serenaded diners with lush arrangements of everything from "Malagueña" to "The Sound of Music."

Steve had forsaken the V-necked sweater that was his on-air signature and, in his charcoal blazer and white shirt, looked almost as formal as the tuxedo-clad violin corps pouring their souls and double chins out as their sawing elbows plied the violins. Catching the spirit of the outing, Liz had debuted a slinky emerald-green wool jersey dress, all cling and drape, that she could never have worn in Turtle Bend. She felt at least a sophisticated, citified twenty-eight and, for once, like a successful public personality. She felt people were watching them, and caught a speculative firelit glisten from eyes all around the room. (Nearly every Flame Room entrée lived up to the restaurant's name, coming served flambé.) It could have been because of Steve's well-known face; or it could have been, as she had noted in the restaurant's lobby mirrors as they arrived, that Steve and Liz made a striking couple, ash-blond and ebony in contrast.

"So, what do we talk about if not our careers?" Liz asked, concentrating on getting her shrimp cocktail neatly into her mouth without leaving a saucy trail on her draped, dry-clean-only emerald bodice.

"Why not 'what ifs'? What if you hadn't majored in journalism? What would you be doing now?"

Liz thought. "Teaching something, probably on the junior college level. Maybe English. Cramming *Moby Dick* down reluctant throats. Or maybe I would have been . . . an archaeologist and I'd be in the South American jungles looking for the lost tribes of Israel. What about you?"

Steve shook his candlelight-gilded head. "Mine was an unfair question. There never was a 'what if' for me. It was broadcast journalism all the way. Growing up in Idaho—and with a slew of sisters and a widowed mother—a guy gets thirsty for news of the outside world, not to mention basketball scores. I made sure I went to college out-of-state. If I never see another pair of nylons on a shower curtain rod, I'll die happy. So I went to Chicago, majored in broadcasting, worked at a couple radio stations, then broke into TV at WBGO. Lucky me. I guess I'm just single-minded."

Liz put down her fish fork. "You know, that's odd, but I think the reason I stumbled backwards into my career is that there weren't really any women on TV to emulate years ago. Except maybe Nancy Dickerson. And now there's Barbara Walters on the *Today* program, of course. So being where I am can't have been a lifelong dream. It's just an accident."

Steve sipped the Scotch and soda still melting its ice cubes. He was deliberate at everything he did. No obsessive haste to consume drove him. For a time-conscious television man, he lived an oddly unclocked life. Liz admired that.

"You know what we're doing here?" Steve asked suddenly.

She didn't want to answer. The setting, her mood, had become irredeemably romantic. Liz decided she wasn't ready for that.

"We're talking *careers*, silly!" he said as she groped for an answer light enough, or safe enough. "We're workaholics, that's all. We love our servitude, our agony." He was teasing.

"Not true! Nobody wants to be oppressed, not blacks or women or any subculture group."

"Women are a subculture? They're a pretty pervasive minority."

"So are ants, but they hardly rule the world. Power has nothing to do with numbers. Power is Mike Roth never giving me a meaty assignment. He doesn't even think about it; he just avoids me. He'd send Gene the Weatherman on a fire before he'd send me, even if all he got was the time and temperature of the blaze."

"No women's lib. I've done my bit for the cause on my show. I even had Germaine Greer on." Steve's hands fanned in a mock attempt to stop an invisible onslaught. "It's not just you, not just women. It's all of us at the station. The management isn't sexist; it's simply bad. You're being oversensitive."

"Maybe. But NOW wouldn't be using the FCC to force stations to hire a reasonable proportion of women if something weren't going on. The newspaper certainly didn't let me escape a preconceived little niche. Maybe it *is* bad management, and maybe management is bad because it's sexist."

"*I'm* not getting anywhere," Steve pointed out over their arriving main courses. "And I'm fairly obviously male. I think."

"Granted," said Liz, flushing a little as she tackled her broiled red snapper. She'd really wanted the fettuccini Alfredo, but she'd never wear her emerald dress again if she gave in to such unreasonable urges. "I just have this awful feeling that I'll never get anywhere. Never. And for no reason."

"Welcome," said Steve, toasting her with his almost empty lowball glass, "to life."

That evening, their social instincts if not their political ones seemed in synchronization. Liz asked Steve into her apartment for the first time, feeling nervous about her unimpressive furniture, about the appropriateness of the liqueur she'd brought that afternoon with precisely this casually elegant finish to the evening in mind.

"Benedictine?" she asked, hoping she sounded as if she served it routinely.

Steve nodded and sat on the wicker love seat, more involved in taking in the surroundings than watching Liz vanish into the tiny kitchen and clatter her new liqueur glasses together like castanets.

She returned with two shot-size crystal glasses, glittering topaz from their amber burden. Liz handed one to Steve, sat beside him on the love seat, leaned to put her own glass down untasted. Steve was doing the same thing. She laughed as he laughed, leaned toward him as he leaned toward her. Their kiss was accomplished so fast that Liz's first reaction was relief that it had been so simple. The first, awkward leap was behind them; she was in Steve's arms, her senses lost in the dark behind her closed eyes, savoring the excitement of arms pulling her close, of lips pressing unpredictably against hers, feeling the stirring tickle of his mustache. Her arms had folded between them, so Liz had to remain pleasantly passive as Steve minute by minute took what could have been a warm first kiss beyond that limit to a second, demandingly deeper kiss and beyond that still to the repeated probing tender-violent explorations of unrepentant desire, bringing Liz with him. When they parted for breath, they were lovers.

They read each other's eyes, gauging the depth of an expression neither had seen in the other before, both sexual and emotional, blatantly obvious and intensely private.

"More, please?" Steve quipped tenderly, in towheaded Oliver Twist fashion.

Liz nodded. He reached over to switch off her single table lamp. Darkness double-blinded them as they came together close-eyed in swift accord—lips, teeth, tongue, torsos, hands. Their fingers endlessly shifted the clothes upon their bodies; their bodies moved in new inventive patterns.

Liz felt deliriously mindless, but the masculine drive was less distractable. From what seemed a remote distance, Liz felt Steve's hand pull her dress zipper open, felt it stretch the rough fabric off her shoulder, felt the inner binding of her bra surrender suddenly to some unsensed touch.

They both froze, holding their breaths, lips locked but unmoving. In the dark, moving as slow as a leviathan in the deep, Steve's fingertips at last brushed feather-soft along the contour of Liz's bared breast.

"I don't know if it's right."

"Don't you want to go on?"

"Yes, oh God, yes. But . . . I haven't before, Steve. You've done more than anyone—"

"You mean 'gotten away with.'"

"Yes. Isn't that enough for now?"

"Maybe *this* is. But *this* isn't. . . ."

"Steve, please. I'm going crazy with, with . . . something!"

"That something's spelled f-r-u-s-t-r-a-t-i-o-n, and it's been driving men crazy for centuries. I'm glad you feel it; that means you're hot."

"Me? Hot? Come on. . . . Steve, stop it. If you keep—"

"Hmmm? Keep what?"

"Keep . . . doing that. And that. Steve, please! I'm—"

"Not hot. Heaven forbid that a good girl should have any juices. . . ."

"I'm afraid."

"Of what? I'd never do anything to hurt you, Liz. I . . . I guess I love you. And this is a symptom of that. Look at it as a disease. You need treatment, my very personal attention. Here. And here. And . . . here."

"Steve. Oh, Steve. Do you, do you really love me?"

"Let me show you."

"I don't know. . . ."

"Don't you want it?"

"Steve, I think I love you, too, but I've never . . . done it . . . before, and . . . and—oh, yes . . . Oh, no!"

"What now?"

"I'm not . . . protected."

"You're not on the Pill?"

"Well, no. I mean, you don't expect to be . . . Does every girl you date gobble the Pill just in case her lord and master gets a notion?"

"Most single girls in the city are ready for whatever might come up. But it's no hassle. I'll be careful tonight, and next time we'll be ready. What's the matter?"

"*Next* time."

"Don't you like the idea?"

"Too much. Ummmmm. It's just that . . . oh, that's nice, nicer than anything. Just that, I don't know. It's corny, but I assumed I'd be married and no one would care what I did, including me. Now I feel like I could get caught, trapped."

"Not if you're on the Pill."

"But what will I say if I go to a doctor?"

"For Christ's sake, Liz. This isn't Turtle Bend. This is 1973. You say you want a birth control prescription, period. For a lady who's got her head together on the job, you're woefully behind the times."

"I was raised to be. Why do you think I left Turtle Bend? I could have been professionally interred at the *Sentinel*, and no one in town would dare screw around with me without benefit of matrimony, and old Doc Knox would blush to put me on the Pill even if I *was* married, and I'd be too embarrassed to ask him anyway, so I'd have six kids and forget working."

"No one would dare, huh? Looks like you came to the right place. Harmon boldly goes where no man has gone before. This looks like the very right place to me...."

"Steve! Quit grinning; you look like Fu Manchu or something. I don't *have* a doctor here yet."

"Go to Planned Parenthood. If you're over eighteen, they don't ask any questions. Unless, of course, you prefer your current, lonely, celibate, single state—"

"Seducer!"

"Yes? You called?"

"I'm sorry. I don't want to ruin...this with qualms."

"Then lie back, close your mouth, open your eyes, and enjoy it."

"You make it hard not to."

"That's what I want to hear."

"Ummmmm..."

"And that."

"Ohhhh..."

"And this. Come on, Liz, let go and love me. I'll never hurt you. Love'll never hurt you. I promise."

— *Chapter 13* —

"I don't know." Mike Roth was frowning. Liz stood in front of his desk, fidgeting like Mary Tyler Moore called on the carpet by Mr. Grant. "This script...it's not the assignment you suggested."

"It's better," she answered boldly. "I knew a look at the whole question of how Planned Parenthood was handling sexually active teenagers was worth exploring, but until I got out there, I didn't know anything about the rest of it."

"But these are allegations...unsubstantiated."

"Eddie got great film of the defaced car."

"Sure. But that could have happened for some other reason."

"In the Planned Parenthood *parking lot*? After the bomb threat?"

"It's so amorphous."

"I'll talk to Parents Concerned members, get a statement denying they've been harassing Planned Parenthood and its clients. That ought to cover us."

Mike Roth took off his glasses and rubbed his eyes, a bad sign.

"We're not a newspaper, Liz. We can't go into these social issues in depth. You can't cover a lot of complexities in a minute-ten."

"Give me longer."

"Why? How can I justify it to the news director?"

"Look. I covered a Planned Parenthood bombing in Milwaukee, but this is the first case of a threat here. It all began happening when the clinic started encouraging teenagers to come in, in confidence, to get contraceptives. Parents are really going bananas at the idea of losing control over their kids' sexuality and they figure the fear of pregnancy is the only thing keeping teenagers in line. But with the young runaways that started in the sixties, and the street kids today, the pregnancy rate is rising faster than among any other group. Let's do a series on it. None of the newspapers know yet about the threats to clinics that counsel sexually active teenagers. WBGO could scoop everyone."

"Scoop" did it, or maybe "sexually active" did. Roth's beady little black eyes glittered. "I suppose I could check it with the news director and let you know his decision. Either way, we've got to hold the story as now written, which leaves me with a hole to fill," he groused. "You sure nobody else is going to get on this?"

"Not right away. I told you; I literally stumbled over the story."

Liz left Roth's desk, semitriumphantly, and headed for Steve's.

"And?" he asked, knowing full well what had been going on.

She shrugged. "It's in Gus Baer's hands now."

"Your first series. That wouldn't be too bad. I was here a year before I got more than a minute-ten airtime on anything."

"But then they gave you a half-hour talk show!"

"Mere chance. I just happened to be there when they decided to do it. If you get the green light on this teen-age birth control thing, you'll be pretty busy for a few days, I guess."

Liz perched on Steve's desk. "Yeah. So . . . ?"

His fingers discreetly played across her braced hand. "So . . . you've been on the Pill just about long enough to be certified safe. We should celebrate formally."

"Your place or mine?"

"Mine. I've got a decent stereo."

"What's this?" she mocked. "Lights, action, Mantovani?"

Despite playing it cool, Liz still felt, whenever she was near Steve, that she only wanted to get him in a quiet corner and commit intense intimate mayhem. They hadn't dared to consummate their love affair until Liz had faced the music at Planned Parenthood, gotten her pills, and undergone a full cycle of hormones to guarantee her protection. The expedition to PP had tipped her off to the new crisis building over teen–age contraception, but the sexual restraint it necessitated had made the past five weeks a heady period of inventive excess and much regretted caution for her and Steve.

"Are you trying to seduce me?" she asked.

"Something like that."

"I accept. If I get this series, I'll wrap it up at full speed and we'll celebrate two firsts at once."

Steve tugged on her hand, pulling her off balance, pulling her toward him. Liz let him draw her close enough so the electricity they generated these days sparked between them like eye-contact lightning.

"Collaborating?" came an archly disapproving voice. Caralee Koeppers bustled by, her clothes rustling crisply.

"No." Liz was sitting erect again, coldly ironic. "Just comparing notes. Steve had given me a story idea. . . ."

Caralee arched a well-drawn eyebrow. "*Given* you a story idea? I'd no idea it was a free market. Where's your ambition, Steve?"

"It's a ladies' story," Steve answered. "I can be generous."

A defrauded look settled on Caralee's face. Her eyebrows twitched defeat and pretended disinterest before she marched off on assertive high heels.

"'Ladies' story,'" Liz chided. "Sexist."

"And I 'gave' you a story. I'll get a reputation around here as an airhead if people think I give away story leads. Even to the Mata Hari of WBGO."

"If you hadn't sent me to Planned Parenthood for purely personal reasons, I'd have never tumbled to this new angle." Liz leaned near enough to whisper. "It's your own unbridled lust, Steve Harmon, that got you in trouble."

"I know," he shouted after her as she left. "Boy, do I know."

A madras-plaid band swept Mrs. Martin Meyers's brown hair back from her brow. From there her hair curled back around her face in a smooth, tight mushroomlike cap that looked as if it hadn't permitted a lock out of place in perhaps three years. Her dress was tailored forest-green. Her knees were tightly paired and kept that way by folded hands placed precisely atop them. The shoes were brown, sensible-heeled and close-toed. Only a diadem of sweat dewing the broad brow betrayed Mrs. Martin Meyers's severe stage fright.

"Tell me a bit about Parents Concerned, Mrs. Meyers," Liz said encouragingly. She, too, felt the hot lights on their tripods, but had learned months before that sweating is a voluntary reaction and can be controlled by sheer willpower.

Russ Delmonico, the station's most stoic cameraman, stood

behind the big black camera even now recording Mrs. Meyers's every twitch. Liz couldn't avoid thinking that the woman wouldn't help her cause any, compared to the overarticulate, overeducated Planned Parenthood spokesman or the hesitant-voiced pregnant teen-age girl filmed in anonymous shadow at the local unwed mothers home. To counter the report's emotional charge, Liz and Russ had covered a Parents Concerned rally the previous night. Their film revealed rows of grim, well-dressed people exuding stiff terror and blanket condemnation of simple human urges at the advent of values other than their own. But Liz had to give the woman a chance to present her views, however punative.

"As I understand it, Mrs. Meyers, your group wants Planned Parenthood to refuse contraceptives to sexually active teenagers, and then turn their names over to their parents. Doesn't that put Planned Parenthood in the role of policeman?"

"These are *children* we're talking about—seventeen, sixteen, fifteen years old. Such groups have no right to supersede parental wishes and encourage them to behave in ways the parents believe wrong."

"What about the teenagers' needs? Statistics show this age group has a rising number of out-of-wedlock pregnancies. Obviously, the kids are sexually active. How does making contraceptives available do anything but permit them to control their fertility?"

Mrs. Meyers's face tightened triumphantly. "They can control their fertility by abstaining from sex, as their parents, schools, and churches teach them. By making it easy to have sex without having babies, organizations like this teach young people that premarital sex is all right. If they faced the consequences of their acts, they would learn a lesson. And their parents would know what they'd been up to so they could stop it."

"Are you saying that having babies is punishment for having sex?"

"No. No, of course not. Not in properly sanctioned marriages. But that's why we organized Parents Concerned. We can't allow society at large to supersede our roles as instillers of moral values. These are our children; we have a right to say what they should do."

"But if they do it anyway?"

"They should be caught, not helped to hide it."

Mrs. Meyers nodded, satisfied at having delivered her message. She turned to face the camera directly, instead of Liz, and nodded even more militantly.

* * *

The series ran the following week, Monday through Thursday, with advertising in both the Minneapolis and St. Paul papers. "Pill Power—An Issue Between Parent and Child" was the ad department's instant summing up. WBGO wasn't softening its image as shallow sensation-seeker.

There was no celebrating with Steve, carnally or otherwise. Liz got her period, and though her monthly cramps were less severe, she bled like an eviscerated hog for some reason. The Pill promised regularity as a side effect, though, and Liz in turn promised Steve a rain check.

She sat at home, clutching a habitual sofa pillow to her stomach and phantom cramps. Liz intently watched the first installment of her first series, thinking. She basked in pride of production, knowing she had nursed the film that now flickered on her nineteen-inch portable TV through the editors, studied the seemingly endless reels of it to create the perfect interweaving of sound bites from opposing sides, juxtaposing the words and images for confirmation, irony, and challenge.

Emotionally, she was on the kids' side—heck, she hadn't been a teenager that long ago herself. She remembered the fevered, secret world adolescents inhabited, trying desperately to claim some private turf of their own, away from adults. Of course teenagers didn't know much about life and love and sex, but then, did many adults? Not Mrs. Meyers, despite her seven or whatever kids. Not Liz, despite a brief, exciting almost-fling with Steve. She blushed to think of how much the past month of passionate petting had taught her about sex—about men, about herself. Liz found herself angry at the adult world for keeping her ignorant, for making the woman the victim and the man the aggressor at the outset of every intimate alliance.

Zach Jordan had told Liz everything there was to know about the First Amendment and cold print and hot type. He hadn't told her a scintilla about sex. And Myrtle—well, Liz would have died before she'd have sat still for one word about sex from Myrtle, anyway. Was it possible her *father*, her *old* father, had married Myrtle because . . . because he was . . . doing things with *Myrtle*? Liz had fled her speculations, as the town of Turtle Bend fled from confronting its new generations' growing pains, and Parents Concerned concerned themselves with everything about their children's lives but their burgeoning adulthood and its ensuing delights and responsibilities.

Crazy. It was all crazy. Liz hugged the pillow tighter, anticipating, with some residual fear and more excitement, the moment when she would no longer be a virgin in name only. She supposed it was wrong, sex without marriage, but she didn't really believe that where it counted, in her heart and her hormones. Besides, it was too late; she was a fallen woman. (Why wasn't there such a thing as a "fallen man"? What about Adam, for instance?) She and Steve had already done . . . well, things Myrtle and her father had never dreamed of, Liz was sure. Things her father and mother may have neared, once, when they were young, but probably never achieved.

Steve was a subtle and patient lover despite his leash, or maybe because of it. He was hooking her on pleasure and tenderness, on being giver as well as receiver. Her mind dove into the private mental pool they capered in together. Naked. And lying together. Whispering. Laughing. Tangled. Moving, moving, moving. Secret. Open. Making love, not babies. In love. Perhaps teenagers were too young for this power and this glory. But there were worse things, Liz thought. Like being too old in spirit for it, too old for the risk, too old for the sheer play of it, too old to surrender to it.

Liz pitied the old. Maybe she'd do her next series on the plight of the elderly.

— Chapter 14 —

*Turtle Bend in high summer offered a lazy, wind-rippled undu-*lation of hill and river, both land and water steaming July heat and breeding days of swarming mosquitoes and nights of over-vocalizing crickets and frogs.

Liz went home for the Fourth of July, because she might not make it for Christmas—the heaving Wisconsin back roads could choke with winter snow, becoming impassable for weeks except to natives with four-wheel drive vehicles.

Besides, in Turtle Bend, the year's highest holiday was the small town's tribute to its roots, the Fourth of July, not the commercially sanctioned urban feast of fast spending, the twenty-fifth of December.

"Have some yams. I made them especially for you." Myrtle passed Liz the plain white pottery serving dish with its cheerful arrangement of starch to go. Liz weighed both dish and decision, then forked the smallest sweet potato onto her plate. Yams were not her favorite vegetable, but somehow the misconception, once implanted, was difficult to yank out.

"That all?" Myrtle was not one to miss weighing mealtime gestures as indications of malaise or simple contrariness.

"Really, I've got to watch my waistline. TV cameras put on fifteen pounds, you know."

Her father snorted, stabbing two plump yams to his already full Red Willow plate. He'd had a middle-aged spread ever since Liz could remember, a white-shirted, comfortable pillow tied around his middle like a Santa's underwear. He was almost vain about his lack of vanity.

"Don't need to worry about your girth at a *newspaper*, Elizabeth," he chortled, "just the news. You do any *news* at that station of yours?"

"I just did a big series on teen-age contraception."

Myrtle's lips pursed.

Zach nodded while shoveling in heaped forkfuls of potato salad and cold turkey. "Teen-age contraception. I imagine we've got some of that in Turtle Bend, too." He spoke of it as a disease. "Well, you younger generation have got to keep up on that kind of thing, I guess. Me, I can still concentrate on the enduring things—like how it feels to walk down a country road and what road this whole damn country is going down. Contraception! Some new Latinate word that excuses old-fashioned hanky-panky, more like it. You ever get to cover anything *good*, Liz?"

"Don't be crotchety, Zach," admonished Myrtle, who—beyond food—craved peace more than anything at her dinner table.

Liz didn't bother arguing. Even the mayor couldn't argue with Z.J. when he was off for a romp on a favorite hobbyhorse. Besides, Zach Jordan's editorial and personal stance was firmly rooted in days gone by. Only one word would adequately sum up both on his tombstone: Curmudgeon.

Liz decided to walk off Myrtle's farm-style dinner with a stroll downtown, where the three o'clock parade speechifying would unfurl. Her father would play his traditional role—commentator and master of what ceremonies there were, such as introducing the mayor with a certain acidity and the Strawberry Queen with his traditional slightly leering joviality.

Turtle Bend was still a small town. The shady, tokenly paved streets were quiet as Liz strolled the cracked and heaving sidewalks. They'd never been suitable for roller-skating when she was a child, weren't now, and likely would never be. Like most small communities, Turtle Bend just ended. The last row of houses stopped and there was nothing but rolling countryside from there on, inhabited by a cluster of cows or an odd horse or two, and mostly populated by thigh-high grasses and wildflowers. The farms began further out, and there was a clear-cut distinction between "farm folk" and "town folk."

She stopped at Dexter's Hardware Store for an ice cream cone dipped from one of the three stainless steel trapdoors behind the venerable snack counter. "Chocolate, vanilla, or strawberry?" asked the bouncy girl wielding the ice cream scoop these days. Dexter's girls were always bouncy, and Liz had never been one of them.

"Chocolate."

Liz strolled onto Main Street, where the big old-fashioned parking meters were swagged with red, white, and blue bunting and those buildings that had second stories were similarly dressed above the streetlamp level.

A few people—strangers—bustled back and forth on errands concerned with the afternoon's big parade. One woman wore a limp full-length calico dress and a sunbonnet. Several men sported patriarchal lengths of wispy beard cultivated for the afternoon's beard-growing contest.

Tur-tle Bend. Tur-tle Bend. A good place to be from, Liz decided as her tongue paved a smooth road around the roughly piled ice cream. Something buzzed at the edges of her consciousness, a big-city sound out of place here. It hummed nearer, circling a few blocks away with the persistent drone of a bumblebee. Then it swooped suddenly close, close enough to make Liz turn and study the big black motorcycle zooming incongruously down Main Street.

The blue-jeaned, T-shirted rider dragged a booted foot on the pavement and swiveled to a stop just past her.

"Liz?" She stared back. "Lizzie!"

"Herb? Really?"

"Really." He didn't wear a safety helmet—for one thing, he didn't have to worry about being tagged in a town as small as Turtle Bend; for another, it was out of character. Liz suspected, studying his casually rebellious attire and the motorcycle now, that Herb had kept a bit of Starbuck to keep him warm over the long, predictable small-town years. She'd bet he was the only guy in town with a full-bore, dirt-kicking, macho-spitting motorcycle.

Herb's run-down boot heel kicked the pavement. "I'm, uh, running sheepdog on the parade later," he explained, as if slightly embarrassed by the cycle, by his profile as official Turtle Bend hell-raiser.

"You still on the farm?" she asked politely.

He nodded, looking down and then glancing up at her, James Dean style. His hair was beginning to thin, she noticed, and the middle of the T-shirt swelled to accommodate a small hummock of stomach. Beer and boredom, that was all there was for small-town men.

"You workin'?" Herb's question wasn't routine. Almost all of Liz's classmates from high school were married now, mothers now. A few had part-time jobs, if they absolutely had to, at the town bank or variety store.

"I'm reporting for a TV station in the Twin Cities."

"Glamour girl, huh?" Herb grinned appreciatively and twisted the motorcycle handles idly. The machine revved throaty approval, idling too.

Liz smiled. "Not so glamorous, Herb. How're things going?"

"Okay." He stared down the vacant street. "Got hitched."

"Really? Who?" It had to be a local girl. It always was.

Herb shrugged. "Karen. Karen Schultz." Liz nodded, remembering. A farmgirl, facing the same social exile on the in-town high school scene, and reacting by being "fast." Liz recalled the thick black eyeliner, false eyelashes, and white lipstick of the mid-sixties high school vamp that she had once mildly envied but never had the nerve to emulate.

"That's great," she said. Herb shrugged again.

"You like city life?" he asked.

"I have to."

"Yeah, well, once they go off to college, they don't come back here, that's for sure."

"Except to visit." Liz smiled.

"Say, it's nice running into you, Lizzie. Maybe I'll see you later." Herb's shoulder muscles worked as he pumped the cycle handles. He smiled, and all the high school handsomeness came flooding back into his features. "It's nice to know someone who's hitched their wagon to a star," he said with a touch of Starbuck charisma. The paraphrase of the play's line turned the street into an intimate stage.

"Why, thank you, Mr. Starbuck," Liz returned in her long-ago Lizzie voice. More than old lines sparked between them; an old alliance flared into brief life, recognition of a time gone that neither would talk about and neither would forget. "I'll be watching you in the parade."

Herb saluted and revved off in a swashbuckling sweep of machine and motion. Liz watched until he vanished around a corner, then turned and ambled back home, warmed with nostalgia. How . . . wise . . . Herb had been to leave her future untampered with. A boy in his position could have used her infatuation with love-making to undo her. He could have knocked her up so easily, out of meanness, out of mistaken manhood, out of envy.

Now, from the safe viewpoint of a maturer, chemically protected sexuality, she could see just how good Herb had been, the boy who "wasn't good enough for her," as she had always secretly known but never admitted.

She was the rainmaker, the dreamer, the visionary, the mover and drifter, the maker of miracles. Herb had always been only a small-town Lizzie who had not been able to resist hitching his wagon to a piece of itinerant stardust. *Why* had she always felt there was something she had to do, someplace she had to go? Why did she still feel that way? Why did Herb catch that same fever? Liz didn't know. It wasn't living up to her father, though, she decided, which was a fear tainting her deepest ambitions. Maybe it was living up to what Herb had seen in her, before anybody else had, for one never-never summer.

Liz came back downtown that afternoon with Myrtle and her father to watch the festivities. Z.J. was a born wisecracker. The crowd giggled and howled in turn as he introduced Turtle Bend fixtures in their new roles as "Longest Beard" "Grayest Beard" "Skinniest Beard."

The floats representing local civic clubs or stores were pulled by farm tractors. Their crepe-paper gaudiness couldn't disguise homely origins.

Herb Boyle growled and throttled his way along the parade route, steering recalcitrant floats back into line, looking like a black motorcycle knight in dusty armor. Liz never got a chance to talk to him again, but the constant distant buzz of his machine kept him on her mind. Just before her father collected his women to go to the picnic in the empty lot known as the town "park," the cycle seethed by.

"That Herb Boyle." Her father's snowy head shook with leisurely dismay. "When will that wild boy settle down to just being a farmer?"

Liz pictured the dismay magnified on her father's face—on Myrtle's—if they'd know about all those precollege summer evenings spent with that "wild boy." She smiled.

The picnic was a predictable smorgasbord of ~~ham and turkey~~, ~~potato~~ egg, and ~~three-bean salads~~, fruited Jell-O squares, and cider and beer. Liz only saw Herb once, from a distance. He was with a short woman who had long, teased, frosted hair, a woman as wide as she was tall, with a toddler clenched to her skirt and a baby draped over one shoulder.

"You're going to college."

No, thought Liz. I went to college. Now I'm going back home to Minneapolis, and WBGO, and Steve. And next, I think I'm going to major in life.

— Chapter 15 —

"*How was Turtle Bend?*"

"Fine. Same as ever."

Steve nodded. "And that. That's breakfast?"

Liz paused in dipping up another dollop of low-fat yogurt to tilt the spoonful his way. "It's not bad. Try it?"

He made a face and leaned away in his chair. "Ugh. It looks like lard. Why do you eat that stuff?"

"It's great when you're in a hurry, as I usually am, and . . . it's low calorie." She popped the spoon into her mouth while Steve grimaced.

It was only eight-fifteen A.M. and the newsroom was still quiet, the clack of manual typewriters silenced for a change.

"You don't have to worry about calories," Steve said.

"You and Stephanie don't have to worry about calories; I do. Especially lately." Her tone and look were significant.

"Why lately?"

She leaned dramatically nearer. "The Pill, silly. The price of being your doxy, or whatever I am. I'm up five pounds. That's a lot on a TV camera."

Steve's puzzlement relaxed into a grin. "Yeah, but it goes on in all the right places." He looked pointedly at her bosom.

"Mae West never had a broadcasting career to consider," Liz answered, licking the last of the yogurt off her spoon. "The Lauren Hutton look is in now."

"What, a gap in your teeth?" Steve demanded scornfully.

"No. Wall-to-wall bones—cheek, collar, and hip. Gotta run. Roth wants me in his office at eight-thirty."

Steve tilted his blond head like a fond watchdog. "Roth, huh? Something up?"

"I doubt it. Watch my yogurt." Liz dumped the spoon in the empty container and plopped it on Steve's desk before dashing off. She'd never been called formally into Roth's office except to consult on a specific story and was more curious than she let on. What he had to say was either very good—or very bad. Maybe he'd noticed her extra five pounds. Maybe he'd noticed Steve and her getting cozy. Maybe . . .

115

Liz came out of Roth's office five minutes later, dazed. This time, Steve was waiting for her by her desk. "Well?"

Liz sat, picked up a pencil, doodled vaguely on some botched story forms. "I've got a new assignment."

"Oh, yeah?"

She shrugged. "I *think* it's a promotion. Kind of."

Steve straightened, narrowed his eyes.

"I'm to do a five-minute anchor spot twice a morning on the farm show, before we pick up the network morning program. I think that means that I'm the first anchor*woman* at WBGO."

Steve was momentarily speechless. "There's no news spot on *Farmers' Forum*."

"There will be."

"Holy cow." They both laughed.

"Just call me 'Hayseed.' I feel like I've been drafted for *Hee-Haw*. Well, I am from a small town. . . ."

"But . . . let's see. The *Forum* is on from six to . . ."

"Seven-thirty. I'll do a news segment at six-twenty-five and seven-twenty-five. It's just reading a script. I do scarier stuff on my off-the-cuff stand-ups. Why am I shaking, then?" Liz elevated her Venus Velvet no. 2 and watched the slender yellow pencil vibrate in her fingers.

"Anchor fever. You think I don't get it now and again? Face it, Jordan, being anchor is the name of the game in this business. I can do a talk show riff till I'm blue in the face, improvise daily out of my own head and instincts in half-hour doses. But it's those stints as a TelePrompTer-reading desk jockey that make your name in broadcasting. Well, congratulations."

Liz shook Steve's extended hand. "The first woman. There aren't many in the country."

"No, there aren't," he said, "but there'll be more. I don't want to prick your bubble. . . ." She looked up with arched eyebrows, playfully underlining the unintentional sexual imagery of his words. "Let me rephrase that. I don't want to rain on your parade, Liz, but even stations as impervious to change as WBGO are beginning to feel pressure to put more ethnics and women on the air—and at the anchor desks. Your promotion more likely reflects of that than any high regard the management holds you in."

"Maybe. But let me wallow in it." Liz laughed. "Just think how jealous Caralee will be!"

Liz's new status merited a mention on the *Minneapolis Tribune* TV page, a snide comment from the evening *Star*'s TV columnist, who claimed to have searched for but not found a beauty-pageant win in her background, and a bland "that's nice" letter from her father, who asked if that meant she'd be able to do more hard news stories.

"I'll be able to *write* more of the news—the stuff that comes over the wires and such. I'll be able to *shape* the newscast, even though it's a brief one," she wrote back, unfortunately before she started.

Five minutes—with one minute devoted to a commercial and one to the weather—didn't allow for much "shaping," Liz found when she reported to work at five-fifty on a Monday morning and with cold hands nervously shuffled news wire material and warmed-over rewrites of last night's major *Star* stories. There was almost no time to update stories, much less rewrite them, and no way to call anybody for new information. Who was up at six-twenty-five in the morning? Liz asked herself as she sat at the set desk and watched a monitor behind the camera unreel a root-worm insecticide commercial. Farmers. Great. If the station signal reached that far, she'd have the reward of knowing that Herb Boyle would be watching her hollow-eyed morning face over his Wheaties.

The seven-twenty-five stint was better. She already felt more in control, and this time the commercial was for a chain of metropolitan discount carpet stores, the chain owner huckstering his own products. He was a portly man whose command of public speaking was slightly above the level of a guppy's. But at least Liz had the illusion of addressing a bustling, work-readying Big-City audience with her brief items on the latest battered woman's body found around the Twin Cities, the announcement that senior citizens should be thinking of fall flu shots, the report of a bomb threat at another Bank of America in California.

For the first time, the station management showed an interest in her appearance. She was flattered at the end of the third week when Mike Roth caught her in passing later that morning and winked. "Sharp outfit today, Liz. Looked good on camera."

That night after work, she confided the compliment to Steve, who snorted. "Mike's a womanizer; he's just started to get going on you. Besides, don't kid yourself that he pops open his bleary beads at seven A.M. to eyeball you on the tube. He's watching the commercials mostly; he uses some fancy videotape machine that automatically records the broadcast for review later. The only ones who get up early to watch you, sweetheart, are Elsie the Cow. And me." He leaned near and nuzzled her fondly, but she playfully pushed him away.

"And I only have *your* word on it. I wish I still had a mother; at least *she'd* watch me."

"Don't. All mine is good for is reminding me to wear galoshes and ask me when I'm going to get married."

Liz grimaced and nibbled a few Tater Tots from the aluminum tray on her coffee table. She and Steve were sharing a TV dinner and TV night in, their usual entertainment these Friday nights when Liz was too exhausted from her long days to go anywhere or cook anything at home. So it was *The Magician* at seven with Bill Bixby, the new hit *Sanford and Son* at eight with Redd Foxx, and at eight-thirty an oddball comedy, *Texas Wheelers*, with wall-eyed Jack Elam and a couple of young unknowns, Gary Busey and Mark Hamill. Then came Liz's unabashed favorite at ten—*Night Stalker*, with Darren McGavin playing the down-at-the-heels reporter who kept unearthing unearthly forces, Karl Kolshak.

"You know, we could be watching the *news* now," Steve pointed out as he bussed the trays to the kitchen. Liz was already hunkered down, shoeless toes curled under her, her favorite sofa pillow clutched to her tummy.

"I get enough news all day. This is a classic, I tell you. Look at that grubby office—newsroom chic if I ever saw it."

"I gotta admit that McGavin's pretty funny." Steve rocked the cushions by settling next to her. "Admit it. You got a crush on him."

"Yeah. Look at that flattened-brim hat, that askew bow tie. He kind of reminds me of Gene the Weatherman, like a cross between Cecil the sea serpent and Howdy Doody. Who could resist that? No, really, it's the way men reporters dress. McGavin's just exaggerating a little. They're a bunch of unrefined slobs and closet snobs whose only talent is running to the sniff of a news story—if some bigger daily or national mag has done it before so they recognize it's news."

Steve removed his arm from her shoulders. "Ouch. Maybe I'd better look for a new TV partner."

"Not TV reporters; just newspaper. You electronic media guys have to keep on your toes about grooming. Absolutely suave." Liz ran her palm over Steve's cheek in a parody of an Aqua Velva commercial and cuddled kittenlike into his shoulder.

"That's what they tell me TV reporters are—all style and no content."

"That's better than being no style and no content."

Steve thought about it. "You think the whole news business is in a pretty sorry state, don't you?"

Liz sighed and sat up, sober-faced. "My father would say it always has been, but I'm not a born critic like he is. There's room for that, but I'm an optimist. I look at things, and can't help seeing the way they *should* be."

"Didn't Bobby Kennedy say something like that?"

"Yeah, in the sixties lots of people said things like that, and we all believed it could be. Trouble is, I still believe it. But I saw man after man at the *Observer* magically elevated for no more obvious reason than being there. Everyone knows—every working woman knows—that the women usually work harder than the men and get nowhere. I can't tell you how many local hotshot newsmen I've met here and in Milwaukee, really supposed to be top people, but their minds are mediocre, their personalities a pain, their ideals jaded, their talent nil. Maybe somewhere, once, they accidentally did something good and it sticks with them the rest of their bloody careers, pushing them up and up until they're institutions or executive editors. A woman can do great stuff over and over and nobody cares."

"Whew. I didn't know Turtle Bend bred feminist hard-liners."

"I'm not. I'm just . . . mad at the world for always taking the easy way out, not men in general."

"Glad to hear it. But seriously, Liz. It's not just women. Look at me. My bent is toward softer news. Social issues, changes, the arts. And I get left in the backfield, too, as if hosting a talk show is a slimy, somehow boot-licking job, as if it's much better to be a news reader like Ted Baxter on *Mary Tyler Moore* and make it *sound* like you're on top of things. I'd like to see our anchorman— any local anchorman—handle some of the situations I do live on the studio floor. Or you do on the street."

"It's the pits," Liz agreed, then brightened. "Well, we're changing something. I'm an anchor . . . anchor*lady* now. Or is that sexist?"

"That may not be, but this is." Steve leaned close to kiss her. "I'm definitely sexually discriminating." The kiss repeated, prolonged, became more intimate.

Liz warmed to it, let the sudden spark of anger their discussion had lit pale to a small, cold, hard lump of coal. Like the icy heart animating Kay in Hans Christian Andersen's "The Snow Queen," it was still there, stubborn and enduring. But Steve's warmth drove it back and far away, so she only felt the sensual serenity of being with him, beyond words, and acting only on gestures. She flicked her career worries off, as they would the television in a moment, before they moved to the bedroom.

"You're falling asleep."

"Am I? Keep doing that anyway; it's nice."

"Maybe it's because you hardly eat anything these days."

"I can't eat like that anymore on the Pill; I told you. The pounds just go on. Ummmmm."

"Liz. I'm beginning to feel like I'm romancing the pillow."

"I'm sorry. It's those damn early-morning newscasts. Even

getting off at four P.M. doesn't seem to make up for getting up so early."

"Maybe I'll have to arrange for a midday rendezvous, while you're still awake."

"Hmmm-hmmm. In the editing room. Under the counter. Just go on without me. I'm feeling something, really. . . . Hey!"

"You are awake. Just testing."

"Why don't you set the alarm for later? Then we'll both be wide awake."

"Look. I've got to work by the clock; I don't want to make love by it."

"Okay, okay. Maybe I just don't feel like to tonight. Is that all right?"

"Fine. Let's forget it. I'll go home."

"You . . . don't have to."

"I want to."

"Steve. If you'd just understand—"

"That's the trouble. I understand too much. I'll see you at work. Maybe you can find a place in your schedule for me next week."

"Steve! Don't be childish. Walking out is dumb. . . . Steve, come back! Oh . . . shit."

— Chapter 16 —

"*Skip breakfast tomorrow, Liz. Nan Harding of the State Agri-*cultural Extension Service is comin' in with goodies!"

Liz smiled wanly at Marv Hubbard, the man who hosted *Farmers' Forum*. It was hard for her to smile—or get excited about a set-cooked breakfast using Minnesota's home-raised bacon and butter—before six in the morning. WBGO should be glad she got there, particularly this November morning, when an all-night drizzle and subsequent freeze had turned streets and highways into obsidian skating rinks. Her Pinto was parked sideways in the lot outside right now, the best she and it had been able to manage.

"Cheer up, girl! It's a country morning!" Marv grinned, which for him wasn't hard at any hour, since he was the unlucky owner of a face that was all Bugs Bunny teeth and ears, and spread his gangly fingers across the set piano's keyboard. A ragtime tune tinkled out. Marv insisted on singing the show open to his own accompaniment, and though his voice was mediocre, his playing was top-notch and his showmanship as infectious as a wink. Around the station, reporters giggled at Marv's approach as corny. Liz was beginning to see that routine cheerfulness at an early hour was an asset beyond price for anyone assigned to the lonely "dawn patrol" of broadcasting.

"I don't know if I can take it," she admitted wryly.

Marv's manic fingers hit a final, dismayed chord. "Can't take it. Why, shucks, Liz. You're a country girl from way back yourself. Getting up early isn't hard if you like who you get up with." He winked.

"I get up with myself," she said sourly. Steve and she had not exchanged more than a few frosty greetings since the weekend.

"Then that applies even more." Marv winked more broadly yet and rippled his big-knuckled hands across the keys.

"I see what you mean. It's just that it's dark when I come to work and now it's so dark and gloomy going home these evenings since daylight saving time came off—"

An incredibly loose-jointed hand elevated, stopping her in mid-sentence. "Speak not evil against DST coming off, the farmers' savior. At least it puts the cows back on schedule like God meant 'em to be."

"That's right; when we city folk rearrange the clock every spring, the cows don't know when to be milked anymore. Dumb cows."

"Mooooo," Marv crooned. "This is a dairy state; don't bite the hoof that feeds you." More free-form melody, while Liz finally found herself begrudgingly nodding her head to the music. "I know what's bothering you, Liz," Marv declaimed in time as if he were serenading her. She stiffened, expecting mention of Steve. "It ain't them early mornings, and it ain't them dark evenings. It ain't even them swishy-tailed bossies or the biiiig bosses in the front office. It's the 'I Been Handed the Down-time, Small-town Anchor-slot Blues.'"

"Huh? I'm *thrilled* to be doing this newscast. Maybe nobody watches but a few farmers over the knobby backs of their Guernseys, but this is my chance to anchor. What's wrong with that?"

"It's a chance for the station to sucker some dumb reporter into getting up at an ungodly hour for an eight-minute stint. How come they don't rotate the shift? Let some of the *guys* take the dawn patrol?"

"Maybe they wanted me to get the experience; maybe they plan to move me up to weekend anchoring. Jeff Stone's been pushing for a Saturday/Sunday replacement for months."

"And you figure you're it?" The piano chords had changed

ominously, forming staccato punctuation to Marv's words, as if he were the pianist at his own not-so-silent movie.

"Maybe," Liz answered defensively.

"Fat chance, hon." The facile fingers waltzed down the keys to a forbidding bass finish. "No one with any brains wants the early-morning shift. The station doesn't even get viewer ratings on it. All they want is the Treflan grass and weed-killer commercials and for us to fill in the rest of the time respectably. Or maybe not respectably." He grinned again.

"There are all those city people getting up for work. Maybe they'd start watching for the news. . . ."

"They're getting ready for work, not standing glued to a TV set. They listen to the radio. Who even sits down for breakfast anymore? 'Cept the farmers' friend, Marvin Hubbard." Glissando.

"What about the *Today* program? That's early-morning fare that's been on for years."

"One of a kind, like you, Liz." The teeth were in full porcelain shimmer and the fingertips danced on the keys like popcorn fresh from the wood stove skillet.

"You're more of a realist than you pretend. How come you put up with it, then?"

Marv stopped. "I'm a broadcaster, but I don't look like Chuck Scarborough. You think anybody'd take this mug seriously declaiming war dead statistics? We all do what we can."

Liz swallowed. She hadn't thought about it, but Marv was the most engagingly homely man she'd met in broadcasting. Talented, quick-witted, lively. But ugly as homemade sin. It reminded her of that public service commercial that touted getting your high school degree, where a degreeless Abraham Lincoln, top hat in hand, sat before a crass interviewer who snarled, "You ain't going nowhere without that sheepskin, Lincoln." Marv wasn't going to get anywhere without a "face," no matter his talent.

"Never fear, Liz." Marv was still, somehow, grinning. "You'll never have to worry with those eyes, those lips, that hair. . . ." He'd segued into song again, into half-sincere serenade and semi-serious jest. Liz smiled.

"Are we on for breakfast?" The piano stilled breathlessly.

"Why not? I've got nobody else to wake up with."

Liz was angry that what she'd naively viewed as an opportunity was merely a dead-end trap, and considered suggesting a rotation schedule to Mike Roth. Trouble was, she wasn't sure she'd get it. The management couldn't be sure of netting a gullible fish a second time, and besides, she sensed that the male reporters had too high an opinion of themselves—and too inbred a conviction that they all were anchorman material—to grasp at the straw of experience no matter how unimpressive.

So she entered the winter of her discontent, the affair with Steve on mutual ice, her regular daily work never seeming to slack off despite the demands of an early-morning schedule, a series of head colds coming and going with depressing regularity, 1974 and her twenty-fourth birthday looming. To top it all off, Caralee Koeppers turned solicitous, as if finally sensing a fellow victim and not a rival.

"Would you like to go to lunch?" she asked one day after Liz had spent half an hour ripping unsatisfying narrative tracks out of her typewriter.

"I really shouldn't take the time today. . . . Oh, why not?" Liz tore the current story form out of the platen. "Give me a minute to freshen up and I'll meet you in the lobby."

It was an overcast late November day. The snowless sidewalks felt like iced marble under the soles of Liz's smart new wine leather boots. Caralee led them to a quaint, old-fashioned tearoom near the station, where gilt-painted radiators banged and hissed out the comforting sound of heat coursing through elderly cast iron.

They settled at a wooden table for two and studied the menu before talking, as uneasy acquaintances often will. Only when the waitress skimmed away with their order did Caralee set aside the plastic carnation in its cut-glass vase and begin her pitch.

"How do you like working mornings?"

Liz rolled her eyes, deciding not to be coy, even though she knew Caralee might use whatever information she got to her own ends. "It's a living."

"You *are* the first woman anchor here," Caralee said fastidiously, neither envy nor smugness tingeing her voice.

"I hear you were the first woman talk-show host," Liz returned brutally.

The woman's guard dropped like an iron weight, hard and fast. "That was in the fifties. Nobody thought much about women being 'first' then. I was an 'only'—a phenomenon. It was nice."

"I imagine."

"I mean, a *man* would have been insulted to have been offered a talk show then. It was a woman's world, aimed at a woman's audience. We interviewed home sewers and Aquatennial queens and lady authors." Caralee smiled, her teeth shark-sharp. "I don't suppose that was too tactful to say, with Steve Harmon doing the talk show now. But you and Steve aren't exactly cozy anymore, are you?"

"I guess not." Liz toyed with her water glass. "But I don't

think men should be barred from doing talk shows any more than women should be kept from doing fires and murders and wars— it all depends what a person has a bent for."

"Your bent is the anchor desk."

Their plates descended between them in concert. "No. I don't know. My bent is doing the best I can with the talents I have, that's all."

"That's not enough." Caralee stabbed her fork into a pink curl of shrimp and devoured it. "It's a man's world now, ever since the managers discovered news was profitable about three years ago. That made it a money game, a man's game. Women are just pawns."

"Maybe. But sometimes a pawn can paralyze the whole board." Liz was sorry she'd ordered the chef salad. It was cold, like the day, like Caralee, and she needed a small flare of warmth. She sipped the lukewarm coffee she'd been unwise enough to doctor with cream substitute before testing it for heat.

"Well. You've got the right idea. Maybe you should try sleeping with Roth. He likes young girls." Caralee's voice was garnished with the acidity of her forty-five years. Liz couldn't imagine being that old and embittered.

"I sleep with those I like. And lunch with them."

"Touché. Maybe you'll do all right at chess. But I'm just speaking the truth. Here's the dope on the TV news game." Caralee leaned forward, her fork pointing empty tines Liz's way and jabbing in unconscious emphasis. "They'll use you, flatter you, woo you. They'll ignore you, overlook you, insult you, and never pay you. You get extra money for anchoring the crack-of-dawn newscast? No? You should. Jeff Stone's new substitute is getting more money. A hundred a week, I hear via the grapevine."

"Jeff Stone's new substitute? They picked somebody?"

Caralee's face was expressionless. "One of the men, of course. Should be announced in a day or two. There isn't much left for me to do around here but gossip, you know. I keep my ear to the ground."

"Maybe if you keep your ear to the ground you only pick up dirt."

"Look. You don't like me; I don't like you. I just thought I'd let you know what the score was. It might save you from getting a few wrinkles worrying about a future. There is none, not for a woman in this business."

"What about Nancy Dickerson?"

"Friend of LBJ's. You do *know* about Johnson and young lady reporters?"

"Barbara Walters."

"Set dressing. And she's getting older. You watch; she'll be shuffled aside."

"What's the matter, Caralee, can't you credit or admire any woman who's achieved something? Are we all bound to fail because you did?"

The woman stiffened. "I didn't fail. They just changed things, and decided I didn't fit. Wait until you get 'laugh' lines, or a gray hair, and some man in an office somewhere with a potbelly and three chins decides you're too old to be on-screen! It'll happen, Liz baby, whether you're Daddy's darling or Steven's sweetheart or the Queen of Persia. Then nothing will matter, except hanging on somewhere, somehow, because it's the only thing you do and there's never been time for a man and a wedding ring and you simply need the money until you collect Social Security. I'm fifty-one years old." Liz's gaze shot up from her salad. "I don't tell my best friend that; I don't know why I'm telling my worst enemy—you're just so impervious, so immortal. Fourteen years. Give me fourteen years and I'll be too old to care about who sleeps with who or who's sliding into whose job. Until then, I have to keep alert my way, even if it's just keeping my eyes, ears, nose, and teeth on the ground and at the grindstone."

Caralee threw a crumpled five-dollar bill to the table between them. "I've got to get back. I've got my own deadlines, too. That ought to cover my share." She scraped back her chair and minced out on stiletto heels, her overcurled head stiff.

Liz let out a breath, then shuddered down the rest of her salad, needing some fuel for what might be a long afternoon. She was beginning to perceive the grim picture both Marv Hubbard and Caralee Koeppers painted so accurately from their temperamentally opposite sides of the palette—sunny optimism or bitter pessimism. Liz was beginning to understand that there was no way to escape becoming part of it.

Back at her desk, she took a hard look at the story that was so stubbornly refusing to arrange itself into the 150 words or so she had to tell it in. It was standard stuff, a piece on post-Thanksgiving department store displays. Tim the cameraman had gotten some enchanting footage of mechanically animated elves and Victorian waltzers; if he could get into the subject matter, why couldn't Liz? Maybe because she was beginning to think she was too good for certain assignments, certain kinds of stories. The Christmas windows meant something to people who weren't too busy rushing by pretending to be important—the young, the old, anyone with eyes to see and time to spend on a momentary tableau of sheer imagination. Liz got up and went to the editing room to check out the film again. This time she would *look* at it. Maybe then she'd find a way to write about it.

She was pulling the final story form out of the tight platen on her vintage Royal when she realized Steve was standing nearby, waiting to be noticed. "Oh."

"You were really concentrating. How can you do that in this chaos? What's so engrossing, the return of Ed Gein?"

She laughed. "Christ-mas win-dows. Wait a minute. I've got to race this in to the desk." Waving her various carbon copies like handkerchiefs, Liz dashed around the desks in her way, efficiently slapping story forms down on the proper worktops. First she'd rediscovered the spirit of Christmas; now Steve was at her desk. Locating the old morgue reel of *Miracle on 34th Street* had inspired her story; she wondered what scenario had inspired Steve to approach her again.

"What can I do for you?" She braced herself against her desk edge and waited for Steve to clue her in.

His hands hit his pockets in tandem. "I've been pretty busy lately, too." Tacit apology for three weeks of silence. "Not as busy as you, Liz." Gray eyes glancing up, more persuasive than apologetic. "I guess it's hard for me to realize what a crack-of-dawn schedule must be like. I was thinking . . ." Liz held her breath. "With the crazy hours we're both on, we've been finding it too easy to collapse and eat junk food and get on each other's nerves. Why don't we go out again? I mean for dinner. Someplace civilized, no 'steaks over at your place and you cook 'em.' Candlelight and roses. The works. My treat. What do you . . . think?"

"Does that mean you want to sleep with me again?"

His eyes darted around the staff-full newsroom. "Shit . . . Liz." Steve's voice lowered. "That, too."

"Hmmm." Liz appeared to be contemplating it.

"Jordan, so help me, I'll wring your neck. . . ."

"Oh, well, since you put it that way. I never could resist sweet nothings, Harmon. Saturday night?"

Steve nodded, glanced sideways, turned a half step away, pivoted back to face her. "How about—Friday?"

She gave up and giggled.

"I didn't know I was so patriotic until I saw you in that blue." Marv Hubbard applauded Liz's ensemble with an intricate run up the piano keys. "What's the occasion?"

"Dinner. I don't have to get up early for *Farmers' Forum* tomorrow. So you do think this combination is all right?" Liz glanced worriedly at her white wool skirt, which she'd paired with a sapphire blouse and raspberry jacket.

Marv launched into "Yankee Doodle Dandy." "Delicious. You seem more chipper these days."

Liz nodded, checking to make sure her earrings were anchored. She was letting her hair grow, but still wanted the finished look of earrings on-screen if she happened to tilt her head.

"I've decided to make the best of things, Marv. Not a very original philosophy, but more fun than making the worst of them. I'm young yet; I've got a lot to learn. Rushing myself isn't going to help anyone."

"Bravo. I, in the meantime, have got to bone up on milk price supports; the dairy commissioner is honoring the set with a live interview this A.M."

"How do you stay interested in all that dry stuff?"

"Milk is wet; it's the commissioner who's dry."

Marv moved onto the set, with its hokey backdrop of checkered country-kitchen paraphernalia, and Liz went to skim the wires for any news worth writing into the show.

By five P.M., she was exhausted, but happily so. Everything seemed to have turned around at once. She'd gone through all the story carbons in her file drawer, organizing them into subject matter groups until a clear profile emerged: the socially relevant stories she had sought out and fought out herself, the routine junk Roth kept assigning her, and the serendipitous "small" human-interest stories that she had somehow nursed into especially nice pieces. The trick would be to increase the first and the last, and somehow squeeze out the middle. The method might be initiating a clandestine beat system for herself, like at a newspaper. It was a radical idea. Station managers were forever griping that they had to run every story assigned. No luxury of having a reporter or cameraman wasting time learning a subject; just see it, shoot it, and show it.

But if Liz could sell enough stories around a nucleus of socially relevant subject matter—contraception, abortion, battered wives— she'd make contacts who'd refer her to other developing stories. Then she'd stand a chance of filming sensitive issues, things people normally wouldn't go on television to talk about. She'd even have a shot at scooping her fellow reporters, breaking big stories. . . . The key was not to let anyone—*anyone*—know what she was doing, and doing purposefully.

She hummed to herself as she restacked the manila folders labeled "Meat," "Desserts," and "Rutabaga" and shoveled them back into her desk drawer.

"Ready?" Steve looked impeccably groomed, wearing a soft gray suit she'd never seen before that made his hair and mustache look gilt in contrast and his eyes seem minted of sheer silver. "You look . . . great."

"Thanks, date." Liz took his offered arm, and they left the newsroom together, through a gantlet of openly speculative looks. Caralee Koepper's were the most corrosive eyes among them, seeming to burn through Liz's raspberry wool-suited back like a pair of careless cigarettes at at a party.

"Charlie's," Liz approved as Steve drove into the tiny parking lot that served downtown Minneapolis's premier old-posh restaurant. Inside, Liz celebrated by ordering the famous Charlie's Brandy Alexander and a very expensive pepper steak.

Steve grinned at her across the sparkling white tablecloth. "I see you're allowing me to atone royally."

"I'm very generous with my repentant lovers," Liz teased, eyeing him languorously over her second Brandy Alexander.

"That *is* present tense?"

"*Mais oui.* I ne-vair toy with my men."

"You do kind of look like Mata Hari across the table. Have you got something up your sleeve?"

"No, but you do, darling."

Steve's fingers had slipped from holding her hand on the table to her wrist, caressing it lightly just inside the sleeve.

"This isn't solely a celebration of our unwedded state, Liz."

"What else?" She smiled, warmed by the creamy chocolate cocktails, soothed by the secret pendulum stroke of Steve's finger on the sensitive skin of her inner wrist.

His motion stopped and pulled back to guard his cocktail with his caged fingers. Liz recognized the signs of a momentous announcement, and wondered for a moment. . . .

"I've got the weekend anchor spot. They'll announce it Monday!"

"*You* have!" Liz's mixed emotions seemed to hang in mid-juggle above her head: surprise, joy, a needle-thin stab of loss. "That's *wonderful*, Steve."

Steve, launched on his story, hardly heard her. "They've been dangling it in front of me for a long time now. You know, be patient and you'll get rewarded. I've been pretty restless, thinking of leaving. But with you here . . ." He looked up; maybe a man couldn't glow, but he could burn. Steve burned happiness. "Well, I didn't want to leave right now. Now I don't have to. This is an expression of faith in me, anyway, and with some anchor experience under my belt . . . Besides, I almost forgot the main reason for taking the assignment." His fingers inched over her hand again. "You don't work weekend mornings. I'll be working weekend nights. There'll be all those Saturday and Sunday mornings to get down and get indecent."

Liz glanced at their clasped hands. She had missed him; she'd been a cold, empty, scared desert inside since two seconds after he'd left her apartment three weeks ago. Her body had missed him; just how much it was telling her now. An undeniably sexual ache throbbed between her decorously crossed legs. She kicked off her shoe and insinuated her stocking foot on Steve's ankle, running her toes up under his pants leg. His fingers tightened on her wrist.

"Either this place has roaches or..."

"*C'est moi.*"

"I've missed you, Moi."

"Moi, too."

They laughed and made it through the entrées, drinking in each other's eyes between bites of steak and baked potato, running out of conversation from sheer sexual tension. Liz felt like an over-revved motor by the time the check was paid and they walked out into the cold November darkness. The car was even icier, but Steve stopped after starting the engine to pull Liz across the freezing vinyl seat. Her senses leaped to the impress of a hot mouth, a cold hand boldly sweeping up her skirt, shattering propriety and custom to touch her innermost warmth without foreplay or warning.

Her body surged against him as if electrified. "Home, James. Quick!"

"No way" Steve was kissing her as wildly as she wanted to be kissed, the cold night around them serving as a kind of elemental aphrodisiac that only emphasized their overheated impulses. "I booked a hotel room."

Strange ceiling. King-size bed. Familiar body. His, hers. Unfamiliar sensations. Eroticized to the ultimate. Tired. Sleepless. Wanting to again....

"I missed you, Liz, damn, I missed you."

"Me, too. Don't squeeze so hard."

"I want to squeeze myself right into you."

"I thought you had. Steve..."

"Too much?"

"No, no...never too much."

"Why did I act like such an ass?"

"You make an adorable ass."

"Well, you let me leave."

"You were out the door before I knew it."

"But how could we let something . . . great, like this . . . take a dumb, wrong turn?"

"People do it all the time."

"Not us. Not anymore. Look, it'll be better now that this anchor thing isn't gnawing at me. I found out, this past week, I love you, Liz, just like I said I did, but didn't quite believe. I love you."

"Oh, Steve—"

Kisses tender. Kisses fierce. Fingers claiming, limbs intertwining. Gasps, moans. Silences. Intercourse. Ragged breaths. Collapse.

Liz speaking first, regretfully.

"I suppose we have to get out by noon."

"Probably. I've haven't looked at check-out time. Anyway, we've got things to do tomorrow."

"What?"

"Apartment hunting."

"You're kidding!"

"I thought it out. Separate places, more hassle being together, double rents. We get paid little enough as it is. I figure we should . . . merge our resources—"

"I like your idea of merging."

"Merge our resources, be more accessible to each other—"

"Yes . . ."

"Trouble was, before we were playing at living together without going . . . all . . . the . . . way."

"So true. I agree with everything you say."

"And they say at work you're hard to get along with."

"They . . . do?"

"Want your own way. They just don't know how to appeal to your more reasonable side."

"I'm about as reasonable as a time bomb right now. Steve, shut up and . . . and—"

"I'm a reasonable man myself, and I do have better things to do than talk."

— *Chapter 17* —

It was murder finding an apartment just before Christmas, but Steve had been eyeing a new high-rise near the university. A spot there opened up so fortuitously that Liz suspected their locally famous video profiles had contributed some unconscious pressure.

"Don't be paranoid," Steve had teased. "You'd be surprised how many people *don't* watch television."

"Yeah," she responded with world-weary cynicism. "They must be the ones who are always asking me to speak at this luncheon or commentate that fashion show."

"It's good exposure to make personal appearances like that," Steve diagnosed. "You're not turning them down?"

"No." She sighed. "But it cuts into my weekends, and I thought you had me all booked up."

"Only mornings. You can still dash out at noon, discuss the new role of working woman to a politely applauding audience of hausfraus, and come home in time to make me dinner."

"Do liberated women descend to domestic violence?"

"Speaking of domestic violence, how's your new series on battered wives going?"

"Heavy plodding. Nobody wants to be filmed, and Roth and Baer are afraid to air the damn thing."

"Gutless wonders."

"Speaking of guts, Harmon, how is it going to look, us rooming together? You said yourself we had a public profile. How can I go narrate the, um, Women's Christian Temperance Union annual charity fashion show with a straight, sanctimonious face?"

"The WCTU just doesn't want you to drink. They don't care about fornication."

"Look. All women have a big stake in fornication. We're the ones society throws stones at if a couple gets caught. You're just 'feeling your oats.' I'm officially a fallen woman."

With that Liz took a slow turn in the empty apartment, surveying it with narrowed eyes. Steve caught her and whirled her around. The two of them in their winter coats waltzed like dancing bears through the adjoining eating area, down the hall, and into first one bedroom and then the other.

Laughing, she finally slowed him to a stop by dragging her

boot heels. "*Two* bedrooms. Lavish. Or did you have something kinky in mind?"

"It's only three hundred fifty a month split between the two of us. We'll need office space, and with our different schedules, we'll stay out of each other's hair."

"Already the rift," Liz declaimed dramatically. She walked to the bedroom sliding door, which opened onto a balcony barely big enough for two folding chairs and a potted plant. Steve's bicycle was parked out there now. Below her, eight floors down, the white winter street hosted a slow stream of cars. She'd never lived higher than two stories before.

"Hey." Steve had joined her, his back to the rail, leaning against it in a way that made her unreasonably nervous. "You're not having second thoughts?" His breath came out in steam-engine puffs that dissipated instantly.

"I don't know." She couldn't take her eyes off the street, or forget their height. She'd never be comfortable on the balcony. "I guess I'm nervous about everybody 'finding out.'"

"Like who?" His eyes were concerned but challenging. "Caralee?"

"No." Ridiculous. "She already thinks the worst."

"The guys at work?"

"I can handle those bozos."

"Roth?"

"Well . . . he might take a dim view of it."

"He's just a flirt, and he'd be miffed that you're off limits, that's all."

"The . . . neighbors, then."

Steve grinned devilishly. "They're proably all shacked up, too."

"Crude," she disapproved playfully, and went back into the warm room.

Steve followed her. "Your father?" His voice was serious for the first time.

"Dad? How's he going to find out in Turtle Bend?"

"But would it bother you if he knew?"

"I don't know. I wouldn't go out of my way to tell him. What about your mother?"

"Well, I wouldn't advertise it. She was very protective about my three older sisters. Mom has certain illusions about what a good boy would do—and wouldn't."

Poor Steve. Liz came and wrapped cold hands around his warm neck. Steve shivered, unzipped his down jacket, and pulled her palms inside, against his chest.

"You only kids have got it made," he said. "I was lucky not to have to wear hand-me-down dresses. I sure had a lot of built-in baby-sitters, though. You know, Liz, it doesn't have to be live-in forever. If we play house for a while, maybe we can make it formal. I'm not averse to . . . marriage." He watched her carefully.

"I've never mentioned—"

"No. And I haven't either. We've been very nonpossessive. But once our career tracks are set—say I get an anchor job here or somewhere else and some real money's coming in regularly—then, why not? Maybe even perambulators, what do you think?"

Their voices had softened; their foreheads had lowered together so they were locked like loving rams, not looking at each other, but inextricably joined for the moment. Liz's hands grew hot in the grip of Steve's, but her feet for some reason felt cold. Marriage. Babies. Tea for two, and two for tea. An anchor for you, a baby for me. . . . Women worked and had babies these days. Hell, she'd done a series on it. Married. Rings and things. Joint checking accounts. Accountability. Responsibility. Credibility. Respectibility. Mrs. Steve Harmon. Liz Jordan-Harmon. Nice ring. Rings and things.

"Let's see how all this togetherness goes, huh?" Steve was suggesting softly. "Then we'll think about it. In the meantime, I recommend heavy doses of fornication."

Their laughter twined, private and warming, like their hands. Steve's levity had let him gracefully off the marital hook. Had let her off the hook, too. But that was wrong, Liz thought; marriage wasn't a trap for a woman, but a safety net, right, Jordan?

Liz couldn't help feeling that living with Steve showed, that if caught, she'd have her chest branded with a scarlet *F*. So she approached Mike Roth about the morning newscast with a secret chip on her shoulder much heavier than the one she had a right to bear.

It was a Monday, and so far the assignment board didn't show much happening.

"Got a few minutes, Mike?"

He looked up, flashed an insincere smile he didn't know was false. "Liz. Sit down. Sharp outfit. Christmas red. Like it. Good for the viewers."

She felt like a cheerleader trying to seduce the coach. "Listen, Mike. I'd like to take a couple days off for Christmas. I know it's a bad time, but my father's getting older and—"

"How old *is* the old devil?" Mike leaned back in his swivel chair and cocked his shirt-sleeved elbows behind his head.

"Gosh . . . sixty-seven. Not so old, I guess." *eleven to go*

Mike nodded sagely. "Ripe old age for a newspaperman. God, that business'll kill you. Well, I'd like to, Liz. I know you haven't put in for any vacation yet, and you're entitled." His chair squeaked as he leaned forward to plant his arms on his desk and lower his voice confidentially. "It's just that you're pretty crucial to the *Farmers' Forum* you know. Anchor jobs are like that. Got to be there. Every day of the year."

Liz smiled as insincerely as Mike. "It's nice to feel indispensable, but even Jeff Stone has a weekend sub now. Couldn't one of the guys sit in for me?"

Roth's face remained frozen while he thought about it. Liz could read the concerns on his face as if they'd been printed there in banner headlines or a slow-moving TV crawl. He was paging through the possibilities, crossing off anyone who'd give him any trouble about the assignment. He mentally crossed off a lot of guys. Liz decided to apply pressure.

"You know I take my airtime responsibilities seriously, Mike. I've done that A.M. newscast with a fever of one-oh-two. And asking for a day or two off doesn't mean I don't want to move on to prime-time news achoring. . . ." Mike's bushy eyebrows shot up in shock like telegraphing caterpillars before he could corral them. Liz smiled confidentially. "But Dad's blood pressure's been acting up and—"

"I'll see what I can do and let you know Monday." It was her anchor ambitions, not her father's health, that mobilized him, Liz knew. He was probably toying already with the idea of rotating the morning anchor spot, so Liz didn't get too uppity, too hard to pass over when a real opportunity came. Slimy bastard.

He saw her to the door. "You, uh, didn't have your eye on the weekend sub slot? We've been promising that to Steve Harmon for months, long before you came."

"Steve's very qualified; I think you made a good choice," Liz answered demurely. Roth started breathing again. NOW had been twisting the FCC's arm lately for more women in responsible positions. The statistical representation of women in broadcasting was shockingly low, as it was in print journalism.

Liz arranged to be near Mike's office whenever she was in. A parade of males came and went all that day—all the reporters except Gene the Weatherman, the regular anchor, and Steve. Keith, the new guy who was a borderline incompetent, was the loudest refuser.

"Six-thirty in the morning! Shit, Mike, I'm a *newsman*. I'm too good to baby-sit Hubbard and his hayseed hoeboys. Not even for anchor experience and extra pay."

Liz, sipping lukewarm coffee, felt herself boiling over. Too good. That goldbrick was notorious for relying on the print reporters' questions at press conferences. What he knew about news coverage you could put in Donald Duck's ear. And he was turning his nose up at a mere two days of what Liz did day after day after day with no extra pay.

In the end they asked Caralee to do it. That alone should have convinced Liz what a dead-end assignment she had. But Liz didn't care by then. She just wanted to not have to get up at five for a couple of mornings, to get away from WBGO, and to get out of town for a few days, even if it meant seeing her father and Myrtle just when she didn't feel up to pretending that everything was wonderful in the big city.

Turtle Bend took Christmas seriously. A crèche ornamented the Episcopal church facade; pine boughs and psalms wafted piercing scent and sound through the gracious church interior. Her father loaded the Oldsmobile with excess canned goods, which they dropped off at the VFW hall for the town's annual Christmas dinner for its few needy.

Liz was appalled at how easily she buckled under to Myrtle's domestic routine, something she realized when she slipped into the kitchen for a post-midnight snack of chocolate chip cookies and caught herself eating them over the sink and washing up afterward. The one visible drive in Myrtle's life was to keep the house spotless.

She sighed, had another cookie to fill a sudden, unphysical hole, and went back to bed.

In the morning after church, Myrtle quickly drafted Liz for her old household duties, cheating her of the opportunity to volunteer. Liz whipped the potatoes, timed the turkey, warmed the buns, and set the table. Her father came five minutes later than when summoned, but the serving dishes burdening the table still steamed.

Grace was Z.J.'s sole inside domestic duty, which he performed with grandiose improvisation. "Oh, Lord, bless this food which has been so well prepared for us, and bless us gathered here for this holiday honoring the birth of your Son, Our Lord Jesus Christ, in Bethlehem so many centuries ago. Bless Myrtle, for never-failing good temper and patience—and bless my lovely, too-thin daughter, Elizabeth. May she find a husband before another Christmas settles on your respectful servant, Zachariah Jordan. Amen."

"Fath-er."

"Yes, Elizabeth? You wanted to add a suitable sentiment?"

She nodded. "Not suitable, though. Censorable."

Her father flapped his napkin open, thrusting a corner between his top shirt buttons so it covered his expansive stomach. "Nothing's censorable in this house, Lizzie. The First Amendment reigns.

Speaking of which, how's—as the commercial goes—your social life?"

Myrtle clucked. She knew the toothpaste commercial really asked "How's your love life?"

Z.J. persisted. "Any worthwhile fellows work for that station of yours?"

"Several. Some admirers of yours."

"Oh? Smart chaps. Snap one up." He winked while Myrtle pointedly passed the beans almondine.

"Don't oversell the girl on matrimony, Zach. She probably hasn't got that career notion out of her head yet. There's nothing worse than a working mother."

Since Myrtle had never been either—except what titular step-mothering she'd faced—Liz didn't see what business she had speaking to such issues, and was tempted to say so. A headache began knocking tensely at the back of her neck.

"First you got to find a working father," Zach teased. "You doing any dating yet, Elizabeth?"

"As a matter of fact, yes." Both looked intently at her.

"Yes?" Myrtle was being so prissy-polite, Liz could have hurled the relish tray at her instead of taking one stick of carrot, one of celery, and a candied apple slice.

"I'm seeing a man at the station, a reporter like me. And substitute anchor," she couldn't help boasting. "He does the weekend shift. Steve. Steve Harmon."

Marriage. And coming home for holidays and sitting around family dining tables until your derriere goes numb. And not smoking, not even you, Steve, with the few cigarettes you consume. No rules bent, not even for you.

Her father squinted speculatively. "Just good-lookin'? Or smart, too?"

"Yes!" Liz was so indignant she didn't know which question she answered.

Her father assumed the best for once. He shook his head. "Lot of them TV types are all twenty-dollar haircuts and no brains, you know."

"What about me?"

"You've always been looks *and* IQ, just like your mother." He winked at her.

Myrtle tightened. "Have some more whipped potatoes, Elizabeth," she said. "They do seem a bit lumpy today, but I'm sure they're tasty enough."

Liz took them, finessed into eating what she'd didn't want because of the slight to her domesticity.

"Tell us some more about this Steve Harmon, Elizabeth," her

father urged through his own second helping of potatoes. Apparently lumps were only detectable to Myrtle's tender palate.

"Well, he's twenty-seven. A communications major. His father's dead. He grew up with his mother and three sisters—"

"Now that's a nice family size. Four. Your mother and I would never have stopped with you, if she hadn't of . . . gotten sick like that. You have four kids, Lizzie. None of this one or two stuff. That's not like a real family."

"I may not get *married*, Daddy!" Liz exploded.

"Course you'll get married, nice-looking girl like you. Your mother was past twenty-eight herself when we got hitched. And you didn't come along for another ten years or so."

"Why?" They could probe her private life, but she, being the younger, could never question theirs. So why had she been such a late and only? Maybe—gasp—birth control.

Her father put down his fork. "It's not fair, I suppose, to grow up an only child with just a father—and a stepmother—to raise you. We didn't plan it that way, honey. Your mother, she simply had trouble conceivin'. Sorry to speak so plain at the dinner table, Myrtle, but maybe that's been bothering Elizabeth awhile."

"I understand," Liz muttered to her potatoes, slapping another pat of butter atop them. She did. Too well.

Had her parents no dark secrets, nothing to conceal from *their* parents? No diaphragm buried in some long-ago drawer? No humiliating case of male infertility to haunt her father's self-image? The woman, again. Guilty, again. As Liz was guilty of living a life without husband and child. Oh, it was unfair. Liz didn't want freaks for parents, just human beings. And Myrtle, married before, and widowed. No children. Must be another "couldn't." Maybe Liz was a "couldn't" and didn't know it. Or maybe she was just a closet "wouldn't." She had thought that when she was older, she wouldn't always lose when the family circle closed ranks and left her out. Maybe she wasn't old enough yet.

Liz added her own fervent addendum to her father's closing grace. "When, oh Lord, when will I be old enough?"

— *Chapter 18* —

Mari Sue Gunn was twenty-seven years old. She looked sev- enteen, a bedraggled, burned-out seventeen. Her hair hung lank and tangled; her sallow face, despite an absence of wrinkles, had fallen into a spiritless, world-weary sag. Her voice was an almost inaudible monotone. You had a feeling this woman would call for help so softly you couldn't hear her, if she'd call at all.

But she had called for help, finally, in a fashion. That's why she sat—on a donated easy chair that sagged as dispiritedly as she—in the Ione V. Hazlett women's shelter.

Liz sat opposite her, notebook on lap, breaking all the rules of TV journalism by interviewing without filming. "Wasting" time. Spending time to find out what made Mari Sue Gunn tick, searching for insight into what made her husband, Harvey Gunn, the kind of wife-beating monster Liz shuddered to contemplate.

But he was Mari Sue's husband. Proof of it squirmed on the woman's blue-jeaned lap in fourteen-month-old Karri and sat in wide-eyed three-year-old awe at her tennis shoe–clad feet. They watched Liz with wary eyes—the woman, the boy at her feet named Barry, the babe in arms. Liz perceived her own inborn advantages as almost physically felt burdens now, an awkward load of education, privilege, and economic security, a lifetime lived under the benefits of mostly benign love. None of the trio before her could take any of that for granted.

"How long have you and the children been here?" Liz asked.

"Three days." If Mari Sue Gunn could be persuaded to go on camera, the microphone would practically have to be applied to her voice box, so effacing was her speech. Each monosyllable was dragged into a vowel-drawled sound, as if the effort to produce it taxed even the simplest response. It reminded Liz of recordings of Patty Hearst just after she'd been kidnapped.

"Have you ever left your husband before?"

The limp brown hair shook, obscuring the face. Baby Karri produced a short, worrisome sound. Her mother lethargically jiggled her knees, but the motion only made the child's bland round head bobble disconcertingly, as if it were about to shake loose and roll away across the faded floral carpeting.

"Why not?"

Mari Sue shrugged in answer while Liz quelled a rising irritation. Most of the battered women she had met were "bad" interviews—unresponsive, nonverbal, unsympathetic; washed-out women who had so little self-esteem that they could barely function.

"Then why leave him now?"

"I got tired, I guess. Tired of taking it."

"What did he . . . do?"

"Hit me. Mostly he likes hitting on me. Pushing sometimes, across the room. Wasn't a very big room, but he sure could get me from one wall to the other fast." Mari Sue's lips lifted in a wan smile. Liz found no humor in Mari Sue's too-routine reality.

"How badly were you hurt?"

The shrug again. "Black eyes. Lost some teeth. Bruises. Lots of bruises. Cuts. Once I hit the wall so hard I didn't wake up until the next day. Maybe he hit me after I was out and that's why. I don't know. Harvey can hurt you real good." She rocked the baby, who had started fretting.

"Did you see a doctor after the . . . incidents?"

The woman regarded Liz blankly. "Harvey wouldn't let anybody *see* me like that. Besides, we didn't have the money."

"How long did this go on?"

"He hit me before we were married a couple times. But he said he was sorry, and it didn't hurt so much."

"And you married him anyway?"

"He said it wouldn't happen again. He got real . . . sad, real sorry. He was real sweet for a while."

"Was it . . . did it have anything to do with . . . sex?"

Mari Sue shook her head, animated for the first time. "Harvey didn't rape me or anything. Maybe it'd happen after sex. Maybe not, more often. It wasn't a sex thing," she said firmly. "I wouldn't put up with no sex thing."

"But you couldn't have felt . . . easy . . . about having sex with a man who could at any moment—"

For the first time, Mari Sue looked at Liz with something like pity. "It's just the way it is. My pa hit us when we were kids. Hit my ma. They do it, men do. It has nothing to do with . . . that other stuff." Her pale hazel eyes looked to the tops of the kids' heads.

Liz understood; sex was not casually discussed among these people. Of course sex had something to do with it, if only because men were physically larger, thanks to nature, and psychologically dominant, thanks to a sexist society. Women and children were possessions from which to demand certain responses—obedience, quiet, catering to the men's needs, demonstrating love when called for, serving as punching bags when not called for—if it satisfied some twisted male need of the moment.

Later came the tears, the pleading, the sweet talk and promises of no more abuse. Battered wives believed their repentant husbands, said the psychologist Liz had consulted. Or wanted to. Such women were reared to have almost no self-esteem, and had less yet after years of physical abuse. Even if they later wanted to escape a situation that had become hopeless, few had the strength or skills to step out into a sink-or-swim society on their own. So they stayed. And took it. Usually it got worse; bullies by nature become increasingly contemptuous of passive victims, almost trying to drive them to rebellion to justify their own escalating aggression.

"Did he hit the kids?"

Mari Sue's arms tightened around the baby. "Not at first. I was there. Then . . . he hit 'em, too. It was getting worse. That's when I decided. He could say he was sorry till doomsday, but he'd always do it. I came here. I don't know what I'll do after."

"What about . . . your husband?"

"They want him to talk to a counselor, like I do. He says no. He says he's gonna come and get us. That's why they have the security men here; there's always some husband or boyfriend threatening to fry us all."

"Why does he want you back?" Liz asked. "You've left him. You don't want to be hit anymore, or have the children hit. Surely he must see that things can't go on as they have in the past?"

The woman sighed, her dead features flickering with sad contempt. Not for her husband, but for Liz, who didn't understand. "Harvey's my husband. We'll probably go back."

Liz's notebook slapped the desk. She confronted the woman behind it. Her unmade-up face was as drab as Mari Sue's, but a lively intelligence animated it, outshining the coarse, gray-threaded hair that hung roughly to her shoulders. Rebecca Murphy was the director of the Ione V. Hazlett House, an impassioned advocate for battered women who had talked herself hoarse in the cause.

"I'm . . . stymied," Liz confessed. "I've talked to several women. They not only won't allow an on-film interview; they're the most . . . wishy-washy, self-defeating lot. I'm sorry, but they're stupid, and I don't mean just uneducated. Mari Sue says she'll probably go back to that maniac—and take her kids with her."

"Did she?" Rebecca's lips pursed, but she looked resigned. "That's what we do here. We try to keep them away long enough so they don't slide back into the old abusive patterns. It doesn't work more often than not."

"You're no better than she is!" Liz exploded. "You just give in to the hopelessness of these situations." Liz took a temper-cooling turn around the dark old room. Ione Violet Hazlett had been a rich man's widow and had left her many-roomed mansion as a shelter for women fleeing abuse. Not many had taken refuge here until recently, when society as a whole had awakened with mildly bewildered concern to recognize a pattern in marriage that was now being labeled "domestic violence."

"I'm sorry." Liz came back to the desk and to the placid woman she'd come prepared to admire but now found as perplexing as the victims who couldn't or wouldn't help themselves, even with the aid of foundation-funded "programs" and people like Rebecca Murphy. "Since I started researching this story . . . I thought it would be simple; black-and-white villains and victims. Men bru-talizing women. And they do. It's just that the women are so pigheadedly helpless, so spineless, so accepting. I could . . . hit 'em myself."

"You're frustrated," Rebecca pointed out in her deep, ever-even voice. "So are the men. And the women *are* as helpless as they seem, trained by society, by the hopeless homes they come from, to be effacing, to never stand up for themselves. They're easy to hit."

"I didn't mean literally," Liz said. "I wouldn't—but I can see why people say they must like their situations; they stay there and take it. Even Mari Sue, you can just see her tipping back into it. If her husband came and pleaded and yelled at her, she'd probably go with him."

Rebecca nodded soberly. "Probably. Many women have done just that; that's why we have a policy of forbidding men here, and only bringing the couple together in therapy."

"But if the separation is that tenuous, if the women are that stupid or masochistic, why interfere at all? Why risk berserk hus-bands?"

"To try and break the cycle. It's not easy. Some of our coun-selors have been beaten themselves by the husbands, who literally will break into Hazlett House and drag their women out by their hair, like cavemen. I've been called a meddling bitch, even a lesbian. We've had three incidents of arson in the past year." She smiled at Liz's shocked face. "It's not safe—even here. Especially here. You see, that's why the women have given up—or maybe never had any resistance to give up. The men are in control. The police can't protect them before the fact, and can do little after the attack. The men will always be out there to come back and get them—and likely it will be worse than if the women hadn't blown the whistle on them, hadn't pointed an accusing finger at them by the mere act of seeking shelter."

Liz turned over another blank page on her notebook. "Maybe. But if a man ever hit me, I'd never put up with it. Once, that's it. I'd be gone!"

Rebecca stood up. Liz couldn't help reading condemnation into her silence. She didn't understand why; she had a particular sensitivity for stories of social deprivation. She was, face it, a borderline bleeding heart.

"Have you talked to Elsie yet?" was all Rebecca said.

"No. No one named Elsie."

"I think you should. Come on. We'd planned on lunch, but I think you need food for thought." As Liz gathered up her purse and notebook, Rebecca smiled and fished out her car keys.

Rebecca drove a green Ford as battered as some of her residents; no one could accuse her of doing her job for other than altruistic motives. Liz sat uncomfortably on the ripped front seat as they left the shelter, aware of paperwork clutter lurching in the back seat and at her feet on the dusty floorboard. Everything surrounding this story was tawdry and mean and taking up more time than it was worth. Her ambitions for a series withered—wrong topic. Maybe she'd try the trend to home births or vasectomies or something that provided her and the viewers with a more upbeat outlook.

Rebecca steered the old Ford away from the old homes that matched Hazlett House's genteel decay toward a grander area of St. Paul. A broad elm tree—lined boulevard kept the residents of prestigious Summit Avenue from staring into each other's lofty mullioned windows. Summit Avenue homes ranged from stone mansions to substantial johnny-come-later single-family dwellings of brick, all echoing the architectural grandeur of European villas and English country estates.

The Ford pulled into the porte cochere of a mansion that was more stately, but as sprawling as the rest.

"Elsie's always at home. I've brought her surprise guests before," Rebecca noted, slamming the decrepit car door doubly hard to close it. "Usually I bring her reluctant foundation board members who aren't sure Hazlett House is a cause worthy even of the pittance we get. She's my number-one recruiter."

Liz tried not to be awed by the high carved ceilings, the tiled reverberating space, the scent of money in the furniture polish and fresh flowers decking entry hall tables. The place felt like the governor's mansion, which his PR people always tried to describe as a "residence" rather than a mansion. Mansion stuck.

A plump middle-aged woman met them in the vast entry hall. "Why, Mrs. Murphy, you're just in time for lunch. Mrs. Grace will be so glad." She took their coats, hanging them in a closet that Liz glimpsed—wood-paneled and about the size of a small library.

"Elsie doesn't leave the house much," Rebecca mentioned quietly as the two women waited in the house's real library, a room replete with ceiling-high walnut bookshelves, a raised semicircular reading area, and a ladder that slid along the walls to make books on twelve-foot-high shelves accessible.

"Who *is* she?" Liz hissed back impolitely.

"A very wealthy woman, and my secret benefactor."

So Liz was prepared to be impressed when the double doors opened. A tall, white-haired woman came through them, dressed in slacks and sweater, youthful at first glance, but in her well-preserved sixties at second look.

"Rebecca, you haven't made an emergency call for a while; I thought all was calm in your world," she said.

"Only on the surface. This is Liz Jordan, who—"

"Channel Eight. Of course. I see you do the newsbreak every morning."

"You *do*? That's great. I thought only the birds were up at that hour."

The woman brushed a hand to her gently waved hair. "I'm an insomniac, I'm afraid. I even watch the monster movies at three A.M. You TV people don't give us night owls much to choose from," she lectured lightly. "But it's a pleasure to meet you."

"Liz is doing a story on the shelter," Rebecca put in.

Elsie Grace's eyes, bright as bachelors' buttons, shifted with uncanny sharpness back to Liz's face. "I see." Liz stood there momentarily speechless as a schoolgirl, struck by some deep interior judgment being made within the woman before her. She felt every iota of her small-town, modest-means origin, every callowness of her youth, and didn't know why.

Lunch was served in the long formal dining room, at one cozy extreme of the endlessly extended mahogany table. Embroidered linen place mats replaced a formal tablecloth, but the fineness of the workmanship made it no sacrifice of elegance.

"Belgian," said Elsie Grace, smiling. Liz's fingers self-consciously stopped stroking the pattern. Money didn't normally awe her; Z.J. had seen to that. But family descent, a privileged heritage passed down for generations, reflected in everything from the finely articulated bones of the face to the bone china from which one nibbled one's luncheon crab salad. . . . Liz speared a particularly succulent chunk of white meat with a sterling fork so heavy it felt unbalanced in her hand. This was all something of a shock after a morning in the dark, dismally ruined rooms of the shelter. Why had Rebecca brought her here? More wasted time, however luxuriously spent. Liz listened to her internal lecture and suddenly relaxed. She worked hard. Why shouldn't she have an unexpected interval in her day?

"Rebecca tells me you help support the Hazlett Home, Mrs. Grace," Liz said politely to her hostess. "It's very enlightened to be sympathetic to an . . . well, an issue that strikes society at large as a bit seamy."

"You misunderstood." The woman poured a refill into Liz's delicate cup from a tall silver coffee pot. "I haven't given a penny to Rebecca or the shelter."

"I understand your role is discreet. I'm not here as a reporter; I just thought—"

"Of course you're here as a reporter; Rebecca wouldn't have brought you otherwise." Liz's mouth opened to protest and shut again, this time on a sugary after-luncheon mint. "You see, Miss Jordan—or can I call you Liz?" Liz nodded. "You see, Liz, my contribution to the Hazlett Home, unlike Ione's, is not monetary. I am not a donor, whether anonymous or open."

"Then . . ." Liz looked at Rebecca, mystified.

Elsie smiled mysteriously, but remained silent as the housekeeper came to remove the luncheon china. "Shall we adjourn to the library with our coffee?" she suggested.

It was in that room, surrounded by leather-bound volumes of great literature and encyclopedic reference, sipping coffee from Haviland china, that Liz learned who Elsie Grace was and what role she played in Rebecca's scheme of things.

"I call myself Rebecca's guilt-edged conscience. I spell that g-u-i-l-t, Liz. Mrs. Murphy there is not above using me to bludgeon the benighted into true belief."

Liz flushed, still puzzled, but well aware that she had somehow ended up among the "benighted." It rankled her to be thought ignorant or insensitive.

"I suppose . . ." Elsie's fingers flattened the wrinkled hummocks of fabric over her knee, pressing them from one side to the other. "I suppose you might call me an object lesson. I 'testify' to the Reverend Murphy's message. Privately perhaps, but where it is most effective. For thirty-five years, I was the abused wife of Carter Phillips Grace the fourth, until he died five years ago. I had and reared three lovely children, who—thank heaven—do not suspect the truth. I was a leading civic volunteer, sat on the boards of a dozen charities and worthy political causes over the past three decades. My picture was often in the paper's society pages, when they had society pages. The only oddity that was publicly perceivable about my life was my tendency to abruptly excuse myself from commitments. The, ah, reason, rumor had it, was an exotic physical affliction. Lupus, some thought. I was suspected also of disappearing for cosmetic surgery. On occasion, it got back to me; some people thought they had detected telltale bruises. . . ."

Liz shuddered, physically shuddered. Her cup bottom chattered against the saucer as she put it down. Elsie Grace did not appear to notice. Her mild blue eyes stared vaguely toward the book-shelves as she told her story.

"Carter had been born to money and privilege, to a certain role in society, as I had. Somehow he had become deeply uncertain of playing that role. He began by shouting at me when we were newlyweds. Later, he slapped me. Then there were blows, hard, as a man would hit another man. Punches, kicks. He would pick up anything handy and beat me and beat me. I tried to talk him into rationality at first. I always tried to muffle my cries." Elsie's eyes moved to Liz's. "The servants, you see. The rich have no real privacy. I threatened to leave him, which made him more volatile. His rages came without warning, but he was selective in his choice of location. It was always in our bedroom, where our privacy was most inviolate. Later, I detected a method to his madness. Instead of simply seizing a nearby belt to beat me with, he had . . . things . . . that had struck him as new and suitably inter-esting weapons . . . conveniently near when his rages came on. Those broke bones as well as skin."

Elsie had not meant to be interrupted here, but Liz couldn't help it.

"He was a sadist!"

The woman frowned. "Not really. He was afraid, of something he couldn't even name. I think he wished to reduce me to the same kind of abject fear. It . . . worked. I was afraid the children would witness something, afraid the servants would hear. I was more afraid of somebody finding out than the actual attacks. The attacks themselves came as a kind of relief—not that I ever wanted them, or felt I deserved them. But I could always say, as I became too weak to run away or too feeble to fight back . . . I could always say to myself: at least the children are at camp now; at least it's in the bedroom and no one can hear."

"And no one suspected?"

"Servants make the best accomplices; they're prepaid to silence. I had more than my share of mishaps and broken bones. 'Falls,' I called them. My friends began to tease me for being accident-prone."

"My God, why didn't you say something, simply to get your husband psychiatric help?"

Elsie Grace laughed; there was an ugly light mockery in the

sound. "My dear Miss Liz, I was young and naive when it first happened. I mentioned it to the family doctor who tended my first wounds. I merely suggested that my injuries were not accidental. He made it instantly clear that my sanity would be the one in question. That my 'hormones' or 'hysteria' was causing me to 'exaggerate' the facts or even 'harm myself.' It was all quite between the lines, you understand, but he made it obvious to me that there would be such a scandal. . . ."

"You surely didn't need your husband's money that badly——"

"The money. The money was incidental. I came from well-to-do people, and they would no more see me as blameless than anyone else. I saw that, almost at the same time I comprehended how incurably violent my husband was. You don't know until you claim something society considers a disease how set apart you are. It would be tantamount to naming myself a leper."

"You could have left anyway——"

"And the children. Leave the children with him? For the family lawyer and the family doctor would see I never got them. . . . Leave the children? And Carter without a nearby whipping girl? He would have turned on them and been as safe."

"So you became a martyr."

"No. I became an abysmally unhappy, wounded, fearful woman who could never let anyone around me, least of all Carter, suspect my agony. For he would have become even more . . . vicious . . . if I'd weakened. And I didn't really want to tell on him, you see." The woman's voice took on emotion for the first time. "I was so ashamed, ashamed of Carter, of the whole human race, of myself for not somehow having *seen* that it would go this way before I'd married him. I was highly educated, you know. Intelligent. Articulate. I was not used to being abused. At least . . . I thank God that I never became used to it. And . . . I kept hoping that my husband would somehow become in private the genteel, well-respected member of society he appeared to be to the outside world. He was a tormented man, Liz, and his children did not grow up to love him, despite the fact that he had never abused them. I think he hated that worse than he did me. That either way—with abuse or without it—he was not loved."

"I don't understand. Are you saying that with all your advantages, you were as helpless in your situation as all those poor, spiritless, washed-out women at the shelter?"

"Yes! The situation is such . . . it makes the person in it helpless, whether woman or child. Society views the man as protector of the family, as head of the family, so the Scriptures say. The rest of us are viewed as irresponsible really, liable to lie if we're bad, to be mindlessly happy as we should be if we're good. Men have been hitting the hell out of women and children for centuries. Why have Channel 8 and the *Chicago Tribune* and *60 Minutes* all discovered it at once? It's *fashionable* for the moment. A cause. An issue. Something worthy for the foundations to throw their money at. That's why I've never given money to Hazlett House. That's too easy. Instead, I do something I could never do while Carter lived. I give testimony; I admit what I never could admit for thirty-five years to people who may derive some small, lasting insight. When I'm gone, I'll leave a bequest for Hazlett House. But while I'm here, it's comforting, perhaps, to know that by telling the truth I might change someone's understanding of this problem—someone influential, who'll remember and do something about it long after I'm gone. And, too, I'm what you might call Rebecca's shock troops. I don't look like an abused wife. I scare the liver out of everyone. If it could happen to me, it could happen to you, Liz. Or your daughter someday. It isn't a problem that doesn't cross class lines. You have no right to judge the women at Hazlett House until you've been through what they have."

Liz leaned forward. "I think I begin to understand. And I'm grateful for your courage in sharing your past with me. Would you consider sharing it with a wider audience? You could change many minds, not just one or two at a time." Elsie's glance to Rebecca reflected a sad uncertainty, but Liz went on. "You've convinced me; you could convince a whole lot of somebodies. Would you let me interview you on camera?"

A gum-snap went off like a shotgun blast over Liz's bent head. She jerked her eyes up to find Mike Roth leaning over her, fists braced on her desk edge.

"How's the wife-beating story coming? This gonna be the Cecil B. deMille epic of Twin Cities television, or what? I hear you haven't started filming yet."

"No . . . but have I got the material to film. Better get the promotion department working on some gut-grabbing title, Mike. This is going to be powerful stuff."

He continued looking so dubious that Liz laughed. "Cheer up. Two days filming and it'll all be in the can, I promise. And could I get Andy Lewis on camera for this? Exclusively?"

"We don't usually assign cameramen on reporter request. Or exclusively."

"I think he's the right man for the job."

"Okay, Liz. Your last series was pretty good. This one better be a barn-burner. And done soon."

Roth rolled away on his cocky, sailor's gait, hitching up his pants. Stephanie leaned across the aisle that intervened between their desks.

"Liz, are you nuts? *Asking* for Andy Lewis? That guy gives me the creeps."

Liz stacked her papers. "I think he's a good cameraman, and that's what I need."

"If your battered ladies are scared now, they'll go bananas when they see Andy."

"Maybe not."

"I *hate* going out on assignment with him," Stephanie confessed, a mock shudder vibrating to the tips of her blond flip. "He says things . . . well, that could be interpreted as too personal. I think he's got a thing about women like us."

"Maybe." "Women like us" meant white. "But he's a good cameraman, and that's the bottom line as far as I'm concerned." Liz let the piled papers between her hands hit the desk sharply, then stacked them at one corner, leaning back to admire the impression of orderliness. She had the same misgivings about Andy Lewis that every woman on the newsdesk had; she just wasn't going to let them interfere with doing her job the best way she could.

Rebecca Murphy called later that afternoon.

"Elsie hasn't backed out?" Liz asked nervously. "We're all set for tomorrow afternoon."

"No, she hasn't, though I can't believe it. It's quite a step for Elsie to go this public. And maybe she inspired some of the others. Mari Sue agreed to be interviewed, and so did her husband—"

"Terrific. Him, too, huh? Wow."

"And there's a new resident, Beth Becker—really tragic case. She may be simply overangry right now, but she's eager to talk about her situation. Husband scalded her with a kettleful of boiling water. She just got out of the burn ward."

"Good Lord. Look, I'll take whatever 'testimony' comes my way. I just hope I do the story justice. I've arranged for a good cameraman—" Stephanie hooted behind her. "—so I'll see you tomorrow."

Liz hung up, knowing "tomorrow" always came sooner than it should. So she was nervous the next morning. Given how touchy these interviews would be, she hoped Andy Lewis would live up to her expectations.

He didn't say much as they walked out to the car together. He never said much. It was only nine A.M. when they left, and the downtown streets were still jammed with pedestrians. They all looked intently at Liz and Andy as they passed. Liz hoped she'd get used to it, and ignored them with not quite the natural ease that Andy did. Andy ignored attention as easily as he attracted it. He was young, hip, and black in a way that permitted no one to miss the fact, even if so inclined. Liz hadn't figured out if it was simply that he was less dilutely black than other black men, or if there was something invisible in his attitude that shouted "BLACK" when most people would have whispered "black."

He'd learned camerawork in Vietnam, where he'd been assigned to film battlefield engagements. Liz suspected that if she'd seen half of what Andy had through his mud-spattered camera lens, her hair would be snow white by now. But he had something because of his training, a terse sensitivity Liz had seen in the way he handled his camera, in the images that always seemed closer, starker, more affecting than the work of the other cameramen. She had a feeling that on the inside Andy Lewis was a pussycat in inverse ratio to the tiger he played on the surface. She could be completely wrong.

"I hear you asked for me," he noted as they backed out of the parking lot.

"Yeah," Liz said, content to leave it at that.

So was Andy. His silences unnerved the other women reporters as much as anything he chose to say. They passed the Granada Theater near the fringe of downtown Minneapolis, where the ancient marquee trumpeted with modern frankness, "Kittens Go Topless."

"Sounds like a hot movie," Andy said just as Liz had finished deciphering the tilted black letters.

"That's how they sell tickets," she commented, unflustered.

"You ever see any X-rated movies?" Here was where Stephanie or Caralee would squeeze her knees together and get nervous.

Liz watched Andy's dark-skinned profile, waiting for his glance to slide her way. It did. "I see enough bad film in my job. Who needs all that out-of-focus, jerky camerawork off the job?"

Andy's full lips twitched, but he never said another word until they got to Hazlett House. They got out and studied the towering, three-story stone mansion.

"Shelter, huh?" Andy prowled the sidewalk, quiet as a big black cat on his soft-soled shoes, back and forth, looking at the house like a panther would eyeball a mouse, as if he was waiting for it to betray itself by moving. "Might get some good exterior shots. You know, mood stuff."

"No, *you* know," Liz said. "Take whatever you think helps show that there are a lot of scared ladies in there."

Two old ladies ambled uncertainly onto the stretch of crumbling sidewalk in front of the house, eyeing them both, stopping, stiffening, moving quickly on. It often happened when Liz was on assignment with Andy and they were checking out the scene first,

without equipment. People automatically took them for a couple—
the ages were close enough—and they always registered mute
shock. Andy, she supposed, was used to having that effect when
in the company of a white woman. She wasn't.

Andy had gone back to the car to pull his equipment from the
trunk. "Lots of scared ladies," he noted, nodding to the disappearing backs.

"Some men give them reasons," Liz answered.

"Some men give *men* reasons to be scared." It was the most
Liz had ever heard him say about Vietnam, and probably all she'd
ever hear about it. Andy picked up the heavy sound pack; he'd
agreed to do the sound, too, because of the subject's sensitivity.
He never let her carry any of the equipment, so Liz went directly
up the wide concrete stairs to the dark porch. Behind her, she
heard the camera whirring, but she didn't turn or question it. She
had thought Andy might be the best cameraman for this story.
Now was the time to have faith in her own judgment.

Liz pressed the doorbell and heard the deep, interior chime
literally wrung out of it. The women of Hazlett House always
froze at the sound, wondering who . . . But it was only Liz Jordan,
girl reporter, invading their sanctuary. She would do them a lot
of good, win them community sympathy, pinpoint their terrible
and lonely problems. So she thought. So she always thought when
she went on a story; that it was important, that she would do some
good.

This story could be the best of her career. It also was the most
dangerous to its subjects, to Mari Sue and to the unmet Beth
Becker, burned as well as beaten. The burning woman. Liz heard
the big wooden door crack as its locks were released, saw it draw
open into inner darkness. She cross the threshold—Andy at her
back, filming, filming—hoping she was right.

— Chapter 19 —

Steve reached lazily across the rumpled sheets, but Liz was
already wiggling out of bed. He snatched at the hem of her convict-
striped sleep T-shirt and missed.

"What time is it?" he demanded in tones of sleepy deprivation.

"Only eight. Go back to sleep. I've got to get to the station."

"It's Saturday morning. I thought that was our time to relax. What're you doing at the station today?"

Steve looked as rumpled as the bed, and as warm and inviting. Liz hated to rise earlier than noon on her two days off of dawn patrol each week, but her fingers shook with excitement as she dressed.

"Andy promised to get all the film processed on my battered women series. I want to run through it, do some preliminary organization."

"That'll take hours!" Steve was sitting up, scratching his bare shoulder, looking dazed.

"Probably."

"They don't pay you for weekends," he shouted after Liz as she vanished into the outer room.

Her head poked back into the doorway. "Neither do you." She grinned and was gone.

Liz's fingers still were shaky as she threaded the film into the machine. Reels to go through—not only of Elsie in her stately mansion telling her unstately story, but of the various beaten women at the shelter, and Rebecca, plus the earlier footage Russ Delmonico had taken of the psychologist and the "enacted" battering the psychodrama seminar members of the state university had performed especially for the series. Liz backed up the film until she found the segment she was most excited about. Talk about manna from heaven, just waiting to drop into the reportorial palm. . . . There. Beth Becker. Liz sat back in the small viewing booth, notepad flat and pencil posied. This was the most emotional interview, with the woman freshly scarred both physically and emotionally by her husband's abuse. Her face, her bandaged body, told the story in no uncertain terms. So did her harsh, unforgiving voice.

"He's an alcoholic. Always has been, I guess. But he keeps getting jobs. And losing jobs. And getting jobs again. He'll just drink and suddenly . . . I've got second-degree burns over a quarter of my body. My back, my arms. He hit me, too. I don't know. Several times. Who counts a thing like that? Anyway, I'd fallen to the floor and as I was trying to get up, he just shoved the kettle of hot water off the stove. At me. Only the water hit me, not the kettle. It was enough."

Liz's voice. "What then? Did he . . . did he call for help?"

A weary laugh. "Help. He left, still cursing me. I couldn't hear him anymore; it hurt too much. I knew I was really . . . oh, God . . . *hurt* this time. I crawled to the phone, called the operator. I was passing out from pain. I wanted to rip my wet clothes off; and they felt like acid, you know? But it was too hard to move."

"Why did you decide to come here?"

"Had no choice. I mean, this time I was hurt too bad to dare go back and take some more. I've got to heal before I can be Mrs. Jack Becker again."

Liz stopped the film. Beth Becker's voice was strong, heavy with hopelessness but bitter, too. The mike had picked up every weary nuance. The film itself showed a plain woman—muddy features and complexion, her hair bleached into an undisciplined blond haystack, the dark roots showing now she was unable to touch them up. Unkempt, uncared for. And why should she look any other way? According to her story, she'd spent seven hellish years with an abusive husband and had finally been pushed into public outrage. For the interview at Hazlett House, she sat propped up like a semidecayed mummy in a lumpish easy chair arranged against a leaded glass window. Andy's restless camera had caught the faded, glorious glitter of turn-of-the-century glass, the disquieting expressions that played across Beth Becker's semishadowed face as she talked; had dwelled on the mute testimony of the elastic bandages sheathing her arms up to her blouse's short sleeves and beyond.

"Will there be scars?" Liz's voice gently inquired from off camera.

The lens zoomed relentlessly near.

"Scars. There've always been scars, only nobody saw them but him and me. Now maybe everybody'll know. Maybe some of the scars'll rub off on him a little. But these . . ." The woman lifted her wrapped arms in unison. The mummy rises from the dead to extract revenge. . . . "They say it won't be pretty, but I should be able to use my arms ninety-eight percent again. They say I was lucky. What do you say?"

What a place to end one of the segments. Liz jotted down the woman's last question and the number on the film counter that marked it. She'd been right about Randy Andy; his filmwork was spectacular, a silent indictment in 16 mm. How many parts did she have here? Liz paged through her notes. There were miles of film. Organizing it seemed like wrestling with the world's largest plate of spaghetti. But it would be a smashing series—Mari Sue's inarticulate sense of defeat playing off Elsie's long-suffering wisdom and Beth's still half-choked rage. . . .

After three hours of running through film, Liz had jotted down highlights enough to fill five two-minute segments. It was unnerving to think of displaying dissecting, and suggesting solutions to so devastating a social problem in ten minutes of airtime. But that was the exciting, despairing challenge of TV journalism. Liz sat for a while in the soundproof room, sobered by the effectiveness of her own work. How lucky she was to have Steve to go home to. The idea of him—or any man—raising a hand against her was foreign. Even Z.J. had never so much as slapped her as a child. She still didn't understand how other women, no matter how beaten down, could accept physical abuse. She had seen men who reacted to life with a blow. Men like that in Turtle Bend had usually restricted their blows to their kids, or a dog that they beat into some imagined standard of obedience until it came to them on its belly every time it was called. Perhaps a battered woman became like those pitifully loyal dogs, knowing a brutal blow was their lot yet always hoping a kind word miraculously would take its place someday.

She got back to the apartment at one. Steve was arrayed before the TV, Hamm's beer on one side, Cheetos on the other, watching a college football game.

"All set to win a Peabody?" he greeted her.

"Hardly." Liz unbuttoned her coat and collapsed on the chair near the door. "Filming is only half the battle. Organizing all that great stuff into a few paltry sound bites is murder. I wish I had your half hour to do the subject."

Steve finally took his eyes off a goal-line stand. "Hey, that's a great idea. I bet Roth'll love it. Why don't I have you and one of your guest experts on *Mid-Morning* the week before your series airs. That way, I get some protein for my talk show and we promo your series."

Liz slid to the floor beside him. "That's a great idea, Harmon. Has WBGO ever done that before?"

"No, but it never had us before. Look, I envy you your blood 'n' guts story subjects; you envy me my time. Let's join forces."

Liz snagged a fistful of Cheetos. "That was the idea way back when, you know."

"Huh?"

"Joining forces. *On* the job."

Steve shrugged. "We just got around to it backwards. I'll talk to my producer first, then Roth. Make it seem like my idea."

"It *was*, dummy." Liz jabbed his arm playfully, but he was caught up in a fourth-and-goal situation. "I guess Rebecca Murphy and I would make the best guests. Or do you want the shrink instead?"

"They got it! They're in!" Steve was yelling and rolling around the rug. "What a play."

Liz yawned. She never seemed to get fully rested anymore. "Rebecca, I guess. I'm gonna take a nap. See you later."

The bedroom, shades drawn, was quiet and dark, a kind of sleep tank. It nagged at her conscience, to sleep during waking hours, but she needed it. And maybe Steve would come in later, tiptoeing elaborately, and wake her up anyway for some off-hour loving. But she must have slept heavily, for the apartment was dark and deserted when she woke. The bedside clock read five-thirty, and for a guilty moment she felt she should be on her way to the station, except it was the opposite end of the day and a weekend to boot.

Liz dragged the TV stand into the bedroom and plugged it in, quickly curling up in the warm bed again. In minutes the *News at Six* was on, Steve Harmon at anchor. The news set was like a bad print; it looked so much more impressive framed by something, even a TV screen. In bald studio guise it was barren and jumbled. But Steve looked impressive on camera, the klieg lights making his thick blond mane sheen, bringing out the subtle pattern in his tie. Few anchormen were blond, Liz realized as she watched with both a lover's and a professional's eyes. Brown was the authority color for men—brown eyes, brown hair, with maybe a dab of gray dusting the temples for an intellectual, been-around-the-world air. Liz's fingers combed her own tousled strands, pulling them around into her view. Dark brown. And blond hair is the TV newswoman's occupational badge. Think about it, Jordan, she advised herself. Except for born-brown Barbara Walters and raven-haired Connie Chung in San Francisco, Liz couldn't think of any dark-haired women broadcasters. They were all blondes nowadays, like Stephanie. And like Stephanie, most were blond by virtue of bleach, not birth.

Liz curled a dark lock of hair around her forefinger. Maybe she and Steve were doomed by their off-color in-hair-itance. She yawned, then giggled. Maybe they should consider role reversal or sex-change surgery. Liz tilted her head to study Steve with impersonally proprietary eyes. No, let the station PR department worry about surfaces. All she and Steve had to concentrate on was doing their jobs, doing the best job possible in this worst of all possible TV worlds—WBGO.

— *Chapter 20* —

The phone rang, for the fourteenth time that morning. Liz sent the same pile of papers skidding that she always did in reaching for it. Someday she'd have to organize her desk, crawl out from under this constant avalanche of unstable paperwork. . . .

"Liz Jordan," she announced to the unknown caller.

"Hello. I just wanted to call and tell you how great your series was. My cousin Ellen had a husband who—"

Liz nodded, her pencil seesawing between her fingertips as she prepared to put in a good long spell of listening. The praise was great, and the public had been unanimous in its sudden, emotional response to *Battered Women, Broken Vows*, as the advertising department had encapsulated Liz's series for the TV page ads. But a big story like that always brought its disappointing aftermath— calls telling of cases that would have added so much to the story had Liz only known about them before the story aired, the crazies who took sick pleasure in other people's misery, whose phone voices would suddenly lower and whose praise would turn into overpersonal questions about the victim's injuries. These Liz had learned to cut off quickly, mercilessly, and efficiently, her sprightly vocal pattern indicating well-concealed disgust only to the reporters round her. Hearing that brisk, tell-me-no-more tone, Stephanie or Steve or Keith would look up, eyebrows raised, waiting patiently for Liz to hang up and then explosively denounce the latest anonymous grossness. Why not? They expected the same support in turn when they got their sick calls.

"Just a lady with a half dozen horror stories," Liz explained to a waiting Stephanie. "No sweat."

"They've really been calling on this one, haven't they?" Stephanie's sympathy sounded envy-tinged. With Liz's successful appearance on Steve's daytime talk show to plug the series, a small flurry of station-generated advertising, and the fact that the April TV scene was well launched in the rerun season, *Battered Women, Broken Vows* had hit the Twin Cities' consciousness like a sack of cement.

"Yeah. I guess this sort of thing was kept in the closet for generations. Women just wouldn't tell, and nobody in the community would support them, anyway. Not even their parents. If

155

you believe a fourth of the callers, half the women in the world have been victims of domestic abuse."

"Well, your series made it plain it happens in the best of families."

"Rebecca says that the calls have been pouring in at the shelter— more people want sanctuary than they can take. And a lot of people are offering monetary support. That's the best part of doing a story like this."

Caralee Koeppers had edged over, embarrassed but eager to discuss the topic of the hour. "The power of the press," she observed acidly. "And the danger. We're not here to pimp for causes— good or not."

"We do Girl Scout cookies every damn year," Liz returned.

"But that's not sensational, dear. It's easy to do sensational stories, a whole string of them, and think you're doing the community some good. Nobody ignores something juicy about sex or violence. You're playing right into Roth's hands in the name of crusading for 'women.' Who do you think got WBGO the nickname of 'Blood, Guts, and Orgasms'?"

"I don't care who thinks they're benefiting; it was a story that needed telling."

Caralee shrugged. "It won't do you any good to be the messenger. The station'll take the credit when the awards come through, and all you'll get is a lot of kooks calling you—"

The phone rang again and Liz picked up the receiver with some relief. Goodbye, Caralee Carper. "Yes, this is Liz Jordan. Umhmmm. Saturday the fourteenth. I normally don't do speeches. . . . I see. Well, I suppose I could. Certainly. I'll look forward to your confirmation letter." She hung up.

"Not a kook. The university president's wife. Wants me to address a big faculty wives' function on my career and the stories I cover." Everything was said loud enough to carry to Caralee's desk. "Not much of a stipend, they said, only three hundred dollars. And I don't have to give a major address. Just a few words. More of a . . . personal appearance, don't you know?" By the end of her spiel, Liz was pointedly preening.

"Three hundred! That's what Jeff Stone gets all the time! Really?" Stephanie excited resembled an elegant blond stork in cardiac arrest.

Liz patted the back of her shiny dark hair in mock self-congratulation. "That's what we sensational journalists get, you know. Mon-ey. Fame. Perhaps the *National Enquirer* will want a column."

No doubt about it, Liz mused. A noteworthy series left a definite afterglow. Letters from prominent citizens on official stationery arriving two weeks later: ". . . sorry not to have contacted you sooner . . . first-rate job . . . public service . . . congratulations." Phone calls and speaking engagements still dribbling in. Reporters from competing stations edging over at press conferences with respectful murmurs of congratulation. . . .

Liz got so she couldn't pick up the phone without expecting a gratifying stroke. "Liz Jordan."

"Miss Jordan?" The woman's voice was not tentative, despite the question.

"Yes?"

"I'm calling about that story you did on men who beat their wives."

"Yes." What now? Another invitation to speak? Another round of praise and verbal applause?

"I'm afraid it's not true."

Pause. Gauge the caller's sanity—or lack of it. "Of course it's true. It's been covered up, but it's an all-too-common social problem. That's why we showed the cases of so many women——"

"I don't know about 'many' women. I just saw it Wednesday night. When you had *her* on. I know something about her background. She lied."

"Wednesday. Wednesday was——" Not Elsie Grace? Impossible! None of her interviewees had lied; why would they?

"She called herself Beth Becker, and that's her husband's last name, all right. Her first name's really Janine. I know them both. Jack Becker wouldn't hurt a fly. She's the one that's a bit teched."

"The woman was severely *burned*——"

"I'm not saying she ain't hurt, though it strikes me that nobody would look under all them bandages. I just know her, and she's lying."

"How do you know them?"

"That's not for me to say. But if I were Jack Becker, I'd think about suing you and that station you work for, WBGO or whatever. He's got friends. He put up with a lot from that woman, and never made a public spectacle of himself. But she lied. You've got a lot of nerve putting lies on the television set, into people's homes. Especially about real people."

"All the women we filmed were at the Hazlett Home for abused women; they were there for a reason." Liz was starting to hedge. I just went where the women were, where they *said* they were because they were abused. I wasn't there when they were abused. Nobody was but them and their abuser. We, of course, are taking their word for it. . . .

"I'm sure they were, and maybe most of them have been beat by their husbands. But not by Jack Becker. That Janine's a liar.

Always has been. It makes me mad, you pointing the finger at Jack Becker like that and not giving him a chance to defend himself—"

"I interviewed several other husbands, or gave them an opportunity to present their side. Most of them refused to go on camera."

"You talk to Jack Becker?"

"No. . . ." Beth had said he was an over-the-road trucker, out of town and unreachable for two weeks.

"Well, you may be talkin' to him now. Or his lawyer, if he's got any smarts."

"How can you be so sure that—hello? Hello? Oh, shoot."

Stephanie was directing an inquiring smile Liz's way.

"Nothing, Steph. Just a nut call. I think I'll get an unlisted number at the office."

Spring was announcing its imminence in typical Minnesota fashion—with a string of overcast, dreary, sopping days, so only the gradually greening grass offered hope of more cheerful weather.

Liz hopped parking lot puddles in her too-new-to-ruin red Capezio pumps. She'd planned to stay in all day, writing up yesterday's stories. Her next project was to be on couples who choose not to have children, and it was proving to be a hotter topic than the battering story in terms of no one being willing to talk about it.

She started the Pinto after a few preliminary gargles of the motor and drove the slick, wet streets at a cautiously fast clip. With luck, she'd get to Hazlett House and back on her supposed lunch hour, all nagging questions answered.

Rebecca Murphy had been happy to see Liz even on short notice. The shelter itself looked more dismal than ever, but Liz was startled by the activity inside, by the swelled numbers of women and the sense of upbeat bustle the very entry hall exuded despite dripping umbrellas and water-soaked shoes lined up by the radiator.

"Come into my parlor," invited Rebecca, her plain face beaming like a misplaced sun. Liz followed her into the office as tall as it was wide. The stacks of papers were higher, but Rebecca happily waved to them.

"Sit down if you can find a vacant spot. I can't tell you what your series has done for us. I meant to write you and your boss a glowing letter, but I've been swamped. I'll get to it next week, once I deal with this outpouring of support. Look, Liz." She waved a sheaf of correspondence. "People are sending money; foundations are writing to ask how they can underwrite our program, perhaps another shelter. . . . It's incredible. Even the residents are feeling more hopeful. You've done us an unbelievable turn. Now. What can I do for you?"

Liz, frozen at the door, shut it. She picked her way across the magazine-cluttered floor to a side chair only half-covered with papers and sat gingerly, the papers in her lap.

"Rebecca. I've had a call about Beth Becker. I'd like to check it out. Is she here?"

"Beth? Why, no. . . . Her husband wasn't in town, so she felt she'd be safe at a hotel. And we had so many applying here, once your series started. From the first night. It was overwhelming."

Liz sighed. "Do you know where she's gone?"

"She might have said so, but she could have moved on since then. They don't have to stay in touch, and we can't hold them here. They come and they go; you know that. What's the problem?"

"I got a call saying that Beth Becker was . . . unstable. A liar. That her husband didn't beat her or burn her. Is that possible?" She waited for Rebecca's easy reassurances.

"You mean, is it possible that Beth, that any of them, made it up?"

"Yes."

Rebecca leaned back in her rickety golden oak armchair. The day hung in the big window behind her like a dirty blue-gray blanket damp from dangling on some eternal interplanetary line. Liz could envision the same dreary day extending all the way to Mars and depressing little green men as much as it dispirited her. She had a terrible feeling that her vaunted nose for news was about to get a bloody blow.

"I suppose they could . . . exaggerate. Lie, even. But their bodies bear the proof, and they've nothing to gain. We take them at their word. We have to. Nobody else will—their families, the police, their neighbors—"

"That's what we do in my business, too. Tell stories as we hear them. It's just that once in a while someone tries to use us to tell a story that's pure fiction."

Rebecca had flipped through a file drawer of manila folders. "Here's all I've got on her. Hotel where she went, two weeks ago. I doubt she's till there. You could try the home number."

"And get Jack Becker?" Liz blanched as she copied the number. "He could come looking for me."

"According to this, Beth Becker *was* burned, Liz. I have the report from St. Paul-Ramsey Hospital. Boiling water, second-degree burns. Isn't that what she told you?"

"So she was at the hospital. That's something. Look, don't

worry, Rebecca. Maybe this was just a crank call. We get them all the time."

"So do we. You do see how impossible it is to answer your question? These women are running, for the first time in their lives, *for* their lives. We're a first stop on the path to freedom. We do what we can, try for continuity, try to get them into therapy. But mostly they run, to a sympathetic friend or sister, to another state, to another man. We may never hear of Beth Becker again."

Liz nodded and finished jotting down a sketchy series of notes from the slim Becker file. "I just hope that we never hear from Jack Becker."

Steve whistled that night when she told him about the call, about how Beth Becker had disappeared. Even though Liz had spent the afternoon following the paper trail the woman had left, she had come up blank as a fresh ream of twenty-pound bond.

"The phantom Becker," he teased.

"Her? Or *him*?" Liz asked grimly. "I hope it's him. The worst part is, Roth comes bouncing up to me this afternoon, all dimples and ill-trimmed mustache. He's entering my series for everything but the Nobel."

"Terrific!" The bedsprings bounced as Steve shook her ecstatically.

"I'd rather there weren't a shadow hanging over this piece."

"Phantom," Steve corrected. "Look, Liz, I get people on my show making incredible statements every day. 'This book has sold one hundred fifty thousand copies in hardcover.' Who's to say it didn't sell fifteen hundred copies under the counter at Woolworth's? We've got to take people's word to a certain degree."

"But by testifying to her injuries, Beth Becker as good as used me and WBGO to accuse him."

"Didn't other women?"

"Nobody used their names. She wanted to. I thought it was just because she was so angry. And it wasn't just a few bruises. Those burns were real; that I believe. The hospital wouldn't lie. I mean, who would figure that kind of victim for not being the victim, but maybe some twisted kind of liar?"

"Nobody." Steve shook her again, a bit admonishingly. "You're just a worrywart. You can't do these front-line stories without taking risks. Forget it; that's my advice. Doesn't Roth see you as the salvation of WBGO now? A kind of unofficial social ills reporter?"

"I guess. I'm working on another series. It's less sensational, but, boy, does nobody want to talk about it. Nobody."

"Sounds right up your alley." When she glared glumly at Steve, he was winking. "Who are you subjecting to public discussion and ridicule now?"

"Well, it might seem dull, but it's about married couples who choose not to have children and get all kinds of pressure from their parents and friends and society in general. Do you realize that no generation until now has had that choice?"

"Didn't stop to think about it. If you're going to work on these sexy stories, you might need a collaborator." He nuzzled nearer.

"Steve, be serious. It's an important issue. Just think, those poor people have to be on birth control forever! I think I'd rather have the kids."

"The Pill's not so bad."

"You don't take it. It's not *your* sleek physique that has to battle an extra five pounds every month."

"Still pretty sleek," Steve said consolingly, exploring under the sheets.

"It should be interesting," Liz said after a minute of silence. "There may be something to it."

"Sleekness?"

"Not having kids. I mean, people don't *have* to. It's not inevitable anymore. Think of the possibilities that opens up."

"I do, constantly."

"Have you decided? Is your heart set on parenthood?"

"I don't know, Liz. Most guys don't personalize the idea too much until they're married, or older. I guess I'll have kids. What about you?"

"I don't know. I've never, ever thought about it, which is kind of weird. Maybe I'll learn something from NON. That's the name of this group for couples who don't want kids."

Steve groaned. "Is there a group for everything these days? What about this?" He pulled Liz under the covers and began performing nameless incursions.

"It's a good thing there isn't," Liz said after a while. "I'm sure it would be illegal."

— *Chapter 21* —

News stories hit the public consciousness like the classic stone in a pond, spawning tight concentric circles of shock shortly after impact that soon dwindled to limpid ripples coming at greater and greater intervals. Then the pond silvers over again, glass-smooth until the next stone is cast by the next journalistic sensation.

A gentle wave from the wife-battering story still rippled the surface of Liz's life now and again, but no repercussions from the Beth Becker segment roiled the calming waters. Liz began to breathe again. Steve had been right, as usual. No sweat.

The child-free couples series came and went, solidifying Liz's laurels but causing no overt stir. It was a topic nobody wanted to talk about, but not one to raise community passions. Summer was busy. Liz and Steve took their first vacation together, backpacking in Yellowstone Park, his idea. They both came back tan and leaner-looking, earning envious newsroom glances. Liz didn't make it back to Turtle Bend for the Fourth that year. Or Labor Day. Or Halloween.

By Thanksgiving she could put it off no longer. While Steve headed west to Idaho to see his mother and sisters, Liz made the pleasant, half-day's drive <u>east to western Wisconsin</u>. Thanksgiving was early that year; a blush of faded leaf color still rouged the ground beneath stripped stands of trees. The November landscape had a muted, run-together look, like once-vibrant multicolored wool mittens that had been left out in the fall rain until the dyes mingled in new and softer shades. Roadside evergreens were plumes of smoky emerald; birches resembled slender contrails of ash from lit cigarettes abandoned to burn themselves out; wind and rain had buffed (elm) trunks into well-aged, leathery expanses of bark.

The road was damp blacktop, a charcoal slash through the faded tapestry of countryside, and few other cars traversed it. A gold carpet of long-fallen leaves, as soggy as Liz's morning Wheaties, cushioned her steps as she made her way up the familiar walk to the house. It was twilight now, and the windows glowed subtly, lit either by the mellow, sinking sun outside or by lamps inside that had not yet been given enough dark to glare at full strength.

It was a halfway season, a halfway time of day, and Liz felt more than ever before that she was only halfway home.

Her father was ensconced in his favorite easy chair, the green-vinyl upholstered recliner that took over much of the cramped living room when fully extended. He was, as usual, attempting to read in the dark.

"Hi, Daddy." Liz kissed him and turned up the table lamp. Z.J.'s face squinched with dislike; whether from the sign of affection or the extra light, Liz didn't know.

"Drive all right?"

"Piece of cake. Where's Myrtle?" Liz always had to remind herself to ask after her stepmother.

"Kitchen. Wants to have some supper for you."

"That's not necessary. I said I'd have a big lunch on the way up."

Z.J. shook his paper pointedly as he resumed reading; he wasn't about to mediate domestic matters. The newspaper was not his own. Zach Jordan, Editor, read every comma of that in raw copy form, page proof, and first edition. For recreation, at home in his own living room, he read what he termed "the rival rags," which could range from the *Rankin County Record* to the *Wall Street Journal*. Z.J. took himself seriously.

Liz set down her overnight case in the hall leading to the bedrooms and dutifully went into the kitchen to succor Myrtle, who took one look at her, glanced reproachfully at the clock, and clucked, "My, it's late, isn't it?"

"I said I wouldn't get here until six."

"These Swiss steaks have to be eaten at just the right moment." Myrtle yanked down the squeaky oven door (Z.J. was no handyman) and prodded the contents of a baking pan with her lethal meat fork. Liz snatched up a woven hotpad and stood by, trying to look helpful. "Get me that platter, will you, Liz? Not *that* one; that's for the dinner rolls. The big one with the flowers on it."

Liz assisted as best she could in the kitchen until the dinner was safely transferred to the dining room table.

"Dinner, Zach," Myrtle announced then, big-boned hands wringing the chair's top rail as she anchored the foot of the table. Liz's father always sat at the head, with his back to the hallway. Myrtle's spot was in a direct line to the swinging door to the kitchen, although she tried to orchestrate meals so that no one would need to get up and get something. "Zach!"

A thick blue plume of cigar smoke waved affably over the summit of the easy chair.

"Must you smoke those things just before dinner?"

"Only one, my dear, at a time," he responded, sounding remarkably like W. C. Fields. The newspaper crinkled noisily as it was ostentatiously folded and set aside. The smoke screen dissipated. Z.J.'s white head surfaced above the green hummock of chair like the riffle of surf heralding the ascension of a submarine to the surface of the sea. Zachariah Jordan's mind had risen from the mysterious, guarded depths it normally cruised to sport among the ordinary flotsam of domestic ritual.

It had not always been like that, Liz thought as her father took his place at the table and rattled off his everyday grace before sitting. When she was twelve or thirteen or sixteen, the grace often would be invoked over soup bowls of Campbell's Scotch broth and plates of sandwiches ranging from ham and mustard to cream cheese and red onion. Her meals were more inventive than substantial, but Z.J.'s graces had lost not a whit of gratitude or rhetoric.

Liz didn't like Myrtle's cooking, and always had to simulate appetite when she came home from college. She still did. It was farm cooking—relying on fatty sauces and butter and Crisco by the can. Z.J. had gained twenty pounds and a case of hypertension since Myrtle came, but Liz doubted anyone but her had made a connection, not even old Doc Dupree. Liz never thought of Myrtle's advent in terms of a marriage, though she vividly remembered the small and oddly formal ceremony in the Episcopal church. Myrtle, like winter every year or one's first period, had just "come," and once it had arrived, there was no going back to endless halcyon summers or life without periodic pain. Or innocence. Liz divided her life, as the historians arbitrarily dissected centuries, into two utterly different sections requiring individual calculation: B.M. and A.M.: Before Myrtle and After Myrtle.

This evening, as they sat around the dimly lit table, passing platter and serving dish laden with everything she didn't want, it occurred clearly and irrevocably to Liz that she didn't like Myrtle, and that everything on the Jordan domestic scene had soured upon her arrival.

"Take something worth eating," Myrtle urged. "You couldn't keep a canary alive on those portions."

"I did have a big lunch in Stillwater. . . ."

Myrtle snorted. "It's this modern mania for thinness. You girls all look like Halloween skeletons. I wouldn't be surprised if you hadn't come down with that, that nervosa disease in the Cities."

"Anorexia nervosa. And you don't 'come down' with it; it's a mental disorder."

"Nothing wrong with Elizabeth's brain," put in her father, winking over his serving of Swiss steak. "You still dating that Pepsodent man? Well, he must have pretty teeth if he's a TV announcer."

"He hosts a talk show and does the weekend news anchoring, Dad. And his name is Steve and, yes, his teeth are quite satisfactory—"

"Aha! Got to have good teeth in that game. Of course, you came by yours naturally. . . ." Z.J. flashed his frankly false choppers.

"Da-ad. Honestly. Yes, I'm still seeing Steve."

"Should have invited him up for tomorrow."

Myrtle stiffened.

"Or would you have had sleeping arrangement problems?" Z.J. went on. Myrtle and Liz for once did something in concert; they drew in audible breaths. "Happened to Mrs. Swenson last Christmas. Daughter brought up a live-in boyfriend and insisted on installing him in her bed, under Mrs. Swenson's mother's handmade quilt. Terrible scandal. The *Sentinel*, of course, didn't report it, though every tattler in town did. You're not in that kind of pickle, are you, Elizabeth? Hell, we're broad-minded. We'd let you and your friend have the garage, so don't be shy on that account."

"Dad, you are as impossible as ever." Liz was toying with the Swiss steak, hoping she sounded innocent, however that was supposed to sound. "Steve would love to come, I'm sure." Lie. "But he has family in Idaho. His father's dead, so his mother and sisters count on seeing him on holidays." Steve, the brave-hearted boy rushing home to his unprotected womenfolk. Oh, brother. But it was better than leaving impressions of carnal knowledge in the big city.

"Just teasing, Elizabeth. I know you were raised right. But don't be shy about bringing your young men home. I want to meet the guy before I turn you over to some bozo at the foot of the altar steps."

That night, Liz had to dislodge her line of stuffed animals from their spot at the base of her pillow. Her bedroom was frozen in time, fixed to the way it had looked when she'd left for college. She studied the bric-a-brac with new, alien insight—the doilies on the dresser, the cheap china cats and dogs collected for reasons she no longer remembered, the drugstore perfume bottle she'd bought as a present for a girlfriend's birthday and then kept for herself because it seemed too beautiful to surrender. The bottle looked cheap now, and the perfume had turned the color of brandy and probably smelled as strong. Liz sat on the bed and with her feet moved the small oval rug that her mother had made. It was faded and old-fashioned, not really worth saving.

Liz caressed the ears of the grimy fuzzy rabbit with the once white satin belly. He drooped at every limb. The oversize poodle was an award for some long-forgotten school contest and still wore the perky look of the unloved toy for a too-old child. The pink felt–eared cat of white rabbit fur, irrevocably yellowed, still winked with the bright green glass eyes Liz once had fancied were emeralds. She stroked it nostalgically. It felt as inconceivably soft as ever it had in the dark. But it reminded her of Whizzy, and she set it aside as if it were furred in nettles at the memory.

Reinstalled on the dresser, the stuffed animals made eerie, unexpected reflections in the mirror. Liz slid into the bed, uneasy. She had grown used to another body in her bed, to the Valium of another person's regular breathing. The house was quiet in an unfamiliar way; the single bed seemed punishingly small, as if she were Alice and had been unknowingly imbibing some growth potion until she shot out of fit with the familiar and the old. She dreaded Thanksgiving dinner the next noon and, with that thought for a theme song, found herself lulled fitfully to sleep.

"Turkey and all the trimmings? For three? Really, Mrytle, you should have let me bring up a pumpkin pie or something."

"You bake now?"

"No, but there's a pie shop near my apartment—"

"This is better." Myrtle elevated a dark and runny pie, its top crosshatched with pastry. Liz's mouth puckered at the idea of sweet-rich mincemeat on top of everything else. Besides, she dared not risk the calories. . . .

"Looks good, ladies." Her father had made his ritual holiday foray into the kitchen. His hand rested on Liz's shoulder, a rare touch. She turned to find his brown eyes twinkling. "Elizabeth, why don't you come into the living room and let Myrtle finish preparing the feast? There's someone I'd like you to meet." When Liz's eyebrows rose in surprise at the idea of an outsider being invited to a family occasion, her father patted her shoulder reassuringly. "Since you wouldn't bring a beau to dinner, I thought I'd better supply one." Liz's mouth dropped. "Come on, honey. You'll see."

Liz was even more bewildered to see a young man sitting suitor-like on the living room sofa, wearing a white shirt and dark suit sadly too large for him, as if they'd been bought by someone like his mother who hoped he would still grow. He was Liz's age, or a bit younger, and sported a pasty skin, rat-flat light brown hair, and a distant look that she took for shyness.

"This here's Neil Wetland. My daughter, Elizabeth. This lad's gonna help me run the *Sentinel*."

Liz turned to her father. "Dad, you're not ill . . . ?"

"No," he pooh-poohed. "I'm just getting a little tired of relying on after-class high-schoolers and a bunch of feeble-minded old-timers. Neil will be full-time; he's a bona fide journalist, Elizabeth. Got a degree and all. I'm gonna make a *newspaper* man of him."

Z.J.'s distinction between journalists and newspaper men amounted to the difference between a dilettante and a ditchdigger.

"I'll be a jack-of-all-trades—printer's devil, so to speak," Neil himself explained. "Sell ads, learn the customers, report here and there. Do a garden column in the spring and summer and a knitting column in the winter, if that's what it takes."

Liz sat slowly on the sofa. "Well, great. Everyone's been telling Dad for years he could use some help. We just thought he'd never listen."

Z.J. laughed. "I was bowled over by his credentials. When a young man shows up on the doorstep beggin' for work in hard times . . . why, I couldn't resist."

"I've got my M.A. from Medill in Chicago," explained Neil, naming one of the country's most prestigious journalism schools. "Where's yours from?"

"University of Milwaukee. Then I went to the *Milwaukee Observer.*"

Neil nodded sourly. "The *Milwaukee Observer*, huh? Not a bad place to begin. What'd you work there?"

"Features."

Neil could express no more enthusiasm for features than he could for the *Milwaukee Observer*. "And now you're in television?" he inquired with devastating politeness.

"More good-looking men there," Z.J. exploded triumphantly. "Elizabeth's a smart one. Newspaper men are a scurvy lot, right, Neil?"

The young man smiled tolerantly as Liz yelped in disagreement. "I'm sure TV news is an interesting field," he said. "And the Twin Cities must be much more exciting than Turtle Bend."

"Dad's got it all wrong about my motives. I'm out to change the face of TV news—namely, to get my face on good stories. But what about you? Isn't Turtle Bend a good deal slower-paced than Chicago? Why come here?"

Myrtle hovered in the archway to the dining room, her very presence silently announcing dinner. When guests were there, she summoned via moral superiority rather than lung power.

They filed into the dining room, Z.J. especially eloquent with grace now that he had a fresh audience member. "And thank you, oh Lord, for the comforting presence of my loved ones: Myrtle, my daughter, Elizabeth, and my new friend, Neil, who will lift the burdens from my weary old back and keep the lead hot."

"I thought your plant was all offset these days," Liz said, shaking out her napkin.

"A figure of speech, Elizabeth. Figure of speech. The Lord

understands hyperbole. He invented it, according to the Good Book."

"Hot lead sounds more like a newspaper," put in Neil, heaping his plate with Myrtle's passing bounty despite his slight size. "Technology may be changing our business, but the spirit remains the same."

Liz noticed the "our" and reflected that she was not included. "How did you happen to choose Turtle Bend, Neil? Are you from here?"

"Kansas. Like Dorothy. No, I studied your father's work in grad school, and when I got out, jobs were few and far between." Neil passed the sweet potatoes to Liz, having commandeered two. She passed them on. "You were smart to switch media fast. By the time my class graduated, all the jobs were snapped up. Too many grads, too many mergers of papers, too many Watergate-inspired would-be journalists."

"I left a nice spot at the *Observer* when I went to TV," Liz noted acidly.

Neil smiled, gently. "Features isn't my field. It's really the old Women's Department warmed over. I'm looking for journalism-in-the round. The little stuff, big stuff, everyday stuff, and stuff that shakes the world. Your father is a genius, Liz; he's used this little paper to speak softly and carry a big stick all over the country. He's got more influence than one of your TV networks, I bet. That's what I want to study. An American classic. The good small-town newspaper."

"That's admirable. But you can do good work anywhere and on any level, if you fight for the opportunity."

Neil was leaning forward, colorless eyes shining. "And I want to do that right here, in Turtle Bend."

"Whoa there, young man." Z.J. was wiping his fingers daintily on his chest-covering napkin, more W.C.-like than ever. "Good work comes after the basics. There are more obituaries to do in Turtle Bend than you'd think, and on ordinary people, too, not your fancy folk who merit a half column in the big dailies. It's mostly boring, you know," he went on, committed to his favorite mealtime lecture, "news is. Half of it's what you don't know, and never do find out in time. And then—poof—it's all another day, the *next* day, and you're off chasing some new will-o'-the-wisp until you're garter-high in swamp gas. I'll either break you of journalism, you young pup, or make a damn good newsman of you."

The jocular threat set Neil Wetland's figurative tail wagging. He lifted the small glass of burgundy that accompanied all Jordan holiday dinners, whether the meat was white or red.

"To damn good newsmen, sir," he toasted his host.

Z.J. toasted back. Mrytle never drank. Liz tightened her fingers on her glass stem and contemplated how the *Turtle Bend Sentinel* would play a story of justifiable homicide involving the editor-in-chief's only daughter.

— *Chapter 22* —

Nothing conveyed an aimless, unused aura like an empty apartment. When Liz turned her key in the lock Friday afternoon, the hoarded air infected her with the same malaise. Steve would be gone until Sunday night, having turned the holiday into a long weekend. Liz had thought she'd welcome some privacy, that it would hit her like a breath of fresh air. Instead, privacy whiffed of newsprint, slowly aging fruit, and undone laundry.

Liz picked her way through the apartment, gathering and folding tented newspapers skimmed once and cast aside, stacking magazines and dishes, and collecting discarded shoes, shirts, and socks, all Steve's. Tidying up kept her busy for an hour and a half. Then she made a light supper, peeling the blackened banana in the fruit bowl, finding it semiconsumable, and slicing it over a soup bowl of slightly stale Frosted Flakes.

She ate the milk-drowned mess slowly, watching—what else?— the news, this time on rival Channel 4. The Walter Cronkite of the Twin Cities, and probably the only other balding, avuncular anchorman in the United States, Dave Moore was doing his usual crisp broadcasting job. He was a man you believed. Maybe it was the freckles and the fact that no razorcut at any price would have any effect whatsoever on his ebbing hairline. Like Cronkite, he projected an overall mousiness of person that oddly added to his credibility. Certainly it made sideburns and wide Technicolor ties seem redundant.

Liz wondered how Steve would age; he was already inspecting his hairline for signs of retreat. But she had no image of a middle-aged Steve, as she had none of herself. It was as if she'd not only swallowed the late 1960s adage to "trust no one over thirty," but had assumed that no one she knew, certainly none of her contemporaries in what *Vogue* magazine had termed the "youthquake" generation, would ever *get* over thirty. But now skirt lengths, newly decorous, had rolled down over knees like discreet shades called back to duty after a decade of window-peeping, men's bell-bottom pants were shrinking back to stovepipe dimensions, flowered skirts were car-waxing rags, and Nehru jackets were something you saw in old still photos of Sammy Davis Jr. And everybody was—surprise—getting older.

Even Zachariah Jordan. Liz poured herself a solitary Scotch and water, unusual behavior for her, and sat in front of the TV again. The changing images flickered like summer lightning in the unlighted room. It was amazing how much television she watched—mostly the news whenever it was on. It was on in increasingly larger doses now that networks and stations had discovered that the news, a once-obligatory "public service" required by the FCC, actually could run for the ratings roses and make the advertising department smell like a rose. And always she watched with a measuring, critical, professional eye. Entertainment might be what she and Steve called a "junk night" now and then, like Fridays with *Night Stalker*. But usually their favorite TV series were doomed to go belly-up for some reason. Liz found it safer to invest her time in the likes of Louis Rukeyser and *Wall Street Week* or the current Lord Peter Wimsey mystery on *Masterpiece Theatre*.

Television, not newspapers, had become the centerpiece of her life, reflecting the trend of the entire country. Her father and his one-man type and tirade act were nineteenth-century leftovers. That's why they were considered so charming, so teachable at learned universities. And why wet-behind-his-granny-glasses-bows nerds like Neil Wetland made pilgrimages to places like Turtle Bend.

Liz squirmed on the old wicker love seat until it squeaked. He grated on her, this stranger from a fancy J-school, freshly loaded M.A. belted to his almost-nonexistent hip, green eyeshade pulled low over his young, trigger-happy eyes—yes, even the clichéd garter binding one shirt-sleeve. It grated on her to think of him making Turtle Bend and the *Sentinel* his own, coming there as subservient as a second-born son to assist Z.J. in his titular old age. He would "do anything to work on a real paper." Sell ads, even, the journalist's most despised chore, but necessary at a small-town paper. Set type. Take photos of the Turtle Bend African Violeteers. Run errands. Become indispensable; you don't go through Medill without learning something. Claim a heritage not his own. He should be making some city editor miserable on a big-city daily. Instead, he was making himself at home on Liz's turf, ostentatiously accepting what she had never rejected, just outgrown. And looking down his nose at her every minute.

Her dad had always let her play at the paper. He had told her the proper names of things, and the importance of such journalistic principles as fairness, freedom, accuracy. She had been drawn to journalism despite this cradle-to-graduation indoctrination, against something within her that stood its ground and said, "me; me is different from what anyone thinks, even me," paradox though it was.

Liz knew the ins and outs of small-town life and newspapering; she knew that, like most icons, this one was painted thin on a very flat surface. She had only contempt for idealistic ninnies seeking fresher air and purer principles in the boondocks, where they believed houses were better built, people were nicer, and even the manure smelled sweeter. It was a retreat from contemporary life and it's challenges—gritty, urban, and often despairing as that life was.

So, she thought, privacy did stir some unbidden reflections. Liz was beginning to know what she was not: she was not, as Herb Boyle had seen so clearly seven years ago, Turtle Bend bound; she was not born to be a wife and mother in quick and sole succession; she was not, despite the same profession, her father's daughter; she was not one to swallow mass-consumption movements wholesale, even when they wore the seductive guise of individualism; she was not one to take no for an answer.

What she was, time would tell.

"Hey. The place looks great. What happened?"

"I cleaned it."

"No kidding." Steve dumped his duffel bag on the living room floor, and began pulling dirty laundry out of it the way a magician pulls scarves from his sleeve. "I brought something back for you—"

"How about putting those clothes in the laundry basket in the closet?"

"Huh? Oh, sure." He punched the pile into a mass and carried it to the large living room storage closet, where an empty aqua plastic laundry basket waited. Steve's burden filled it totally. "Anyway . . ." He was back pawing at the duffel bag, and finally pulled out a small square box. Still squatting, he watched her take and open it.

It held a silver ring, wide, with bands of turquoise and carnelian set in alternate channels.

"You can't wear bracelets on the air, earrings don't show, and necklaces rattle on the mike, so . . ."

"It's lovely."

"Indian work. I don't know which finger it'll fit. . . ."

Liz tried it on her fourth finger, right hand. "Perfect."

"Really?" Steve studied her hand, dubious of his luck.

"Really." Liz demonstrated with a quick shake; the ring stayed put. "See? That was sweet. I'm afraid I didn't bring anything back for you from Turtle Bend but a foul temper."

"Really?" Steve pulled her down on the floor beside him, beguiling her with a kiss. "I missed you, temper and all." His hands rubbed soothingly between her shoulder blades.

"But it's getting better. I've made a few decisions," Liz said, surprising even herself.

"Like what?"

"Like we're both going to pay more attention to keeping up this place. No more dishes sitting sinkside until the food is baked on, no more clothes carpeting the floor, no more refrigerator rot— do you know what I threw out of there this weekend?"

"Okay, okay. I don't want to know. I'll rinse every dish, so help me. . . ."

"And put them in the dishwasher right after you use them? What's it for if—"

"In the dishwasher. And socks in the closet basket and tooth-brush back on the little rack. Anything else?"

"We make the bed. Every other day." Steve's eyebrows rose. "I mean, we're not here at the same time, but every other day one of us makes the bed."

He nodded amiably.

"And . . ."

Steve was beginning to look the slightest bit rebellious.

"And tomorrow morning, I'm seeing Roth and telling him I want out of *Farmers' Forum.*"

"That's a pretty sudden decision," said Mike Roth, leaning back in his chair and twitching his mustache from side to side.

"It was a sudden assignment," Liz returned coolly.

"But your news segment is vital to *Farmers' Forum.*"

"Maybe *a* news segment is vital to *Farmers' Forum*, but I've done it for more than a year now. Why can't you switch around the staff?"

Roth scratched his neck. "I could . . . but I thought you'd be unwilling to share your anchor spot; not that many women get an opportunity—"

"—to get up at four-thirty in the morning, I know. Me and Barbara Walters. Lucky us. I think I'm ready to share the wealth."

"It was an assignment."

"And I can . . . ask . . . to be transferred."

Roth's hands made an impatient gesture. "Maybe a bonus for doing it—"

"It's been over a year. I've bent my life out of shape to come in every morning and tell a rapt audience of Future Farmers of America all the news that's fit to rehash from yesterday night. I want out. That's my bonus."

Roth leaned forward, finally taking her seriously. He twirled a pencil between his stubby fingers the way a melodrama villain twirls his mustache. "So, what's to bend out of shape, Liz? I didn't know your personal life was so touchy."

She held her breath. No one at the station knew that she and Steve lived together. It had been an unlikely piece of luck, but one that Liz wanted to hang on to. While she debated, indecisive about what to say next, Roth leaned nearer and his voice dropped.

"Maybe we should have a drink after work and talk it over someplace quiet."

Apparently, her private life was *too* discreet. Liz sighed, wearily. "Try Caralee," she suggested flatly, whether for the morning anchor spot or the drink, she left up to him.

— Chapter 23 —

Liz spent the first Friday morning she hadn't had to get up before the sun speeding down State Highway 52 in a rickety camera van, toward Rochester, Minnesota. With Fast Eddie Andersen.

Steve couldn't believe it when she'd told him.

"An overnight in Rochester? What's Rochester got worth staying overnight for, except the Mayo Clinic? Hey, you're doing some red-hot celebrity interview; that's it. . . . There's always a world-class personality checking in there. Come on, Liz. Level with me. No secrets between—" His voice had lowered to sexy bass. "—lovers."

"Actually, I'm meeting Omar Sharif for a quickie in the Rochester Radisson."

"Omar Sharif! You're kidding. He's got something! Something fatal, is that it?"

"Steve, what he's got I don't want. I interviewed him at the *Observer* when he came through town with some touring bridge tournament. Believe me, bridge and horses are his only passions. Women rank right down there with dogs and house slippers. Even the hotel staff thought he was the rudest celebrity they'd seen. I wouldn't go to the corner 7–11 to see Omar Sharif. He had the nerve to be absolutely uncooperative during my interview, then try to kiss my hand when I gave up and wanted to leave. Get serious."

"Well, it's got to be big. You've been doing nothing but Peabody Award–candidate stuff lately."

"That was before I bowed out of *Farmers' Forum*."

"Oh. You mean Roth's got you on his shit list."

"Check." Liz sighed. "Would you believe a series on the Rochester Pantomine Players? Tots and teens onstage in tights. Bright lights. No sound, just movement and music. Should be a joy to script."

Steve laughed and handed Liz the big bowl of popcorn as a consoling gesture. His arm went around her shoulders as she drowned her sorrow in a fistful of no-salt, no butter, no-zip pop-corn.

"It's nice to have you home in bed in the mornings," he pointed out.

"Yeah. But what price sleep? And Fast Eddie, too. I *know* Roth did that just to be vile."

"Yah want to stop for lunch?" Fast Eddie's chin jerked in the direction of a Dairy Queen.

"I suppose," Liz agreed. When they got to the window, she was so depressed she ordered a hamburger and a Peanutbuster Parfait for dessert.

They ate their food in the van, not speaking to each other, mostly because there was simply nothing to say. Fast Eddie didn't have time for reporters, and tolerated them the way a bear will put up with gnats. Liz he had no love for at all.

She paged through the press kit on the RPP, remembering the earnest young woman who did PR for the theater—besmocked, makeupless, long brown hair flowing across her bony shoulder blades. Arts groups attracted those professionally sincere, soberly dedicated young staff people, who took low wages without com-plaint in hopes they were advancing the cause of Art with a capital Advance.

But the color slides of the Pantomime Players' productions were spectacular; it looked as if the Players were fully worthy of the ecstatic press they'd earned everywhere except their home state over the past few years. Young Earnestine had explained that, too.

"The group has been hailed everywhere," she said earnestly, tossing a limp rope of brown hair back over her shoulder. "They've received the highest awards in theatrical circles, and Donn Cole

Bryson, the director, is brilliant. He gets so much out of these kids. People can hardly believe they're child performers."

Liz studied the black-and-white glossies again while the van bounced along the winter-pitted highway. The children, made up in whiteface and clothed fancifully in tights and doublets and pinwheel collars, did look like ageless elves, eminently graceful and almost preternaturally skilled.

The roadside fast-food joints and motels came faster and thicker and turned into the outskirts of the city of Rochester. The buildings that came closest to looming downtown were eight or ten or twelve stories of surprisingly new brick. Rochester was a town of hospitals and hotels, a medical mecca that drew the great and beneficent and low and meek. All were sick, or feared they were, and at this famous diagnostic center hope was fanned or fears were confirmed, and all who came went away convinced they'd done all they could, whatever the outcome.

Liz knew about Rochester. Everyone in the neighboring four states did. But the preponderance of doctors and medical personnel had done more to shape the small city than an international flow of famous patients. The people of Rochester were orthodox, conservative, and tight-lipped down to their high-button shoes.

Eddie checked the battered watch on his wrist. "Not bad time. We should make the theater by two. You just watch the show and let me worry about filming."

"Fine." The last thing Liz wanted to worry about was Fast Eddie.

She was impressed, though, when the van pulled up behind a line of yellow school buses at a sleek new concrete bunker near the downtown. "Rochester Art Center and Theater," brushed chrome lettering indicated in a modern, modestly arrogant way. A towering entry area carpeted in emerald green led to the theater, where triple lines of coat-clad children, red-cheeked from the winter winds or merely the excitement of an outing, streamed into the darkened house beyond.

"Enjoy yourself," suggested Fast Eddie, sliding equipment cases around the green carpeting.

Liz rolled her eyes. Joining a mob of antsy kids wasn't her idea of fun, or an assignment. She'd have an interview with the director and a backstage tour later. And tomorrow she and Eddie would come back to film dance, pantomime, and makeup classes. Still, big building or not, national reputation or not, kiddie frolics were not her cup of tea. Glumly reminding herself never to underestimate a story, Liz followed the children into the auditorium, feeling like a Pied Piper in reverse.

She came out ninety minutes later, surprised and blinking at the daylight pouring into the lobby through the glass doors. Numb, she felt stranded midlobby while children by the dozens poured past her to mount the buses outside. Fast Eddie was nowhere to be seen, but the PR girl had finally spotted Liz.

"Oh, you made it. How great. I knew your cameraman was backstage—"

"He was? I seem to have lost him."

"He's still back there, filming. Did you like the show?"

"It was . . . marvelous. Completely enrapturing. Those kids are really good."

The woman, whose name was really Gretchen, Liz recalled, laughed as she led Liz on a merry chase down stairs, through tunnels, and into the bowels and back of the theater building. "They *are* incredible. It's a school as well as a performing facility, you know. These kids take dance and fencing and character-building classes—not their own, but fictional characters. We've done *Sleeping Beauty* and adaptations of things like *The Wind in the Willows*, all in pantomime."

"But it's not really a dance theater. . . ."

"No. It's more than dance. And it's not just a children's theater, either. We have adult staff members and actors, too. Despite the kids we draw from neighboring schools, forty percent of our audience is adult." She beamed at Liz's surprised look. "True. Adults respond to the magic of imaginative theater. Even Richard Burton came to see us once when he was at the clinic."

"Really." Liz was already searching her memory for the Burton recording. . . . "Each evening from December to December, before you sink to sleep upon your cot, think back on all the tales that you remember . . . of Cam-e-lot." They could run that sound track behind some of Fast Eddie's film, flash a picture of the famed actor's craggy face among stills of rapt children's faces in the audience. . . . By golly, maybe there was a story to tell here after all, Roth be damned.

Liz and Gretchen found Fast Eddie enthusiastically filming while the stage crew struck the elaborate set, worked the ropes, and dragged off the many and inventive props. Liz was startled to find youngsters three feet tall brushing by her on urgent errands, directing themselves and one another. The set was stored as economically and gracefully as the onstage action was conducted.

"It's a tremendous opportunity for these children," Gretchen went on. "Some of their parents move here just so they can attend the school. Have you ever thought what happens to talented children in regular school? How bored and unstimulated they are? And if they do express their creativity, they can be ridiculed, even by insensitive teachers. Here, everything is directed by the art of learning and performing."

"They take it so seriously," Liz said, turning slowly, like a large, clumsy ballerina amidst a corps of wood nymphs.

"It *is* serious," lectured Gretchen, her pale, overintellectual face taking on a fierce intensity. "It's work to them; their job; the most important thing they do. That's what we teach them. Just because they're children doesn't mean that what they do doesn't matter."

Liz stepped over several tracks of thick cable. "But doesn't that put terrible pressures on them? To perform, to be overachievers?"

Gretchen smiled. "You'll see some classes tomorrow, and talk to Donn Bryson. I think you'll understand better. In the meantime, we do have an evening show for the adults and the youngsters they let stay up late. I'm sure you'll want to film part of that."

"And interview the audience as they leave."

"Anything you like. If you need something, just call on me. Or any of the staff. Including the children. You'd be surprised how much they know." Gretchen bustled off, little-red-hen style.

Liz spent the rest of that afternoon and evening watching and marveling. Eddie found plenty to shoot on his own, so she gave him his head. There was nothing more irritable than a cameraman interfered with.

But they did get together long enough to conduct off-the-cuff interviews with kids cramming themselves into tights and painting themselves into character. They all answered Liz's questions with sweet maturity, even the littlest ones. She knew as she heard Eddie's camera whirring over her shoulder that these small, polite half-beclowned faces would look even more endearing on film.

Later, the pair waited in the spotlit lobby for the audience to stream out and plucked at passing sleeves to catch a word of reaction. The adults' faces shone as delightedly as the children's. Everyone loved the Rochester Pantomime Theater. Everyone marveled at the sophisticated stagecraft that brought to life fairy tales and legends and half-remembered dreams of innocence and beauty and, yes, pain and fear, but above all the triumph of the youthful human spirit.

Fast Eddie nodded thoughtfully in the dark, cold van during the drive back to the Best Western on the edge of town. It was after ten o'clock; Liz was beat and even Fast Eddie had slowed down.

"You know," he ventured after a long while. "That's all right. That was okay. These kids really are something, aren't they?" His body adjusted on the seat as if to take a more affirmative posture.

"Now that's not a bad assignment, even if it is kid stuff. You should do more of these."

Liz's smile was wry. "I have a feeling I will be."

In her room, predictable in size and furnishings, she sat on the floral bedspread and studied the phone on its wall-attached, Formica-topped table. She felt, for some strange reason, like calling Steve, although there was nothing to tell him. The motel sheets were tucked in tight, like at a hospital. Liz wrenched back the bedding and sat gingerly on the icy percale. There was no reason to call anyone, but she felt vaguely like sharing something with someone. Maybe it was the shock of being on a "normal" story, an upper, a heart-warmer. Maybe she, heaven forbid, owed Mike Roth thanks for giving her the penance of a simple story in a small city.

That's how she would do the narration track, she thought, turning off the lamp and inching down into the unwarmed sheets. Like a story. "Once upon a time there was a troupe of merry, dancing children following a Pied Piper, not to vanish forever over the next hill, but to step soundlessly into the spotlight and enchant thousands of other children and anyone who has ever been a child. . . ."

Like most of the world's immortal leads, this one vanished over the hill of consciousness into an enchanting empire of—sleep.

The lit stage glowed amber below, a rectangle of distant warmth against the velvet darkness of the house. Liz stood studying it through another rectangle—the slice of glass that made up most of one wall of Donn Cole Bryson's stage-facing office high above the last row of seats.

"Don't you ever fear getting carried away, stepping out, falling down from here?" Liz asked.

Bryson didn't answer. Liz turned to see Fast Eddie casting the shards of his dismembered equipment on the two leather Barcelona chairs that faced a suede camelback sofa across a Chinese rug. Donn Cole Bryson was watching Fast Eddie with a fleeting expression of pain on his blandly genial face.

Liz sighed. Telling Fast Eddie to be careful was a waste of oxygen and might only result in some reactive gesture more dangerous to the furnishings than his current careless mode. She studied the large, impeccably furnished office again, surprised. She knew Bryon had spent twelve years of his life nursing the Pantomime Players from a church basement to a troupe meriting international press and its architecturally polished setting in a new building. She hadn't expected the high-profile power office. But why not? If even the child performers took themselves seriously, shouldn't the dedicated adult who'd piped them to this unheard-of eminence have his own summit to stand on?

The adulatory articles called him a theatrical genius. Liz hadn't met a genius yet, but she was prepared to be humbled. When Fast Eddie was ready, they took the places he indicated on the Barcelona chairs—Bryson with his sweatered shoulders against the black sky of the towering house, lit with constellations of baby spots, Liz out of camera range unless Eddie chose to turn it on her.

She knew all the press release background: how Bryson and four PTA women had founded the group, the housewives dropping out one by one with the usual spats group ventures engender until only the theater major from Elk River remained. The lean early days of begging for performing space, costumes, audiences even. . . . Then local recognition becoming regional. The summer five-state tours; the winter invitations to prestigious festivals, even in Europe. The explosion of success, to the point of surfeit. And still the absolute dedication to the theater itself and the stream of children who came, performed, stayed until they grew beyond high school and moved on beyond the limits of Rochester while another new pint-size wave swept up from below to take their places.

"You spend sixteen hours a day here, I understand," Liz began.

Bryson smiled. His smile was always a bit sad, and a bit superior. She was yet to be convinced that this was a mark of genius. "Sometimes eighteen," he said precisely. "I have a house very near. Postwar rambler. I can just dash over if I'm needed."

"This is such a professional operation." Bryson's moon face waxed warmer with the tribute. "Did you ever have trouble being accepted this way? Parents don't expect their children to be so . . . intensely involved in an extracurricular activity. Unless it's football."

Bryson laughed, as she had intended him to. "Of course. No one questions it in the slightest if a boy spends all his time wrenching his limbs on a muddy field and the coach calls it football or baseball or even soccer these days. But art. Theater. Movement. I don't call it dance—what we do is less than dance, and more than dance. It is interpretive movement in its purest sense. . . . At any rate, it's amazing how likely parents are to look down on their children's activities when they involve self-expression. But not our parents here in Rochester. They've been most supportive."

"No parents object to their children coming out at night to rehearsals? No bedtimes interfere with art?"

"The parents make a wonderful contribution. They drive their kids here in carpools, and pick them up. It wasn't always this way, but when they began to realize the growth and development, this theater provided their children . . . well, they're my most avid supporters."

"You mention supporters; that implies detractors. Do you have any, or is all sweetness and light?"

Bryson pointed to the stage casting a campfirelike glow through the dark. "In performance, it's all sweetness and light. Anywhere else it's damn hard, demanding work, whether you're a child or an adult. And it was hard work for me to convince all segments of the community that what I was . . . we're doing here enhances us all. The educational community is sometimes the last to truly challenge the child's creativity. There is a certain fear that children should be seen and not heard." Bryson smiled impishly. With his mid-thirties receding hairline he looked oddly childlike. Puckish. "That's why I created a pantomime theater. All gesture and no voice."

All gesture and no voice. That phrase haunted Liz long after the interview was tightly rolled into Eddie's film canister. Seen and not heard. Bryson himself was a quiet, slight man. Perhaps he had been a quieter, slighter child. Children were too often ignored, as Bryson had so succinctly said and perhaps knew better than most. All right, his pantomime theater mutely answered the deaf, blind adult world, see this—this wonder—and ignore it.

Liz and Eddie drove back to the Twin Cities late that Saturday afternoon as a red westering sun warmed the brown fields and concrete ribbons of road with crimson. All gesture and no voice. That's how most of this film should be presented, Liz thought. With music, a random comment here and there, and as little of the reporter as possible. She liked what Bryson and the Pantomime Players had to say so silently to the world of ververbalizing adults; she liked what she could say with the piece if she did it right. Maybe even go farther. Interview former Pantomime Players, find out what they were doing now. Check out children's theaters and schools around the Twin Cities. Hell, do a whole *series* on it.

Liz wrapped her arms tight around her stomach for illusory warmth and scooted down in the oversize bucket seat, chuckling to herself. Fast Eddie lived up to his name and drove, ignoring her. A series on the Pied Piper of Pint-size Players. Roth was going to eat . . . rats.

— *Chapter 24* —

Liz had collapsed on the white Formica makeup room counter.
Steve sat on one of the vacant stools, patting Pan Stik around his
eyes while Liz observed.

It was always fascinating to watch the men make up. Most,
like Steve, used highlighter to counter the intense studio lights'
most vicious shadows, which could make even Robert Redford
look hung-over. Some old-timers, like Gene Malone the Weatherman, would only pat a bit of powder over their bald spots. The
new breed went further; dark, slightly overripe Jeff Stone actually
ran eyeliner around his already soot-lashed eyes.

Steve gave his freshly combed hair a swift dusting of hair spray
and spun his stool away from the mirror to face Liz.

"I'm sure glad I don't have to do anchor duty anymore," she
noted. "No more primping for the live camera." Jeff Stone was
on vacation and Steve was anchoring the entire week.

"What are you doing here so late?" he asked.

Liz groaned. "You once said you were the most sexually sophisticated guy in the place. I'm becoming the resident expert on kid
creativity. I've been going through miles of that film I've been
getting on young people's theater groups. We are what we interview."

"Hey, no complaints here. I've been getting a better grade of
guests on my show lately. A Berrigan brother now and again,
Ralph Nader, repentant CREEP members, Zsa Zsa Gabor with a
new wig collection only once. I'm now the most *politically* sophisticated guy in the place."

"How the mighty have fallen. Too bad. Well, if you want a
reading from *Peter Pan*, I'm your girl. But I've gotten great film,
really. Just so damn much of it."

"Your fault. Series mania. Think how nice it'll be when all the
local TV stations convert to videotape in the next couple years,
if this penurious third-rate station ever springs for the dough. All
our shots neatly encapsulated in casettes. You could stack the tapes
for a whole series in that bottomless pit you call a purse. But this
kids' theater trip—aren't you about finished?"

"You sound like Roth. Oh, it's going to be a sweet, artsy piece;
Our Gal Liz doing a Pollyanna turn for a change. Ought to shock

my audience." She braced her palms and lowered her weary weight to the floor. "Got to get back to the editing room. Is this all you do when you anchor, Harmon? Primp and sit around?"

"Like all great artists, I just make it look easy," he returned, pulling her close for a quick kiss.

Liz submitted, but jumped back quickly, checking the parallel row of mirrors. "Someone might come. Besides, you'll ruin your makeup." She ducked out the door, just avoiding the small triangle of makeup sponge hurled after her. Liz smiled as she headed down the hall back to the newsroom. In grade school, if boys threw erasers at girls, it meant they liked them.

The Pantomime Players were a good lesson. It wasn't Liz's meaty kind of story, but an exercise in being open-minded and getting the most out of an assignment, even one meant to punish. Liz guessed it would happen again. From what she had observed on the *Milwaukee Observer*, at WBGO, and on the stories that brought her into brief, intense contact with organizations ranging from political to social to artistic, she had come to the strikingly unoriginal conclusion that life was a struggle. Not against competitive animals, the elements, or fellow Homo sapiens anymore, but against an inbred characteristic of humans in groups: the ineluctable force pulling all effort and aspiration down to a level of comfortable, surrendered mediocrity.

Liz had never seen anyone win free of that cardinal principle. Even her idol, Barbara Walters, a tough and sensitive interviewer who did her homework, had strict limitations as to what she could do on the *Today* program, and was contractually forced to defer to her male anchorman/host on interviews she herself had initiated once the prize was ushered onto the set. She could bring 'em back alive, but she couldn't mount the celebrated head on her trophy wall in public.

So it fascinated Liz that Donn Cole Bryson had somehow managed to erect an institution on a changing cast of talented tykes, sticking it all together with charisma, wheedles, and spit. He wasn't a prepossessing man on film or in person. Intelligent, yes, but so were many of the people Liz had interviewed; most were not nationally acclaimed as founder and guiding spirits of a hallowed institution. And when Liz ran the film she got later of Twin Cities children's theater directors, she saw members of a dedicated, often unsung educational group. She did not see anything in them, their work, or their students that matched the shining professional purity and ongoing magic act practiced daily on the stage of the Rochester Pantomime Players.

And of course everyone hailed the Players as the pinnacle of achievement in its class of one. There were no detractors. No one questioned the kids' hard work or late, lonely hours; the effect of too much imagination on the imaginative; the pressures of being chosen or not chosen, being cast or not cast, being as good as or not good enough introduced too early into the child's world.

The parents were all as supportive as Moira O'Toole, hard-working, widowed, worry-visaged mother of six, who had gone to the extreme of moving to Rochester so her talented cluster of sons could each progress through performance school the way some boys are funneled through military school.

"That's Sean. He was the first. He was playing *Puss 'n Boots* in that photograph. He's gone on to college now." Moira worked two jobs to help pay the extra tuition the Pantomime Players required, but several of her younger sons were on scholarship. "And here's Patrick. He's twelve and so talented." Patrick, beside her on the worn sofa, blushed at his mother's unbridled pride. They were all black Irish, the O'Toole boys, dark of hair, white of skin, blue of eye. Swashbuckling Sean, the eldest, glimpsed only in miniature on the wide-angle photograph, had looks to make a maiden's heart stop. But Jack, fifteen, also on the couch, was still unfully formed in his older brother's mold, more delicate of feature and sensibility. He was to have the lead in an upcoming production of *Pinocchio*, and remained uncommunicative despite his mother's prodding.

"It's great," Jack said for Eddie's rolling camera. "It's hard work, too, but it's a chance to do something terrific."

"Do you think you'd like a career on the stage?" Liz asked.

Jack glanced at Patrick, then his mother, and shrugged. She saw it then, the seeds of his brother's handsomeness obscured by the androgynous aura that surrounds males of a certain age between rowdy boyhood and the mysterious threshold of manhood. He could be an actor, or a model, with looks like that. It was a realistic career goal.

"I don't know," he said shyly. "I like working with the Players. We're a group. It's like football, you know, something you do because you . . . because you feel you have to. Not everybody goes pro."

Mrs. O'Toole beamed and the segment ended. No wonder parents loved Donn Cole Bryson and his theater. Their kids got all the limelight they could handle for now, yet the parents were spared the terror of seeing a child led astray into the wilds of a theatrical career. The Players was the youngsters' work, their passion, their play. Yet Bryson evidently prevented them from becoming unrealistically enamored of a performing career. It was real life—in the safe lane.

Perhaps Liz was jaded by too many sad stories, but she felt

uneasy about the fact that no reservations raised their ugly little heads. Her Pantomime Players series would be total sunshine and tribute, decorated by stunning color footage of well-drilled tots in tights and handsome teenagers in leotards executing gravity-defying combinations of acrobatics, acting, and ballet. Like the guy said, beauty is truth, and truth, beauty. That is all we know of life, and all we need to know.

Then she heard about Wendell Banks and her "need to know" changed—dramatically.

Wendell Banks was one of Liz's last round of interview subjects, a renowned set designer who'd got his start doing hand-painted backdrops for the Pantomime Players when they were moving to the plinkle of a hollow-toned upright piano in a Rochester church basement. Now he mounted *Carmen* for the Met, and still came back to his native Minneapolis to design an occasional set for the renowned Guthrie Theater. Liz caught him on a trip home and filmed an interview in the Guthrie basement, while Banks labored over a drawing board littered with working sketches of *Two Gentlemen of Verona*.

The vast, subterranean gray space underlying the Guthrie's multicolored seats in the theater's house above fascinated Liz, as did Banks, a soft-spoken man of thirty whose prematurely graying hair and ink-stained fingers couldn't erase a kind of gamin grace and whose well-considered words contributed to an air of unshakable integrity.

Fast Eddie had done his duty and skipped as soon as the interview was formally over, telling Liz not to hurry, as he had to film the latest modern art exhibit at the semiattached Walker Art Center building. So she lingered, enjoying the dramatic ambience. Papier-mâché masks and rubber daggers silvered with aluminum paint surrounded Liz and Wendell Banks; as a visiting artist, Banks cheerfully made do with a workspace carved from the perennial theatrical clutter.

"I've worked under far worse conditions," he said as Liz, touring the effluvia, commented on the crowding.

"I suppose during the early days of the Players all you got was a breadboard or something to draw on, and that was it."

"Or something," Banks said noncommittally, his stubby fingers executing lines of amazing delicacy on the paper before him.

Liz perched on a neighboring stool. Something bothered her; something missing or unsaid that made her want to stay until satisfied. "Do you mind if I watch?"

"Not at all. I could design *Otello* in the men's room of the *Titanic*. You learn how to function any which way in the theater."

"Sounds like TV news."

Banks looked up, a frown on his placid, friendly face. "Not really. Theater's a closed, hothouse atmosphere. The public doesn't see us daily, but only the outcome of weeks of work they don't see. It's a good thing," he added grimly.

"What—" Liz leaped into the chasm of opportunity Banks had opened up for her. "—doesn't the public see about the Rochester Pantomime Players?"

The hand and the charcoal pencil it held so lightly stopped moving. The Guthrie basement seemed grayer, stiller, ready for the Three Weird Sisters to materialize from behind a pile of discarded armor.

Banks looked at Liz, his eyes somehow franker. The pencil moved again, brushing faint strokes over the battered paper. Nothing was neat about the act of creation but the illusion of it.

"The pressure," he said shortly. "Performance pressure. It'll burn out a man or woman of forty; think what it could do to someone who's fourteen. Or four."

"I've wondered about that." Liz clasped her crossed knee. "But no one seems concerned. It's such a great opportunity for the kids. I've interviewed professional actors, or seen them interviewed, and they're like writers—always bewailing the late start they got in their careers. The Pantomime Players give these kids a chance to start off running and never stop."

Banks set down the pen, pushed the paper away as if his work wearied him. "How many of these 'youngsters' continue their performing careers?" he asked quietly.

"I don't know. . . . The Players have only been going a dozen years or so. The youngest beginner would be about eighteen now."

"What about the teenagers back then?" Banks pressed. Their roles were reversed; Liz felt she was not only being interviewed but was being gently prodded into a cluttered gray corner of her mind she was not yet ready or willing to explore. "The Twin Cities are full of pro and amateur theater and dance groups," he went on. "Haven't any of the Pantomime Players' 'graduates' past high school age moved on to straight acting or dancing in university or community theaters?"

"I've been looking for some to interview, but struck out so far."

"There aren't any."

". . . aren't any Pantomime Player graduates?"

"Not in the performing arts. If getting this kind of intense theatrical experience at an early age is so great, why don't any of the kids who've been through it stick with it? Maybe not all, but *some*?"

"You mean, nobody ever got anywhere after being in the Players?"

"Bryson did. I did. The adults do fine. The staff members do fine; take the praise and bow out and do their thing somewhere else. The kids . . . One I know is a sheepherder in Montana. Another's riding the rails around the country. Those are from the first 'graduating class.' I don't know about recently. I was last with the Players nine years ago."

"Why did you . . . move on?"

Banks picked up his pencil and drew it softly across the paper. "Theater's a pressure cooker. Especially the performing part. You're always judged on how you look as well as what you can do. That's devastating for adults; think what it does for adolescents or pre-adolescents. Then . . . in any performing group there are pressure relievers—alcohol, affairs, drugs are the most common. Adult staff members can't escape the pressures or the pain relievers, either, so the example is always there—"

"And kids nowadays are especially vulnerable to experimenting with drugs and sex," Liz finished. "You're saying early exposure to an adult world could corrupt the kids, that it's not all sweetness and light."

"If there are performing art groups," Banks said obliquely, "there's booze and dope and sex somewhere, maybe only among a minority. But with a children's group, the majority of the performers are minors."

"And its illegal as well as immoral."

Banks shrugged. "I work in the field. I don't judge." The lines around his eyes deepened as he smiled. "You don't know what I'm into."

"Straight," Liz guessed boldly. "From sea to shining sea."

Banks grinned an affirmative.

"What about . . . Bryson?" Liz watched Banks's smile slowly fade. "It's not unusual for men in the dance world, theater world, to be—"

"No," he agreed, a bit quickly.

"I wondered about, oh, some of those kids I saw. A lot are kid kids, if you know what I mean. But some, well, you can just sort of see them teetering on the edge of their identities. Sexually, I mean. I wondered if seeing or admiring somebody who was . . . committed to a life-style that was . . . same sex . . . might not influence some of the boys to follow in their hero's footsteps in their own lives."

"It isn't catching, you know." Banks was watching her carefully.

"I know," Liz answered. But she didn't know. She didn't have children, and hadn't confronted such concerns before. Conservatives said gay teachers corrupted students; liberal said gayness made no difference and to even notice it was discriminatory. "I know, but . . ." *Something* was wrong at the theater. . . .

The artist was drawing again, head bent, hand moving rhythmically, scratching across the mostly blank paper. Confidences were over; Liz had a feeling it was something she had just said. Usually she was perceptive. Why did she feel right now as if she'd been handed the key piece in a jigsaw puzzle and had tried to force it into the wrong place?

Her shoes scratched the semilittered floor as she dropped her weight to the ground. Banks didn't look up.

"Well, I guess I better get back to work." That implied the just-past conversation was off the record. "Got to find Super-Eight Eddie and get back to the station. Thanks for your . . . help."

Banks nodded and glanced over his hunched shoulder. "Take care now," he said, smiling again, friendly but ineffably regretful.

Take care now. Liz repeated it to herself as a warning as well as a farewell as she wove her way through the Guthrie basement's tangled web of props, costumes, and set pieces. Banks had told her all he could, as directly as he could, without violating confidences, she guessed. It was up to her to interpret it correctly. Was her basic suspicion right—that brilliant, unmarried, mid-thirties, balding Donn Cole Bryson was gay? Would she even suspect that if he were a single woman who had dedicated her life to kids? An old maid schoolteacher? But how could a three-part, seven-minute "happy" series address complex issues like that? Who would talk? Who would listen? Most important of all, who would care?

Liz was quiet on the way back to the station, but Fast Eddie whistled. "Good stuff," he announced once, leaning practically across Liz's lap to adjust the police radio. "You should do more of these."

— Chapter 25 —

"*What do you mean, you haven't done enough background* work on the story? I gave you lots of rope to shoot here and in Rochester." Roth was steaming. "Andersen could wrap the Foshay Tower twice in the film he's got."

Liz held her ground.

"There are questions that aren't answered. What if this guy isn't the Willie Wonka of the toe-shoe set? What if there's something . . . strange . . . about him?"

Roth stood, fists on hips, and confronted Liz across his desk. "You mean he's queer. Jesus, Liz, these theater guys are all fruitcakes; everybody knows that. I bet even that big English guy that founded the Guthrie Theater was—" *doesn't mean a thing, Liz*

"Sir Tyrone Guthrie was married!" Liz was indignant; the famous stage director had been one of her first *Observer* interviews before his death in 1971. *Gay is one thing / pedophile another*

✓ "So was Charles Laughton, but I guess it didn't get in his way," Roth smirked.

"Look, Mike. Unlike you, I don't believe that homosexuality is a given in the arts. Some are; some aren't. But what if the 'some' are working exclusively with impressionable kids?"

"How the hell you gonna prove a thing like that? It's none of our business. This isn't an investigative unit, and even if it were, I'd never let you go after an angle like that. The guy gets arrested trailing midnight lace down Hennepin Avenue some night, okay. There's basis for a story. Not until then. Go with what you got— a nice, uplifting piece about kids making magic." Roth's voice grew dangerously wheedlesome. "Fairy tales, Liz." The iron resurfaced. "Not fairies!"

The day after the Pantomime Players series had run, Liz came in to a fistful of caller notes praising the piece and one nerve-wracking memo from Mike Roth, too carefully tucked into a sealed envelope bearing the station letterhead.

Liz got a cup of coffee from the communal pot, then stopped by Stephanie's desk to compliment her on her new haircut and discuss frosting her own unrepentantly dark brown hair. They both concluded, as usual, that a frost job would only make Liz look "hard," whatever that was.

She came back to her desk, sat down, sorted through the praise notes. Most callers hadn't left their names or numbers, and the overworked operator had only jotted down key words. "Great story." "Adorable kids." "Bryson must be a saint." "Beautiful." "Didn't like your hair up." "Nice to see good news." An outpouring like this <u>was unusual</u> for any story. Liz concluded her professional misgivings were worth their weight in candy floss.

Finally, a stubborn sodden feeling in her chest, she opened Roth's memo. It was bound to be bad; you never heard from management formally unless it was bad. Liz read the terse note inside. She sat up straighter. She read it again. She stood up. She looked around for witnesses. Where the hell was Steve, anyway?

"Stephanie!" The blond woman glanced up, her face inquiring. "I don't believe it. It won. My series on battered women won a <u>Peabody Award</u>!" Across the room, Caralee Koeppers heard and looked Liz's way, her face tinged green by the newsroom's overhead fluorescent lights. Everyone looked green, even Steve coming through the far door, a Styrofoam cup of machine-made coffee in his hand; Steve didn't trust the sterile conditions of the newsroom pot. "I won," said Liz, more softly. Everybody looked at her, as disbelieving as she was. <u>Trust Roth to break</u> the news so sneakily, the rat, to leave it up to Liz to spread her own glad tidings. "I won," she said, sitting down and reading the brief memo one last time.

It was a Thursday night and weekend rates didn't apply, but Liz didn't care. She heard the dim ring repeat four, five times.

"Hello."

"Myrtle?" She was always sorry to get her stepmother first. "It's Liz."

"Just a minute; your Dad's in the living room." Myrtle never hung around to talk to Liz, but immediately relinquished the phone to her husband, perhaps out of wifely duty, perhaps because she felt as alien to Liz as Liz did to her.

"Liz?" Her father's voice boomed over the long distance line, seeming to fill the small apartment. "You rascal. Got me away from the news. Haven't you got anything better to do than spend big money on long distance?"

"It's worth it. I have some wonderful news...."

"You're bringing that mysterious boyfriend of yours home for Christmas?" her father teased.

"Maybe. If we're both off work. No, this is better than that.

A series I did on battered women just won a Peabody Award. That's the biggest thing in broadcasting news reporting."

"I've heard of it," her father said dryly. "Station sending you to pick it up?"

"New York. Too far. I guess I'll get a plaque or something."

"That's nice, Elizabeth. Good news, but not news to me. I've known you were a prizewinner since you were small enough to swing from my suspenders. Bring that plaque along when you come for Christmas. And bring that boy! I want to see the cut of his jib."

"Sure, Dad. How are you feeling?"

"Tip-top. Quit treating me like an old fogy, daughter mine. I bet I could still outrace you to the postbox."

"I bet," Liz agreed, laughing. They'd never had those fabled races; it was part of Z.J.'s legendry for Liz's childhood, which become more elaborately embroidered with every passing year until she hardly knew what was truth and what was fiction. "Well, take it easy anyway, Dad. Say good-bye to Myrtle," she added guiltily, knowing she never even wanted to say hello to her.

"Good-bye," Liz told the phone, her father had already hung up, and Liz's good news had gone flat as one of Myrtle's anemic Sunday-morning pancakes. . . .

Who was there left to tell who had not already been told? And yet it was not enough. Liz went to the apartment window, a wide, empty frame, seldom washed and therefore scummed with a patina of dust and rain, that trapped a changing urban landscape unremarkable for anything but its ordinariness. She stared at the colored metal rooftops of cars scattered over the blacktop, automatically locating the familiar hump of her red Pinto. Steve was still at the station but had suggested going out to dinner in celebration when he got home. He no longer "took" her anywhere; they "went." They had become an old married couple in all but fact, sharing space, time, money, beds, and head colds. . . . That, too, did not seem quite enough.

"There must be something wrong with me," Liz told the gray winter day, which returned her blank stare with an uncommitted façade of its own. The world at large did not disagree.

It was only a courtesy to inform Mike Roth of Liz's winning entry by wire; the formal notification came to Roth and Liz on Monday, on letterhead bearing the names of broadcast journalism's most photogenic flowers as well as academicians less well known by face than by philosophy.

Liz ran her forefinger over the blue type. Engraved. She read through the illustrious names on the Award Committee. Sevareid,

Sander Vanocur, Huntley, Harvard's Dean of Journalism, a professor from Medill School of Journalism at Chicago. Take that, Neil Wetland, you sanctimonious wimp. Judged by her peers, her more eminent peers, and found worthy. Not quite her peers. Liz studied the long column of names down the letter's left-hand margin. No women among them. Not a one. She began rereading the letter portion, which mentioned winners in other categories. All men and damn few white women, or black women, although the joke going around the station nowadays was that the next anchor would be Shirley Chisholm, the logic being that only a black woman would quiet charges of broadcasting racism and sexism.

Still, most of the women on the air remained unremittingly blond, and confined to cutesy weather spots or bottom-of-the-barrel assignments or—like Caralee—to the rooster-shift news.

Roth called Liz into his office a half hour later to wave his matching letter at her. "I assume you got the official news."

"Right. The plaque will be coming soon," she said.

"Should be a nice addition to the station trophy case in the lobby."

The case was a janitor-built monstrosity halfheartedly filled with overbloated concoctions of walnut and fake brass, featuring phallic-shaped objects apparently on the verge of taking off for outer space.

"I kind of wanted to take it home to Turtle Bend to show my father."

"It's station property, Liz, just like all your stories. But if you want to flash it for your old man sometime, Harry the janitor can unlock the case for you before a weekend."

"It's not important. I guess Dad's seen a few awards."

Roth tapped his vilely scented cigar into a huge glass ashtray inset in a green leather square. "Yup, I guess he's gotten a few of his own, and now his little girl's in the running. You'll get more. Gus Baer and the owner are real pleased about this recognition. They wouldn't be unhappy with another one. So why don't you put your thinking cap on and come up with another barn burner, huh?"

"Any old thing?"

"That's contest material." Roth grinned. "We can't waste your valuable time now, can we?"

"I'll mull it over. But it might not be obvious."

"None of your stuff is. Think about it, come up with something, sell it to me, and I'll give you carte blanche and any cameraman you want on it."

"I'm overwhelmed."

"No, Jordan, you're just lucky that the old man and Gus Baer are award-happy this month, that's all."

After lunch, Liz found a spare minute to make a thoughtful phone call. Most reporters were too harried to afford the time to be thoughtful, but Liz prided herself on somehow managing it. Few of the recipients realized at what cost such ordinary gestures as a note or a phone call were made.

"Hi, Rebecca? Liz Jordan at WBGO-TV. I thought you'd like to know—the series on battered women I did last spring? It won a Peabody Award. Right. Best of its class for a station of our size. Thank you. Yes, I'm pleased."

Rebecca's congratulations held a hesitant note. Liz, who'd had to do entire interviews over the phone at the *Observer* and whose job now meant she had to read any uncertainty and follow up on it in an instant, marked the unspoken reservation.

"So. How are things going?" Were funding problems distracting Rebecca Murphy from welcoming in the good news with real exuberance? Was Hazlett House in trouble? Was there another story in it?

"Things are fine . . . here." Rebecca paused. "I don't know if it matters, but . . . Beth Becker's been burned again, Liz. And it wasn't done by her husband this time. Maybe you'd better come out and talk about it."

"Poor woman. You mean I should go there for a follow-up . . . ?" Burned again. Not by her husband? By whom, then?

"No . . . just for your own . . . information."

"Who burned her this time?"

"She did it herself, Liz. Just like the first time. We know that's what happened now."

— Chapter 26 —

Rebecca's parlor office was more cluttered than ever, and Rebecca's face sagged as disheartedly as the old lined drapes covering the narrow bay windows.

"Where is she?" Liz asked as soon as she'd arrived and sat down.

"Hennepin County General burn unit. It's an even worse injury this time. The hospital contacted us because her social worker's records showed she'd spent a week here." Rebecca moved a pile of manila folders, which did little to tidy the work area, but cleared a small valley of space between herself and Liz. "We had to ask her to leave last time, you know. We felt other people were in more need of shelter and . . . it had become obvious that Beth Becker craved drama and attention in larger amounts than she was entitled to."

"Is she crazy, to burn herself?"

"Not functionally crazy. We can't lock her up. And we can't prove she burned herself, but the fire department, the police, the social worker, the hospital, and us have put it all together. We think that Beth is determined to harass her ex-husband and make him the villain—yes, they're divorced now—and to keep the spotlight on herself, no matter the cost. Although we think she got more than she bargained for this time. Fires aren't as fast and easy to put out as they are to start," Rebecca noted grimly. "And Beth's landlord had turned off the water that day to work on the plumbing, so she lost the quick source of dousing she'd expected from the kitchen tap."

"God." Liz sat back, imagining a woman in the market for a limited amount of self-immolation suddenly realizing the flames were beyond easy quenching. "And you think the first burn—the kettle of boiling water . . . ?"

Rebecca sighed so heavily even the massive draperies behind her seemed to stir like a bellows. "We think that, yes; she burned herself both times. But we can't prove or disprove it. I know you were concerned about the story. Does this endanger your award?"

It was Liz's turn to sigh. She rose and walked to the windows behind Rebecca, facing the flat gray winter day.

"I don't know, Rebecca. Beth Becker's story was only a small part of the series. Yet . . . I may be obligated to alert the Award Committee, give it the option of citing another piece. I just don't know yet." Liz idly counted the old-fashioned sidewalk blocks leading from the house steps to her parked car. "Will she be all right?"

"She's in for a lot of therapy, physical and emotional. She's one sick lady."

"Yeah." Liz smiled and turned back to the room that was as February-drab as the day outside. "Let me know if anything more happens."

"You mean finding any more ladies that cried wolf!?"

"Yes. And, I hope, no."

As she left, Liz noticed by the crowded main floor rooms how Hazlett House's population had risen in the few months since the series had aired. A lot of good had been done. Was one bad apple with self-inflicted bruises going to infect the returning health of the whole barrel?

Liz was half-distracted at the station the rest of the day, forcing words to fit the narrow narration column, handling stories that hitherto had been fighting her with emotionless dispatch.

For a change, Steve was ready to leave when she was, or vice versa, but they still had separate cars to drive home. Liz didn't feel like driving, didn't feel like attempting to control any aspect of her life, no matter how minor. But she steered over the snow-packed streets, past eroding snowbanks showing winter-long cinder-pocks of dirt beneath a layer of fresh snow the way a dirty slip might sag below the hem of a white lace Nipon frock.

"Dinner out or dinner in?" Steve asked when they met in the apartment parking lot. He'd seen her face.

"No dinner, unless it's hemlock."

"That bad, hmmmm?" Steve trailed her into the elevator and, though they were alone, tactfully refrained from inquiring into the source of her despondency. Men who lived with women became used to treading lightly at times. Liz wished they—he—wouldn't.

Steve made them both a Scotch and water, sinfully pulled out one of his infrequent cigarettes, and sat on the love seat.

"What's the problem?"

She filled him in, then waited, the Scotch stinging her tongue less than the ugly truth she'd just told. It was worse than making a confession, admitting to a flaw in a story already aired, already honored. Liz waited for all the inevitable questions that began with "Did you . . . Could you have . . . Why didn't you . . . ?" Steve's first question wasn't any of those.

"What about the maligned husband?"

"I asked Rebecca, but no one can find him. Apparently he skipped months ago, just after his wife got him in 'hot water,' so to speak."

"Well, then . . . if the guy's not around to raise holy hell, it's moot. Reporters don't get certified as infallible, you know."

"I know. But why this story, why—?"

"Why'd it have to muck up your award-winning effort?" Steve ran his fingers through his temples, loosening the control of the light hair spray he used. "When glitches show up, it's usually in the most sensitive pieces. If they filmed an eighth of the dumb things I've said on the air . . . Anyway, my advice is forget it unless some lawyer contacts the station. Are you sure you don't want any dinner?"

"Sure," said Liz, now firmly entrenched in her own personal foxhole of funk.

"Okay." Steve stood up, looking innocently sly. "But at least take off those clothes, get comfortable. . . ." He was drawing her into the shade-darkened bedroom, where the sheets were still rumpled from the morning flurry to escape the apartment in time to get to work. Hastily rejected shoes and earrings lay lackadaisically paired on dresser top and by the bed.

He had half her clothes off and Liz down on the covers before she knew what was happening; then she was under the thorough, sensitive strokes of his hands and she didn't care what was happening. They didn't speak, but Steve soothed her slowly with the motions of his warm, dry palms and his warmer mouth over the most far-flung but erotically responsive limits of her body. It was a long time before they actually came together, but by then the day had dwindled to nothing but this familiar twilight room, and to the familiarities, which could never grow stale, that they practiced upon each other. Liz felt utterly coddled and catered to, letting Steve move above her and beside her and finally within her as a pond accepts the refreshing wind that riffles its surface.

They lay beside each other, not tired, but placidly sated, listening to the silence, considering sleep. Liz finally sat up.

"What's up?" Steve's hand raised, fell ponderously to her bare shoulder blade, rested there.

"It worked," she answered, standing up in her half-slip, which had somehow remained on although disarranged by their lovemaking. "I'm going to the kitchen to see if we've got a frozen pizza. Want any?"

"That Steve is terrific," said Stephanie in April, fanning an oversize hardcover beauty book in her hands as she stood by Liz's desk. "He just interviewed the author of this and had her autograph it to me. It's a thirteen-ninety-five book! He's a sweetheart."

"I know." Liz smiled at the idea of *her* lover giving beauty books to other women. She had a collection of other such booty at home. An interviewer always got a free copy of visiting authors' books ahead of time. Steve had stunned Liz within a week of meeting her by presenting her with a lush hardcover of *America*.

"It's so expensive," she had demurred politely, still opening it to turn the lavishly illustrated pages. "I can't take it."

"You have to. It's got your name on it." He had flipped back to the title page, where a delicate black tracery stated in indelible ink: "To Liz, by repute a first-class lady and reporter. Alistair Cooke."

"I'm *crazy* about anything Alistair Cooke does! How did you know?"

"I figured you'd be into Alistair Cooke."

"Well?" she had demanded.

"Well what?"

"Well, is he as nice, as intelligent, articulate, and British as he is on *Masterpiece Theatre*?"

"Yes, yes, yes, yes." Steve had laughed and closed the book. "It's yours. My bookshelves at home would break if I kept every tome that came my way."

Now Steve's bookshelves sat next to Liz's in their apartment, and a number of other autographed books resided there: novels by the prolific Garson Kanin, who made an annual trip through town, dispensing breezy anecdotes like a millionaire distributing silver dollars; rich theatrical memoirs by Helen Hayes and Ruth Gordon; social histories by eminent academicians. Not one of them was a beauty book.

Stephanie cradled hers, open, on her arms. "Gosh, they're putting the eye shadow color *under* the bottom lid now. I don't like it. What do you think?"

"Ish," Liz said after a mechanical glance. She needed to get back to writing her story.

Stephanie lingered. "When are you going to take him home to meet Daddy?"

Liz's train of thought had been rudely derailed. "Who?"

"Steve, dummy."

"Oh." Liz knew some of the women at the station had guessed she and Steve lived together; she hadn't known they knew the affair had never been parentally sanctioned. She glanced up again, pursing her lips. "Charged"—that was the word she wanted, not "accused." It was a subtle difference. "Easter," she told Stephanie. "How about Easter?"

Roth studied the two typed pages on his desk. Liz couldn't read his body language—another book that Steve hadn't given her. She wished she'd mastered pop psych now.

"You're sure there's a series in this, a good series?"

"Everybody's into restoration of inner city neighborhoods, but the blacks and old people have nowhere to go. It's a classic confrontation, not to mention the developers turning all the cheap old apartment buildings into condos. I've got a feeling this could be great."

"It's so great and you don't want to start it until this fall?"

"I don't want to *run* it until fall. I want to start filming now, while the weather's still drab; the old houses will look tackier. Then, as we keep filming and spring comes, the weather will mirror the process of rehabilitating the old houses. I want to follow two or three through from wreck to resurrection. Some of them are really gorgeous under the weathered wood."

"Old mansions . . . Yeah, should be fairly graphic. 'Wreck to resurrection.' Remember that. Might make a good tagline for the ads. Still, it seems kind of tame subject matter for a series, Liz."

"Not when I get through with it." She had deliberately soft-pedaled the story's seamier and more controversial aspects—the young sweat-equity white couples, both straight and now increasingly gay, elbowing blacks out of their once unwanted ghetto; the condominium developers evicting feeble old folks from their long-time residences onto the mean streets; the vandalism and fires, the hot neighborhood tempers. Roth would shy from such sensitive issues. Oh, it was a juicy story, all right, and nobody was really telling it. Gentrification was a big new word for an old and brutal social process.

Roth swiveled importantly, letting his cigar burn a long, ashen train in the oversize ashtray on his desk.

"I think you're making a mistake, Liz." Her heart stopped. "With Lewis. I know I promised you whatever cameraman you wanted, but I don't think you realize that Lewis has been arrested twice by the Minneapolis police. While on the job. Once he insisted on crossing a fireline to film. Another time, he was parked in a No Parking zone and refused the ticket."

"The Minneapolis police are Nazis; they have trouble with blacks they think are out of place for some reason. Besides, I knew about that before I asked for him."

"Why did you ask for him?" Roth's little dark eyes cast a very narrow net and it was gathered tight around Liz.

"He's the best cameraman we've got, simple as that."

"Is it? Did you also know that the other girls . . . women reporters are scared stiff of him? There've been complaints he's made improper advances on assignment. They say he's some kind of sex pervert."

Liz looked away, making a disgusted *tsk*. "I'll tell you what he is; he's the first black man on the staff besides the janitor. They're Nervous Nellies. He hasn't bothered me a bit."

"Maybe what he does just doesn't bother you." Roth's smile was overfamiliar and momentarily unpleasant. He still didn't know about Steve, though after Easter, everyone probably would.

"Right. Two of a kind. So let us get on with the job. We'll bring back film you won't believe."

Roth surrendered with a raised palm. "I believe it."

But Liz's face felt hot as she left his office.

She hadn't mentioned the female reporters' fear of Lewis to Steve; he would be puzzled by it. When male reporters went out with male cameramen—or found themselves taking cabs with male drivers—it was routine. They didn't realize that both cameramen and cab drivers often came from blue-collar backgrounds and felt an ugly itch wherever they stored their macho identity papers when a professional woman, particularly a young, attractive professional woman, was there to literally tell them where to go. Liz and her fellow lady reporters had to put up with a lot of open male hostility, not just in the newsroom and from their superiors. Their inferiors were even touchier about the women's presence and their new equality. No, Andy Lewis was like all the other male chauvinist pigs Liz worked with daily and sometimes grew to like despite their blind spots. He only came in a different color, and ought to have known better. Maybe Caralee and Stephanie, or green girls and tittering menopausal matrons, couldn't handle Randy Andy, but Liz could.

Zachariah Jordan's daughter could handle anything.

— Chapter 27 —

Easter snow fell that year, fluffy and white as the Easter bunny to look at, wet and mushy as Cream of Wheat to walk in.

Liz wore her new shocking pink pumps to Turtle Bend anyway, letting Steve take her arm to keep her from stepping awry as they picked their way up the sidewalk to her father's house. They had "driven up" from the Cities for midafternoon dinner only, and were to return that evening. Liz felt that would be less coercive than staying the awkward night before, or traipsing to St. Clement Episcopal Church en masse and giving Z.J. an opening to bring up wedding ceremonies.

"I could carry you," Steve suggested as he watched Liz mince like a geisha from dry spot to dry spot.

"If my father saw you, he'd call it grounds for matrimony."

Steve shrugged. "Might not be a bad idea."

Liz stopped, collected herself for the leap to the first step, which was sunbaked and therefore snow-free, and glanced up. "You haven't met Z.J. yet." She sprang, her hand clutching the wrought-iron railing, the ball of her foot landing with practiced accuracy on the wooden step. "Used to do this to avoid the snakes in the sidewalk cracks."

Steve looked down at the snow-dappled cement. His shoes shuffled hesitantly. "Snakes? I thought this place was named after turtles."

"They're in the river; snakes are on land. No, it was just a kid game. I used to think snakes lurked in the dark between the sidewalk blocks. Come on in, and try not to look as if a snake got your tongue."

Steve followed her, looking on-air formal in his tweed sport coat and woolen tie. He had refused to wear a topcoat, with typical masculine disregard for the weather. The sun was shining, the skies were blue. It looked warm outside; ergo, no coat, even if the thermometer read thirty degrees. Also, Liz figured, Steve wanted to meet her father unencumbered, even by the clumsiness of outerwear. It was not an innocent Easter Sunday dinner, for the lamb on the menu might be Steve.

"So this is the young fellow." Z.J. rose from his mountainous chair like Buddha from his temple to shake hands with Steve. Somehow, Liz thought, the room seemed smaller—or Steve bigger. She felt crowded by all of them in the modest-size living room—her father, huge and hearty, herself, Steve, Myrtle, and . . .

"Neil Wetland," he said, stepping forward. Neil had matured sartorially. He wore an olive-green three-piece suit and looked as slippery as a record company executive at a road show.

"Sit down, sit down." Her father's hospitable order proved a problem. Liz sat next to Myrtle on the sofa; Neil resumed the barrel chair opposite her father; Steve settled on the battered old hassock in front of the fireplace, the only free seating surface. He nodded at the wall behind Z.J.'s head.

"So that's Our Gal Sunday in pigtails."

"You would have to notice that," Liz complained good-naturedly.

Z.J. turned with difficulty to study the gold-framed high school graduation photograph of Liz that hovered over his white head like a kind of rectangular gilt halo. "That's Elizabeth, all right. Petty little thing then. Still is," he added a bit too late and too quickly.

"Prettier," Steve said amiably.

"Now, what a man my age would like to see there," Z.J. went on inexorably, "is a row of his grandchildren, too."

"Well, you certainly wouldn't expect to see a row of your own children—at your age," Steve agreed.

Zach's eyes narrowed at the bland riposte. "You a pretty good newsman?"

"Some say."

"How about Liz?"

Steve glanced her way, warmly. "She's told you about her award—"

"Right, right. You didn't bring that trophy with you, did you, honey?"

"Sorry. No show and tell. The station keeps it locked in a case; doesn't want it out of its hands."

Z.J. nodded. "The station. It can't be the same as a newspaper, eh, Neil? Working for an institution with an antenna tower for a standard. The station. It sounds like so much air, sound, and fury; not real, like the grit of a printing press."

"It's real, Mr. Jordan," Steve put in before Wetland could second his first-in-command. "The transmittal process may be invisible, but our work is as concrete as anything old-time reporters did. It's just in a different form."

"But it's not *writing*," put in Neil.

"How do you think those words get into the TV reporters' mouths?" Liz demanded. "Mental telepathy? It's not only economical writing of a kind most newspaper reporters never have to practice, but we have to interweave film images with our words to create a cohesive whole."

"But it's gone as soon as it's said, Elizabeth," put in her father. He leaned forward to extract one of his cigars from a box of Muriels prominent on the end table near his chair, and began the complicated ritual of lighting it, talking through the process all the while, as if he were a ventriloquist demonstrating his command of his smoking dummy. Cigars were a new prop for his old age.

"Now take your—" Scratching farmer's match on worn side of box. "—your award-winning piece, that one on wife-beaters."

"It was on battered women. Some of them were married, some not. And it focused on the women, not the men."

"Whatever." Z.J. inhaled intently on the cigar, his forehead corrugated in concentration. "Now you sent them bits of film with your 'story' on it, mostly in the words of these unfortunate women, I would guess . . . ?"

"Yeah. Think of my interviews as graphic 'quotes.'"

"Nicely put, Elizabeth." Z.J. finally sucked the cigar alight, waved the match out with a flourish, and leaned back in the chair to the accompaniment of its unfurling squeaks. "Graphic quotes. So you send it in, they look at it, give you the award. But what's left? I mean, suppose a historian from 2015 wants to see what you saw here in 1974? Are there going to be libraries full of it? Will he run across it lining the bottom of his Aunt Sarah's shoe box? Will anyone have *saved* it 'cuz he or his cousin Quincey was in it? It's gone, Elizabeth, and that's why it's not an art form. Not like what Addison and Steele and Franklin and even William Randolph Hearst, God forgive him and his granddaughter, practiced."

Steve had pulled out a cigarette himself, lighting it with casual efficiency. "You're right to an extent, Mr. Jordan—"

"Z.J."

"But there are news film libraries now throughout the country, and some people are getting home videotape recorders—"

"Spoiled rich folks."

"Maybe now; maybe not next year or the next. The technology is changing. Size and prices of equipment are shrinking. Video may be an elite world now, but it's on its way to becoming as common and accessible as type, maybe more so."

"But will it educate the people, as the press has for more than four hundred years?" Z.J.'s eyes radiated a fierce, committed light. "Who can learn anything from a bunch of folks who can't even get the difference between subjective and objective case right? Between you and *me*, Mr. Harmon, if the future of the English language depends on being plucked out of the airwaves, relying on the tin ears of whosoever wants to appear on our little gray screens and orate in atrocious syntax, why, Mr. Harmon, that little box in the corner of my living room isn't much good, except for storing fish or serving as a bird cage!" He pointed, indicting as Perry Mason, to the blank TV set.

They all chuckled at Z.J.'s turning the classic recycled newspaper joke into an antitelevision gibe. They all did, except Myrtle, who sat solemn and outwardly attentive at these philosophical diatribes of her husband, much like a Buckingham Palace guard forcing himself to remain stoic in the face of great temptation— or great boredom. Liz, feeling vaguely guilty, leaned toward the silent woman.

"Everything under control? Would you like some kitchen help?"

"It's fine," she answered discreetly, loath to interrupt "man" talk. "It's just taking a while for the ham to bake."

So acid was Myrtle's tone that—had Liz not known she was humorless—she would have suspected her of sarcasm directed toward Z.J., whose Socratic dialogue with Steve was rapidly becoming a W.C. Fieldsian monologue.

"You defend your profession; it's only natural," he was saying. "As I defend mine."

"They're not that different," Steve interjected.

"In substance, no. In form, yes. And form is the key difference. Look at athletics—boxing, golf, tennis. Form's the thing. And journalism is, at base, writing, and you can't write on a cathode-ray tube!"

"You write *for* it, Dad." Liz could no longer let Steve fend off Z.J. solo. "And maybe you don't use as many words, and maybe an anchor on live doesn't always hit the perfect grammar when improvising, but they're hard-won skills, and they can influence a lot of people and carry a lot of responsibility with them. If that doesn't describe what you do at the *Turtle Bend Sentinel*, I'll eat the next edition."

"Let's eat Sunday dinner instead," said Myrtle, rising. The men stood with her, as if pulled to their feet by matriarchal prerogative.

They filed in, talking, while Liz trailed Myrtle to the kitchen to help bear various steaming dishes to the festive dining room table. There was something "family" about a full table at a holiday occasion. Z.J. held forth, as if impressing a touring group from Turtle Bend High's junior journalism class. Steve held his own, his blond hair seemingly star-dusted among the brown and grizzled company, his smooth voice easily counterbalancing the host's good-natured bellowing.

Liz let the two men dominate the conversation; the whole idea was for her father and her lover to get to know each other. Neil Wetland, she noted with pleasure, had drawn the day's dummy hand, along with Myrtle, and played the afternoon mostly silent. But perhaps he could afford it, she thought later, long after the peach cobbler and the coffee had been served and the men had enjoyed their after-dinner smokes. Neil didn't smoke. He didn't do much but sit and watch and wait. And be there.

"What do you think?" she asked Steve on the drive home. They'd tried to leave before dark, but protracted farewells had delayed them just enough so that the patchy snow shone skim-milk blue-white in the twilight, and a smoky scarlet banner of sunset stained the rumpled horizon that rolled past as if seen from a sedate roller coaster.

"Your father's a funny old coot—all bombast and bite. Just as I thought. Just as he writes. He's easy to love. From afar."

"What about . . . Neil?"

"Yeah, who is that guy, anyway? Some flunky from the paper or what?"

"I don't know. He says he came to do anything and everything for my father."

Steve grinned Liz's way, unable to read her face in the demi-dark. "Must be one of the new breed who finds journalism purer as practiced in the hustings. Give him a few more quilting bees to cover and he'll hightail it back to Grime City."

"I don't know." Anxiety touched Liz's voice. "Dad never wanted, never accepted help before. I wonder if there's something I don't know about."

"He looks pretty robust to me. And a man who's not afraid to nag about grandchildren when his daughter's brought a boyfriend home must anticipate being around awhile."

"Oh, God. You didn't pay any attention to that, I hope?"

Steve laughed. "You should hear my mother and sister when

I go home; they make your father look like Mr. Discreet on the subject. It's not a bad idea."

"You want grandchildren?"

"Not me. But the next time I come up here, I think I should check out the architectural style of old St. Clement Church. If it's up to snuff, and the rest of the relatives aren't too bad, I might let you marry into my ancient and honored name."

"Oh, you have a brother?" Liz asked acidly.

"I told you, all sisters, and all blondes like me. We've got to get a brunette in the family somehow."

Liz spent that spring, when she thought about it in retrospect, up to her boot tops in mud, thrashing around the sites of mired architectural grandes dames who still looked down their long-staired noses at her from under raised eyebrow windows.

Most of the houses she and Andy filmed were disreputable clapboard mausoleums, seemingly beyond redemption. Wind had scoured much of the paint off their boards; snow had saddled their roofs with permanent swaybacks; time had tumbled their porches and stairs. They sat on the crumbling inner-city streets in desolate, deserted rows, some with their windows and doors roughly boarded up. Only a few, sprinkled here and there like bright new pennies in a mountain of use-dulled coppers, sported fresh paint and reconstructed gingerbread. They stood clapboard by porch post with their run-down neighbors, and their very pristine new facades seemed to invite the midnight vandal and the hit-and-run spray-can graffiti artist.

"I've got to admire these people," said Liz one day as she and Andy drove the streets of St. Paul's Summit-University area, where the restoration movement was as insignificant and fragile as spring crocuses against the neighborhood's overall aura of drab decay. "It takes a lot of courage to invest everything they've got in one of these run-down barns."

"You think the neighborhood's bad?" Andy asked, his tone flat.

Liz tensed. The neighborhood was mostly black, as close as St. Paul could come to a ghetto with a piddling three percent black population. It was delicate business bringing a black man into it to record its dissolution. She had thought Andy Lewis could handle it with some professional detachment.

Instead of answering directly, Liz checked her notebook for an address. "I want to go to Marshall Avenue. There's an old lady in the eight hundred block who's supposed to have lived here sixty years."

"I got to make a stop," he responded. Liz said nothing. Cameramen were in the driver's seat. They'd call out the Canadian

Mounties if a reporter requested a pause or diversion for a personal errand; if the cameraman got the urge, station business waited.

The station compact turned onto Selby Avenue, the only spine remaining to the black neighborhood since the interstate had razed infamous Rondo Street and blazed a house-leveling trail right through it in the sixties. Selby was a sad corridor of one-story storefronts with chicken-wired shop windows and tattered facades. Big out-of-date cars, rusted and dented, cruised the street like battle-scarred sharks; the compact felt as vulnerable as a tin can among them. Selby was semideserted even at eleven A.M. on a spring morning, except for aimless men wearing fancy clothes and a predatory look. No one in sight was white, except Liz.

"I'll be right out." Andy smirked as he left the car at the curb and vanished into an odd-looking storefront, which featured bright lengths of African fabrics, gaudy lingerie, and an odd assortment of three-dimensional objects, including hookah pipes, that Liz was just as glad she couldn't see clearly. There was no name or sign on the shop front, but that didn't seem to prevent business.

The men on the sidewalks veered closer to the stranded car, put their hands in their pockets, and peered in, mouthing phrases Liz couldn't hear though the thankfully rolled up windows.

Damn you, Andy, she told herself; crummy, juvenile stunt to pull. She doubted he had any business inside the bizarre store except killing time while she was marooned, obvious as a single snowflake on a lump of coal, on the ghetto street. Liz pretended to make memos to herself in the notebook, keeping a casual eye on the cruising blacks. Cool, she told herself. Alert but cool. She was a liberal by education, but right then she wished she could succumb to an Archie Bunker knee-jerk reaction and slide across the seat to lock all four doors. That might make her feel easier among the gathering black men; it would ruin her forever with Andy Lewis.

A couple of men had stopped pretending to walk by and leaned against the storefront, talking, grinning, looking at her. Street intimidation. *You're out of your element, mama. We can, we could . . . do just about anything. Anything, baby . . .* Shit. It wasn't only black men who did this kind of thing to women; it was black men most women figured might do more than threaten. Why not? They had so little to lose, locked out of white society for generations, locked into poverty. Liz could understand it; she just didn't want to be a sacrificial statistic to it. She doodled uselessly in her notebook. Come on! Enough's enough, Andy. What if you start something only the police can finish . . . ?

He came out finally, walking in that aimless, easy street way that makes cops and women uptight, and eyeing the gathered men insolently, got into the car. Liz burned, knowing she'd been paraded as Andy's white woman to his peers, at the same time feeling a flare of relief at his return. Sexist and racist games, in spades, she thought, using the old racist term almost as an interior cuss-word to vent her frustration.

Andy laid a small brown bag on the seat between them as he drove away. Something illegal? Liz wondered. Another wordless challenge to her equanimity? Relax, she told herself. He's just a cat playing with a mouse. You know he won't hurt you; the prob-lem is, he wants to.

Then, driving, still watching the road, Andy slid an oily glance Liz's way. "You ever heard about this new thing they got nowa-days?" he asked softly. Liz fell for it and looked his way, hoping things were back to normal. "Candypants," Andy explained qui-etly. "They come in strawberry, banana, and licorice. You can eat 'em right off."

"Sounds . . . inventive," Liz said neutrally.

"They're real popular. Yup. Strawberry, banana, and licorice." Liz almost expected him to smack his lips. "You ever try any?"

"No, I'm happily shacked up," she explained pleasantly, look-ing levelly at Andy.

There was a silence. Andy turned the car onto Marshall Avenue; they had come up on the eight hundred block. Whatever games he was playing, he knew where he was going.

The car pulled up before a graceful gray house stacked three stories high. Leaded glass twinkled from the many window tops. It was Elida Jackson's house, and they were right on time for their appointment with her.

Andy looked ahead, through the badly wiped windshield, rum-inating. "Strawberry's supposed to be awfully good, but then some folks like licorice."

"And some folks like to put other people on. Cut out the shit, Andy, and let's just get to work."

Andy's palms hit the wheel. "Okay, Jordan, since you got nothing better to do . . ." He paused in sliding out of the seat and moved his arm toward the brown paper bag between them. "You wanta see what I got?"

Liz raised a cautionary spread-fingered hand. "No, thanks. It's your bag," she pointed out sardonically.

He laughed then, as if a long, overinvolved joke had finally reached the release of a punch line. "All *right*. Give me five."

Liz extended her pale white hand toward the big pink-and-mocha palm, hoping she wouldn't regret it. Andy's open hand slapped lightly down on hers. "That's all right," he repeated, and rolled out of the car seat. "Let's go shoot this mother."

— *Chapter 28* —

An oaken newel post. A tile-faced fireplace tucked into the wall opposite the front door. A spindle-work screen between entry hall and front parlor. A baby grand, elaborately carved, occupying the opposite parlor on four fat mahogany legs. Lace curtains. Clutter. Dolls dressed in satin and sequins. Doilies on the upholstery. The scent of peppermint tea, potpourri, and a genteel veil of dust. Sheet music, frayed, worn rag-soft, dating to the turn of the century.

And amid it all, sitting as stiff and starched as one of her china-faced dolls, was Elida Jackson, doyenne of a house far too large for her that held the best part of her past and sat along the worst part of Marshall Avenue.

She insisted on serving them cookies and tea. While she rustled back and forth in her vaguely old-fashioned dress, Andy unpacked his equipment and began filming her so discreetly that he seemed no more than another ghost from the haunting past.

"Do I remember the neighborhood? Why, honey, I was born here. Born here, raised here, went to school here, taught dancin' school here. I'll never leave, never.

"No, the 'neighborhood' don't bother me. Course, I do hate to see them fine houses along Marshall and all the side streets wear down, look shabby. But my house was painted three years ago; don't it look fine? So fine . . .

"White folks coming in don't worry me. There were always a few white folks here. What bothers me is seeing those houses empty, those fine old houses that used to have so many happy families in them. I don't know what happened to all the *young* people you used to see in this neighborhood! The children playing hopscotch on the sidewalks, and jumping rope. . . . They just seemed to get swallowed up—somewhere—the children.

"Now it's mostly old folks like me. Oh, I don't like those rooming houses they make by partitioning up these old houses. No, sir. Too crowded. They burn down, too, you know, every once in a while. I hear the sirens. . . .

"I'm not afraid. Me and Lovey get along fine. Lovey's my cat. Yes, she's pretty. Came to me one wet Halloween night. But she isn't black. Just a calico, I guess you'd say. I can make more tea just like nothin'. . . . No? Well, if you say so, but have another cookie. You, too, young man.

"I have scrapbooks, you know. Somewhere here . . . Things get so heavy. . . . Taught them to tap-dance, so smart. And the ballet. Lots of tiny little things with spindly legs. My, we had such good times. The piano going thumpety-thump, plink, plink, plink, and those little black legs pumping, pumping. . . . Oh, they were fast. Faster than I ever was, I guess.

"I'm not so fast now. But we manage, Lovey and I. You can pet her if you want. She is the lovingest cat. . . . So hungry she was, scrawny when she came. Kind of like I am now. I get enough to eat, sure do. I'm just made stringy; always was. Wait'll I show you this picture. Those were pink satin rompers I had on, and a little top hat tilted just so. Oh, I was something. Miss Elida Jackson and the Jacksonettes. Kick and tap and turn. You folks sure you don't want to finish these cookies? They're only store-bought, but I don't have the strength I used to.

"Sure you can take pictures of the scrapbooks; what are memories for? Television, my goodness. Never got one, you know. With my piano and all this old sheet music, I got enough entertainment to last me into my personal pine box, you understand, honey?

"No, nobody troubles me. Never been robbed. Oh, there's some folks buying houses along here and turning them into—what do you call them nowadays, row houses . . . ? Con-do-min-i-ums, that's right. I said no. Ain't never gonna leave my house. Me and Lovey's gonna stay forever. You write that down, honey. Make sure those con-do-min-ium folks hear that real good.

"Well, 'bye. Come back, if you want. We'll be here, me and Lovey. See, Lovey's waving good-bye. Folks do say I dote on her, but she is the lovingest cat. . . . Watch those steps. They're a little rickety, but I don't have the strength I used to, to find somebody to fix 'em. That's awful kind of you to offer, young man, but you don't have to. . . . 'Bye now. You want to hear anything about the neighborhood, you come back, you hear? I like young folks. . . ."

Liz sat in the car while Andy loaded his equipment into the back seat and came around to get behind the wheel. The brown bag lay on the seat between them, forgotten.

"Did you get as much as I think you did?" asked Liz.

Andy nodded slowly. "That was some lady."

"She kind of says it for the whole neighborhood, doesn't she?"

"Yeah." The car started with a grating turn. With so many different drivers, the station garage never could keep the fleet in smooth running order. "I know a couple guys," he volunteered. "They're redoing a house over on Ashland. You might want to see if they'll let you film."

". . . let *you* film." The tune had changed since the sex shop. Liz thanked her own hard head and the soft touch of the little black gingerbread lady in the big gray house for Andy Lewis's change of heart. It was "their" story now, not just hers, and that's the way it had to be if it was going to be good.

The car jerked away from the curb. Liz saw Lovey's patchwork face peering through the lace curtain in the piano room as they left.

Every story has its turning point, the hinge on which the before and after, the good and bad, this side and that, the opening and wrap-up turn. Elida Jackson was Liz's turning point. Studying the film, the close-ups Andy had taken of the wry old face as dry and wrinkled as a walnut, Liz knew she had her central image. Elida Jackson and her voluble memories would bracket the other images and interviews, almost like the living spirit of the neighborhood come to conduct a guided tour.

Liz was no longer thinking series; she was thinking half-hour special.

"That's unprecedented!" Steve tossed another palmful of popcorn into his mouth and looked up from a rerun of *America* on the educational channel.

"I just mentioned it; I don't want to distract you from Alistair Cooke."

"No reporter's ever had his own—or her—half-hour special."

"It's just a one-time thing; don't you think the subject matter's worth it?"

"Not intrinsically, no. It sounds like you've dug up a lot of interesting issues—'Robin Hood' theft to preserve the old wood that would otherwise be burned in vandalized houses; old people losing their homes to condominium projects; gays moving in; sweat-equity renovators making a profit on fixing up houses and selling them and moving on to the next one. All these things are important, Liz. I just don't see them having enough impact for a whole show."

"If you saw the stuff Andy's shot, though . . . I can't bear to snip most of it out. It's really the film that tells the story, and some of the house transformations are stupendous. I want to edit one like Cinderella being dressed in the Disney movie, you know? Kind of speed frame, with little birds flying in and out. . . . Maybe even get the staff artist to overlay some cartoon bluebirds carrying paint buckets and stuff."

"You're going to endear yourself to the staff editors if you keep messing with their jobs," Steve interrupted grimly. "This is not a one-woman operation."

"It just has so much *potential*!"

"So do we all," he said peevishly, "but you don't see the rest of us trying to hit everybody over the head with it."

Liz said no more, and settled back to try to concentrate on Cooke's learned and witty discussion of the massive influence barbed wire had on the American West. *He* had his own series, for God's sake. Couldn't a mild-mannered TV reporter from the Midwest try for a project worth doing when it cried for exclusive attention?

Within twenty-four hours, Steve had developed a head-ringing respiratory infection by the time he came home from work. Liz bedded him down with a nightstand full of aspirin, orange juice, cough medicine, and cold medicine. No wonder he had seemed a bit crabby the night before.

"Are you sure it's all right for me to go to the SDX meeting?" Liz asked, feeling guilty about looking healthy even in her black crepe goin'-to-meeting dress. She dipped to check her makeup in the mirror; everyday foundation and eye shadow always seemed underdone compared to the heavy makeup TV cameras required.

"Go ahead." Steve blew his red nose into a pink Kleenex. "It's so seldom that the journalism society schedules someone of interest to broadcast people. Damn, I'd like to have heard Jay McGovern."

"Well, I'll listen for you," promised Liz, pausing by the bed to stare down at a miserable-looking Steve. "Get some sleep; I'll be back by ten-thirty."

She blew him a farewell kiss—dared not risk *two* sick TV reporters—and rushed out, feeling late. It was odd taking her car out of its darkened stall in the parking ramp, odder still to realize that she was driving herself somewhere, alone, to a social engagement, not that SDX meetings offered much in the way of society. She and Steve had been in discreet but constant tandem so long that Liz felt, well, widowed almost. It was good for her, she told herself, to get out on her own now and again, and worth the trouble of trying to find a parking spot in downtown Minneapolis on a Thursday night.

The Press Club was in the Radisson Hotel, anchored by a bar— what else?—and a dining room. The decor was early railroad car. The walls were covered with journalistic memorabilia, mostly photographs of famous men who had spoken there. There were a good number of women at meetings these days, many of them from professions ancillary to journalism—public relations, public information, and so on. They enjoyed the "status" of being eligible for membership, but Liz had found it was still a men's club—male-run, male-oriented, male-benefitting.

She also found herself seated at a round table of men only and girded herself for being unremittingly trivial all night.

Where was Steve when she needed him?

The men already seated made some obligatory remarks about their luck in drawing such an attractive young lady as a table partner. Liz smiled mechanically and checked the other tables, hoping to spot a long-lost bosom friend who'd provide a pretext for moving.

"You've lost your name tag," pointed out a new arrival, another man, on her left as she impolitely craned her neck around the room.

"Those things never do stick." Liz patted the shoulder where the blue-edged rectangle had ridden just a moment before. "Somebody's probably walking all over me right now."

"Who is 'me,' so I can mourn the corpse properly?"

"Sorry. Liz Jordan, WBGO-TV."

"I'm TV, too. Jay McGovern." He extended a hand for a shake while Liz frankly stared.

"I'm sorry! I should have recognized you. I just didn't expect to end up sitting next to the guest of honor."

"The guest speaker. There's a difference, believe me, that comes sickeningly home when one rises to compete for attention with the ice cream torte."

Liz laughed. "It'll be vanilla and mint. It always is. I hate to say this, but—"

"—I look different than I do on TV. I never know if people mean better or worse."

Liz smiled and unfolded her napkin. She certainly wasn't going to desert ship with the guest speaker at her disposal. McGovern was a man in his late forties, a network broadcaster of the old school. There was something about him that spelled "newspaper"—maybe it was his pleasant but far from chiseled looks. In a field where fat hair and thin waistlines were the standard for both men and women, he was comfortingly and unconcernedly headed in the opposite direction. He looked like a "real" person.

"Jordan. That rings a bell," he said after sipping from his lowball glass.

"You're probably thinking of my father. . . ."

"No." McGovern squinted at her face, seeing past it. "Jordan. That Peabody piece on battered women, that's it!" McGovern's eyes focused on Liz again, and he smiled. "You owe me a drink.

"I do?"

"If I took after-the-fact bribes. I voted for you. I was on the jury last year."

"Oh. Well, thanks. I take it you liked the piece."

He nodded. "Good feeling to it, almost newspaperish, if you'll forgive me. I didn't feel the viewers got the gloss and the goose, so to speak. Or the subjects. What are you working on now?"

"The usual mixed-bag, jill-of-all-trades stuff. I anchored the morning news for a while, but got tired of getting up at the crack of dawn for an audience of moo-cows."

"Morning news is coming up. Even the networks are antsy nowadays to challenge *Today* for morning primacy. The local stations will jump into the race with both tripods one of these days; you watch."

"Anyway, I'm doing a great piece on gentrification in the ghetto, which is a fancy way of saying a lot of people are being pushed around by progress, and what's the cost?"

McGovern nodded and passed the rolls. "You ever thought of going the network route?"

Liz squeezed a roll to paste in her hand, then dropped its remains on her bread plate. "You mean a correspondent? I don't know; international travel doesn't turn me on. I like the American scene." She didn't say anything about how remote a chance she had at a network job. Many slaver but few are slavered after back.

"That's not the only way to New York," McGovern said obliquely. He patted in his dark suit jacket and pulled out a card. "Here's my office number. If you happen to be in New York sometime, give me a call. I'd be interested in what you're doing. The network's looking for good people all the time."

"They don't find too many," Liz said, smiling despite a sinking heart.

"Maybe they don't have good scouts like me," he answered. Then the man on his left, who'd been openly chafing at McGovern's attention to Liz, broke in with some pompous question about Watergate and the First Amendment.

Liz half heard the man's rambling sentences; he was clearly more interested in impressing McGovern with what *he* thought than drawing out the guest of honor. She studied the plain card with the New York area code before the phone number and the three-letter network logo. A contact in New York. Why not? Liz slipped the card into her too-tiny dress purse and tried to butter her flattened dinner roll.

McGovern tried to talk to her again that evening, but the men at the table had decided to bag him exclusively for themselves. None of them looked at Liz when they talked—and they talked quite a bit—or even when she talked. Common sense told her she should work to cement the impression she had made on McGovern. Her instincts told her not to bother; if she had to duel an entire dinner table to get a word in edgewise, it wasn't worth it. They were all newspaper men, and talked newspapers till boredom did them part. They cited McGovern's newspaper days, and tried to get him to admit that broadcast journalists weren't cast quite in the same mold. They even dragged up her father's name.

Liz sat silent, and McGovern answered politely until he rose to go to the podium and give his speech. It was witty and thoughtful and made no distinction whatsoever between print and broadcast media. Liz, lulled by the dull, starchy dinner fare, listened abstractedly. Then she heard her name mentioned—by McGovern.

"That broadcast and print journalism are only two sides of the same coin can best be demonstrated by one of your members," said McGovern. "Liz Jordan was weaned on the printer's ink at the knee of her esteemed editor-father, Zachariah Jordan, yet she works as a television reporter and does rather well for herself, to judge from the award her work has received." He went on to cite other local notables, such as Dave Moore, WCCO's eternally excellent anchorman.

The men at Liz's table turned injured eyes on her, but she sat smugly next to the empty chair on her left. For once, being Zachariah Jordan's daughter had come in handy.

— Chapter 29 —

elevenyears ago   Liz is 25,

It was a grim spring, that year of 1975. The Minnesota Vikings had lost the Super Bowl for the third time that January, a better omen than a groundhog that spring would be hard coming. But that was only a local disappointment. Aristotle Onassis died in March, ending a legend and widowing Jacqueline Kennedy Onassis a second time, but with none of the poignancy of the first occasion, with only a last drawn-out whimper in a drama that once had beguiled a world now weary of it. Nationally, the country seemed headed for a let down, too. Thieu resigned. The triumphant North Vietnamese finally swept into Saigon, sweeping the Vietnam War into the American history books as a lost cause both at home and abroad.

Liz read the papers and studied the fuzzy, front-page wire photos of new men and war machines patrolling a subdued Saigon.

and Mary Lou stopped teaching March 25th

With Watergate and Vietnam finally behind the country, it was as if there was no real news left to report. Everybody wanted something upbeat; people were tired of the oil crisis and rising prices, of distant military standoffs and corrupt politics too close to home, of Idi Amin.

Liz could almost smell the country's new mood—brisk, lemony as dishwashing liquid, capable of scrubbing away the stale political aftertaste of the past few years. Newspaper life-style pages were even more tenaciously trivial, resurrecting etiquette columns and fashion and home furnishing spreads, sermonizing with grim repetition how to save money on food, on clothes, on housing, on cars. Save, save, save. There was a recession on—didn't we know it—and saving would be our salvation. . . .

Liz wondered about her gentrification story and its contradictions as she reeled the miles of film onto the editing screen. It seemed to typify the national needs and divisions. On the one hand, saving vintage houses, making do with the old and making it better than the new, reflected the self-help trend. On the other hand, the dislodged minority and elderly populations, no longer welcome in their own newly chic neighborhoods, no longer able to pay for what no one had wanted until last month or last year or last week, seemed to be remnants from an earlier age of social concern who were silent now simply because there was no one to speak for them. The Vietnam War protesters were off the streets and easing into three-piece suits. Times were purportedly "hard" for everyone, so there wasn't much sympathy left for the truly impoverished; it was needed too close to home.

She and Steve were doing fine; the extra money he made as weekend anchor was being banked. Neither said what for, but the unspoken implication was a house. "There's one thousand eight hundred sixty-three dollars and fifty-four cents in the bank," he'd announce from time to time. Or "two thousand two hundred eighteen dollars and seventy cents." It was growing, and so was the need for more money down to buy houses, the prices of which kept escalating. They mildly envied Jeff Stone and his wife, who'd bought their house in the early seventies, and who, whenever the discussion turned to houses, would bring up their six percent interest rate.

That spring Steve and Liz began touring model homes at housing developments, treading carefully on boardwalks over mud to reach designer-furnished homes set down complete on empty acres given pretentious names like Pheasant Run and Valley Green.

"I'd never buy an old house and restore it," Liz would swear after every working expedition to the inner city. "They're gorgeous when they're done, but those high ceilings to heat and cool, and paint and paper . . . We're too busy to fool with that."

Steve smiled and listened. Houses were her bailiwick; his mind was more on station politics, which bored Liz blind.

"The grapevine has it that Jeff is being wooed by Philadelphia," Steve told her one Saturday morning.

"He wouldn't go there; Crime City."

"If they gave him enough money he would."

"You're thinking an anchor spot might open up for you?"

"Maybe." Steve crumpled the Sunday *Trib* into a pile and shoved it aside on the love seat. "But not likely. Even WBGO likes to import its anchormen full-grown. If I'm ever to anchor, it'll probably be somewhere else. That's why it isn't much use house-hunting here."

"It's consumer education. Besides, what else are we supposed to do on Sunday afternoons?" Liz settled down in her rattan chair. "So where do you think you'd like to go?"

"Wherever anybody'll take me. I don't know; I don't think things will ever get better at WBGO. If there was a chance of that, I might stick it out here. But the management's got all the imagination of a sardine."

"Maybe if you went somewhere else as anchor, I could switch to talk-show hostess," Liz speculated. "Then *I* could get Alistair Cooke for a change. Not bad."

Steve's gray eyes were knowing. "Try it for a while; you'll find out no silver lining is without its clouds."

It was fun to dream of a house, of going to another station somewhere else and doing something different. In the meantime, the days and nights at WBGO moved relentlessly on, one by one, newscast by newscast, story by story.

Liz almost had her series on gentrification shaped up when she skimmed the *Trib* one morning and was stopped cold by a small news item on the second front.

"Senior citizen found dead," read the headline. Liz didn't even know why she had paused to scan such a routine item. Maybe the name had flagged her subconsious.

> *Police found an 84-year-old woman, Elida Mae Jackson, dead in her home at 853 Marshall Avenue Thursday morning. There were no signs of forced entry or foul play at the home in St. Paul's Summit-University area, and preliminary findings indicate death by natural causes. Neighbors had not seen Mrs. Jackson for several days, but said that was common.*
>
> *Nothing was disturbed in the house. An autopsy will*

*be performed today to determine the cause of death. Mrs.
Jackson was a noted dance teacher in the Summit-
University area for several decades, and performed at
variety theaters in both Minneapolis and St. Paul during
the 1920s and '30s. She lived alone in the house, <u>which
had been in her family since 1916</u>, and had no known
living relatives.*

Liz let the paper sag in her hands. That wonderful film...
They could still use it, but she'd have to weave the awkward
fact that the woman was now dead into her narration. That
memorabilia-filled house. Who would get all the scrapbooks,
the dolls, and the wrinkled sheet music? Maybe the historical
society should be alerted. To die alone in your own home. That
wasn't so bad. Yet Elida Jackson had seemed so *alive* only—
what?—three weeks ago. Liz set the newspaper aside, already
planning how to adjust her narration track to accommodate the
inconvenient demise of the star interviewee. Halfway to sitting
down, she stopped.

"She *didn't* live alone!"

"Huh? Who?" Stephanie looked up, puzzled.

"This lady who died. I interviewed her for my house restoration
series. It says she was found dead and lived alone, but she didn't.
Why didn't they mention Lovey?"

"Lovey?"

"Her cat. It was the prize of her life. That's good human interest
material. Why didn't they mention the cat?"

Stephanie looked agreeably blank. "You tell me."

Liz picked up the St. Paul phone book. "Maybe nobody found
the cat; that was a big house. Maybe..." She dialed the St. Paul
Police Department and identified herself. "About that woman who
was found dead on Marshall Avenue, Elida Jackson. Was there a
cat there?"

"A cat?" The policeman on the other end sounded stunned.

"A cat. White and gold and black. Calico. I was just out at
Mrs. Jackson's house, and there was a cat there. I'm concerned
it might have been overlooked, might be stranded in the empty
house."

"The report doesn't say anything about no cat. I'm sure some
neighbor took it in."

"But she had very little to do with her neighbors; I doubt any
of them would even know she had a cat."

"Well, I'm sure it's okay."

"Well, I'm not. Is there any way to get permission to get into
the house and find out?"

"And you want to do this just because of a *cat*? Lady, there are *people* out there in real trouble, and we never get citizens calling up about them. But if it's an animal, everybody's concerned."

"That cat meant a lot to Mrs. Jackson. I'm sure she wouldn't want it starving to death simply because she had no relatives. Besides..." Liz felt suddenly inspired. "I might want to film the finding of it—if it's found—to go with the film I got on Mrs. Jackson several weeks ago."

"Oh, I see. Well, you'll have to talk to somebody higher up. Just a minute."

Liz hung on, growing more enamored of what had began as a lie to manipulate an unreasonable policeman and now sounded like a damn good idea. She finally got the media liaison officer, who—with some reservations—agreed that she could meet a squad car at the house and inspect it, with cameraman.

Luckily, Andy was in the building. Liz found him and dragged him to Roth's office, where she wisely left the cat out of it.

"Mike, that great old lady I interviewed for the series—she was just found dead in her house. I want Andy and me to go out and film a sort of silent farewell. The police will meet us there and let us in. Can you scrub any assignments you had us down for this morning?"

Roth looked pained, but then he always did. "You need this?"

"Oh, it'll really make the story—just a slow camera tour of the empty house, the dressed-up dolls, the piano. Great stuff, right, Andy?"

"Uh, yeah. Sure."

Roth glowered. "And this wraps up the series?"

"I swear." Liz flattened her palm on her chest in pledge-of-allegiance position.

"All right. But be back by noon. Somebody's got to do some daily work around here."

By the time Andy and Liz were on I-35 speeding—and that was exactly what they were doing—toward St. Paul, Andy was beginning to buy the idea, and Liz was beginning to get cold feet about the whole thing.

First there was the problem of confronting two policemen with a cameraman notorious for flouting authority. If Andy wanted to film something in the house and the police said no, there'd be trouble. Then, how was she to surreptitiously comb a strange three-story house for a frightened cat that might not want itself found? The only thing to do was come clean.

"I hope we find Lovey," she remarked to Andy as they exited the freeway at breakneck speed.

"Lovey?"

"You remember. Mrs. Jackson's cat she was so crazy about. When they found her, there was no cat around. Wouldn't it be neat if we found Lovey at the back of a closet or something? You know: one small happy ending for series, one giant step for cat-kind."

Andy scratched his nose, his jaw setting stubbornly. "Jordan, you're not doing this just because of that dumb cat, are you?"

"Don't you think it'll make great film?"

"Maybe. But only 'cause I'll be filming it," he answered with typical modesty. "This series of yours had better be good, or Roth's gonna want your ass on a platter, Candypants or no Candypants."

"Roth! I'm not worried about him. But I am wondering what happened to that cat. It'd be so easy to get lost in that big old house, particularly if it was scared."

Andy sighed. "Okay. I'll shoot the premises and if I happen to step on some raggedy cat's tail, I'll let you know.

The squad car was waiting for them—and a pair of young cops with mustaches and sideburns who didn't look too reactionary. They even helped Andy haul his equipment up to the front porch.

While one officer wrestled with the big safety lock, the other studied the narrow wood slats of the porch ceiling. The central glass globe light was black with years of trapped bugs, Liz noticed, shuddering slightly at the idea of probing too deeply into the old house's nooks and crannies. No restorer, she.

"Nice." The young policeman gave his verdict. "Sure don't build 'em like they used to."

"That's what my story's about," Liz said, darting inside as soon as the first policeman had the wide wooden door pushed open.

It was still in the house, absolutely quiet with the silence that comes from abandonment. Everything looked as it had before— the grand piano that flashed a grin of white keys from the parlor on the left, the stiff row of gaudy dolls sitting at attention.

Then Andy's equipment began hitting the tiled foyer floor in bursts as startling as gunfire.

"I'll shoot downstairs first," he said. "Go over the ground we got when we were here last. When the old lady was alive. Why don't you go upstairs, see if you can dig up that cat?"

"I hope that's not what I'll do." Liz shivered. "A cat wouldn't die in three days without food, would it?" she asked the policemen.

"Nah, they hang on longer than that. What do you want the cat for?"

"It was Mrs. Jackson's most cherished friend. I don't think anybody's found it, and it'd make a wonderful piece of film if we could rescue it."

The two policemen exchanged glances. Here it comes, thought Liz, the accusations, the recriminations. You brought us out here just to find and film a blankety-blank cat?

"You take the basement, Harvey; I'll try the attic. Why don't you stick to the second floor, Miss?"

"Right," Liz said in relief as they fanned out through the house. "Remember, call it softly. And her name is Lovey."

Afterward, she collapsed laughing when regaling Steve with a description of the event. "So these two big cops go crawling all over the top and bottom of the house. I can hear them even on the second floor—'Lovey, here Lovey,' in little, wee voices—above me and below me. And on the first floor, the baaadest, cop-hatingest cameraman in the Twin Cities is filming close-ups of dolls and doilies. . . ."

The expedition was a triumph of persistent police work combined with the guesswork of an inspired amateur. The cops could find neither scrawny hide nor hair of the cat at either extremity of the house, but Liz herself found Lovey huddled at the back of a closet and bore her triumphantly down the stairs, Andy filming the procession as the attic cop and the basement cop met her in the foyer and marched abreast into the front room.

"She's all right! I think." Liz scratched the cat behind its worry-flattened ears, the merest hum of a purr starting under her caressing fingers. Then the cops took turns petting Lovey. Andy filmed it all, and finally filmed the off-the-cuff stand-up Liz did outside the big, gray, empty house, the cat in her arms.

"So Elida Jackson is gone now," Liz said directly into the camera's single solemn eye. "But the house remains, and so does the creature she loved most in all the world. They say developers will turn this whole block of houses into trendy condominiums for the young professional set, who will never know Elida Jackson's world, or much miss it. And what of Lovey, the last survivor of eight fifty-three Marshall Avenue and an era? Someone will find her a good home and a new name. Something to fit the times. How about calling her . . . 'Condominium'?"

The television audience that finally saw the segment would never know that Liz brought the cat home with her. Steve was nonplussed at the new addition to their arrangement, but Liz pointed out that the cat was a well-behaved adult and very little trouble, save for food and litter box. She wasn't going to give it up, and Steve, seeing that, gave in gracefully. "Condominium" was too cumbersome a name for ten pounds of fur, even if it did make for good TV. Liz tagged her series *A Cat Called Condominium*, but Lovey was known in the bosom of her family ever after as, simply and sensibly, "Kitty."

— Chapter 30 —

Liz's overburdened shoulderbag hit her desk with a plop; some- times it felt so heavy she wondered if the cameramen weren't sneaking their equipment into it for a free ride.

It was two-ten P.M. and she didn't have much time to write some sort of piece on the latest and dullest of a series of govern-mental announcements issuing from the state capitol in St. Paul.

Stephanie Lynch came over to Liz's desk as soon as she saw her, odd behavior for a woman whose strongest characteristic was well-mannered reticence.

"Have you heard from Steve? Anything new?" Stephanie demanded.

Liz turned toward her, puzzled. "Not since last night...."

"Didn't you hear on the police radio?"

"I've been stranded in the halls of governmental gobbledygook since eleven this morning. What's happened? Someone kidnap Idi Amin or something?"

"Riot at Stillwater Prison. Then you don't know," Stephanie said, rather obviously. Caralee, too, had come over, silent and subdued for once.

"Know what?" Liz demanded with exasperation.

"Steve's gone out there to meet with the rioters. They asked for him. He's supposed to bring out their list of demands."

"Oh, God." Liz sat down. "When did he leave?"

"Must have been just after you—ten o'clock. The police called us in on it. We're the only station aware of it so far, I think. Of course, by going in, Steve gets the scoop."

"Why Steve?" Liz asked dully.

"He had the inmate spokesmen on *Mid-Morning* a few months back, remember? I guess the prisoners were impressed with him, thought he'd give them an honest break. Steve heard about it, and just went."

"Oh, great." Liz idly hit the return lever on her typewriter. "This story was complicated enough to write without worrying about Steve getting his throat cut."

"Roth's arranging for some film to be sent back in time for the ten o'clock news," put in Caralee.

"Great for WBGO. And in the meantime Steve's risking his neck. Have you heard anything yet from the prison?"

Stephanie's head shook. "It's all the way to Stillwater; must be thirty miles. I guess we won't know until the news tonight, just like the rest of the public."

"Well, I will. I'm going to ask Roth."

Stephanie stepped in front of Liz to block her. "You don't want to tackle Roth now; he's wired about this prison story."

"No time like the present." While Caralee and Stephanie watched numbly, Liz strode through the newsroom to the closed door to Roth's office. Liz didn't know if they were holding their breaths, but hers released with a sigh when Roth barked "come in." At least he was there to answer some questions.

"I just heard about Stillwater."

"So what's the matter? Sore because you weren't here to go on it?"

"No. I hear they asked for Steve."

Roth nodded. "It happens. Big break for the kid, to be dragged into a breaking news story like this. The network will probably run it, need a local follow-up."

"But it's so dangerous! How could you let him go?"

Roth leaned back, palms cupped behind his head, his smile sly. "Is this the same cub reporter who insisted on doing a stand-up outside a house where a crazed gunman was holed up her first day on the job?"

"That was different. I wasn't alone with said 'crazed gunman.' Convicts can really go berserk."

Roth leaned forward again, shuffling papers on his oversize desk. "Never happen; they're too media-smart to hurt a reporter. Hell, they need to *use* us. You get that government committee piece?"

"For what it's worth."

"It'd better be worth forty–five seconds, Liz. I need it. Oh, and that series on old houses ready to roll yet?"

"Yes, but . . ." She didn't want to get into it now, while only half her mind was on it.

"But what?"

"I edited it as a half-hour special. Lewis's film is superb. The people are fascinating, and so is the subject matter. I thought if we had a public service slot open—"

"A half-hour piece?" Roth frowned. "Okay. I'll look at it." That was a big concession coming from Mike Roth. Liz wondered why he was being so open-minded. Maybe the thought of the scoop he'd have if Steve perished in a prison uprising had made him generous, she thought ungenerously.

At any rate she left Roth's office with violently mixed feelings: unallayed fear for Steve's safety and a prickle of hope that Roth would buy her gentrification piece as she had packaged it.

The Stillwater siege went on, as prison uprisings often do, hour after weary, grinding hour. Liz somehow wrote her capitol piece, but hung around the station, anxious for news. By seven-thirty it became ironically obvious that she'd learn more from her TV screen at home than here in this supposed nerve center of news reporting, and guarded eyes wouldn't be watching her there.

The apartment was uncannily still and dark. She switched on the TV as soon as the lights were on, listening subconsciously for news bulletins. She wasn't hungry herself, but Kitty accepted a refresher of cat tuna with good appetite, then bathed and climbed onto Liz's lap. They waited together for the ten o'clock newscast, mesmerized by the television's image-changing flicker, Kitty dreaming slit-eyed and facing the screen.

Jeff Stone came on, his voice as charged as if he were announcing another presidential assassination attempt. "And reporting for WBGO from the riot scene at Stillwater State Prison is Steve Harmon, in footage filmed earlier this evening," he trumpeted like a ringmaster hailing the wild animal act.

Steve stood inside the prison walls, against a nondescript cement-block wall. He talked of prisoner grievances, poor physical conditions, overcrowding, and inmate racial tensions, enumerating the whole litany of ills plaguing so-called modern prison systems. He talked of the inmates' demands, and their threats if those demands were not met. He told of hours listening to the convicts and conveying their message to the warden. He talked of the long night it would be as they—and he—waited and watched inside a prison surrounded by state troopers. And then the film ended and Steve vanished, to be replaced by Jeff Stone's aggressively pleasant face. "In other news," the anchorman segued smoothly, "President Carter told an audience that the Russians' human rights policies . . ." *FORD* *TOOK OFFICE JAN   1977 author error*

"In other news," Liz softly told Kitty, "it's going to be a long, lonely night, Lovey."

Steve got back to the newsroom at five the next afternoon, beard stubble shadowing his face, dark circles making targets of his eyes, his clothes wilted. Yet he exhibited all the insouciance of a twelve-year-old boy who'd slept overnight in a riverbank cave without telling his parents.

Everyone clustered around him, crowding Liz out of the picture. Everyone had congratulations to offer, leaving Liz the only one still silent. Everyone seemed to regard the whole episode as an exciting game whose time clock had run down too soon, leaving Liz the only one feeling that eternity had slowly sloughed an aeon or two in the last twenty-seven hours.

She finally caught up with Steve, alone, in the makeup room, where he made faces at himself in the mirror as he shaved with the community Schick.

"You look like a foreign correspondent," she said, coming up behind him. Steve didn't stop shaving.

"Yeah. Hate to lose the only genuine five o'clock shadow I've had in my life, but I'm going on live with Jeff at six."

"No thanks to you," Liz said direly.

Steve flicked off the shaver's drone. "Live. An expert summation. What a break. The network wants an in-depth postmortem tomorrow, too."

"You couldn't tell me somehow?"

"No time. You know how it is, Liz. Wouldn't you have gone?"

She thought about it. "I don't know. Into a rioting prison? It's different for a man than a woman."

"I thought there were no differences."

"Women worry more," she said severely.

Steve put down the electric razor and pulled her into his arms. "It's all over and I'm fine. Plus I got a great story. Nothing to worry about—unless you're a competing station out in the cold, huh?"

She laughed, finally forgiving, and caught a glimpse of Jeff Stone retreating in the mirror, leaving them time to reassemble, to dissemble again for the rest of the newsroom.

Once a reporter covers a hot topic, he becomes an instant expert. Steve appeared on the public channel's local news show and for months afterward went before civic groups, with or without prominent former convicts, to discuss prison unrest and inmate grievances.

Roth didn't get around to viewing Liz's gentrification special until the prison story hubbub and the consultations with network brass had cooled down. Then he declared that the news department couldn't assign half-hour spots on the whim of a reporter. He offered her a two-minute, five-day run time for a series.

"That's ten minutes, Liz, an eternity in television news. Look, the half-hour version—and it's a pretty job, I admit it—ran twenty-four minutes. You only have to trim fifteen minutes. Most stories benefit from cutting, anyway." He smiled broadly before turning back to his eternal paperwork.

"Newspaperman!" Liz swore when reporting the verdict to Steve. "That's where he comes from. Doesn't believe the average

American has an attention span longer than five inches of type or thirty seconds of air time. And those figures probably reflect his own sexual performance statistics."

"Liz!" But Steve was breaking up. "Sorry. You're so funny when you're mad."

"Not beautiful? Cut the clichés. I'm funny when I'm mad only because you men think women are impotent. If I could really do something about an unimaginative boob shafting my story . . . it wouldn't be funny, not at all."

The only person whose rage—and expletives—matched Liz's was Andy Lewis. "I shot my ass off on that story. Can't that honkie see it's prize-winning footage?"

"I'll try to keep your best stuff in," Liz promised, and meant it, even at the cost of rewriting her perfectly polished script.

As a series, the piece was very good. It was just that the half-hour version was so devastating, so poignant, so . . . unique. She ached to prove it, but didn't even have the option of entering the uncut version in an awards competition. Only pieces that had aired were eligible. She even became paranoid enough to wonder if the special hadn't been *too* good to air. Steve was convinced that doing an outstanding job was the way to move up the television news ladder. He considered the Stillwater uprising a feather in his razorcut. Liz was beginning to wonder if standing out only made one an easier target for jealousy from above and below. *Amen*.

They argued about it as they had not argued before. He said she was losing perspective and becoming bitter, that nobody was holding her back but her own attitude. She said he was selling out.

And then the news consultants came to town.

They arrived like the angel Gabriel, with no warning but much blowing of trumpets once they were on the scene. And as on Judgment Day, the moment they descended on the station in their three-piece suits with their sinister locked briefcases and fat sheafs of computer printouts, all peace at WBGO-TV evaporated into intimations of job mortality.

There were long meetings with Gus Baer, the seldom-seen station manager, the owner, and Mike Roth. Newsroom rumors cut the air in group formation and veered wildly from one day to the next.

"They've been secretly 'studying' us for months," said Caralee. "Analyzing how much viewer recognition we each get. What we're seeing here is the death squad. There are termination notices in those briefcases. All the groundwork was done without us even knowing it. They just have fancier methods nowadays. I've seen this movie before."

"Not to panic, people," said Steve, holding forth by his desk. "It only shows this backward little operation has finally smartened up, is going to do things like the big network boys do."

"—and girls," Liz corrected automatically. Everyone who was gathered around grinned. How could things go wrong when Steve and Liz were doing their Man and Liberated Lady act?

"I don't know," said Stephanie. "I hear when these guys come in, the first thing they do is fire people."

"We've got contracts." Steve was trying hard to reassure.

"But they say *we* can't work at any stations around here if *we* leave *them*," Liz pointed out. "The contracts don't say *they* can't continue operating beautifully if *they* ditch *us*."

"You're overreacting, Liz." Steve was becoming distressingly prone to use buzzwords, Liz had noticed lately.

"I just know that nobody in the news business likes Maggot and Associates, or their ilk," added Caralee.

The name of Frank Magid and the thought of his semisecret computerized Iowa headquarters had put terror into sophisticated TV newsrooms ringing the country's coast since Magid began implementing his "happy talk" news formula at WABC in New York City in the early seventies. Most people reading the name "Magid" pronounced it Maa-jhid, as if it were kissing kin to "magic." TV news pros knew the *g* was hard, and that the only magic was how Magid kept getting big money for turning a TV news into a formula dog and pony show.

"Heck," said Gene Malone, the rotund weatherman who anchored his moon-shaped face with a bow tie, "I've seen an awful lot of changes, folks. I don't think anything too startling is going to happen this time, either."

"Is that a prediction, Gene?" Caralee asked morosely.

Gene beamed reassurance, the same way he did when a tornado watch was in effect. Looking at that unsophisticated face, viewers just knew any tornado that touched down would only sweep them to Oz and back, and they'd all be at the same old stand tomorrow—them, the house and movables, Dorothy, and Toto . . . and Gene the Weatherman.

Gene Malone was given notice the following day. A series of house ads appeared out of nowhere, fully scripted, filmed, and edited, touting the exciting advent of Dr. Lance Lambert, the new WBGO-TV meteorologist. In the promo pieces, Dr. Lance had lots of hair, dressed like a rock promoter, and displayed an unflagging grin. He pounced on the weather map playfully, a fond father cheerfully pointing out nearing bogeymen to a gathering of his simple-minded offspring. The air was rife with "T-storms" instead of Gene's old-fashioned thunderstorms, and the weather map seemed to have spawned fluffy flocks of cartoon clouds and formations of scowling thunderbolts. Dr. Lance, the narrator stated, wouldn't just *tell* you the weather like an ordinary, unapproved weatherman; he would *diagnose* the climatic conditions.

"What the hell does that mean?" Liz demanded of the TV set at home when one of the mysterious ads interrupted the ten o'clock news. "Diagnose the weather? Has it got a cold or something?"

"That's peripheral stuff." Steve dismissed it. "Weather's always been a service area. And Gene has been around a long time."

"The operator says people are calling in like crazy, wondering what's happening. They *like* Gene; he's as safe as houses. This guy looks like a yo-yo, a Gene Shalit who's gone to positive thinking school. Would you buy a used thermal chart from this man?"

"I think it's great," Steve said stoutly. "WBGO's like an old gray mare; it needs some new riders."

"Yeah, well, I've got a diagnosis for you," Liz returned. "You think you're sitting pretty because you did that star turn out at Stillwater. You think you'll come out smelling like a rose from an upheaval."

"Probably. And you should, too, Liz. You've done some good stuff. See, there's no point in worrying about a shake-up unless you're a slug."

The next day at work, there was more news. Marv Hubbard, 2 the piano-playing wake-up man for the country set, was leaving WBGO. Not fired. Leaving. For another position.

"A mid-morning talk show in L.A.?" Steve sounded incredulous.

"Not a bad spot," said Liz at lunch. They were lunching together almost every day if they could manage it; there was a lot to keep track of. "It's still unofficial, but I heard it from the *Farmers' Forum* cameraman. He liked working with me, and *hates* Caralee Koeppers."

"Yeah, but we don't know what kind of station it is; it might be a big risk."

"It's got to be a big *opportunity*, Steve. This is the Coast we're talking about. Home of Johnny Carson. Who knows, maybe someday we'll see Marv Hubbard on—*ta-dum*—national TV."

"That scarecrow." Scornfully.

"He's an ingratiating guy. Maybe nobody tuned in to see it, but because WBGO doesn't recognize worth doesn't mean that somebody bigger and better won't. You're just jealous," Liz teased, "because you'd love a Tinseltown talk-show spot yourself."

"No way. I'm going for anchorman."

"Here, you think?"

Steve shrugged. "Heads are rolling."

"Even Jeff's?" Liz was shocked. Jeff Stone was competent and popular; he seemed unassailable. "You don't *know* something, do you?"

"Wouldn't I tell you?" Steve smiled and downed the last of his chili sprinkled with grated Cheddar cheese and sour cream. Liz gobbled a spinach salad sans dressing.

She smiled back. Of course he would tell her if the management offered him an anchor spot. They lived together, didn't they?

When she stopped in the ladies' room after lunch, she found Caralee engrossed in pitching some makeup system to Stephanie. It would not only make you look good, but improve your skin while you wore it. Liz watched Caralee rub the lotions on Stephanie's hand in demonstration.

"What is that stuff?" Liz asked. "Something new?"

Caralee turned a blinding saleswoman's smile on Liz. "It's been around for some time, but it's not sold in stores, only privately by approved demonstrators. It's called Mary Kay Cosmetics."

"Never heard of it," said Liz, brushing her dark hair back from her face. *Eek*. Was that a tiny wrinkle running from her nose to her mouth? Were Maggot & Co. even now studying it in a film still of Liz with a magnifying glass? Maybe she needed Caralee's Mary Kay makeup after all. Mary Kay. It sounded so fly-by-night. What was Caralee doing selling the stuff, anyway? Selling. Liz turned. Stephanie was intent; Caralee was demonstrating as if her livelihood depended on it. Maybe it does—or will soon, Liz told herself, throwing her brush in her purse. Paranoia. They all had it. Except Steve, who seemed serenely confident.

Liz went back to her desk and fished through her top junk drawer, where she usually threw the few business cards she got in the course of a story. People like Elida Jackson and Beth Becker didn't carry cards. But Jay McGovern did.

The network logo looked bright and confident, just three little raised letters that meant in the TV news business what "I love you" meant to lovers. Bingo. Liz banged out a professional-looking letter on her ancient typewriter, then casually headed for the station morgue—where dead film was stored—and swiped the can that contained the unexpurgated version of her gentrification story. It would be intriguing to see what Jay McGovern would think of it. If he'd answer her letter. If he'd even give a damn. If he was still there. Who knows? Maybe the Maggot's boys in navy pinstripes had hit the network this week, too.

— Chapter 31 —

The summer of seventy-five. Two fixtures of Liz's childhood— from vastly different spheres—died that summer, Ivy Baker Priest and Rod Serling. In Liz's grade school in the fifties, Ivy Baker Priest, the national treasurer and only woman in high office, was held up as singular example of what a woman could achieve. From all Liz could figure out, that meant the exercise of signing her name to a bunch of one dollar bills—the highest denomination Liz ever saw in her allowance until she got to high school. Liz was unimpressed by Ivy Baker Priest's spidery but pervasive signature. Girls always got asked to do things like that because of their neat penmanship.

Rod Serling was a deeper loss; he had enthralled and terrified a whole postwar generation of kids. Commentators said that _fifty_ was a sadly y̲o̲u̲n̲g̲ a̲g̲e̲ to die, e̲v̲e̲n̲ f̲r̲o̲m̲ c̲a̲n̲c̲e̲r̲.̲ The person on *is* the street, newly health-conscious, gave a direr, more disapproving *57?* epitaph: "He smoked, didn't he?" And Liz and her contemporaries were simply shocked that their long-revered clipped-voiced guide to the televised bizarre was "so old." Liz herself turned twenty-five that summer of 1975, and shuddered at her accelerating maturity.

It was a dull news season, a summer of media discontent made dimmer by the stodgy stories that dominated the tube. The Rocke-feller Commission on the CIA found some hanky-panky but was accused of laundering facts until they came out in your basic government whitewash. They opened the Suez Canal again. An Episcopal priest allowed a woman to celebrate communion. The church's ecclesiastical court begrudgingly ruled that nothing but male tradition kept women from being ordained. Liz found local Episcopal would-be women priests for an "in-depth report," which meant that it was a s̲e̲r̲i̲e̲s̲ w̲i̲t̲h̲o̲u̲t̲ s̲t̲a̲t̲i̲o̲n̲ promotion *again again*

In Uganda, Idi Amin was acting outrageously, as usual, and in Athens, Christina Onassis got married. The hit of the summer movie season was a well-made cross between Ibsen's *The Enemy of the People* and *Moby Dick*. Steve and Liz huddled, like every-body else, in a dim, over-air-conditioned theater, and Liz jumped, like everyone else, when the dead body rolled bug-eyed and head-down from the submerged boat.

"I rooted for the shark," Liz groused as they slowly filed out of the movie theater into the heavy humid air of the street. "It was there first."

The station staff began referring to Gus Baer as "Jaws," but besides Gene Malone's firing and Marv Hubbard's defection, there was no more staff turnover. Talk of hirings and firings remained at fever pitch, however, although Caralee became more tight-lipped and silent as the summer wore on. Liz stayed out of it, sunk into her own personal summer slump, convinced that all her good work would go unnoticed by the visiting consultants if the cut of her hair was judged too long or the register of her voice was found inappropriate.

So it was a normal summer, in every way. It was also the summer that changed Liz's life, radically and forever. Steve gleamed that June, July, and August. He'd gotten lightly tanned, more the golden boy than ever, and seemed the calm, confident eye of an anxious storm.

"You *know* something," Liz teased him, hanging on his neck at home one Saturday before he left for weekend anchor duty. "Tell me, come on, tell me!"

He brushed it off, both physically and verbally. "Cut it out, Liz. You'll wrinkle my shirt. Don't you think I'd tell you if something were going on?"

Her eyes narrowed. "I don't know. Management doesn't like loose lips."

"Well, I do." He gave her a farewell peck and slipped away, safely unmussed.

That was on Saturday. Monday noon, Caralee Koeppers cleaned out her desk, grimly shoveling the contents of the drawers into plastic dress bags. No one dared approach her except Liz.

"Caralee?" Liz stood behind the woman, feeling awkward.

Caralee didn't turn, but kept on sweeping personal effects into the jumble in her bags. Liz noticed several boxes of Mary Kay cosmetics. Then Caralee spoke. "My contract's up today, they didn't renew."

"But surely there was some warning . . . ?"

"Forget the farewell luncheon, Jordan." Caralee turned, eyes bright and fierce. "We were 'in negotiation' the last two weeks. I wanted off *Farmers' Forum*. Like you got. Maybe that's what did it." Caralee turned back to the desk, her voice leaden. "Or maybe it was just an excuse."

"Who's going to do the *Forum* news, then?"

"Don't worry; it won't be you. They're bringing in 'a young new morning team.' Weather, news, the whole schmear. Sure, young." She snorted, a sound strangely out of sync with her normal, exaggeratedly elegant demeanor. "Only young fools would tolerate those hours with the kind of treatment you get around here. They don't even need me for the graveyard shift anymore."

"Caralee . . . don't rush off like this. It may sound silly, but— I'd *like* to take you to lunch. Come on. Stephie will come, too. We can have a good bitch session."

"No thanks." Caralee slammed the empty metal drawers shut in ringing sequence. She turned to face Liz and the watching newsroom. "Don't feel sorry for me; I'm out of this rat race. You're just past the starting gate, you poor young fool. Wait'll they throw you away like a used Kleenex—"

Her face and voice broke simultaneously, cracked like parched earth into deep, instant fissures of ruin. Caralee Koeppers looked old, older than Liz had ever seen her, and she suddenly sounded old. It was as if by considering her such, the news consultants had cursed Caralee to live up to the billing. Liz instinctively backed off.

Caralee looped the full bags over her arms and stalked out on her high heels, looking like an aristocratic bag lady.

"Too bad," Steve said over lunch when he heard the story. "I'm glad I was on assignment when the Dragon Lady left, though. She must have been smoking."

"She was too devastated to make much fire. I really felt sorry for her, Steve. She's a professional; she's been in this business for twenty years. My God, she's practically a pioneer."

"Pioneers shuffle off, Liz. It's a young *man's* business now— okay, a young *person's* business. That's just the way it is."

"You wouldn't be so blithe if you were the one past fifty."

"But I'm not." Steve smiled tolerantly. "Relax, Liz. The stations' going through a lot of changes now. For the good. Caralee and Gene Malone should have been axed years ago."

Liz did not relax. She felt a positively moral unease. She began looking at her colleagues, estimating their survival chances. Stephanie looked terrific but had a bland delivery. Keith was obnoxious but projected energy on camera. Steve was . . . well, Steve, and still looked good to her. Liz . . . what about Liz? Liz examined herself in the long slash of mirror over the rest room sinks. She didn't look a day older than when she'd come to the station. Her hair was more fashionably cut; her figure was under control, despite the Pill, thanks to having no fun in restaurants. Apparently, for the modern woman, it was either food or sex. But she was brunette. Dark brown. Not black and not blond, either one an advantage in TV news right now. Steve was calm, as relaxed as he told Liz to be. If Liz's job was on the line and he knew it, he couldn't possibly be so unruffled. And if his own were endangered, he'd be expressing audition tapes to every major-market station within the continental United States.

So relax, Liz told herself, brushing her lamentably dark hair. She didn't.

By late August, WBGO again had a whole new *Farmers' Forum* staff, including a newscaster. It had a new host duet named Scotty (him) and Stacey (her). He did the news and the agricultural interviews; she did chitchat and "Baking with Bacon Grease," as Liz had christened the cooking tips section of the revamped show. They were both blond, lean, hyperactive, and incredibly vacant.

"I'm going to barf." Stephanie eloquently clasped her concave middle when she heard the news from Liz.

"Don't panic; you've got the right hair color."

"Cut it out, Liz. Everybody knows you're the best reporter on the staff; they'll never toilet you."

Liz smiled ruefully. Peer praise usually only came in dire moments of honesty. These days, every day felt dire. Her phone rang, and Liz was grateful to retreat to her desk. In Liz's private analysis, Stephanie's job security was a toss-up.

The phone line scintillated subtly with a long-distance crackle; Liz perked up. Long-distance calls were always more glamorous than local ones, the way Marlene Dietrich always could outblond Hollywood starlets.

"Liz Jordan?"

"Yes."

"This is Jay McGovern. . . ." He paused for her reaction.

"Oh, sure! How're things in New York?" Pulses pounding foolishly, Liz sat down and—optimistic—turned her back to the newsroom and any eavesdroppers.

"Hot. In the high nineties. And there?" he inquired politely.

Come on, you didn't call about the weather. "It's dog days here."

"Is that a judgment made in your capacity as a weatherperson, or a newsperson?"

"Maybe . . . both." Here it came. Why he had called. Her damn film, of course, that she'd forgotten after the first hopeful weeks of waiting to hear.

"Listen, uh, Liz . . ." Uh-oh. Nice stuff, kid, but not what the network is looking for. "I've shown your film around—not easy; we've all converted to videotape. But I got the top people to eyeball it." He paused again, forcing Liz to say something.

"That's wonderful. I'd hoped—"

"They like it. They like you. They liked you both very much.

You'll be hearing from a Leonard Slater. He's a vice president. He'll be making an offer."

"An offer?"

"Right. I called to warn you, and to warn you to . . . Look, Liz. Don't, uh, play hard to get. Take it. Take what they offer for now. There are a lot of bright, pretty young women out there. . . ."

"—and a lot of bright, pretty young men," Liz interjected.

Pause. McGovern laughed lustily. He was old enough, and ordinary enough, to appreciate the dig. "All right. You don't sound like you're going to lose your head about this. The spot they offer may not be what you want, but go along. It's an in; there aren't a lot of them."

"But . . . don't they have to . . . interview me? See me?"

"They've seen you. The tape. It's too damn good to ignore. And I told them about your piece on battered women; the Peabody Committee lent it for review. You're in, kid. Don't fight it. See you in New York."

"Jay! Wait! Thank you. . . . I thought you'd only get somebody to look at the tape, consider me. I've got a contract here—"

"It's almost up; you think they don't check on those things? They're sure they can find a spot for you, Liz. And maybe . . . maybe they have some future spot in mind I don't know about. Believe me, if that's the case, you'll know you're competing for it. For now, you've just been promoted to national. Congratulations."

splitsville for Stevie

The line was empty, except for the usual monotone drone. Liz studied the receiver, reluctant to hang up until she understood what had happened. Jay said her tape was a huge success. The network people loved it; ergo, they hired her. Simple, if you were network people—maybe. Not so simple if you were small-town people working in a middling-sized city that didn't do things that way.

She looked around the newsroom, dazed. Everything seemed frozen, as if a ghostly figure in a network blazer had drifted through to whisper, "Come. Leave your minute-tens and follow me." If this were a commercial, Liz would spring from behind her dreary desk in ballet slippers, pirouette happily, and go leaping down the desktops and out the door, no questions asked.

Leave. Move. New York. Just go. Move up. Leave. Leave WGBO. Hallelujah! Leave upper Midwest cold. Hooray. Leave . . . Steve. Oh. Steve. Had to tell him. Where . . . ? Liz looked wildly around the newsroom, as if suddenly transported to a totally unfamiliar place and trying to orient herself. Of course, Steve was out for the rest of the day. Not due home until late. Shoot. Tell . . . Stephanie? No. Can't tell anyone. Tell . . . tell—Dad? Not yet. Just do your work today and wait for the call. Or tomorrow. It could come tomorrow. Or tomorrow, and tomorrow, and tomorrow. What agony. To know and to have to wait anyway. No wonder the Greeks hated prophets. And when he called—oh, God! The name. She'd forgotten the name. Um, um, Slater . . . Leonard Slater. So she wasn't a total nincompoop. And then tell—Mr. Slater—tell him . . . tell him yes! Anywhere, anything, Mr. Network Man. So easy, so idiotically easy. Liz threw her billfold into the air and caught it on the third spin, out of sheer exuberance.

"Liz! You going crackers?" Stephanie asked.

"Yes, Steph." She leaned confidentially across the aisle, whispering in an elaborately hushed stage voice. "As a matter of fact, *they're coming to take me away!*"

"I don't doubt it," Stephanie whispered back, humoring Liz with a solemn and exaggerated nod.

Steve, naturally, didn't get back to the apartment that evening until forty-five minutes later than he had estimated. While waiting, Liz restlessly rambled from the kitchen to the sofa in front of the television. Nibbling and loathing herself—the network wouldn't want a butterball; trying to watch television, failing—the network wouldn't want a nervous wreck, either; testing the chilling of the celebratory bottle of Asti Spumante bought on the way home.

It came to her then how few friends she had. Only through work, and then only if their friendship didn't trespass on common career ground. How few women friends. Most were "professional acquaintances," good for an amiable lunch now and again, a discreet exchange of vital statistics or life situation. "My husband's going to grad school . . ." "My father was always in journalism . . ." None of these throwaway lines ever merited more follow-up than a genial "Oh, I didn't know that."

If it came down to it, Steve was Liz's best friend, and vice versa. That was nice, she decided while pretending to watch *Petrocelli*. Men and women should be friends as well as lovers. Very advanced social thinking, or at least, more than most people achieved.

While musing, she had completely lost the plot of *Petrocelli*, and turned down the sound so she could listen for the nearing throb of a motor, the bang of a car door. Silly . . . but she wanted to tell somebody so bad she thought she'd explode.

When Steve's key finally scraped the lock, Liz was sitting tensely on the love seat. She jumped up the minute the opening door revealed a slice of his familiar figure.

"Steve! How'd it go?"

"Great. The governor's staff likes the idea." Steve had been pitching an idea to use *Mid-Morning* for mini political debates between Minnesota's Independent Republican and Democratic-Farmer-Labor parties. "And they even sprang for dinner at the The Blue Horse," he added, naming St. Paul's famous Esquire-endorsed restaurant on Grand Avenue.

"No wonder they put the governor's 'mansion' on Summit Avenue," Liz noted cynically. "Nice neighborhood diner to have." Prestigious Summit ran parallel to Grand, and when an official governor's residence was chosen a few years before, the opposition party carped heavily about its environment of mansions and old money, though it certainly made an impressive setting for state dinners, visiting Nordic royalty, and—occasionally—lowly local media types.

"So the shows are pretty well set?" Liz asked.

"Right."

"Then . . . maybe you can apply yourself to cracking the bottle in the refrigerator."

"Oh?" Steve followed her to the tiny alley kitchen, where Liz produced the wine bottle with a maître d'–like flourish. He took it and began wrestling with the typically resistant cork. "What are we celebrating? The gubernatorial nod to *Mid-Morning*?"

"That, and . . ." Liz stretched to bring down two wineglasses from a top shelf. A festive pop announced a ready flood of pale gold, bubble-bedewed Italian champagne into two slightly dusty everyday wineglasses.

"A toast," proposed Liz. "To my new job."

Steve's light eyebrows rose. "To your new job," he parroted amiably. "What is it?"

"Maybe . . . we'd better sit down."

"Come on, Liz." He trailed her into the living room. "Roth can't pull anything that surprising out of his assignment roster. Let's see. He can't have assigned you the dawn patrol again— WBGO has Scotty and Stacey to perk up our mornings."

"Yuck. Don't remind me. No, this has nothing to do with Mr. High and Mighty Roth at all." Liz kicked off her shoes and curled up on the love seat next to Steve.

"Well, you must be happy about it, and that doesn't sound like WBGO . . ."

"Nooo," Liz cooed over the lip of her wineglass. "That doesn't sound like WBGO at all. Precisely, my dear Watson."

Steve slowly lowered his glass to the glass-topped coffee table; the foot hit too hard anyway, striking a discordant chime. "You . . . haven't switched stations? Liz, you can't. Even if another local station made an offer, your contract won't let you work for a rival—"

"What if it's not 'another local station'?"

"Somewhere else?" Steve looked stunned. "That's flattering that they want to recruit you, but that's a big move for us, Liz. We're not ready—"

"Why not? You've been talking about going somewhere else ever since I've known you."

"Yes, but . . . that was talk, Liz. Daydream talk. We've invested a lot of time and effort in this place, this city, this station. You don't just go flying off someplace else for some will-o'-the-wisp of a better offer."

Somewhere midway through the speech Liz realized with sinking spirits that Steve might not receive her "good news" as she had expected. It made her defensive.

"You're the original 'rolling stone' when it comes to talking about leaving, Steve. You've always said WBGO is a third-rate operation. Why *shouldn't* we look farther afield—especially if it drops into our laps?"

"Nothing 'drops into anybody's lap' unless it's rotten. I hope you didn't go and do anything foolish, like commit yourself to something. What is the deal, anyway?"

"It's no 'deal.'" Liz's glass hit the coffee table, spilling a bit of the wine. "Honestly, Steve, if you'd just listen; it's the most exciting thing that's ever happened to me!" Her excitement was flooding back again, headier than champagne. She could feel her face glowing with the high of it.

"I thought I was the most exciting thing that had ever happened to you," Steve said coolly.

"Steve . . . This isn't going right. Let me tell you. It's the network. The Network! They want me."

"*Our* network?"

"Right. You know, those three little letters they announce every hour during the station breaks?"

"What do they want you for?"

"I don't know yet. I just got a call today that they'd be calling me."

"Oh." Steve leaned back, relaxed. "It's just hearsay. Honey, if the network really wanted to hire you, it wouldn't be just like that—you're hired. There'd be auditions and interviews." He smiled. "Who put this bug in your bonnet?"

"Don't be condescending. I could live with Neil Wetland for that. Jay McGovern called today with the news. I hardly think he qualifies as a tipster."

"McGovern." Steve was finally taking her seriously. "Jay McGovern. He was in town—"

"Right. I met him at the Sigma Delta Chi dinner. Remember, when you were sick?"

"That's right. You went alone. And you never mentioned meeting McGovern."

"It was hardly 'meeting' him, for heaven's sake. He sat next to me at the dinner table for a while, and the men at the table monopolized him anyway."

"You must have gotten something in edgewise."

"He was a judge on the Peabody panel. He'd seen *Battered Wives, Broken Vows*. Anyway, he told me to keep in touch—"

"So you called him up on the QT and hit him for a job."

"That's not the way it happened."

"Oh, now we're talking about an 'it.'"

Liz leaned away from Steve, angry and puzzled. "Steve, I'm trying to tell you the best news of my life, and you're acting like ... you're *grilling* me like a criminal, like I'm being *unfaithful* or something."

Steve folded his arms and looked blank. "Sorry. Go on, tell your story."

"That's what I mean. It's not a 'story'; it's what happened. Anyway, when all this upheaval with the consultants came up, I, ah, sent McGovern my unrun gentrification special, just to see what he thought. I never dreamed he'd show it around at the network, that they'd hire me on the basis of it."

"And that's what McGovern called today to say?"

"Yes! By George, he's got it! The network wants to hire me, Steve. On the basis of this one crazy fluke. Can you believe it?"

"It's tough, but if McGovern called ... He's a credible newsman," Steve conceded.

"So." Liz picked up her glass again, her nerves unfrazzling. It was almost ten, and they were both tired after long workdays. "So that's why the wine. We've got an out from WBGO. They can can us—hear that, can-can?—they can can us until hell ices over; we're off the hook."

"You are," Steve said.

"Well, me, yes. But you, too. You've been talking of leaving; now's your chance. McGovern said New York. The big time. I'm sure there'll be lots of opportunities for you."

"I don't want an 'opportunity.' I want an anchor job; and you don't just move and then pound shoe leather looking for those. I'm not ready to leave WBGO, Liz."

"Not ready to leave? But you've always wanted to, talked about it—until lately. Gosh, you can't love a management that canned Caralee and Gene the way they did; and the consultants, they're donkeys in Brooks Brothers suits ..."

Steve's mouth set stubbornly under the gold bristles of his mustache. His hands were tucked under his folded arms, so there was nothing of him to latch on to, to lean on, to touch, persuade. He was as self-contained as an Oriental idol, carved from emotions Liz had never read in him before.

"I think you're wrong," Steve answered. "The new WBGO could be a great place to be. But we've never had a chance to discuss that. You just went off into the wild blue yonder and secretly sent your precious, self-serving tape to your contact at the network. Talk about high-handed; you're doing a good imitation of Zachariah Jordan's daughter! You didn't even tell me."

"Tell you? These things have to be top secret, you know that. And what was to tell? Aren't I telling you now?"

"Oh, sure, now that it's all fait accompli. And anyway, what is the network offering you? You don't even know and you're ready to race off into the sunrise and drag me with you. Well, no thanks. I'm not sure I want someone as sneaky as you for a traveling partner."

Liz shouldn't have drunk the little wine she had; she could feel tears pushing to the surface like bitter, salt-laden bubbles.

"Steve, this was supposed to be a happy occasion..."

"That's because you were just thinking of yourself, Liz. Did you ever consider that I might not be ready to move east—or move at all? That I might have to give up something to traipse in your footsteps?"

"Give up? WBGO?"

"Yes!" Steve was angry now, his face flushed under his tan. "I'm going to get anchor when all the changes are made. They've been promising me that for a couple of months. This station has a chance to be good under proper management, and I've put in too many years of struggle here to walk out on it when a plum is finally dropping into my lap."

"Anchor. I didn't know..."

"It's not general knowledge."

"No, Steve. I mean...you didn't tell me, either. And you've known about it much longer than I've known about the network. How could you not tell me? I might not have sent off that tape. I might have reconsidered my own future..."

"Well, you did. And you didn't. Go to New York, Liz. Run right after that rolling golden ring you're so determined to snatch. Do what you have to to get there, to get ahead there; sleep with McGovern if you haven't already—"

"Damn it, Steve—!" She was standing, shaking, the wineglass in her hand, thinking of dousing him with it. "You know you have no right to imply that."

"I don't know anything about you." Steve's voice was distant. "Tonight's shown me that. There's one thing I do want you to know, though. That vague 'network job' someone will be calling you about. There's only one reason you got it so miraculously. They need women. And minorities. That's all. You're part of a catch-up quota system. The last thing they'd hire now is a white male. We're a very fragile majority, us white males; nobody wants us but the Ku Klux Klan. So don't preen yourself that you were hired for your news judgement or your way with a script or even your big brown eyes. You were just the right sex. And I suppose being Zachariah Jordan's daughter didn't hurt, either. It even <u>sounds like</u> you have journalistic credentials—"

Thank goodness there are NASTY men!

She threw the champagne. Not at Steve, at the floor. A frothy arc of droplets baptized the coffee table, Liz idly wondering if it would be too hard to clean up. For she would clean it up. Herself. Alone. After Steve had gone.

He was halfway to the door already. "Sure. Make a mess. Try to make a bigger mess than you made tonight!" The door slammed, shaking the apartment building, making neighbors freeze in their chairs and wonder what had happened—and to whom.

Liz sat there, in the light of a single floor lamp, watching the wine drops flung like a broken string of pearls on the glass tabletop, trying to figure it out. She'd done something extraordinary and unexpected. She was being sought, for whatever reason; she had the reason to lead. And Steve did not want to follow her.

What *had* happened—and to whom? *A jealous, threatened male!*

— *Chapter 32* —

"*If that network wanted you so bad, how come they're taking* so long to call you to New York, Elizabeth?"

"They have to wait for my contract with WBGO to expire at the end of November."

"Contract, networks..." Z.J. pulled another stogie from the Muriel box and huffed and puffed until he blew the smoke out. "It's hard for me to keep up with all this. You sound like you're becoming a movie star."

Liz smiled, glad the dimly lit living room couldn't illuminate the new hollows in her face, the dull quality to her hair. It had been a <u>harrowing three weeks</u>—<u>finding a new apartment</u>, working, surviving.

"What about that beau of yours?"

"Steve?" Her voice radiated blithe unconcern. Maybe Z.J. was right; she *was* becoming more of an actress than a newswoman. "Oh, he's doing great, too. WBGO made him anchorman. He starts next week."

"Hmph. Anchorman. *That* sounds more like some sailor than a newsman. What are they going to call *you* when you get too New York?"

"I'll be a correspondent. Now doesn't that sound like a writer, Dad?"

Z.J. chuckled. He liked to be cornered when he had asked for it. "Cor-res-pon-dent. Sounds writerly to me. Well, don't you worry, Elizabeth. I've got Myrtle to bake my biscuits and Neil to correct any typos my fading eyesight overlooks. . . . I'll get along fine. You sure you can't come back for Christmas?"

"Oh, Dad, I wish I could. But I'm supposed to fly to New York December tenth and get familiarized there and—well, they haven't assigned me yet, but it'll be a domestic post. No Middle East and bombs bursting in air."

"I should hope not; sending a delicate female into that sort of brouhaha. . . . Now, don't glare, Elizabeth; you'll scare Myrtle."

As if on cue, her stepmother emerged from the kitchen, bearing homemade fudge. Liz took a piece without her usual evasions. She'd lost enough weight in the past few weeks to afford a smidgen of gorging.

Myrtle sat down and the conversation turned desultory, Liz giving no clue to the physical, mental, and emotional turmoil that agitated her life at the moment. Here, at home, such upheaval seemed fleeting, as remote from the life of her father and stepmother lived as the real world is from the time-frozen inhabitants of a bell jar. Yet such conflicts, disappointments, and passions must stir small-town hearts as equally as those of city dwellers. Despite this conviction, Liz could never detect a trace of similar storms in her house or her old hometown. Today was no different. She had broken abruptly with a lover, even tearfully given Kitty to Stephanie, moved alone to a tiny new apartment she'd soon desert for yet another unknown residence in the country's largest strange city, and here in her father's living room, nothing seemed to have changed. It was a lazy, late October Turtle Bend weekend. No special occasion, no Sunday dinner ritual convened them. Except . . . Liz had come home to say good-bye.

She had driven up Friday, made a farewell tour downtown Saturday, and had gone to St. Clement Church with her father and Myrtle Sunday morning. She expected to come back again, but she didn't expect ever to be the same again. Liz saw everything through new, finally adult eyes. She saw it with nostalgia, the nostalgia Halley's comet would feel for the earth it saw barreling by again for the fortieth time. Ah, yes, I remember it well. . . . It was no longer her arena; there was no longer any illusion left of it being her arena. It was past, as past as the interlude with Steve. Interlude. That word implied a point between one thing and another, between past and future. Liz wasn't sure she had an emotional future. She felt as void as space, yet her so-called success made her seem like a dazzling, fiery comet in passing, burning itself out and making a spectacular show of it.

"I think I'll take a last walk around town," she told her father, bracing her hand on his knee as she rose. Old men's knees became vital domestic fixtures somehow, maybe only because their owners were less prone to rise. Z.J. habitually hooked his summer straw boater and his fall checked cap on his knee; perhaps he would have preferred grandchildren. Liz glanced to her solo photograph on the wall. Too bad; grandchildren were busy *not* aborning back in Minneapolis, with Steve. Maybe her father could adopt Steve to have grandchildren, as he had adopted Neil Wetland to become his journalistic heir.

"Walking again, Liz?" Myrtle sounded, for the first time, shrill. She was no spring chicken, either, Liz reminded herself. "Isn't much to see in town."

"No. But I may not be able to come back for a while." Silence greeted this subtle reminder that Liz's life was no longer fully her own, but the property of that mysterious, distant, and all-commanding "network."

In her old bedroom, Liz pulled tennis shoes from her suitcase; she'd had a hunch she'd want to leave the house a lot this weekend. The stuffed animals watched from the bureau as she sat on the sagging mattress to pull sneakers over her panty hose and don a headkerchief—a square cotton scarf—and tie it under her chin.

"Sharp, huh?" Liz asked her row of mute onlookers. There she stood in an odd amalgam of past and present, of the mature Liz of today and little Lizzie of tennis shoes and headkerchiefs. She petted the rabbit-fur cat, cradling it for a moment. Could a big, grown-up network correspondent take a stuffed cat to New York? She set the cat down and glanced at the sadly untouched pink dog. Perhaps it wasn't only getting it at too old an age that had made this stuffed toy so redundant. Perhaps it was because it had arrived after Whizzy had departed.

"You've got to think of it like an allergy, Elizabeth," her father had said. In her mind's eye he looked the same as he did today, as he had always looked to her—big and white-capped, like a mountain or a wave.

Liz swept the fat pink toothlessly grinning stuffed dog off the bureau. It hit the floor soundlessly, and she felt foolish, looking like a refugee in the mirror with her chin-tied scarf, tears streaking her cheeks. She wiped them away with her palms and picked up the stuffed dog to reinstate it in the accusatory row of mute animal faces. She remembered now; she hadn't won it at school. Her father had brought it back from the county fair just before her senior year began that summer of 1966. Just after Whizzy had vanished to the "better place." That was why she'd never named the foolish pink dog, and why she had never dared throw it away. It was a consolation prize.

She restored it to its post now, feeling a wave of sorrow for it—poor unloved, unwanted, inanimate thing. It hadn't asked to be an inadequate substitute, an unarticulated attempted bribe from father to daughter. . . . Liz turned and headed quickly through the house, calling a fast "good-bye" to anyone who could hear so she didn't have to pause and be seen.

Outside, the potpourri-scented October air glinted with sunshine and glittering motes of gold dust—leaf chaff fallen from mighty oak, towering elm, and graceful birch trees. The dead leaves crackled beneath her rubber-soled shoes, conjuring memories of leaf forts and suicidal leaps into piles of caramel-colored leaves as high as her head, of the smoky autumn fog exhaled by burning leaves diffusing an odor like incense to spread against the twilight benediction of the small-town sunset.

There would never be autumns to match Turtle Bend's, Liz knew. Tree-starved cities celebrated seasons—like winter—that you could mark by buying things . . . Halloween, Christmas, Easter. She kicked her way down the quiet afternoon streets. In cities the odd fanatic jogger would have shared the street with her; in Turtle Bend nobody jogged yet and maybe nobody ever would.

She made her way, purposefully aimless, all the way to St. Clement Church, neat and spire-marked, and passed under the lych gate to the churchyard.

Liz had never considered her mother an early death, although she'd visited the grave many times as a child, enraptured by the chill glamour of death as only the young can be. Now she paused before the familiar double headstone with "Jordan" written large at the top, one shiny marble side vacant, waiting for her father, the other carved with the rudiments of a life Liz knew nothing of. "Dorothy Marie. September 3, 1912—May 28, 1951." Now thirty-nine didn't sound so old.

She wondered if her father would rest here when he, too, died, as he had taken for granted in 1951. Or would a new plot be bought, so Myrtle could someday take up a position beside him? It was an awkward dilemma and would be resolved, inevitably, by Myrtle; Liz couldn't picture that stringy, hard-bitten woman predeceasing her father. No, Z.J. would go out like a firecracker—suddenly and spitting sparks. Myrtle would shrink, slowly, slowly, until only her arid bones remained, and then they would bury her.

The leaves chattered dryly against the headstones as Liz left the graveyard, thinking of Walt Whitman's reassuring poetic fancy that grass was the hair of the dead, new growth from old bodies, that the earth returned its death to life in every leaf that grew. She herself was, she supposed, a single leaf on the ancient, ever-spreading tree of humanity.

Beyond the Episcopal cemetery a stone-studded brook ran through a grassy gorge. Liz crossed the wooden footbridge, hearing the rilling water below choke on its annual fall meal of dried leaves. In a month or two it would ice over, and then freeze, only to break out gurgling again in the spring. How nice, she thought, to be a brook, to be temperamentally certain that the winter freeze that numbed all motion would be followed by a spring thaw.

Liz felt as if she would never thaw again, as if everything touched her from a respectful distance. She felt the cool fall wind burnish her cheeks, and was grateful for the kerchief protecting her ears. She felt the sunshine warm the top of her head. The warmth went no further.

Eventually, she came to the River. The River. It had a name, originally French in honor of the region's first white settlers, now flattened to a set of syllables a French fry wouldn't recognize. The brownish trench of water rippled, letting the breeze rumple its broad breast at will. Liz stood at the curve of it, where it angled west for a bit before making a lazy S and heading east again. It was like standing at the inside angle of a boomerang, the river almost forking around her. Ahead of her, amid the constantly moving water, was a small, flattened limestone plateau, a Hollywood miniature maker's Lost World sticking its stubby neck out of the enormity of The Flood.

Turtle Rock. They sunned on it, the hand-size snapping turtles whose periscopelike heads often dappled the muddy waters. One sat there now, motionless, letting time and the river run by, to wherever they both thought they were going so fast.

Liz sat on the bank, even though she knew the ground's autumn cold would soon impress itself on her derriere. She clasped her hands around her knees and watched the water. And then she let herself think, for the first time in three weeks.

As enduring, as cooperative, as supportive, as rational as her relationship with Steve had been for more than two years, so had its disintegration been swift, bitter, excessive, and irrevocable. He had not come back after storming out the night she told him of her network offer. Liz had pulled a blanket from the linen closet shelf and slept on the wicker love seat; she didn't want to be in bed if he did come back. He didn't come back the next day, either; Liz began packing her belongings, not sure where she'd take them.

Steve finally returned—they'd caught glimpses of each other at work and immediately pretended they hadn't— and surveyed Liz's semipacked boxes.

He nodded, approvingly. She spoke first.

"You scouted this apartment; I guess it's yours."

He nodded.

"I guess you can afford to pay all the rent, anyway, with anchor pay."

He nodded.

"Andy Lewis is going to help me move my stuff tomorrow. He's got a van."

Steve's light eyebrows raised the roof of his bony frontal ridge. "Great; that'll look just great around the station."

"So what." Liz was angry and stomped into the bedroom to get some more clothes.

Steve stood by and watched her. It was awkward. She had relinquished claim to the space, but had to stay another night. She didn't know where Steve had been the last two nights, and didn't care.

"The network call?" he finally asked, so sullenly she didn't feel like answering.

Liz straightened from wrestling a carton of books shut, interweaving the stubborn flaps into the classical position. "Yesterday." She smiled grimly to think how she would have felt if McGovern's warning had been false, if all this had been for nothing.

"And . . ."

"I'm going to New York in December, after my contract's up."

"To do what?"

"Correspondent," she spat out.

There was silence while she shoved her belongings into a tidy moving-day pile. Steve had not offered or made any motions to help. It was just as well; the struggle was burning off Liz's destructive energy.

"I guess I'll get lost, then," Steve announced to the room in general. He paused on the threshold. "There's no need to let the newsroom staff in on this. I'm staying, after all . . ."

"Of course," Liz snapped. "You'll still be Sir Galahad at WBGO."

"I never pretended to be your knight in shining armor."

"I wasn't thinking of that. I was thinking that Sir Galahad was

the one who was so busy chasing that damn Grail that he never
had much time for human relationships."

"*You* say that? You're the one who can't wait to skip town solo
when a hot job offer comes up."

"Hot? I thought the network was throwing me a bone because
it needed to put some women on its personnel lists."

Steve's eyes were flashing silver fire. "Can you say they didn't?
Can you honestly admit that there weren't dozens of more qualified
guys *ready* to go to network, who'd paid their dues, that you
didn't ace them out because you batted your eyelashes at a Peabody
judge at a dinner and you happen to be the fashionable sex at the
moment?"

"If you believe that . . . no! I earned it. You saw me break my
back on my stories. That's why they were good. That's why I'll
make it on the network level. That's why——" Goaded, she spoke
the truth she'd always spared him. "——you'll never get there; you
aren't network material, Steve."

He was silent, stunned maybe, to realize that she had been
judging him professionally all the while he had been judging—
underestimating—her. His look for the long seconds before he
opened the door and left stayed with her a long time.

She saw it again now, reflected in the river's restless, neutrally
colored, shifting water. Steve had looked angry, bewildered,
stricken; he had not looked like a man who had—ever—loved
her.

Was it so easy to not love? Liz didn't find it so. She still loved
Steve, despite realizing that he'd always thought less of her than
he expected her to think of him.

Their breakup had taken all the gloss off the network job. When
Slater had finally called, he found a Liz Jordan who was articulate,
calm, calculatedly upbeat. Professional to her toenails. It was not
the Liz Jordan he would have talked to two days ago, but she
would suffice. She would function smoothly in a fast-paced, hard-
edged, hustle-bustle world with little time for deep and lasting
personal relationships.

And what was deep and lasting? Certainly not the shifting,
shallow river. Certainly no one's grip on life; look at Dorothy
Marie Jordan. Certainly not romantic love; Steve wasn't even a
sentimental milestone to whom she could make fond pilgrimage
in her memory, like Herb Boyle, the farmboy who'd believed in
her more than a college man from Idaho. Betrayals like that were
hard to look in the eye. It would take Liz years to sift the wreckage,
to isolate the seeds of self-destruction in that semiperfect romance,
in Steve. In herself.

In the meantime, she had to walk away from an even earlier,

more easily betrayed part of herself. She was here at the river to say good-bye to little Lizzie. And yet, unawares, something else danced at the edge of her consciousness. Not the ghost of little Lizzie playing near her mother's grave, not an image of herself at all, real or imagined. But still it hovered, unbanishable. It pounced among the long, dry grasses; it rolled like an almost invisible ball of energy down the long slope to the very river's edge. Her ears almost heard a small splash; she almost felt the spatter of fat droplets of river water...

"Whizzy, don't shake!" someone yelled, some girl who'd gotten a puppy when she was six years old and had named it perfectly so she'd be embarrassed ever after. Stupid name. Stupid shaking dog. The bright, foxy face tilted, ever-sensitive to her every twitch, her every mood. In the window, waiting, barking soundlessly through the front window glass, after school, every day. Sitting up, narrow front legs folded beseechingly, waiting for a tidbit flung through the air and leaping, up like a fish, snapping, wriggling back down to earth. Sleeping by the side of her bed on a homemade rug with the fuzzy images of a lamb and a duck worked in, pointed face on pointed paws.

Where was he? She had never asked her father—what farm? Who are the people? She had never asked her father. Had he heard? Was Whizzy well, alive, happy, dead? She had never dared ask. But sometimes she thought... only two years. Whizzy would be twelve. That's not so old for a dog. On college graduation, while her classmates ran their silken tassles through their hands, Liz looked into the distance and saw a summer river and thought, Whizzy would be fifteen. He could still... At the Milwaukee *Observer*, doing the feature story on the local Humane Society, staring through the chicken wire at dozens of eager, loyal, forsaken doggish faces. Whizzy is seventeen and he... could... still...

Liz's palms slapped the hard, frostbitten earth. It is 1975, and Whizzy is twenty, and he could *not* still be anything. Tears were pouring down her face, seemingly shaming the river for speed and volume, while her fingers unearthed fistfuls of dead yellow grass. Her face felt made of Silly Putty, all twisted, as if her features were disowning her, or melting in the acid of her tears. Still Liz kept her hands away from her face as she cried... bawled... as she never had before.

Her palms pounded the ground. "You shouldn't have done it, Daddy. You shouldn't have done it," she sobbed out, voicing what had always been an unspeakable secret before. "It was wrong, Myrtle came second. I was there first. Whizzy was there first. We had a right.... Why? Why? *Why?*"

It was an old question, and there was never any answer. Liz

finally got up, drying her eyes child-style with her dirty palms. Her face would recover on the long walk home; she'd have to remember to wipe it of dirt traces. By the time she got home, she'd look her normal, collected, mature self again. The turtle had left the sunning rock, she saw, and the afternoon was turning cooler. Liz walked home. She had said <u>good-bye</u> to her mother, and <u>to Whizzy, finally.</u> Now she had to say it to the living, who were so much easier to leave.

PART II

Now no matter, child, the name:
Sorrow's springs are the same.
Nor mouth had, no nor mind, expressed
What heart heard of, ghost guessed:
It is the blight man was born for,
It is Margaret you mourn for.

—GERARD MANLEY HOPKINS

— Chapter 33 —

"Your father was a grand man."

"I know. Simply grand."

"It's too bad you, he—" The woman paused to bisect a poppy seed roll with one bite. "—that he didn't live to have any grandchildren, you know? He would have been a wonderful grandpa. We're so sorry to lose him."

There it was, the small-town swipe at the unmothering woman, tucked into the center of an innocuous sentiment like a bitter patch of poppy seed in a bun. Liz hated poppy seed, and it was sprinkled as generously as bad-grade caviar over the donated baked goods ladening the dining room table in her late father's house.

"Have a sweet roll, honey. It'll do you good. Energy. This is harder on you than you think." A faint aurora of hair net haloed the next woman's gray-brown frizzle. This face was more familiar. Liz remembered seeing it a few decades ago over a geography textbook.

"Thank you, no, Mrs. Thompson. But everything's wonderful. This food—I don't know what we'll do with it all. . . ."

"No wonder you're so skinny. Every time I see you I think, There's little Lizzie Jordan and, my, it's a shame how thin they keep her. This one's got homemade currant jelly—"

Liz edged away, her smile as cloying as the offered roll's sugar glaze. This was worse than covering a royal wedding. "Thank you, no," she was still muttering as she edged right into Neil Wetland, who was placidly gumming one of the rolls.

"Welcome back," he observed caustically. "You staying long?"

Liz checked the subtly opulent Piaget on her wrist. "About an hour more. I've got to get back for the show tomorrow."

"They can't give you more than a couple days off for your father's funeral?"

They could, but Liz hadn't asked.

"That's network journalism."

"I'd hardly call *Sunrise* journalism." Wetland finished his sweet roll and licked his lips, watching her carefully.

No. She would not get into the old argument at her father's funeral. Especially not with Neil Wetland.

"It picked up an Emmy nomination," she said coolly. "Speaking of award-winning journalism, how's the *Sentinel*?"

Wetland's shrug did nothing for the fall of his ill-fitting pin-striped suit. He was the world's oldest thirty-five-year-old and didn't look much different from the twenty-five-year-old J-school whiz kid who'd turned up on the *Sentinel*'s doorstep ready to do anything for the legendary Zach Jordan. And he had done every-thing—typesetting, and keylining, selling, even the social column—up to becoming chief reporter and managing editor, always carefully stepping in Z.J.'s shadow.

"The *Sentinel* won't be the same without your father," he said finally. Like most print journalists, Neil had a genius for restating the obvious flatly. Bitchy observation, Liz, bitchy, she told herself.

Liz sighed. "No, it won't." She looked around the crowded rooms of the small clapboard house she'd grown up in. The only framed piece on the wall was her high school graduation photo, the one that made her look like an underage bobby-soxer. She'd sent other photos home from afar—stills of her doing stand-ups in front of the White House, the Scavullo portrait that made her look like Raquel Welch, that had been commissioned when she'd taken over *Sunrise*. Her father had never hung one of them. Or maybe Myrtle was responsible for their absence. Liz wondered if they resided in the same sea of lost photos that held Dorothy Jordan's faded 1940s face.

"Turtle Bend will miss Dad, too," she added, but Wetland and she had edged mutually away from each other. Another late-middle-aged, overweight, unmade-up and uncoiffed woman turned to add eager alleluia.

"Oh, that's true. So true. My, don't you look better! I mean, better than you do on TV. Not but that the funeral's been a strain. Would you like a poppy seed roll, dear?"

"The will won't be read until Friday."

Liz made an uneasy, dismissing gesture, but Myrtle persisted.

"You really should be there, Elizabeth. There may be something in it you'll take exception to."

"Have I ever taken exception to anything?" Liz's tone was innocuously bland. Her eyes were iron.

Myrtle patted her overpermed gray hair and looked away. "Goodness. I think there's a vacancy on the table. I'd better bring out these cold cuts from Mrs. Velezny. . . ."

Three middle-aged women waddled in bearing empty platters and Myrtle was gone. Liz followed, pulling her aside by the dining room plant stand filled with deep purple African violets in full unscented bouquet.

"There's one thing I want. A photo. Of my mother. It was taken in the early forties. A woman with a heart-shaped face. Upswept sides, shoulder-length page boy . . ."

"Oh. There's a good portrait of your father, too. He had it taken for his column."

"That'd be nice. But the one of my mother—I haven't seen it . . . for years."

"You'll have to try one of the boxes in the attic. I really don't know where it is. I wish you'd told me you wanted it sooner. Right now . . ." Well-wishers were ringing the widow again, and the only daughter was about to leave scandalously early.

"That's fine. I'll just run up and hunt for it."

Nobody missed Liz. She shut out the noise of their invading sympathy as she pulled shut the door leading to the unfinished attic. It was the house her father had bought for her mother and himself—neat, then-new 1940s clapboard. The rust-painted attic stairs had always seemed alluring to Liz, a sinister, gory passage to mystery above. But all that lurked overhead were open rafters aged to the color of strong tea. Under the attic's slant-roofed eaves reposed an assortment of ancient suitcases, discarded lamps, and cardboard boxes.

Liz rooted through oddments of clothing, stacks of outdated sheet music, small boxes crammed with thread and broken beads. She found her photos in their original envelopes at the bottom of one carton. In another—the glass cracked and the once-gilded wooden frame dull—she found the photograph of her mother. It was smaller than she remembered, and her mother looked younger. Liz's age. Contemporaries. Two almost-forty women nearly four decades apart.

Liz slipped the frame into the manila envelope with the photos of herself and, squatting in the dust and the unheated November chill, checked her watch again. Damn. Her flight left in two hours. She'd have to drive her rickety rent-a-car like a bat out of hell. Liz stood stiffly, listening to her knees give an eerie attic creak. Amend that cliché for accuracy, Jordan, she told herself. She'd have to drive like an *old* bat out of hell. How Con would have laughed at her vanity. . . . Con. The wrench of another recent funeral, far more public and yet as private, made the empty attic landscape shift erratically, until she felt like a child fleeing imagined demons and clattered too quickly down the steeply raked wooden stairs, the sound simulating a matching heartbeat.

She paused on the step before the closed door and resumed her public face, listening to the murmur of the world beyond. Time to say good-bye to Myrtle, the people of Turtle Bend, the whole damn town itself, and get back to civilization. She'd already said

252

good-bye to her father. Over and over. Many, many years ago. If only he had listened.

"I just don't see why you have to go so far so fast, Elizabeth; there's plenty of news happening here in the heartland. More, maybe. It's like you're running away." Green vinyl squeaked as Z.J. grumpily adjusted his reclining chair.

"It's a super opportunity, Dad—network correspondent after only two years on a local station. . . . People would kill for it. And you don't need help at the *Sentinel*, you say. You have Neil."

Her father's hand dismissed Liz's interest in the family newspaper. "You know what you're gonna end up doing, Elizabeth?" he began in his best addressing-an-audience manner. "You're gonna end up marrying some slick Eastern fellow who can't talk without sounding like he's gargling baked beans; you're gonna quit your job, have a bunch of kids, and you'll be stuck out East so your poor old father'll have to get on a goddamn aeroplane and go fifteen hundred miles just to see his grandkids!"

Z.J.'s cigar puffed defiantly as he gave both Myrtle and Liz a final, wordless nod.

Shards of that ten-year-old conversation with her father, when he had taken her promotion to the network as a kind of rejection, shifted like broken crockery in Liz's memory as she drove away from her father's funeral, her father's town, her past. She wanted to put the pieces together, but there were too many.

Once she had crossed the Minnesota border, she checked her watch and subtly depressed the gas pedal. Her home-state fuzz were notorious for hounding speeders, but Liz was out of their jurisdiction now and she had a plane to catch. There'd be hell and maybe even her so-called career to pay if she wasn't in Studio 8G on Lexington Avenue by five tomorrow morning.

Twin Cities International Airport offered a bustling but oddly lifeless stretch of nondescript concourse and regimented waiting area. It had scared the hell out of Liz the first time she'd been sent there to interview a passing-through celeb for WBGO, never dreaming that within two years she'd be winging her way east from this very airport.

Beyond the interior bustle, a sweep of ashy wan December sky pressed down on the equally gray tarmac. Even the planes' shark-sleek bodies looked insubstantially pale as they silently skimmed the flat winter landscape, at times only the sharp projection of their tail fins leisurely knifing the visible distance.

Liz arranged herself expertly in the black vinyl slings that passed for chairs near her flight gate, studying the ghostly reflection she glimpsed in the windows overlooking the tarmac. She couldn't discern specific features but knew well enough by now what her public appearance was. It had become a network icon, polished, buffed, and refined for years by a series of TV makeup people and Liz herself. Thirty-five now. Liz mulled shaving some numbers off her official bio and as instantly rejected the idea with something of Z.J.'s fabled indignation. She was a journalist, not a movie star. . . . Except that the two professions seemed to be playing footsie these days, both behind and in front of the TV cameras.

The window-mirrored Liz tilted her still-dark head at herself. It wasn't a bad package; magazine and newspaper articles usually admired her "dark good looks and contralto voice."

It was not what she had looked like a decade ago, when she had sat there, perhaps in this very spot, at the same season of the year, and nervously waited to board her first plane to New York City.

"Passengers may now board Northwest Airlines flight 42 to La Guardia." The stewardess's voice thundered over the microphone into the air above Liz, as shrill, sudden, and unnatural as a sonic boom.

For an odd, awful instant, Liz Jordan plummeted through a hole in time. The busy airport noise of echoing voices and baggage trolleys exploded into full volume, as if she'd just removed her own private set of earplugs.

La Guardia. New York bound. A still slightly startling destination, though Liz had flown there enough times to consider it routine. She joined her fellow travelers in gathering her things—a large, businesslike purse and folded garment bag. She had finally learned how to travel light; she had always known how to travel alone.

Her first-class seat bordered a window. Looking down on a remote, somehow alien world in miniature always awed Liz. She buckled her seat belt and tucked her purse under the seat ahead, ignoring the passenger who settled next to her. Solitude was the rule when she traveled, particularly now, when she was hamstrung between the benchmark of burying her father and heading back to New York and the network to examine the terminal carcass of her career.

Time passed quickly. Before Liz had floated fully away from a free-fall into the past, the gray, glittering island of Manhattan was unrolling below her. She knew it from fore to aft now, from Greenwich Village art galleries to SoHo lofts to the co-ops and penthouses of the upper Nineties. She could hail a cab on a windy corner in a typhoon, and probably beat somebody who'd been there first out of it. Her walk was fine-tuned to keep street people clear; she could find her way blindfolded to the most pricey hairdressers along 57th. Liz took for granted eating at restaurants tourists visited after years of longing as pilgrims had flocked to Mecca. She knew Elaine of Elaine's, or—more important—Elaine knew her. So did several of the solid but undistinguished Irish pubs that dewed the sidewalks of Manhattan like shamrocks springing from concrete. As the plane's wheels touched tarmac again, Liz wondered if McGillacuddy's or O'Hara's would ever see her again. . . .

Liz was pushed back in her seat as the whining engines reversed, as if some powerful hand had planted itself on her chest to keep her from disembarking, from making the familiar journey to her midtown apartment, to the network in the wee hours of morning, ever again. As if someone was saying, "No, no, no." What name did that disembodied, demoralizing force wear? Perhaps it was Zachariah.

Liz unbuckled her seat belt and pulled her purse to her lap. Her father's sudden death and funeral had steeped her in the past. Now she was in New York again, in real time, and she'd have to do more than confront the past. She'd have to make some sense of the present. *Amen.*

Home. Liz dropped her efficiently packed carry-on bag in the hall, double-checked that the door was double-locked, kicked off her conservative navy pumps—she'd learned long ago to buy shoes for comfort—and switched on the table lamp just enough to illuminate the huge room without overpowering the electric twinkle of midtown Manhattan through her windows.

A fat pile of mail the doorman had handed her landed noisily on a lacquered console table in the entry hall as Liz advanced on the vast, artificial panorama that never failed to excite her. Civilization. Ugly and gorgeous, dangerous and sometimes even safe—if you knew how to get around in it.

The room smugly waited to acknowledge her presence. Like all apartments of often-gone, single, successful people all over Manhattan, it seemed to look best empty. It had been expensively furnished with the first fruit of her six-figure network salary; it was elegant and she'd learned to live with it. Most of all, it was hers and filled a void in her busy, eleven-hour workday life. Its ambience was almost sentiment, like that of a great, slumbering white Persian cat. And it *was* white—calculatedly, costly non-Midwestern white—from the down-filled overstuffed Italian sofas planted on upholstered bun feet in front of the decorative overmanteled fireplace, where a fluffy ruffle fern unfurled in place of roaring flames, to the off-white Irish mohair carpeting underfoot to the albino walls wearing a pale collection of abstract silkscreen prints. And against it all loomed the glossy, midnight-black backdrop of New York City shaped by a skyline of pulsating pinpoints of light.

Liz unbuttoned her suit jacket and collapsed into the sofa's marshmallow depths. Her mail included nothing intriguing enough to investigate now, and her clothing—wrinkle-resistant—could stay unpacked until tomorrow, or 1995, for that matter.

She reclined, feeling not jet lag but juxtaposition lag. From Turtle Bend to the Big Apple. Will the real Liz Jordan please stand up? The disingenuous photographed face on the Turtle Bend wall or the pointillist visage the airwaves beamed across America every weekday morning? A personality reassembled into so many pixels on a screen. Pixelated. Liz giggled, stretched, and wiggled her toes.

All she had to do was get her makeup off, undress, hit the Porthault sack, and make sure the alarm was set for three A.M., as usual. And . . . rats. But she really should do it tonight. Going in prepared was one reason Liz Jordan was a household name these days.

The walls seemed to reel a bit as she pushed herself up and walked leadenly through an adjoining doorway. The room's gray flannel walls needed more than one stingy light bulb, so she dialed the rheostat that lit the perimeter downlights before going to the wall of teak built-ins and unveiling the TV and VCR. The tape rewound docilely, smooth as high-tech silk. Liz yawned, warmed up the TV, and punched the start button before curling up with the remote control on the semicircular sunken banquette. A technicolor sun exploded onto the gray screen as yellow-orange letters rose with it to spell out . . . *S-u-n-r-i-s-e*, to the tune of inanely peppy theme music. At last, in all its $560,000 glory, came the infamous Plexiglas set that could be accessorized or lighted to reflect any season of the year. November called for sober but not depressing autumn umber.

Liz didn't intend to sit through the whole broadcast, just to fast-forward through and check out the performance of her replacement, a bouncy blond twenty-five-ish anchor named Heather from the Detroit affiliate. It was only a two-day stint, but Heather was smiling as if the corners of her lips were stapled to her gums. They probably were; network would-be's had been known to do stranger things to make a hot impression on a relentlessly cool medium.

Personal competition wasn't Liz's nature. Let the work do the talking was her motto. But network nerves meant no one was particularly safe, at least not since Walter Cronkite had retired.

An entire tier of network vice presidents could have gone with the wind of the ratings in the two days Liz had been gone. No, it was smart to know what was going on—while you were doing your job, and especially while you weren't.

Heather showed promise—as a Dallas Cowboys cheerleader. Ye gods, what a dumb remark. Happy talk, not Howdy Doody talk, honey. Liz stretched, about to click off the tape. Then the camera panned to the *Sunrise* cohost. Not good ole Danny Rogers of the sincere frown and well-capped teeth, recently departed, but a handsome dark-haired Latino man with a Mr. Roark manner.

Liz sat bolt upright in a sofa not designed for it. "Damn it, Alfonso, what the hell are *you* doing on my TV set—and in *my* chair?"

Looking, she answered herself, for a seat that feels just right.

"Liz! Good to have you back. You briefed on the show today?"

"Oops. I thought we didn't say that word."

"Briefed?"

"Today," Liz intoned ominously.

Frank Burton laughed and perched on the Formica counter, careful not to sit in any makeup. Liz kept her eye on the face that Bessie was erecting in the mirror. One slip, and Liz could look jaundiced, hung-over, or cross-eyed in front of eight million Americans.

"How was your trip, kid?" Frank called everybody demeaning nicknames; it was probably why the network had kept kicking him upstairs until they made him *Sunrise* executive producer. But he was basically a nice guy, which was why the entire *Sunrise* staff had a running pool to pick the date he'd be fired.

"Not too bad. A funeral is a funeral is a funeral, even if it's in the family. And my father was seventy-eight . . . ."

Frank's balding head shook. In these merciless makeup lights his bleary gray eyes sported bags the size of Saratoga trunks.

"More cover-up under the baby browns," Liz delicately reminded Bessie. As one of the few brunette media women, she knew the camera's tendency to find bruiselike shadows under each eye, even after a week of marathon sleep. After two days of air travel, Liz's "circles" were carved deep purple wells.

"Well, it's good to have you back," Frank said jovially. He was almost always jovial, believing it made him sound in charge.

"Same here." Liz couldn't chat much, having either to hold her lips immobile for an application of lipliner or look in some unnatural direction while Bessie applied powder dangerously near Liz's touchy contact lenses.

"We've, uh, got a little surprise for you," Frank went on. "After makeup, why don't you hit the editing room, play back yesterday's tape?"

"Surprise? I saw him."

"Alfonso?"

"Big as life. Since when does a *Sunrise* correspondent move into the anchor slot without memos all over the network six months in advance? It was enough to make me turn off the VCR."

"Hey, Liz. No call to be touchy. It was a one-shot deal. It's part of the surprise. Alfonso did a tribute to your father."

"*Alfonso* did a tribute on *my* father? I didn't see *that*."

"Yeah, him being an investigative reporter and all. I think it went real nice. Alfonso worked all night on the script. And you being gone for the funeral, it didn't look like conflict of interest, you know?"

"No, I don't know, but I think I'd better find out."

Liz slid out of the high chair, tore away her makeup cape, and cadged Frank's steaming Styrofoam cup of coffee. "I have a feeling I'll need this more than you. Thanks, kid."

She grabbed a copy of the previous day's tape at the morgue and slid into the first available viewing room, enjoying being locked in her own soundproof, glass-windowed booth.

It wasn't hard to spot the segment where Alfonso came on camera. Liz let the tape roll and sat back to listen.

"... He was not a young man, except in the vibrancy with which he used the tool of journalism to address issues large and small, local and national. Zach Jordan was never afraid to speak his mind. Luckily for the rest of us, that mind had a range and a love for justice and truth that is hard to find nowadays, even in the best of us. He was a man who never believed the worst of us, no matter how damning the evidence."

Alfonso paused, and gazed limpidly into the camera. "I've known and worked with Liz Jordan for several years, and I admire her almost"—ouch—"as much as I revered her father. She couldn't—and wouldn't—have made this public testimonial to him, so I've said the words for her, and for all of us journalists and admirers of good journalism who will sorely miss Zach Jordan. And to Liz, who will miss him most of all, I speak for myself and all our colleagues here at *Sunrise*, when I say: your father was a man worth looking up to ... and living up to. And you can't say more than that about anyone."

Liz recognized a closing line when she heard it; she hit the pause button and Alfonso obediently froze in mid-expression. He was Cuban in ancestry but aggressively New York in upbringing. He'd hit the media scene like a jalapeño pepper and caught the eye of the network, which took him blue jeans, collar-length curls, mustache, and all.

Alfonso was the only network newsman allowed to wear a mustache besides Geraldo Rivera. Networks usually eschewed mustaches and urban cowboys—too blue-collar—but allowing one on-camera mustache made up for years of underemploying ethnic men; it was so vividly different.

Liz couldn't help thinking of Steve, remembering that even his pale, unassuming lip adornment had succumbed to such pressure. For an instant, Steve's blond Midwest image merged with Alfonso's. . . . Liz shook herself into the present. Picturing Steve and Alfonso at the same time was like mixing buttermilk and brandy.

Events seemed to have weighed especially heavy on Liz lately. First the shock of her father's death, then going back to Turtle Bend and finding it such a jolt. Liz was no longer able to stroll down memory lane, she found; her memories whipped her down it. Liz of ten years ago had not been so happy, either, depressed by the breakup with Steve, worrying about entering the network feeding frenzy without an ally anywhere, feeling guilty for some reason about leaving her father. . . .

And then coming here, all that way to New York City, alone.

— Chapter 34 —

Monday morning, a pre-Christmas shopping day in New York in 1975. Monday morning, and Liz Jordan, network correspondent-to-be, didn't know what to wear. The huge hotel room booked by the network suddenly seemed too small to hold her. She ran around like a caged rat, worrying over her Diane Von Furstenburg jersey two-piece—too floral, too clinging?—versus her cinnamon wool dress—too . . . well, dressy? Then there was the boots versus shoes dilemma. No snow or slush marred the streets of New York; the temperature was nearly fifty degrees. Were Liz's caramel suede boots too heavy for the weather; would they be too . . . aggressive during the interview? At least hemlines had settled below the knee nowadays, she thought, turning in the Von Furstenburg before the bureau mirror. She wrenched out of the outfit and zipped herself into the wool dress, still turning, wondering. . . .

Later, she found out what she really should have been worrying about—getting a cab. Eight-thirty was rush hour, she discovered, and even the impressively uniformed doorman couldn't stop one of the countless heartless cabbies who passed them without pausing. Not even a whistle that would wake the dead made a cab do so much as quiver in its headlong path past them. Liz jiggled nervously from foot to chilly foot—she'd decided on the shoes. They were good Italian leather and their forty-five-dollar price had impressed her, so it ought to impress somebody else.

In the end, impatience took the bit in its teeth and pulled her along behind it. She gave up and decided to walk to the network building, glad she'd had the foresight to check the route the night before. She walked as fast as she could without running, the dainty Italian heels infallibly finding every sidewalk grate in New York City, every chink in the concrete, every collapsed curb.

The buildings along Lexington Avenue seemed to occupy entire half blocks at a gulp, apparently such famous landmarks that nobody had deigned to put an address on them. Only catching the sudden sheen of brushed chrome numbers two feet high above a bank of doors here and there assured Liz she was pointed in the right direction. Finally she spotted the proper building and darted through its glass doors with two hundred other people apparently just as fearful of being late. In the lobby, entombed by polished marble, Liz froze in front of a row of elevators. The floor indicators only went to eighteen, and Liz's appointment was on twenty-six.

She panicked. Was it the wrong building after all? The wrong street? Should she go outside, find someone to ask? There was no one to ask; they were all purposefully striding into the building, out of the building, streaming into the elevators, out of the elevators. They never stopped. Puzzled, Liz noticed that some poured past the elevators. Perhaps there was a coffee shop deeper in the building, a human being somewhere held captive by a cash register and therefore obligated to answer out-of-towners.

Moving beyond the elevators, Liz confronted a second row of elevators, this one with its floors labeled nineteen to thirty-six. Relief. Two sets of elevators behind each other. Crazy! Liz was being whisked aloft with her fellow passengers, eyeing the buttons to make sure twenty-six stayed pressed. From crowded chaos, Liz disembarked into tranquil corporate Nirvana, as unreal as another, alien world. She had arrived at the network offices.

Forest-green carpet stretched in all directions, cool and crisp as a pine tree. Sleek, almost amorphous seating pieces upholstered in gray flannel sat in the vast foyer like Henry Moore sculptures. Stainless-steel pediments held up travertine slabs so large one could dissect a walrus on them. They were empty except for a neat display of upscale magazines and the *Wall Street Journal*. At a curved stainless-steel desk, a receptionist presided over the hushed receiving room and, in equally hushed tones, rang Leonard Slater's secretary and informed him that Liz Jordan was here.

Liz perched gingerly on one of the undefined chairs, waiting to be guided into the offices beyond. She was later to learn it was pure coincidence that the reception area had been deserted at the moment she arrived. It normally thronged with various petitioners, like the Sun King's receiving rooms. But for now Liz was the only occupant, and she felt like a lone deceased soul waiting at the afterworld's gate to be ushered into heaven or hell. She could never decide which the network was, and later she wondered if she was qualified to distinguish heaven from hell at all.

Slater was a network vice president. Like all his ilk, Liz learned quickly, he was urbane, ambitious, and endowed with a perilously short corporate life expectancy. For now he was the balding, middle-aged man in an expensive suit who sat Liz down, chatted cordially, inquired about her hotel accommodations, and told her the bad news. She made the mistake of being elated at first.

"Washington? Isn't that a prime assignment for a freshman correspondent?"

Slater beamed at her over his tented fingers. At the time Liz would have said he beamed "benignly." Later, she redefined it as "smugly."

"Ordinarily it would be," he said. "But your qualifications are excellent and what we have in mind is tailor-made for you." Slater smiled yet more broadly. "All the networks have their heavy artillery down there—Rather, Donaldson, Brokaw; you know the names and faces. No network has assigned a correspondent to cover the stuff the big guns miss. Your gentrification piece shows you have a feel for all sides of society—rich, poor, young, old." He leaned forward confidentially. "And Washington has a pretty big minority community, you know. You could start out by redoing your gentrification story down there."

Liz was stunned. "But surely the local stations cover that sort of thing."

"Not the way we'd like it done; classy enough and general-interest enough to hit the network news. And you don't have to look for only downers; we're open to some happy stuff, too, on network news. Maybe background pieces on the movers and shakers who get overlooked—like the political wives." Slater must have read Liz's unguarded expression. His smile faded. "I hope you're not one of these raging feminists who think wives aren't worth covering. . . ." The wide, confident grin was back.

"No . . . not per se—"

"Excellent." He was on his Gucci-shod feet, hand and a whiff of unrecognized expensive men's cologne cocked Liz's way like a pair of dueling pistols, one visible, one not. "Welcome aboard. Our people will take it from here—get you booked, boarded, and relocated before Christmas. You can work out of our affiliate and bureau down there. Happy hunting!" His handshake was firm, his farewell final.

Liz left, referred to an efficient but impersonal woman who handed her a Bible-thick folder of network rules, editorial philosophy, pronunciation caveats, and expense account forms.

In a swift, head-spinning turn of events, Liz was put on salary—$38,000 a year—whisked out of New York, established in the Watergate Hotel in Washington, introduced to the local station and network bureau personnel, and found a spacious though faceless furnished apartment near Georgetown. No sense sending for knickknacks in the news business, the Washington relocation chief told her cheerily. "Keep to clothes, honey. I've seen a lot of 'em come—and go."

Christmas loomed like a guillotine—anticipated but unexpectedly swift. Liz felt cut off, psychologically decapitated. Her head still resided in one place—the Twin Cities or at least the New York, New York, of her fantasies. Her body was in bondage to Washington, D.C., a city that celebrated Christmas with midfifties temperatures and snowless sidewalks unless a surprise blizzard came along to tuck it in for the winter.

She would later regard herself as the hapless hostage of two cities—New York, whence all her instructions flowed, and Washington, where she lived and worked and never felt welcome. In retrospect, she found those Washington years the best of times and the worst of times. She had been spared immediate immersion in the center of the network politics in New York until she got her feet wet as a national correspondent. And she had been consigned to a thankless, ambiguous beat that, despite the opportunity for covering events of moment, in practice became the very model of the female/feature story trivia she'd fought doing all her working life.

And if she didn't want Washington, it was equally clear that Washington didn't want her. Liz had immediately sensed that her position was official but unsanctioned by the local establishment. Someone found her a clear desk at the Washington bureau, but the White House reporters ruled the roost and had little patience for a news hen suddenly plopped in their midst with a vague and, to them, unimportant assignment. They had dibs on the camera crews—first, last, and always. Liz was told she could always draft a crew from the local station, but the news director there seemed as domineering and harried as Mike Roth. Liz doubted she'd ever get what she needed. For now, it didn't matter. The network had told her to get acquainted and not to worry about producing stories until the new year, which was lucky. Liz couldn't have produced a Bicentennial Minute with the little she knew about the city and already was developing an attitude mixed of three parts embarrassment and one part gratitude as she dutifully trailed the affiliate staff members she was assigned to until she got her bearings.

It didn't help that the one most often saddled with Liz was Rosemary Martin, a tall, regal blonde originally from Atlanta whose firm news-anchor voice still wore the soft, melted caramel slide of a Southern accent the expert way runway models trail mink.

"Really, I don't need to shadow you all day," Liz apologized as she killed time sitting by Rosemary's desk and watching her work. The Washington station's newsroom was as crowded and unglamorous as WBGO's, except it was bigger.

"Don't you worry," Rosemary said in the soft drawl she slipped into off-camera. "I love having company. I'm the first woman anchor at the station. The men don't know how to talk to me."

"That's why they saddled you with me," Liz noted ruefully.

Rosemary flashed a Miss America smile. She was amazingly pretty for a tall woman, with no trace of the usual slightly mannish manner. But Rosemary's soft, feminine features were erected on the foundation of a square jaw that toughened her appeal and made any camera lens into a lover. Liz had Jell-O for facial bones, she sometimes thought, although everyone said she filmed well.

"Those old boys just aren't used to womenfolk on their playing fields," Rosemary consoled. "They get nervous. I know."

"You make me nervous," Liz confessed. "You're so together."

Rosemary's laugh was a ladylike glissando. "Me? Liz, if you only knew." Her baby-blue eyes turned shrewd. "Listen, honey, are you doin' anything for Christmas?"

Liz shrugged. "Putting Tinsel on my shower rod, I guess."

"Sounds kinky. You Yankees are always up to something odd. Why don't you forget about that silly old shower rod and have dinner with Joel and me? He's comin' in from New York and we have no family here—and no time to get away to see 'em anyway. I'm gonna make a ham, and candied yams and black-eyed peas. Would you believe these hands"—Rosemary's long-nailed white fingers lilted off the typewriter keyboard and fluttered artfully—"can cook as well as type?"

Liz looked into those bluebell eyes and detected a self-mocking glint.

"I believe you can do anything, Rosemary, including make a very kind offer I can't refuse."

"Good." Her hands hesitated before resuming their pianist's position over the keys. Rosemary sighed. "One thing I can't do, though, is lose that twenty pounds I need to, and home-cooked holiday dinners don't help."

"*You* don't need to lose any weight," Liz protested. Rosemary's arms and chest were tomboy-thin. She could wear a six-inch-thick mohair pullover and still look slim.

Rosemary noted where Liz was looking and rolled her eyes. "The hips, honey; it's all in the hips and legs."

"But that doesn't show on camera!"

"No . . . but I'm not always on camera." Rosemary's face sobered, then unveiled that dazzling, beauty-contest smile. "But thank heaven for dirndle skirts, God's boon to womankind. Even my hairdresser doesn't know for sure." She leaned confidentially near. "And Joel has only begun to suspect. . . ."

Liz had expected Joel Martin to be a mush-mouthed Southern boy, not the wired New Yorker she met over eggnog in the tasteful colonial house the couple owned in Chevy Chase. No wonder she and Steve hadn't lasted; they were too alike. Rosemary and Joel were living, married proof that opposites attract.

"How ya doin, Liz? How do you like Monument City?"

"Why do you call Washington that?" she asked curiously.

Joel, a dark, intense man impeccably dressed in a double-breasted pin-striped suit with a red tie adding a Christmas touch he probably hadn't even thought of, leaned forward on the cushiony sofa until his knees almost touched Liz's. "Because it's filled up to here . . ."—throat-slashing gesture—". . . with these white marble civic landmarks—and it's about as dead as a graveyard."

"Dead?" Rosemary's laughter trilled. She was wearing a full, floor-length plaid taffeta hostess skirt and a lace-frilled white blouse as airy as her laugh. "This is where laws are made, darlin'. Where wars are declared and taxes are raised. This is Yankee headquarters and a hub of worldwide upheaval."

"That stuff." Joel grinned at Liz. "You're not a fanatic news hound like my wife, are you, Liz? I've been tryin' to get her to find some job in New York, and dump this burg."

"Washington is a plum assignment for any newsperson." Liz found herself defending Rosemary. "But . . . well, I thought I'd end up—or start out, rather—in New York myself."

"Sure—everybody wants to be in New York, babe." Joel turned on Rosemary and frowned, watching her delicately bite into a powdered sugar–dipped ball of shortbread. "Right?"

Rosemary chewed hastily and answered. "Right. But wanting to dance and bein' asked are two different things, darlin'. More eggnog, Liz?"

The dinner itself, served by Rosemary at the oval mahogany dining table, was hot, homey, and generally soft in texture. Liz missed the snap of a green salad or a carrot stick but ate even the gooey white blob oozing all over her plate.

"Grits. I made 'em just for you." Rosemary beamed mischievously.

"Don't believe her, Liz. If it's soft and fattening, Rosemary loves it. She doesn't normally eat like this; Christmas she gets to pig out."

The table of three was suddenly silent, and Rosemary's fork had stopped midway to her well made-up mouth. Naturally, it was up to Liz, the stranger, to find a way across the mysterious marital chasm that had opened up before them all. "Well . . . holidays are for eating—and drinking." She eyed the lowball glass of whiskey that had never been absent from Joel's well-manicured hand all afternoon.

Joel's face was expressionless. "But my job doesn't depend on it."

"Neither does Rosemary's, I hope. Goodness, I'll never survive here if the network calorie police get on my case."

"You don't have to worry," Joel threw in, his eyes flicking over Liz in frank evaluation. "You're a lean type. Rosie's a mesomorph, and she has to watch it. Right, lamb chop?"

"Sure, Joel." Rosemary drew the napkin from her lap to the table, then stood. "Coffee, anyone?" she demanded brightly. "No calories. Maybe I should forget dessert."

"What is it?" asked Liz."

"Pecan pie."

Joel whistled. "Good stuff. Nobody makes pecan pie like Rosie, Liz. Secret's in fresh, Southern pecans. But you better keep your own slice paper-thin, Rosie," he yelled after her through the still swinging kitchen door.

Liz wondered what Rosemary was thinking and doing in her hostessly retreat, but she was soon back among them, smiling at a full 350 watts and placing green glass desert plates before them. Joel's portion was huge, apparently a custom. It was so unfair; most men could eat the moon and never show an ounce. Liz's slice was more than she needed but exactly what she wanted. Rosemary sat down and toyed with the narrow portion of pie in front of her, eating slowly and quietly. For a moment the only sound at the table was the clink of the ice cubes against Joel's Baccarat crystal glass. Then he spoke, turning on like an actor.

"So here's to Liz, a holiday toast." The two women hoisted their glasses of Beaujolais. "May she find Washington all she wants, and leave it sooner than she thinks."

It was only through shards of conversation with Rosemary over several more weeks that Liz learned what Joel did in New York. She had guessed advertising, which seemed to be the only field that required Joel's custom blend of smarm and chutzpah. Liz was wrong; he turned out to run a talent agency—mostly for models. That's how Rosemary had met him. "Best hand model in Manhattan," she smiled ruefully, moving her fingers in graceful demonstrations. "Now nobody hardly ever sees my hands on camera."

If Joel's profession surprised Liz, his record as a predictor of futures was predestined to failure. The network showed no sign of withdrawing her assignment.

Liz replayed her gentrification story, with a more dire outlook. In Washington, the issue was further tainted because the press for housing for political, diplomatic, and lobbying personnel was pushing the poor and the black back faster and further, although most Washington bigwigs resided in the posh Virginia suburbs adjacent to the capital.

That spring Liz did a satirical piece on the Cherry Blossom Festival queen contest, exposing it as an out-of-date exercise in states' one-upwomanship, and got several rewardingly vitriolic letters, including several from congressmen, so she felt like she was doing her job. Z.J. always said a journalist's task was not to make people feel comfortable with themselves or their society.

"You really stick your neck out," said Rosemary at one of their called-at-the-last-minute-if-our-schedules-jibe lunches. Liz had never had a woman friend in the same profession before, and she was enjoying the support it gave her. Rosemary was definitely partisan. "I'm amazed you can get away with scattering all those Cherry Blossom queens over the national TV screens and making the whole thing look so vacant."

"It *is* vacant—an annual spring fertility ritual complete with maidens and social patriarchs, i.e., senators and congressmen, permitted to go amongst them and leer for a bit in between lunches with lobbyists and dinners with strippers."

"Oooh. Cynical already. I do not know *what* Washington does to people," Rosemary chided mockingly. She smiled. "I was the Dogwood Days Queen in Tupelo, Mississippi. Did you know that?"

Liz gulped on her scalding cup of coffee. "I didn't mean to imply that *all* beauty pageants or beauty queens were—"

"Oh yes, you did, 'Liz'beth Jordan," Rosemary said in full drawl. "And I'm not sure you aren't right. I envy you, Liz. You've always seemed to be able to concentrate on what's in your head, not what's *on* it—or under it—not that you're not a nice-lookin' lady. But you never needed a beauty contest, did you?"

"I'm not beauty queen material," Liz said, grinning. "Not blond, enough."

"Anybody can be blond, sugar. Not everybody can be . . . well, secure *not* bein' blond. At least not in our business. You ever notice how at football games, when the cameramen do a close-up on a . . . shall we say, a young female fan of certain attractions? It's almost always a blond."

"I don't watch football much."

"You should," Rosemary said earnestly. "You can learn a lot about men that way, and—my goodness—we do have to live with them, don't we?"

"Speak for yourself, sugar. I may never date again. There are so *many* single women in Washington. . . ."

"You'll meet someone nice and available. You'll see. After all, you're a famous lady."

"I don't mean to put down beauty queens, Rosemary. Phyllis George has done okay, too." Liz was still trying to make up for being opinionated on a subject that had touched her friend's life.

"Put us down. Sure, we sometimes get somewhere because of it, but nobody takes us seriously—on the job or off it. I think it's a bad idea, givin' women the notion they've got to be pretty little girls forever. It's hard to turn that kind of expectation off." Rosemary looked down at her huge chef salad and sighed. "I really shouldn't finish this."

"Well, you'd never describe Barbara Walters as a 'pretty little girl,' and look where she's gotten—first woman network news anchor, and she's in her forties. That's kind of neat."

"Isn't that something? You don't spend much time at the station, but the men are just livid, Liz, so help me. You should hear them; they say it's the biggest journalistic sellout ever. ABC givin' her a million dollars a year. They say it's just show business, not news business, and that she isn't worth it."

"I don't know. I've been watching her for years; I think she's good. Why not give her a news anchor slot?"

"Well, the men don't like it. You *do* read the papers?"

Liz sighed. "I know. Every male old enough to hold a color crayon has been raging about how this demeans journalism and it's a travesty." Liz let a smidgen of bitterness seep into her voice. "I've heard men claim before that women get good jobs because the company needs a token or the woman slept with somebody.

Why can't we get promoted because we're good? Every national columnist has gotten on his high horse over poor Barbara's promotion, all claiming that they'd never succumb to all that filthy lucre. . . . Most of them are hardly paupers—Buckley, Baker, and Kilpatrick and Company."

"You sound so riled about this," purred Rosemary. "You ought to write a guest column for the *Washington Post*."

Liz looked up from her soup, startled. "You're right, Rosemary! I'm a writer, aren't I, even if my stuff gets recorded and filmed? I just might do that."

Rosemary smiled. She'd never feel strongly enough about anything—or courageous enough—to speak her own mind so publicly. But she had no hesitancy about leading Liz to the soapbox, maybe because she felt Liz could better take the roar of the crowd—and the smell of the tar and feathers. *She has no feel to put her DOWN !*

Liz soon found her soapbox, a fairly elevated one. Her essay on the Barbara Walters job brouhaha ran in the spring *Columbia Journalism Review*, creating almost as much of a stir in media circles as the Walters move.

Maybe it was the lead. "I wouldn't be Barbara Walters right now for a million dollars," Liz began, citing the cloudburst of criticism that had rained down on the woman merely for having received a promotion and a raise.

Barbara Walters' $5 million, five-year salary wasn't so startling, wrote Liz.

> What's really amazing is how these men stick together when their exclusive territory is threatened. The male newspaper columnists all insist that they don't object to Walters moving up in the world, even if its theirs. No, they say, they're simply concerned with the larger issues, the principle behind the poorly-paid-just-like-the-rest-of-us working journalists.
>
> The Walters contract upsets all this institutionalized poverty, you see. Why, Walter Cronkite, dean of American newscasters, and all those other guys don't get a million a year. (Estimates are that Cronkite and his cronies pull down about $400,000 a year, plus hidden fringe benefits. These are only estimates because none of the boys or their networks make their negotiations public.)

She went on to highlight Walters's achievements in interviewing heads of states and fending off several younger female rivals.

> Anyone whose job security so obviously rests on other

people's fickle perceptions of her age and looks deserves hazardous duty pay. Barbara Walters doesn't strike one as the type to fade because her youth has, but the network powers seemed mighty intrigued by the possibility. Candice Bergen was brought in before Walters left NBC and is now up for the cohost job. Jim Hartz doesn't have to fret about Donny Osmond snapping up *his* job.

I for one will look forward to hearing my news with a less bass approach, and I think Barbara Walters earned every cent of her million during twelve years of predawn rising. But I wouldn't be in her shoes. Her move has made her the most popular moving target for the boys in the peanut gallery. But then that's the way boys always react when a girl beats them at their own game. They cry foul.

The piece debuted quietly a month or so after the original furor. The first reaction Liz saw came in a congratulatory note from a woman correspondent at competing ABC. Other notes arrived, mostly from women, one from a senatorial aide, another from Bella Abzug. The University Women of America invited Liz to address their national convention in June on the role of women in national news reporting.

Liz's male colleagues at the bureau and the affiliate started noticing her comings and goings, and commenting on her pieces when they ran. Eventually they began teasing her, calling her "Liz the Hun." But she wasn't invisible now. The ex-governor of Georgia sent her a note applauding her stand, and was so down-home that he signed it "Jimmy." The bureau chief called her in and, never mentioning the article, told her that her annual salary had been raised to $50,000. The raise didn't thrill Liz; she had learned through delicate probing that her male colleagues had been making that all along. It wasn't five million, but it was a step. When Liz told Rosemary, they giggled together and christened the syndrome that produced the raise the "White-Collar Male Guilty Son of a Sexist Two-Step."

But of all the outpouring of support Liz got in the mail, of all the extra money she garnered in speaking engagements and personal appearances, and even the hefty raise itself, the thing she treasured most was a note that came on ABC stationery and bore Barbara Walters's signature.

"Can I see it?" asked Rosemary when Liz told her. "What'd she say?"

"She liked my piece, thanked me warmly," answered Liz, abnormally reticent.

"That's all?"

Liz sighed. "It's private; I really wouldn't feel right about showing it around. But it hurt her, Rosemary, to reach the pinnacle of her career, of any woman or any *person* in TV journalism's career, and have everybody, every man, turn on her and try to kick the foundation out from under her; to have them say she was no good, not 'serious' enough. Oh, she'll survive. We women always do. But what should have been the best of times became the worst of times. People forget that, that people on the TV screen have feelings and fears and sick children and a right to a little credit now and again."

Rosemary was very quiet. "We can't show it, Liz. That we have any insecurities. One sign of weakness and the sharks swim in for a feeding frenzy. Damnit, sometimes I hate this business!" Her blue eyes swam in sympathetic tears.

"Hey, things are changing. Look at us; we're a younger generation. Maybe if we have enough martyrs it won't be so bad for the ones who come after."

"Maybe," said Rosemary, but she didn't sound like she meant it.

— *Chapter 35* —

Liz hadn't needed her raise. Speaking engagements flooded in, bringing mad money in the form of $1,500 lump sums. Every other weekend she jetted across country to address this women's college annual Founders Day luncheon, or that League of Women Voters banquet. She honed an effective speech, part anger and part inspiration, on the role of women in broadcasting as a mirror of women's roles in other, less public work arenas. Her mixed conclusions: that women now had opportunities in the working world that had never existed before, but that the old stereotypes and chauvinist impediments remained, with invisible barricades manned by threatened males now smart enough to resort to career ambush and subtle discrimination instead of outright sexism or blatant rhetoric that would shock a courtroom. The current feminist movement, she said, had alerted the enemy, not converted him.

The more Liz appeared in person in public, the larger a public demanded her. She became a connoisseur of hotel-served chicken breast, able to diagnose at a glance whether the sauce-disguised lump on her plate was worth testing—or better ignored. She could leave a plane, chic and unwrinkled, on a Saturday morning; ride in a limo to a hotel luncheon making small talk with her institutional hosts; eat or fast, whichever seemed wiser, then speak, answer earnest questions, and sign programs for embarrassed but starstruck autograph seekers after lunch; closet herself for a post-speech sherry reception with the affair's prominent sponsors —and be back home in time for bed.

"Home" was the roomy but faceless Washington apartment the network had found her. Home was a good place to leave.

So she had the work, she had the money, and she was beginning to have the recognition, although she realized her sudden fame resulted from there still being so few women on national news, not the stellar quality of her work—yet. Still, she enjoyed advising the young women who approached her so worshipfully on the ins and outs, the ups and downs of a broadcasting career. She told them to start where she had, at smaller or local stations, and she warned them of pitfalls nobody had told her about. She still had to fight to do good stories and, with the summer political conventions and fall election, found them. She was as amazed at everybody else when that ex–Georgia governor named Jimmy walked off with the Democratic nomination. Remembering his supportive letter, Liz did the first piece on the Carter position on women, meeting Rosalynn, Ruth Carter Stapleton, and the incredible Miz Lillian, and bringing the Carter women to public attention.

Liz was even invited back to the Twin Cities that fall to address members of the Society of Professional Journalists as a local reporter made good. It had to be either her or Bill Stewart of WCCO, who had been plucked for ABC's correspondence corps that same year. But Stewart was assigned abroad—or maybe the SDX committee had just wanted a token broad on a guest speaker list that was traditionally and exclusively male.

Stephanie was there in the Radisson Hotel banquet room. She came up for a quick chat after Liz's speech.

"You look *great*," she said with feeling.

"New hairdresser," Liz demurred.

Stephanie laughed. "Same old Liz; 'Look at what I do and say, not what I look like.' You're a star now, though. My mother always asks me what you're *really* like every time one of your network stories airs."

"I hope you lie. How are things at WBGO?"

"Different but the same. I always come in expecting to see a guillotine set up in the newsroom. Heads are still rolling."

Liz automatically scanned the rest of the room. Too many

people pulled and tugged and clamored for her attention in public these days for her to concentrate on any single one, even an old friend.

"He's not here," Stephanie said abruptly. "You didn't expect him to come?"

Liz's head shook impatiently. "No, but I wasn't really looking for Steve. At least I *think* I wasn't. How is he?"

"Fine. He likes the anchor job. I don't know if they're paying him what they should be. You know, those consultants aren't done with WBGO, not by a long shot. Steve could just be a stopgap until the anchor they really want is contractually free."

Liz looked at Stephanie, her mind suddenly focused. "That'd be a rotten thing to do to Steve."

"Yeah." Stephanie shrugged. "Well, nice seeing you, Liz. I guess I'd better move on and let your fans have at you."

"No, don't go! Hang around and we can have a drink later."

Stephanie's tall blond head was being swallowed by the press of shorter, less familiar heads schooling around Liz. "Next time, maybe," Stephanie said, waving rueful farewell.

And then Liz was talking to a cordon of women—smiling strangers who had seen her or heard her, who liked this or loathed that piece, who wanted to be just like her, or their daughters to be just like her. . . .

Liz wished Z.J. could see this, could hear these parental crows emanate from strangers. She had scheduled a visit to Turtle Bend for the next day.

In her hotel room, finally, Liz caught the tail of the ten o'clock news. Steve on-screen. She smiled. The mustache was gone, and with it was gone something of Steve himself. He was just another pleasant, familiarly strange face on the boob tube. A fleeting image, a teller of other people's stories, a messenger of death and destruction, of clogged sewers and medical miracles, of the sublime and the ridiculous and the just plain awful. . . .

Driving to Turtle Bend through the autumn colors that glazed the countryside to the likeness of kiln-fired pottery, Liz felt returned to another world. She never drove now; her old Pinto reposed in some teenager's parents' Minneapolis garage. There was no need nowadays for Liz to take the wheel. Camera crews squired her around Washington, or cabmen when she arrived separately for some reason. If she left Washington, she flew. Liz smiled. Superwoman. Faster than a speeding teletype, able to leap all obstacles in a single bound. . . .

She liked to drive, and missed the feeling of being in control, of pacing herself to look at things instead of racing by them on the way to somewhere else.

Nothing had changed at home. Z.J. never saw her stories on the news. He was an ardent Walter Cronkite watcher and said he was too old to change channels now. When was Liz going to move to CBS? he pestered, sounding querulous for the first time.

Liz left Turtle Bend in her rented car, feeling more than the usual alienation, feeling a bewildered resentment that assumed almost physical form and deposited a bitter taste in her mouth. The flavor was remarkably familiar, but she couldn't name it. It seemed to taint all she did, so that back on her regular beat in Washington she wondered why nothing she did felt important, why she hadn't moved up after a year, why CBS didn't want her. . . .

Carter won the election, and the network, citing her "special" feeling for small towns (Liz read that as 'small-town mentality'), gave her the job of covering the human side of the Carter White House. It wasn't a bad assignment. The Carter administration hit Washington in early 1977 like a hardy, old-fashioned hazelwood broom sweeping an odor of candor, optimism, goodness, magnolias, and Billy Beer into the stodgy capital city.

Liz worked the crowd when President Jimmy and his wife, Rosalynn, strode down Pennsylvania Avenue in the brisk twenty-degree January air after the inauguration—hatless, long-stepping, waving. It was a performance diametrically opposed to the top-hatted formality of the Kennedy inauguration sixteen years earlier, which Liz remembered watching on TV in grade school. But it seemed to have the same instant, optimistic impact on the public. The common people who spoke into Liz's microphone that day and whose various faces unreeled on the evening network news that night spoke happily of "human rights" and "decency." Carter's election seemed to banish the last bitter aftertaste of the Nixon years and the subsequent Ford pardon of those years. Then Rosalynn dragged out the same dress for the inaugural bashes that she had worn when Jimmy had been inaugurated as governor of Georgia in 1971. People cheered approval for what was a far cry from the fashion-plate perfection for which Jacqueline Kennedy had received rave reviews—and criticism—years earlier.

Not many people in Washington noticed that the Minnesota Vikings had prefaced the inauguration by losing the Super Bowl for the fourth time. Liz did, and smiled. Minnesota would be in the dumps, but she no longer identified with local issues; her beat was national now. Yet, like any reporter reared in one part of the country who moves to a network, she found some of her stories still centered around her former home, no matter how far afield she went.

And she went to Plains, Georgia, a lot, spending some time

collecting homespun aphorisms on Miz Lillian's front porch or chasing Billy Carter down in Americus. She also went to the vice presidential residence in Washington, faultlessly restored during the Rockefeller incumbency and filled with works by American artists donated by the country's museums, large and small.

The Mondales of Minnesota, simple folk from the heartland, lived in the impressive residence now, slightly self-conscious caretakers. Liz's interview with Joan Mondale, a thin, animated woman whose hair and clothing wore the marks of no-nonsense Midwestern simplicity, made a splash. Like most wives of public figures, Joan Mondale proved to be an intelligent, lively lady in her own right. Liz spent a fascinating afternoon talking art, politics, and women's rights.

A stand-up outside the residence summed up her impressions.

"Who is Joan Mondale? A woman who is as passionate about art as she is about politics, who thinks more, says more, does more than anyone who's only seen her on television as the candidate's supportive wife would ever guess.

"She is a wife and mother, and now the nation's Second Lady. Yet those familiar generic titles don't begin to label the facets of a unique and specific Joan Mondale. . . ."

Liz had asked Mrs. Mondale if she still felt a *Minnesota* product. She hadn't answered directly, instead taking Liz on a tour of donated artworks in the vice presidential residence to point out Minnesota-originated items with partisan pride, including a small bronze sculpture by the late Paul Manship.

"It's a very small world," she noted. "Manship also did the famous gilt statue of Prometheus in Rockefeller Center in New York."

"I know it well," returned Liz. "A certain other network which shall remain nameless has its headquarters in the Center and often films outdoors against it."

Mrs. Mondale's narrow face broadened into a Cheshire cat grin. She set down the bronze. "Well, as you must bow to the existence of other networks, I must realize that I'm no longer simply from Minnesota but represent the entire country now. It's as simple as that."

As simple as that. As Liz was no longer of Turtle Bend or the Twin Cities, she was not of Washington or New York. But an election or time would return the Mondales to Minnesota. Liz felt no more links with any place. She felt <u>dislocated</u>, <u>unconnected</u>, as ephemeral as the image of herself the airwaves buffeted across every Middlesex village and town.

She'd also asked Joan Mondale about image versus reality. There were two forms of image, Mrs. Mondale had said: the outer image—whether a woman looked pretty or well-groomed or smart—and the inner image—whether a woman conveyed what was important to her and made others feel they were important to her. Outer image came and went with fashion and others' perceptions; inner image was what a woman came to live with herself.

The trouble was, Liz concluded, that television was a medium that could seriously misrepresent either image. Women were either perpetually portrayed in the background, smiling inanely, or—if in the foreground—couldn't survive the distortions a television camera made to their outer image, given the standards set for them. That's why so many hyperthyroidic bubbleheads populated the television screen in both news and entertainment programming; why women of a certain age almost vanished from the screen— except for Pauline Frederick, the great U.N. correspondent, and "entertaining" caricatures of older women like Phyllis Diller. Media men were not doomed to die out from Late Middle Age Rot, but gained stature with their gray hairs.

It was all very puzzling, and something Liz contemplated more often as her thirtieth birthday neared and she could no longer be considered the "girl" to whom everyone gives latitude but the woman the world sometimes takes in its sharp white teeth and shakes.

She was becoming less and less willing to accommodate herself to that world. As Rosemary had predicted, Liz did attract Washington men, particularly as her presence made itself felt, adding that pleasant dollop of fame atop the hard work and the money it earned her.

The first three years in Washington. Liz dated newspaper reporters, lobbyists, congressional aides, and even an attaché at the Swedish Embassy. She dined at every landmark restaurant in the capital, and saw the interiors of more than a few landmark Georgetown bachelor pads.

Inevitably, it began with quiet dinners and civilized conversation and came down to bed and bored. Maybe part of the trouble was Liz's prickly personal decision. She wasn't going to bloat herself up every month and risk severe hormonal high jinks just to be ready in case some man decided to sleep with her. So she resorted to the diaphragm and jelly method of contraception, relatively safe and intrinsically sorry. It made you sorry you had ever thought of having intercourse. Between relative strangers, its use required a delicate feeling out of intentions and the cautious inquiry of a U.N. negotiator. How "serious" do we intend to get? And when? Where? Do I need to bring "it" along?

Men loathed the contraption, claiming they could feel it. They hated the jelly almost as much as Liz hated repairing to the bathroom and equipping herself for the forthcominig "spontaneous" encounter. When she mentioned condom and foam as another safe method, and one a man could participate in, they freaked out even more, claiming condoms kept them from feeling anything at all.

By then, Liz herself felt nothing but self-disgust anyway. She decided a consequence of sexual liberation was that men were now allowing women to take all the risks and had lost even the chauvinist pretense of protection. She began to conclude that life was simpler and more her own without them. This was, she knew, not a normal decision for a woman not yet thirty, but it was right for her situation, her work, her travel schedule. . . . Z.J. still teased her about boyfriends when she periodically called home. She dazzled him with a litany of her beaux' professions, and no particulars. He didn't seem much impressed, but how could he be? Liz wasn't impressed with her men, either.

Her salary and importance had thrived if her personal life hadn't. When Bill Stewart, the CBS correspondent, was gunned down by Nicaraguan Guardsmen, she got the funeral story because she had been in the Twin Cities, where he had worked before going network, because she had taken Spanish in high school and college— and because she raised holy hell to get the assignment.

She flew to Nicaragua to report the government's disorganized denial of complicity, to interview the shocked American correspondents there. She was filmed at the graveside in the soft Kentucky June when Stewart was buried in his hometown of Ashland. She went back to the Twin Cities and interviewed his coworkers and friends there, all equally shocked to think that serious, never-superficial Bill Stewart, whose looks were a little too normal for network stardom, whose life had been wholly dedicated to broadcast journalism, had lost both past and future in one terrible, unexpected moment of atrocity.

No members of a profession mourn the violent deaths of their own with such solemnity as the police or the media, perhaps because the public seldom recognizes the risks they take. Liz's long piece survived all the way to the network uncut. For a few brief minutes, it froze the routinely familiar face of Bill Stewart in everyone's mind's eye. There, by the grace of senseless, alien upheaval, goes another victim of an undeclared war, the cost of playing professional witness to the world's inequities.

Liz was sick about Stewart's death, and so were her few former colleagues remaining at WBGO who remembered him. She reacquainted herself with them while working out of the station on her network obit. Steve wasn't among them. He'd been replaced by a more "forceful" anchorman, Stephanie reported. Liz viewed the replacement as merely slick. Steve had gone to Philadelphia two years before, Stephanie said, and sent Christmas cards back to the staff. He anchored an NBC affiliate there, liked it, and had married. A schoolteacher. Someone had heard his wife was expecting a baby. And did Liz remember Randy Andy Lewis? He left, too, for Chicago to become a Playboy photographer.

It was while in the Twin Cities that Liz picked up the *Minneapolis Star* one afternoon and read an unbylined "short" datelined Rochester, Minnesota.

"Holy cow!"

Stephanie, on whose desk Liz perched, looked up.

"This story is wild! Its says Donn Cole Bryson has been arrested on child molestation charges in Rochester." *The MIMER*

"So? There's a lot of that going around nowadays."

"Steph—this is the guy that ran the children's pantomime theater. He had dozens of kids in his hands . . . for years."

"Apparently."

"Yeah, but doesn't it blow your mind? The responsibility he had. This story says practically nothing, except that the city council and theater board have initiated a full investigation and the parents have rallied around to keep the 'nationally famous theater' going. Damn!" Liz crumpled the paper to Stephanie's desk. "I *knew* there was something wrong with that whole setup. And my piece added to the Donn Cole Bryson legendary!"

"Liz. Relax. That was a long time ago."

"Maybe, but I sure can do the story right now."

She called the nightly news producer in New York and got a go-ahead to stay on a few more days to report the full story of the Rochester Pantomime Players and the Pied Piper with the feet of clay.

It was a messier story than anyone wanted to let out of the bag. Not only Bryson was arrested, but several adult staff members, including former child members of the troupe who had stayed on as technical or administration staff. One man had had sex with a teenage girl; the others had been involved with boys—boys as young as eleven, twelve, and thirteen.

It had been going on for years, even when Liz had done her piece in 1974. The children had competed for parts. Competing for Bryson's good will was a central stage in that process. Some had simply slept their way into their leading roles. That's how the story broke; a miffed young actor had squealed when he had performed privately for Bryson but didn't get the public role he felt he should have. Hell hath no fury like a child introduced to adult ambitions and then scorned.

Other youngsters had been untouched, although when Liz interviewed them, their long, telling silences showed that they knew what was going on. So must have some of their parents, or the theater board. But nothing breeds complicity like success, and Bryson and the Rochester Pantomime Players had been successful to the point of hubris, luring guest conductors and choreographers from the best adult companies, and even being filmed for *60 Minutes*. Liz suspected that her long-ago story had tipped off the respected TV newsmagazine, which had ironically missed the underlying story, too. Now Liz had it, and had the background to do it right this time.

Liz found Moira O'Toole, grayer, more haggard, less willing to talk than four years ago. The sensitive fifteen-year-old Liz had met and filmed then, Jackie, was one of the young men accused of molesting boys.

"It was so *good* for my boys," a distracted Moira insisted on camera, a Kleenex tucking her tears into the wrinkles around her eyes. "With no father, and me working. To get the recognition, the attention..." Her words were indicting, but she was too confused to realize it. "I trusted the theater and Mr. Bryson. They all did so well there, every last one. We're in family therapy now—I'm sure Jackie didn't do anything that wrong—"

"Or have anything wrong done to him?" Liz interrupted.

Moira O'Toole looked sideways, away from the camera and away from Liz. "I ... didn't think so. I don't believe it. Mr. Bryson is so brilliant, he couldn't ... The theater must survive; it's done so much for the children." *at the sacrifice of children*

Liz got copies of videotapes from the Rochester station showing a handcuffed Bryson, looking grim and furtive, being ushered to jail. Bryson wouldn't talk to her, but she had her old WBGO film of her interview in happier days, which Mike Roth let her borrow from the morgue. "Your instincts were right about that guy, Liz," Roth conceded. "No wonder you went network." Roth's respect was a bit overdue, but Liz let it go just to get the precious, now old-fashioned reel of film out of there. Then she flew back to New York to find Wendell Banks. *the designer*

He was just finishing designing a major remounting of *Lucia di Lammermoor* for the Metropolitan Opera and was due to take off for a German opera season in two days. But he saw her. On camera.

The past five years had been good to him; he lived in a SoHo loft, an artsy elegant expanse of naked brick wall and bare wood floors furnished with an amalgam of antiques, found objects— i.e., attractive trash—and expensive Oriental rugs. A huge skylight roofed the studio area, and his workstands were as cluttered as ever.

Banks was frank on tape. Liz knew after the interview that she had the person who would play Greek chorus and put in perspective the events she had catalogued. She let the camera crew go and stayed for herbal tea on Banks's invitation.

"My friends call me Wendy," he said over a steaming pottery mug of Red Zinger.

"Liz. And you've been a friend in need. I really wanted to tell this Rochester story right. I hate being duped."

Wendy shrugged. There were a few more corrugations in his forehead, his thick hair was a trifle grayer; he still gave off an aura of integrity.

"Why didn't you ..." began Liz. "Why didn't you *tell* me, back then, what was happening at the Players? I think of five more years of kids going through that sick pressure cooker ..."

"I tried." He cupped his hands around the big-bellied cup, as if for warmth. "I tried to give you leading answers, I guess you'd call them. And it was only an instinct on my part. I had no proof."

"I was getting the idea, only ..." Liz groped for words to describe what had happened in the basement of the Guthrie Theater. "... only, you turned off on me, like a faucet, and I thought I'd been imagining the rest. Why?"

"You were worried about Bryson being gay, being a bad example for the kids. You obviously hadn't even considered the darker possibilities. I couldn't point you in that direction on my own suspicions. You just didn't seem ready to believe the worst."

"Like the parents," Liz nodded. "Now I understand. Blind innocence. How'd you get so smart?"

He laughed. "The theater is a wise old whore; she teaches you the facts of life fast."

"Too fast in Rochester. Well, thanks. Maybe I can redeem myself with this piece. You didn't have to speak out after all these years."

"Yes, I did. Because I was right and didn't do anything about it. Listen, do you work twenty-four hours a day like me, or can you go out for dinner?"

"But you're due in Europe...."

"Not tonight."

She measured him. "You're still not married."

"The theater's a jealous mistress."

"And the network's a hard master—but they do let me out to eat once in a while. Sure."

They talked and drank tea in the loft until the light through the square skylight faded to black. Wendy took her to a Village restaurant, fine but off the beaten track, where they ordered wine and veal and talked some more. They could have gone back to each other's equally lonely residences, and made unselfish love. But just knowing that, and seeing it in each other's eyes, was enough—and maybe even better.

"Thank you," said Liz as Wendy opened the door to the cab he'd hailed to take her back to her apartment. "Thank you for my first decent evening out in a long time."

"It's mutual." He smiled and waved. Liz peered out the cab's filthy back window as he turned and walked back toward his loft, a man of average height and average looks, of rare talent and rarer ability to feel comfortable with himself. She settled back into the seat, contemplating what it said about modern sexual mores when *not* sleeping with a man was more emotionally rewarding than ~~making love.~~ having sex.

She finished writing the Bryson piece the next day. Juxtaposing her idealized film of several years ago with tape of the empty theater, and confused parents and children, the sordid scene of Bryson being arrested, made a powerful piece. Beauty and the beast beneath it. Liz flew back to Washington satisfied, not sure she'd ever see Banks again, but pleased by their momentary sympathy. Perhaps she hadn't forgotten how to be with a man.

It was fall again, and 1980 was just a Christmas season away. 30 She mulled going to Turtle Bend for Christmas, and then Leonard Slater called her out of the blue.

"Great piece on that Rochester thing, Liz." The phone thrummed with New York urgency.

"Thanks" was all Liz said, recognizing she shouldn't get in the way of what Slater had really called to say.

"We're pulling you out of D.C. Don't think there's much you can do down there. Carter's out and there isn't much cute stuff ✓ to cover for Reagan, unless you count the dancing son; no Amy. We've got a spot in mind for you here. Anchorwoman spot for a morning newsmagazine. Get up here by the new year and we'll take a long look at you. There's some competition for the job. It's too hush-hush to go into, but you've got a decent shot at it. I recommended you."

Liz stammered thanks and repeated the essentials. Slater had never asked if she wanted a change; of course she did. Slater had just added one more password to the magic duo of "New York" and "network." Anchorwoman. At last, Liz was headed for where she thought she was going in the first place.

— *Chapter 36* —

"What happened to your hair?"

Liz patted the short, windblown waves around her ears. "Network idea. Supposed to make me look younger."

"What are you, thirty?"

She nodded, disappointed by his unflattering accuracy, but Jay McGovern laughed. "Thirty and you gotta look younger. I'm too old for this business, and I certainly don't have the hair for it anymore." He patted the top of his balding head with the same blitheness with which a four-year-old will rub his tummy.

"You're not thinking of leaving the business . . . the network?"

Jay shrugged and let his attention focus on Bobby Short nursing the ebony grand piano into a white-hot jazzy arpeggio. They were in the Carlyle Room of the Carlyle Hotel on Madison, where the network had booked Liz in a $280-a-night room. That's how she knew it was serious about her.

"Jay? You're not leaving, just when I need a friend inside?"

Liz had spent a seemingly pointless month in New York, meeting network veeps, having her looks rearranged, making audition tapes of phony interviews on phony sets. The first thing she'd done on arriving was to contact Jay McGovern and take him out for a long overdue thank-you lunch. Then, she'd discovered that he was divorced, and he'd probably discovered there were worse things than being seen around town with a hot network property, so he had become her reluctant mentor—a ready consultant–cum-wailing wall off whom she could bounce every twitch and tic the network mavens made.

McGovern addressed himself to his vodka gimlet, one of a steady, refillable stream that accompanied his lunches and dinners. He never appeared drunk, or even high. He just drank, constantly.

"Leave the network," he mused. "Yeah, I might." Her gasp drew his easy gaze. "I'm fifty-two, Liz; I'm a newsman, not a pretty boy. I've become a network hack. It wasn't like this when I started. I might move, try something else, say, public TV. Kids are out of school. Wife's gone. Who needs the money anymore?"

"But who'll advise me what to do when Slater drags in the network page boys to decide if my nose is too long?" Liz squeaked. "You got me into this mess. Save me."

"*You* got you into this mess. I just passed a reel of damn good film along. You really want this anchor spot, Liz? Getting up at God knows what hour? You know the networks are all fighting like mad for early-morning dominance. You could be next week's hash browns even if you did get the nod and then the show went belly-up. You know . . ." His hands cosseted the lowball glass. Like most heavy drinkers, Jay felt most infallible when clutching cold, condensation-dewed restaurant crystal. "I didn't know you until you came to New York. You're smart, a lot smarter than these bleached banana-head models the networks are calling news-women these days. But more than that; you care what you do. I don't think you're anchor material. You're too good for that meat grinder."

"But I could do good work; look at *Today*. Okay, the format is old-fashioned, but it's always done a solid job of informing the public without putting them back to sleep in the morning. I'm not a Sally Quinn or a Stephanie Edwards; I'm a TV newswoman. Maybe the network has learned its lesson and will go with sub-stance instead of surface."

Jay shook his head. "If they want you for this job, it'll be because of what you *are*, not what you do. You'll have to get used to that. Sure, what you are is based on what you did all those years you served your apprenticeship. And that could lose out to some bubbly blonde who makes swell on-screen chemistry with whatever beefcake they hire to do male anchor. You know that, Liz. I say, get out before you're in." He took a deep swallow from his glass. "Or . . ." Liz waited breathlessly for wisdom from the voice of experience. ". . . or go to bed with Slater's boss."

"Levin? Wash your mouth out with tap water." Liz turned serious. "That's one thing I've never had to do, never would do." She checked Jay's expression to make sure he believed her. "Not that I haven't been accused of it." Cautiously. "My, uh, old boy-friend in Minneapolis said that's why you helped get my film shown way back when."

"Impudent pup." Jay was secretly flattered. "I hope you dumped him."

Liz smiled. "Something like that."

"Well, Ms. Jordan, even if I do leave that den of snakes, second cousins to the chief and advertising experts, we can still get together for a few drinks and a roast of the surviving network honchos."

"You're going, aren't you?"

Jay winked. "Read the papers."

Two days later it was all over town: Jay McGovern was moving to a special position in public television, part producer, part one-man commentator. Liz envied him the challenge, even though she knew the money was about a fifth of his network salary. Some things were more important than money, and she hoped Jay would find them in a fresh arena.

For herself, there were empty, anxious weeks of being constantly studied and constantly put on hold. She'd been introduced to a craggy-faced, curly-haired "personality," part actor, part headache remedy huckster named Danny Rogers. Liz instinctively distrusted men over forty who still went by childhood diminutives—maybe it was leftover from the disappointing Jimmy Carter years. Danny Rogers seemed to have no reaction to Liz at all and spent the expensive lunch at Lutèce relating uninspiring anecdotes about his acting days.

"Why don't they just get Soupy Sales and forget it!" Liz exploded over the phone to Jay McGovern. He laughed, as only someone who was away from the network could afford to. "I mean it, Jay, if they saddle me with this guy—and it looks like it."

"Don't worry," Jay advised. "They can pull somebody as fast as they hire him. And I love it in public TV. They actually give lip service to putting out a quality product."

So Liz frothed in private, and smiled and smiled and smiled in public. She knew she had the inside track on the job when the show's assistant producer suggested Liz try going blond and the producer gruffly vetoed it.

Well, a blond Sally Quinn and a redheaded Stephanie Edwards had failed a few years ago as lady anchors; maybe a brunette would make it. Still, the revolting Danny Rogers was pervasive, ignoring Liz but showing up in her vicinity, cracking corny jokes and coining snide remarks that sounded innocent but somehow reflected on her.

They all seemed suspended in limbo, like the cast of *Waiting for Godot*. Even the show hadn't been named yet and was jokingly referred to by the crew as *Product X*.

Liz found herself paid a princely salary to remain at loose ends. She rattled around her huge Carlyle Hotel suite when not at the network. Jay was "on assignment" in Europe, lucky dog. The network gavotte was alien to her father. And Wendell Banks was still somewhere in Germany, designing helmets for assorted warbling Valkyries. Liz thought she would go crazy. Then one evening the phone rang and a soft, familiar voice trilled into her ear.

"Liz? It's Rosemary—"

"Rosemary! Oh, God, how good to hear from a real person. It was sweet of you to call. I hope you liked my postcards. It was all I had time for. . . ."

"They were real fun. Say, Liz, I thought maybe you wouldn't

mind having dinner with me tonight. I know it's short notice, but—"

"You're here? In New York? That's terrific. Joel must be ecstatic. You're sure *he* doesn't want you for dinner?"

"Slow down; you're startin' to sound like a New York operator. ... Yes, I'm here, and no, Joel has no claims on me. Heavens, I'll be in town a good, long time. He'll have lots of opportunity to have dinner with me until he's sick of it. And I want to see you, and ask you some things about the network."

"Boy, can I tell you about the network. Be glad they didn't pluck you out of blessed obscurity in Washington for the signal honor of sitting around on your can waiting for them to deign to make a decision about you."

The phone was silent for so long Liz feared the connection had broken. Then Rosemary spoke again, so softly she sounded as if she were talking long-distance.

"Liz ... I didn't want to mention this right off. But they have 'plucked me,' I guess. They've been watchin' my tapes and called me here yesterday. I think ... I think they want me for your job."

— *Chapter 37* —

Once the starring cast had been chosen, it took the network only three weeks to mount the newest contender for the valuable early-morning, scalded-coffee-gulping audience. *Sunrise* was ballyhooed from sunup to sunset at hourly breaks during everything from soap operas to prime-time news. The "secret" set was unveiled with solemn fanfare. It turned out to be a series of semicircular risers apparently custom-designed to trip the hyperactive and portly weatherman as he skipped from the news center to the elaborate "weather center." Promo tapes showed Danny Rogers and Rosemary Martin perched on high stools like college thespians given the unhappy task of reading instead of acting some endlessly talky play.

Liz could see why Rosemary had won the coanchor role. Against the elaborate set, her daffodil-blond head was as cheerful as the graphic of an exploding sunrise that opened the program. Liz couldn't begrudge Rosie her moments in the morning sun. Rosemary was ecstatic to be there, center stage at last, in New York, where she could convert the long-distance marriage with Joel into a daily consummation and convert his bachelor apartment into a domestic nest feathered with wifely care and home cooking.

The network had decided to keep Liz on in New York and found her an apartment as roomy and faceless as the Washington one at four times the monthly rent. So Liz became unwillingly intimate with every step of Rosemary's conversion to morning-news maven and every stage of high-pressure hype lavished on the new show. Rosie leaned on Liz, expressing anxieties she had to keep hidden from her coworkers and her achievement-hooked husband. Liz—staunch, unselfish soul—provided stability for Rosemary's wildly veering spirits, cheered her on, and kept any misgivings to herself.

"I don't know about the high chairs," she told Jay McGovern at lunch after his return from Europe. They were at the Pen and Pencil on 45th, a moderately priced steak-and-potatoes hangout for the print media set. There was little chance of uptown TV types dropping in, and the tables sat well apart, so there was even less chance of them eavesdropping. "High chairs" was Liz's epithet for the stools. "They're hell to sit on gracefully, especially for women."

Jay looked momentarily puzzled. "Ah, you mean managing skirts and showing too much leg," he finally said.

"That, too. Anyway, everybody *knows* that TV newspeople have no nether parts. We're like hoopskirted Southern belles; nobody ever sees our legs on camera. For all the public knows, we're a troupe of paraplegics. Those damn high chairs are a big mistake."

She didn't add that for Rosemary "showing too much leg" was not a matter of length but of width. Rosemary never had complained to Liz that *Sunrise* seating arrangement was the worst possible for her bottom-heavy figure type, that it showcased thick ankles, beefy calves, and the spreading hips and thighs created when her entire weight had to balance on the edge of a small round stool top. If she didn't mention it, Liz knew she was too sick to even talk about it. It would make dressing for work every day a self-defeating ordeal.

"Why wouldn't they make mistakes on the set?" Jay returned stoutly. "They made the mistake of not hiring you."

"Thanks for the gallantry, Jay, but I'm not competitive about *Sunrise*. Rosie's a dear friend; I can't begrudge her success. I just wish I didn't have this awful feeling about it."

"Come on over to public TV, then. The pay is lousy, but the work is fun."

Liz studied him sharply to see if this was an unofficial feeler, but decided it was only a light remark. She couldn't rely on Jay McGovern to bail her out of career impasses forever.

"Thanks, but I think I'll stick with the network awhile. I've got a new beat, as amorphous as the old."

"What is it?" Jay asked between mouthfuls of a perfectly done slab of sirloin.

Liz grinned and dropped her gaze demurely to her filet mignon. "New York. That's all."

It was "New York," and it wasn't. She was assigned to the network flagship station, which shared the headquarters building with the national division. Her mission, now that she had decided to accept it, was simply to find and showcase "interesting people and things about New York City." Her bosses, a large number of vaguely but highly placed men known to the work force merely as "the suits," figured that her fresh Midwestern eye might spot stories of both local and network interest, or so Slater, her immediate liaison with the foggy powers that be, had told her. Liz wondered if there were other, ulterior reasons, but didn't waste time speculating. If they were dumb enough to hand her an ambiguous assignment, she'd make the most of it.

Assigned to find "interesting people in New York," Liz spent two days at the public library, visited the American Film Institute headquarters, peered intently at bicyclists in a certain area of Manhattan, and finally found her quarry—a spare, freckle-faced, trousered, hatted, and scarfed lady on an Italian racing bike. Liz stopped her outside an imposing co-op.

"Miss Hepburn, I'm a network correspondent. New York is my beat, and I'd like to interview you."

"Why?" The expressive eyes were as flat and challenging as the famous voice.

Liz took a deep breath. "I'm from the Midwest, and I've never *seen* anyone navigate a bike through that madhouse of a street the way you do."

The laugh was a staccato bark of surprised delight. "What's your name?"

"Liz Jordan."

"Well, Liz Jordan, I'll let you and your cameras visit me, on one condition."

Liz swallowed. "Yes?"

"That you get yourself some decent wheels—" her age-dappled hand vigorously slapped her bike seat—"and come with me before-hand for a spin."

"Oh . . ." The face that had mesmerized so many generations of moviegoers was tilted Liz's way, waiting, challenging, slightly out of focus with the tremor of Parkinson's disease but commanding nevertheless. Liz waffled. She hadn't ridden a bike since she was thirteen, and then only in the placid streets of Turtle Bend. "Oh . . . okay. If you'll take a risk, I will."

What Liz got was better than an interview, although Katharine Hepburn sat down for three long hours in her tasteful living room and let Liz ask anything she wanted—or almost anything. Liz had skimmed everything she could find on the actress before contacting her. The interview was surprisingly smooth for a subject as prickly as the notoriously independent Hepburn. But Liz knew she had taken her niece, Katherine Houghton, under her wing and suspected she, too, was benefitting from some fallout because she was young and trying to make a career for herself.

But what made the piece were the tortured forty-five minutes in hell Liz spent on the streets of Manhattan on a wobbly, underweight two-wheeler, peddling desperately after the serenely gliding senior citizen ahead of her. The camera crew filmed them both coming and going, etching a portrait of Hepburn confidence against the comic relief of Liz's novice bike riding, both set amongst pressing fenders and honking cabs.

Hepburn almost never gave interviews, so Liz's piece caused quite a stir. It was even run on *Sunrise*.

"What's next after Hepburn?" Slater asked. "Garbo?"

Liz pouted as if thinking. "I think maybe . . . bag ladies."

Liz would never understand what made her insert herself into everything that terrified her about living in New York—the congested streets, the mean sidewalks populated profusely with everybody from high-power executives to low-IQ muggers. But she found and trailed and talked to her bag ladies, the cameras tailing her the whole time, and found them as hardy and admirable in their vastly different way as the esteemed Miss Hepburn. And as tough to interview.

"You ain't dressed for this gig," one ancient crone named Sairy Jane barked one late-December day, disdainfully eyeing Liz's high-heeled leather boots, smart designer coat, hatless coiffure, and Isotoner gloves, a Christmas gift from Turtle Bend. The woman compulsively wrapped her accretion of dresses, sweaters, coats, and scarves more tightly around her. Her weather-rutted face stared out from under an awesome erection of Salvation Army hats of all eras, rhinestone felt and flap-eared fake fur combining to produce a tower of unlabeled fashion Babel. "Better git inside, honey, where summon'll take keer of you."

Off she waddled down the uncaring street, Kickerino toes scuffing the sidewalk and Macy's bags rhythmically bumping against her hems of many lengths. A punk rocker would have killed for those Kickerinos.

The bag lady piece was another triumph, but Liz took Sairy

Jane's unsolicited advice. Face it, Jordan, she told herself, you're a minnow out of a bait pail on the streets of New York. Maybe you'd better hie yourself indoors and uptown.

Her next interview—for it had come down to that; Liz was best on a one-to-one basis—was sculptor Louise Nevelson, another native grande dame of the city that had never been kind to women, children, and immigrants. They were survivors, Liz's subjects, each in her own way, each on her own particular embattled turf.

Nevelson in her eighties was an artist of epic proportion even in person, a black-garbed matriarch festooned with sweeping false eyelashes and tribal neckpieces that hung to her unseen waist, draped rather than attired in voluminous clothing that made a kind of abstract monument of her human form. In that sense she resembled her art works, the wall-size congregations of wooden flotsam plucked from the streets of New York during the 1950s, '60s, and '70s of her artistic discontent and painted flat black. Nowadays there was a high-toned phrase for trash recycled into art. Nevelson's works had made that junkyard technique artistically respectable. "Found objects," they were called.

"I was *poor*," the artist explained wryly. "I couldn't afford art materials." She couldn't even afford the large studios she rented anyway to house her massive works, but eventually the museums solved the storage problem by acquiring them for their collections. Now Nevelson was an art world icon, a just and terrible one, ready to wither anyone who had not been forged in the creative fires she had faced. Liz taped a striking portrait of the artist as an old woman, but did not escape unscorched by the Nevelson scorn.

"You're becoming a regular Barbara Walters," Rosemary enthused one day over lunch at Tavern on the Green.

Liz tried not to wince. After Walters's short-lived anchorwoman stint at ABC, where Harry Reasoner had gone into such an unprofessional snit at being paired with a female coanchor that he sniped at her on the air, even her own professionalism couldn't cover the fact that she was being relegated to host a series of celebrity peep show specials—everything you always wanted to know about Johnny and Jane and Farrah and were afraid to ask, Barbara wasn't.

Liz understood that viewers of the eighties were fascinated by celebrity. There was nothing wrong in trying to bring these mysterious but very human beings to the audience close-up. But media commentators used the more trivial specials as sneering material, as if Barbara Walters had always been the Rona Barrett of the video set and had never done the groundbreaking interviews with Castro, Kissinger, and Haldeman she'd attained on her own. Barbara

Walters had been publicly de-serious-ized; Liz considered any comparisons to her a prescription of doom.

Rosemary never mulled over such issues. "And I think it's great the network is running your personality pieces on *Sunrise*," she went on. "It kind of makes up for, well, you know."

Liz picked at her expensive crab salad. Lunches with Rosemary were a rarity now. The crushing early-morning schedule meant Rosie usually rushed home to primp and cook for Joel when she finished work in the early afternoon, dishing up an early dinner and collapsing into an early bedtime.

"Rosie, the network has nothing to make up for. And neither do you," Liz said firmly. "If you hadn't beaten me out, someone else would have. The network was uneasy with me. I can see that now. I had no live anchor experience, and there you were, dazzling Washington every day.... How are things going?"

"All right." Rosemary dragged her fork through the Linguine Milanese she'd ordered, promising to eat only a third of it. Two-thirds was gone already. The fork paused, moved upright, twirled into the sauce-smothered noodles. "The hours are awful. But I knew that, didn't I? And of course Joel has to be out all hours because of his business."

And of course Joel. Liz sipped her Chablis. She didn't like Joel, but one seldom found a married couple where one liked both parties equally or one even at all. It made Liz wonder about marriage.

"Liz..." Rosemary was being unusually tentative. "Am I bein' unfair? You know that nightlife doesn't excite me—Club 54...."

"Studio 54."

"Whatever. Joel says he has to make that scene; he has to get his clients seen. And I'm so tired evenings. I have to get up at three in the morning to get to the studio on time, and I need my sleep or my face gets all baggy. And I think there are drugs, and things..." Her voice trailed off unhappily.

"Surely you knew what kind of life-style Joel led here."

"But I didn't *see* it! And now he wants to take me out, show me off. At least he isn't gettin' his picture in *W* every month with this or that model or actress. Now I get some equal time. He really is proud about this *Sunrise* thing. Heavens, even if I wanted to get off it, I wouldn't dare." Rosemary laughed. "But what about you? I think you're doin' fine."

"It's fun doing the celebrity beat," Liz admitted. "Celebs are the hardest people to interview in the world. Not that they won't talk; most of them will talk up a storm. But they're very good at not *telling* you anything. Anything about their real selves. It becomes a challenge to ambush them into honesty. I tend to go for people who have something behind the facade. But I can sympathize with you on the morning show. I did a morning anchor in Minneapolis for a while; it was the pits."

"The pits," Rosemary agreed, spinning the last of the linguine onto the fork and popping it into her mouth.

Liz couldn't help mentally paraphrasing that *Mary Poppins* song, "A forkful of starch helps the misery go down, misery go dow-own, misery go down . . ."

"Is this Liz?"

The male voice on the phone wasn't Jay's, but it was vaguely familiar. For a heart-stopping moment she thought—

"It's Wendy Banks. I just got back from Stuttgart, and wondered if you were interested in dinner some night. I never found out how your story on the Pantomime Players came out."

She met him that Friday night, on lower Broadway, at a place called the Acute Cafe. Wendy was already waiting in the foyer when her cab dropped her off.

"This is a cute place," she observed as they were led to a lamplit corner.

"Cute," he responded on cue. "But the food's great. French cuisine. I recommend the veal."

The service was smooth and unobtrusive, the food superb. Liz, being Midwestern-bred, wasn't much for wines to dine by. Wendy came from the same background, but his frequent European sojourns had mellowed the antiwine bias. He ordered an ambrosial Rhine wine that kept Liz lingering over her meal.

The Acute Cafe suited him. It's consciously casual clientele fit perfectly with the laid-back artistic temperament. Liz did much of the talking, Wendy listening with a flattering attention. He was not a verbal man, as so many in broadcasting were. When she had bubbled herself empty of conversation, he just smiled and ordered coffee and cognac.

"Did Germany go well for you?"

He nodded, the candlelight snagging unmercifully on every ragged strand of gray in his shaggy head of hair. But he wasn't a media man; he didn't have to worry about seventy-five-dollar haircuts, gray hair, or wrinkles. He was probably only thirty-five, but a matching set of fine, deep smile lines surrounded his eyes like the etching in a Florentine ring setting circles the stone. Liz felt safe.

"Would you," he asked when the cognac was just a wash of burnt umber in the bottom of their glasses, "like to come back to my place?"

"Yes."

Her heart pounded as they trawled for a cab on the dark street outside. It had been so long since it'd been a question of your place or mine. Now she was doing it again, taking a chance on slipping out of her protective shell and allowing someone else to scrape her emotions raw. Maybe she'd forgotten how—forgotten how to make love, come quickly, leave gracefully. Not cause a scene by expecting too much or not enough.

She'd forgotten how much she'd liked Wendy's bare, spare loft with its midnight population of artist's paraphernalia glimpsed like ghosts in far corners.

"Are you—?" he began.

"I'm not on the Pill," she blurted.

Wendy didn't miss a beat. "Then did you—?" he asked. "Or should I—"

Liz elevated her slightly overlarge-for-evening handbag. "I came prepared. Do you think I'm pushy?"

"Wise," he said, pulling her into his arms in the almost dark. They swayed together, to the rhythm of their pounding circulatory systems, committed now to a course they both felt free to succumb to. Wendy led her carefully up a circular staircase in the dark, to the balcony where a simple, old-fashioned brass bedframe and a scattering of prints on a room-dividing wall made a bedroom.

The bathroom was behind the freestanding wall, an arbitrary assemblage of old porcelain fixtures screened by a jungle of large potted parlor palms. Liz felt very Victorian as she inserted her diaphragm and came, shyly and still fully dressed, around the wall to the bedroom.

Wendy hadn't undressed, but pulled her down on the old quilt with him, where they began with testing kisses, finding each other's tempo and pleasure. He was methodical, precise, as he must be when he drew, Liz thought. He helped her off with her clothes with slow, savoring fingers, until she was shivering from the almost stroke of his hands in places she didn't even know were eroticized. She found her own touch softening at the example of his, until they sought each other like the oversensitive blind in the dark.

They finally joined, Liz gasping as her body spasmed, trying to pull, pull, pull him into itself. She realized how much her celibate self had unknowingly missed this, this penetrating, probing, piercing, filling, plunging contact, again and again, over and over and always over too soon, despite the convulsive sudden satisfaction, first his, then hers.

In the morning they woke, the skylight pouring daylight down on them. Liz rolled over to see Wendy's face, the same calm, unruffled one she had seen last night.

"How come nobody ever married a nice guy like you?"

He smiled, unthreatened by the question. "Travel, the theater. My work doesn't make for marriage. It doesn't even allow for . . ." He hesitated, apparently afraid she'd misinterpret his words. "It doesn't even let me have much . . . decent sex."

But Liz just nodded. "My job, too. And this was pretty— decent." She threw her arms around his bare shoulders. "I think I have just fallen violently in like."

"Me, too," Wendy said equably. "You don't know how damn lucky we are."

— *Chapter 38* —

"*Pass those mashed potatoes my way, Elizabeth. And the gravy* boat."

"And have some more rolls," Myrtle added, extending a plate of over-warmed store-bought buns as soon as Liz's hands were empty of the potatoes and gravy.

Family-style food serving seemed alien now to someone used to ordering what she wanted, eating however much of it she wanted, and tipping the server. These ritual rounds of overburdened serving dishes, with hurt feelings riding on how much or whether or not something was eaten, struck Liz as decadent. She usually felt like a barbarian guest lost in the elaborate etiquette of a Roman feast when she came home for major holidays. That may be why she no longer came home that often.

But this was Christmas 1981, and her father was past seventy.

For once the ever-present Neil Wetland was not available. Liz was surprised to learn he had family in Ohio and had gone to spread his time-soured cheer among them for a change. At least he wasn't here to sneer at any talk of Liz's work, dismissing it all as "features" with a deceptively understanding smile.

Liz sipped the traditional Burgundy and meekly took a roll. She was on the run so much these days she didn't have to be persnickety about her weight.

Her father looked up from the mashed potato mountain he was erecting on the fluted edge of his food-burdened Red Willow plate. He had created a crater and filled it with turkey gravy until a hot brown lava oozed over the top.

"It's nice to have you home for the holidays, Elizabeth. It should happen more often."

"I know. But the network is an absolute Grinch when it comes to scheduling holiday time off."

"The network! It sounds like God, Elizabeth, the way you talk about it. Go here, go there; do this, do that. Thou shalt have no other obligations before me—" *What about his work?*

"It sounds like any assignment editor, Dad. You know there's no rest for the wicked in the news game." Liz had been foresighted enough to have kept her father ignorant of her brief shot at the anchor spot. He never knew she had been considered for any post other than that of correspondent, for now in New York. He never knew she had failed.

"Hmm." Z.J. attacked his potatoes, thinking. "Whatever happened to that anchor fellow who was squiring you around? Steve whatever? Nice young man. . . ."

"He went to Philadelphia and got married, last I heard."

"Married. Well. He didn't look the marrying kind to me. Any young fella now who's got all his hair and his head screwed on right, he'd be crazy to marry, seein' how many young women there are who seem in no hurry to get hitched. . . . You got another young man, Elizabeth?"

"I'm seeing a man, yes, Dad. He's thirty-six and designs sets and costumes for the Metropolitan Opera."

"Thirty-six and never been married?"

Liz nodded wearily.

"Better be careful, Elizabeth; those men in the thee-ay-ter can be a bit . . . odd."

"He's straight as a hat pin, Dad, so don't—"

"And what does this 'seeing' mean? Hell, you can see someone on the bus every day—or do you ride the subways? You dating this guy, or living with him, or what?"

"Zachariah!" Myrtle could take no more at her dinner table.

"Dating," Liz answered sweetly, "is I guess what you would have called it in your day."

"I suppose he isn't the marrying kind, either."

"He works with opera companies all over the world, so, no, I guess he isn't in a position to get married and settle down."

Z.J.'s shock of bleach-white hair shook. "Seems like nobody in New York is ready to settle down. You better get yourself a better assignment, Elizabeth, my girl, if you expect to put some grandchildren up on the wall beside you."

He was old and getting older, while the world was changing. Liz felt she had a child in hand already, a big, rambunctious, crotchety boy who saw the world in the clear primary colors of youth. Certainly he required patience and protection from her, as any cranky infant would.

"The grandchildren will have to wait," Liz said good-naturedly, buttering the last of Myrtle's roll. "I have a piece on I. F. Stone to wrap up first." Liz thought that should please her father; I. F. Stone was a crusading journalist from his own era.

"'Pieces to wrap up.' It sounds like you're selling china or Girl Scout cookies, Elizabeth! Tell me about something I know."

She exchanged a glance with Myrtle, startled to find an expression of knowing sympathy in the usually uncommitted hazel eyes.

"Well, Dad, there isn't much out there that's the way you knew it anymore. Things are changing. . . ."

"Things always change," her father snapped. "People don't."

Ah, but people do change. Back in New York by the new year, Liz found herself at the lavish party Rosemary and Joel always threw. Liz had heard of this fabled affair but had never attended. This year it was held in their new multilevel co-op, affordable thanks to Rosie's *Sunrise* salary, which Liz had never been crass enough to ask after.

"Lots of dough," the man with a martini by the Steinway grand remarked, apropos of nothing more than Liz being handy and engaged at the moment in looking over the crowd and surroundings. "That Joel is some operator. All his properties are *hot*! See that one by the wall with David Susskind? Got the lead in a cable TV miniseries—like that! Did one car commercial and bingo. That Joel doesn't miss an angle."

Liz managed to melt away without appearing to have heard. She ran into Rosemary, who rustled like a sheet of stage thunder in a stiff black taffeta hostess skirt.

"Liz! How could I have missed you so far? That silver silk is spectacular on you. . . . Does the skirt slit all the way? Well, you've got the legs for it. Wait a minute; I'll have another—" Rosemary wafted two full flutes of champagne off a passing waiter's tray and offered Liz one. "Where's your boyfriend?"

"You sound like my dad," Liz chided gently. "Wendy's not here yet; he had to work late on a Met set. Don't worry; I'll introduce you—"

"You're Liz Jordan. Saw your thing on the stage doormen; clever, very clever." The emphatic matron who had swooped by to make the pronouncement sailed on.

Rosemary giggled. "These things get more crowded every year. It's getting so even *I* don't know anyone anymore. Oh, wait—" She snagged a shrimp canapé and devoured it, then sighed. "Oh, Liz, honey. I wish I could sit down; I wish I could hear myself think; I wish we could have time to talk. I'm not used to stayin' up this late, and it turns my brains into chitlins. . . . Oops, Joel wants me in the dining room; must be some other 'must-meet.' Don't let your Wendy slip in without me meetin' him, promise?"

Rosemary rustled away, her departing crackle sounding both harried and desperate. Liz sipped the champagne. Tonight Wendy would whisk her home and she didn't need to keep herself sober. The party itself was enough to drive a teetotaler to drink. People swirled and talked and drank and smoked and—in discreet corners—sniffed cocaine.

Joel, in full black tie, darted among his guests, who were a compendium of Manhattan's "most recognizable" nonentities— rock star live-ins and models who appeared more before the cameras of the *National Enquirer* than any fashion photographers, has-been Hollywood starlets and hungry agents, winners who had become losers and vice versa.

Liz panned the gathering like a camera, looking for one interesting face, one person who seemed to have a story to tell. Everyone there was telling his or her story now, ad nauseam. They had no secrets to conceal. She could target Joel's model clients from across the room. They were the beanstalk-tall, exotically decked women whose heads loomed over everyone else's, including most of the men's. Liz sometimes thought that New York was solely populated by short men and tall women who had come here from somewhere else to compensate for their differences by making good and making each other famous. The Sonny and Cher Syndrome.

Someone bumped into her shoulder blade. She turned, vaguely annoyed, because she'd seen too many careless and drunk people at this party tonight.

"Sorry, sweet." The man was rock-star street-handsome, with Drambuie eyes and a dark mustache just a shade more than pencil-thin. His warm hand tightened on her silken midriff momentarily but too intimately, as if to steady her, although her balance had never wavered. The silk seemed to crackle at his touch. Liz felt her social hackles rising on a primitive wave of resentment—and uninvited response. His eyes gauged the emotions in hers, then he was lost in the crowd—another producer or actor or nobody on the way to somewhere else.

A waiter paused smoothly, his tray poised to receive Liz's empty glass, which she hadn't even noticed was drained. She deposited it with a smile and he glided away. All the waiters were black, the only black people in the string of vast rooms except for one Watusi-like model whose magenta-glittered eyelids screamed alarm from across the smoky room like red lights atop a police car. It made Liz uneasy to be served solely by deferential black men, as if they had always served that way and she had always been so served. To the manner born. Maybe she was paranoid; maybe now blacks could take pride in their work even if it touched on old, racist stereotypes. Maybe. But Liz couldn't sit back and feel comfortable.

No, no one here she could contact for a future story. The guest list was impeccably composed of people she didn't want to see, and people who wouldn't want to see her.

Except for Wendell Banks, here at her invitation. He threaded his way now through the manic crowd, untouched by them, to her side. A waiter, as if alerted to the new arrival, hovered instantly with a full tray of fresh champagne flutes. Wendy offered one to Liz.

"If you'll see me home . . ."

He handed her the flute and took another. "You been here long?"

"Feels like it."

Wendy had risen to the address and donned a suit that hinted at the formal without bowing to it. He surveyed Liz's outfit. "Beautiful fabric." His fingers expertly slid along the platinum crease of a silken shoulder fold.

"You say the nicest things," Liz whispered back. "How about saying something even nicer and suggesting we leave?"

"I just got here."

Liz sighed. "I know. But you can't have an audible word with Rosemary, and she's the only one I'd wanted you to meet. I don't know why I suggested this. I've never been to one of Joel's business bashes before and I felt like a party. They're a bore. Do you mind leaving?"

He just nodded and returned their half-full glasses to one of the peripatetic waiters waltzing by with tray in hand. Liz waved good-bye to Rosemary, pointing in pantomime to Wendy and mouthing, "This is him." But Rosie was trapped in full-skirted grace on the open stairway, her blond hair pale against the grass cloth–papered walls. Liz slipped into her fur jacket and out the door with Wendy. A last look back showed the mob still writhing, like a many-headed monster in its death throes, and Medium, Dark, and Handsome glancing toward her from the edge of a crowd by the fireplace.

The doorman hailed a cab and Wendy gave the driver his address without asking Liz. They never went to her apartment; it was barren and bereft of the care or beauty inherent in Wendy's spare SoHo loft.

Liz basked in Wendy's solo approval of her expensive gown, in her formal and befurred evening out, but she was glad to be back in familiar surroundings, where she could feel free to be herself. Wendy built a fire in his ancient fireplace and established her on some cushions with a glass of B&B. Then he lit up a home-rolled cigarette.

"Great grass." He offered her a puff.

"Don't smoke," said Liz, surprised.

"You can learn this. It's terrific stuff now and again; no head-aches." Gingerly, she took the misshapen cylinder in her fingers and put it to her lips. Flecks clung to her lip gloss as she inhaled deeply and held her breath. Nothing happened. Wendy took the joint back and drew on it deeply before handing it back.

"You do this often?" Liz asked.

"No."

"I didn't know you were into controlled substances."

"There was a lot worse at that party."

"I know." Liz sighed and tried again, holding her breath until her head spun and wondering if that was being high. She exhaled and gave back the roach, watching Wendy put it to his mouth again. "Either this is sexy, like the double cigarette trick in *Now, Voyager*, or it's highly unsanitary."

He laughed, his eyes slitted half-shut like a dozing cat's. He handed her the joint again.

"And I told my father you were straight," Liz accused, dragging far more expertly on the marijuana this time. Something took. The night seemed to pause, then turn up the volume on its colors, sounds, shapes, textures. Wendy's hands were exploring her through the sheer silk, his fingertips liquid as velvet fire. She giggled again, slipping down in the pillows in her $680 designer knockoff as if it were a T-shirt. Fabric writhed against fabric, creating a symphony of subtle sound, with the snap of fireplace logs playing intermittent timpani. Timpani symphony. Sounds made her laugh; touch made her tremble. A flash of fear exploded—what had the stuff done to her? Nothing, nothing. Wendy was over her, about to press his mouth to hers, inhale the acrid air of her lungs, recycle it in his own intoxicated veins, mingling, tingling, turning, spin-ning. For one weird, splintered moment, Wendy's face wore a stranger's mask. He looked like the man in the crowd at the party. . . . It was an incendiary illusion, purely sexual, streaking like St. Elmo's fire through the smoky pathways of her brain.

A phantom mustache seemed to tease the arch of her upper lip—so familiar, so alien. Liz twined herself fiercely around Wendy, trying to find someone else. <u>Trying to find herself</u>.

— Chapter 39 —

Rosemary's mascara had turned traitor, tracing telltale char-
coal smudges under each cornflower-blue eye—or maybe it was
just fatigue from months of a predawn schedule. Her blond hair
looked dull—overteased and undernourished. The face was as
flawlessly underpinned as ever by a bone structure time couldn't
seem to touch, but Liz noticed two small pockets of fleshy sag
on either side of the well-made-up mouth.

Rosemary was stuffing Fettuccini Alfredo into that mouth as
fast as she could and still keep talking.

"That Danny Rogers is a creep. He's taken to holding meetings
without me there, so I only get leftovers. I could be the weather
girl, for all the contribution I make to the show. Everybody thinks
he's Mr. Valium, like Bing Crosby. Relax along with Danny. But
behind that shucks-and-sweater act beats a heart of pure venom."

"I always did think he thought a lot of himself," agreed Liz,
"which is a good excuse for thinking nothing of anyone around
him."

"You're so lucky, Liz, that they didn't pick you for *Sunrise*. I
mean, it's nice that they air your pieces now and again, but you
don't have to *be* there and put up with all that guff. The producers
haven't the foggiest idea of what they're doin' or even *want* to
do. Danny runs them like a ringmaster with a cageful of monkeys.
He hates women, I do believe, but hides it with this phony chivalry
act. And the ratings! Well, honey, it certainly isn't what the powers
that *were* expected. The first tier are all out on their cans and now
they've brought in some whiz kid to revive the act."

The waiter was there to whisk Rosemary's empty plate away.

"Another screwdriver," she tossed over her shoulder as care-
lessly as a sneeze. "Honestly, honey, I am at my wit's end. You
know the reviewers haven't been easy on any of us—"

"It's against their nature. When Jane Pauley got the *Today* spot,
some type assassin described her as having 'the IQ of a cantaloupe.' That comes with the territory, Rosie." Liz sipped her Perrier
water. She hated to be trendy, but it was better than losing her
working edge to a luncheon wine buzz. Rosemary, however, was
through for the day and could drink what she liked.

She took a big slug of the fresh screwdriver. "The *Post* guy said I 'must have been hired for my beauty-queen body, not my brain.'" She laughed, harshly. "Honey, he sure hasn't seen me naked."

"You look terrific on camera, Rosie. You always have. People are going to hold it against you. They always do."

"You're so cool, Liz. You've got it all so together. . . . I don't know—it's like I don't have any glue left inside, you know? I just feel . . ."

"What does Joel say?"

"Oh, he's busy with his business. You don't run a top talent agency with one eye on your wife's career. Joel says what he's always said: If I would just get some discipline and diet off about thirty pounds and work out about ten hours a week, I'd be fine. But I don't have time to exercise, and I used to starve myself and never lose all this poundage below the waist anyway, and I'm too tired to watch what I eat . . . and, it's no use."

"Well, maybe fifteen pounds, but you've got one of those enviable thin faces, Rosie. Has anyone at work mentioned your weight?"

Rosemary scratched her neck nervously. "No . . . no one ever has. But they don't *talk* to me anymore, Liz. I feel . . . extraneous. Who knows what they think about me?"

"That's what I hate about television—the suits in the front office really get into the agony of defeat and make it a self-fulfilling prophecy. Look, relax. That's all I can tell you. This game goes up and down. The trick is to maintain an even course right in the middle somewhere between ecstasy and despair."

But Liz went back to her apartment that night and programmed the fancy videocassette recorder she'd bought on her arrival in New York to record *Sunrise* for a week. She often was en route to work before the program ended at nine A.M., and hadn't really seen it beyond recording her own intermittent segments and watching its debut week, when Rosemary had been eager for a friendly verdict.

Each night, tired but loyal, Liz reviewed the tape. Rosemary still looked good on camera; those bones would never let her down, not even in old age. But her manner was taut, jerky, partly in contrast to Danny Rogers's sublimely laid-back veneer. He acted like he could sing a cup of coffee to sleep.

The problem was, Danny was also energyless. Rosemary's new nervousness was not the right counter to his patented laissez-faire. Liz could see why the *Sunrise* producers had become fond of running her segments; they brought some life and fresh air to the costly but stagnant set. The brass had imported other reporters, she discovered, pausing in fast forward to play a gritty piece on street people in real time. This was her bag ladies with a vengeance. The reporter had gone into the parks, the flophouses, and the seedy bars to find the men who lived out of their empty pockets the way Liz's ladies lived out of their secondhand clothes and shopping bags. The camera dwelled on young faces made old, old faces made into icons of filth and neglect, crazed faces. Alcohol-cured voices slurred into the microphone in answer to the off-camera voice that never stopped probing. It was a damn good piece. Liz hadn't know anyone was reporting scroungy reality for the networks besides Geraldo Rivera on ABC and free-lance crusaders like John Alpert for *Today*. She waited for the final stand-up, filmed beside a soup line.

"And so men like Dingo and Lefty and Punch inhabit these mean streets, living on an expensive elixir of cheap alcohol and despair, always poor, often cold, and seldom visible to the eye of the passerby. We pass them and try not to see them. And we succeed at that as much as they failed at whatever feeble opportunity life once offered them. But they are our brothers. And they are there. This is Alfonso Delgado, at breakfast on the Bowery, for *Sunrise*."

It was a moving finale. Liz hit the pause button and studied the man who had written and delivered it. He was there on network film for the same reason she was. The networks had responded to the social agitation of the late sixties and early seventies, now so quietly ebbed. They had hired a sprinkling of women and what TV insiders called "the beautiful ethnic," minority men and women whose black, brown, or yellow skins shouted "equal opportunity" to millions of viewers every day. Oddly enough, there were few minority women on a network level. Apparently being female alone was enough of a sop to liberals. For minorities, networks usually went to the slim stock of qualified men—they found Geraldo Rivera when he was an activist lawyer and demonstrated natural on-camera charisma while speaking for his clients. Bryant Gumbel had worked his way up through the side door of sports. Connie Chung found her opportunity in multiracial San Francisco.

But there weren't many of them, and Alfonso Delgado, good as he was, was one Liz had never seen before. Or not quite "never seen before." He was the man who had bumped into her at Joel's New Year's party.

Slater's boss was Levin, and Levin's boss was Mahan.

Liz was called into Slater's office one day to find Levin and Mahan there before her. Slater was hanging on and his office was big, but not that big. The only reason for this powpow could be that it was officially secret.

"Miss Jordan." The top men stood and shook hands with her, eyeing her all the while as if she were rare roast beef and it was their lunchtime. Another man came in, obviously late and not worried about it—short, brusque, balding, and sharp as an X-Acto blade in a hurry.

Slater did the honors. "Barry Hoffman. Liz Jordan. Barry's the new executive producer of *Sunrise*. Frank Burton's out."

Hoffman sat on the edge of Slater's desk, a sign of organizational confidence. "No use beating around the bush. I've seen your tryout tapes for the first round of *Sunrise* casting. I think Weintraub made a mistake. I've got the show now, and I'd like to go with you as female anchor."

Liz was . . . flabbergasted. "Me? Look, Mr. Hoffman, I'm surprised. I'm flattered—"

"Don't be. The show's in the toilet. You could be on a garbage scow headed right toward the bottom. It's a suicide mission."

"Hmm . . . thanks. But *you* volunteered, I see."

Hoffman shrugged. "I'm a gambler. I'm behind the scenes, too. I can outlive a flop. You're frontline talent. It dies, you do."

"I like what I'm doing now."

"Why wouldn't you? As far as I can figure, you're out there in some limbo making your own mark. Somehow you managed to bamboozle both the network and the affiliate into feeling they don't have an overriding claim on you. But *Sunrise*, such as it is, is an opportunity to make a real national impact. I'd let you keep up those in-depth interviews and street pieces of yours; they're classy."

"Thanks," Liz said wryly. "What else are you going to keep?"

"Rogers." He immediately saw her face change. "The public likes him; you can't argue with on-camera charisma. We'll get a new weather jester; try something there. And I want to continue those taped segments—you and Delgado have saved the show's ass. I'm putting Delgado on as roving *Sunrise* reporter, with some desk time to introduce his stuff, make him part of the *Sunrise* family."

Liz jumped. "Why don't you make Delgado the anchor and use me as the free agent? That's what I've been doing, and Delgado at the anchor desk would be as much of a coup to the liberal set as another woman 'hostess.'"

Hoffman, amazingly, agreed. "Could. But—sorry, Liz—your stuff is inherently soft. Great, well-written, creatively filmed—and I know that's partly your doing—and insightful. But soft. The Fonz gets the hard stuff. He's the outside man."

She knew it was true.

"Besides," Hoffman persuaded, "there isn't anybody you can't interview as coanchor on *Sunrise*—statesmen, stars, Pulitzer Prize winners, Muhammed Ali. . . ."

Liz laughed. "When would this *Sunrise* . . . make-over . . . start?"

"Soon as possible." Hoffman's sheaf of papers dealt the desktop a karate chop. "The patient is croaking. If you're agreeable, have your agent call me and we'll work out a deal to your liking."

Liz, dismissed, started to rise, then sat back. "What about . . . Rosemary Martin?"

"What about her?"

"She's a good friend of mine."

Hoffman cracked his first smile. "There are no friends in this business, only competitors. She didn't cut it, that's all. Viewers didn't warm up to her."

"You could be saying that about me in six months."

Hoffman's smile widened. "Six weeks, baby. Or I could be putting a bonus into that fat contract your agent will be perusing tomorrow."

"And if I say no?"

"Fine. But find another network."

Liz stood. "At least you're honest. I think you've just made an offer I can't afford to refuse."

Hoffman's hand thrust into her path as she left the room, and Liz paused to shake his hard dry palm. She didn't like him, didn't trust him, but knew it took exactly what she disliked in him to save a program like *Sunrise* once it hit the skids.

She wondered what it would take to save her friendship with Rosemary Martin.

"It's all right; don't you fret about it, Liz, honey. After all, I got first crack at the job when you didn't expect me to even be in the runnin' for it. It's only fair that I'm out and you're in."

"What will you do now?"

Rosemary stared out over the newsprint-gray collage of sky-scrapers spread like Tinkertoys below them. Lunch was on Liz, so she had chosen Windows on the World at the top of the World Trade Center. From 107 stories up, you could see what a jammed, tiny island Manhattan was, how looming and yet so small, and maybe look at your problems in the same way. She hoped Rosemary would.

"I don't know what I'll do, Liz. Tell Joel first, I guess. It was nice of you to break the news, instead of lettin' that new producer do it, or hearin' it from Danny Rogers."

"Nice. Rosie, you know I've been sitting on this for over two weeks. But everything's been hush-hush. I've known you were out and didn't tip you off—"

Rosemary rearranged the heavy silverware on their cozy round table and gazed again through the giant vertical slices of window. "I've never been up here at night. Oh, Joel's entertained clients here, but with *Sunrise* I've always been too tired to come along. Now, maybe I can."

She looked back, direct and calm. "Don't feel guilty, Liz. It's the business, not any single person in it, that's so inhumane. I know what you couldn't tell me before now."

"I wish Steve had been so understanding," Liz said suddenly.

Rosemary smiled wanly. "He wasn't, was he? Understanding. Most men just expect to be understood and forget that it works both ways. His loss. But it's better that *you* should have *Sunrise*; it's a tough schedule to meet if you're married or have a family. And your friend at the Metropolitan Opera, who I never did meet—"

"Wendy Banks."

"Wendy. Will he still fit into your schedule?"

"I hope so. I'm kind of hooked on Wendy. But it's nothing . . . serious, Rosie. For either of us. And he's off to Europe half the time."

She nodded. They sat in the corner of the restaurant's topmost tier, which made an exclusive little island within an exclusive bigger island upon the world's most exclusive piece of waterbound real estate. Liz finally was no longer awed by it, by the size and the scurry of New York City. It was just a place, like any other, with its own peculiar rules of survival.

"Wendy sounds . . . understanding." Rosemary smiled. The shock of the news had deflated all her pumped-up energy. She seemed sad, but more herself. "I'm happy for you, Liz. I wish you all the best and only the best." She reached for her handbag and installed it on her lap, under the napkin, as if ready to leave. "I hope you'll find time to have lunch with me now and again—I'll have all the time in the world. But you'll find the schedule wears you out, doesn't leave much time or energy for a personal life. If there's anything you want to know . . . any survival tips, just ask me."

"I will," Liz said warmly, mentally noting that Rosemary Martin was the last person in Manhattan she would turn to for survival tips.

She waited to call Turtle Bend with the news until that evening; somehow she couldn't crow about her success in a personal arena with an uninformed Rosemary still on her conscience.

"Dad—?"

"Shout out, Elizabeth; this line's all fuzzy. Must be that New York smog."

"That's Los Angeles. New York just has muggers."

"This isn't even the weekend. Why're you calling?"

"I have great news. I think."

"If you don't know good news from bad by this time, Elizabeth, you must have forgotten everything I taught you."

"It's about my job. I'm going to be the new coanchor on *Sunrise*."

"Coanchor?"

"You know, they have a man and a woman who run the show; I'm going to be the token woman. It's a big promotion and ... and they're paying me more money than I've ever heard of."

"Oh? Guess there is money in television. Well, that's swell, Elizabeth. This mean I'll be seeing more of you on TV?"

"Every morning from seven to nine."

"When does it start?"

"The show's already on, but I don't join it for two weeks. This is an inside tip. It hasn't been announced to the public yet."

"Well, I'd better get a word or two in the *Sentinel* then, even if I'm accused of nepotism ... I could always run your high school photo with it."

"Da-ad! I wanted you to know. It's really a big break, a big responsibility."

"You can handle it, Elizabeth; you always took to responsibility like a muskrat to water. You call again, but when the rates are cheaper. These things cost nowadays."

"Dad. I could practically *buy* Ma Bell now! Well, not quite, but at least a substation. How are you feeling?"

"Fine, fine; long as my blood pressure isn't rising at the thought of big phone bills—"

"All right, I'm going. Take it easy."

"Sure will. And I'll give your regards to Myrtle."

The network was paying her $280,000 a year plus nontaxable fringe benefits. It was a one-year contract, a mute reminder that nobody was guaranteeing anything. She'd heard that Danny Rogers was making $500,000 or more.

To earn the money, Liz had to pay the price; they went over her with an ultrafine-tooth comb. The show's producers gathered into an informal jury in the makeup room while imported hair and makeup specialists "played with her look." The staff makeup and hairdo people would maintain whatever the outside experts came up with, so they hung around the fringes of the hubbub, eyeing

Liz as if she were an extraordinarily overgrown and miraculous vegetable imported from some exec's Long Island hobby garden.

"Down," one expert decreed on her hair. "Up," decided another. "Permed." "Straight." They brushed it and sprayed it and blew it and twirled it on an assortment of heated devices that looked like surplus from the Spanish Inquisition. The "suits" looked on, all indecisively puckered brows and lips. "Blond," they suggested, a knee-jerk reaction. The experts and Liz turned on them, all too aware that there was little you could do with a natural brunette but live with her coloring the way it was.

At first the make-over was fun. Then Liz's neck cricked from keeping her face tilted to the overhead lights. Her ears burned from where the hot rollers and blow combs had seared the sensitive skin. At least six eyelining pencils slipped into her eye. Powder gathered behind her contact lenses, creating a cloudy, cataractlike gel to view the world through. Her scalp began to feel as if it housed a hill of fire ants.

In the end, like most committees, they came to no conclusion, and turned her over to Scavullo.

Liz was in terminal awe. Francesco Scavullo was the current dean of portrait photographers. His studio occupied a modest portion in a building too upscale to house the usual photographer. Inside, it was the same arid empty space populated by tripods, silver umbrellas, and white cardboard backdrops Liz had seen at other photographers'. What, then, was the magic of this small, intense dark man who had made even middle-aged-dowdy Martha Mitchell look like a blond bombshell on the cover of *New York* magazine a few years back?

"Can you do anything with a brunette?" quipped Liz, holding out a strand.

Scavullo's black eyes narrowed gleefully. "My favorite."

That's how he did it. When you "sat" for Scavullo, you were the be all and end all of his universe. You were the core. He worked with his makeup artistry—and the man was an artist, Liz thought as she saw her face "painted" into perfection in the mirror beneath her restyled hair—to stamp a commercially recognizable beauty on the individual face before his camera without sacrificing the personality beneath the surface gloss.

Before he began shooting, Liz semireclined self-consciously on a sheet of white matboard, draped in an alien magenta silk blouse and cobalt scarf, with only a black sheet wrapped around her below the waist, feeling naked.

Scavullo winked. "You know how to make the camera like you. That's your job. My camera will like you even more than the others. That's *my* job."

She relaxed, got into it, let expressions play across her features, did what models do, concentrated on the camera, seduced the camera.

The photos, when they finally came, were spectacular. Liz looked like an intellectual Racquel Welch, gorgeous but to be taken seriously. The sitting had cost thousands, but Hoffman was so pleased he gave Liz the largest color print for her own use and a black-and-white version to send home to her father.

"Guess what? It's me, Dad," Liz penned quickly in a note she attached to the carefully padded photo before sending it. "Not 'Liz' Taylor, but your very own daughter. If you must run anything on me in the *Sentinel*, at least use a decent picture, Love, Liz."

Of course, it was as much a product of Scavullo as of Dorothy and Zachariah Jordan, or even Liz herself, that newspapers across the country dutifully ran in noting her rise to *Sunrise* anchor. The *Ladies Home Journal* featured the color version on their cover six months later, along with an in-depth interview with Liz inside. She was the hot new rising TV news star, female variety. Even blond Jessica Savitch's icily and efficiently twinkling natal planet seemed to go into temporary retrograde as Liz's face and name streaked across the public's star-watching consciousness, all carefully choreographed by the network flacks. Jane Pauley was married and reclusively dull. Liz was still single and viewed as a cross between a starlet and a trained pony. She put her foot down when the network attempted to arrange a blind date between herself and a rock star of questionable gender for a charity gala.

"I run my own private life," she told Hoffman. "You do want me and *Sunrise* to be taken seriously, don't you?"

He shrugged. "I want *Sunrise* to succeed" was all he answered. Liz was expendable.

So she knew that on the first, benchmark Monday when the network limo drew silently up her still street. Liz darted into the predawn darkness and into the deeper dark behind the heavily tinted windows. A script of the show had been sent by messenger the night before, giving her time to study it in that crucial period before sleeping when the memory is supposed to be at its sharpest. By the time she got to the studio, Liz wasn't sure she could remember her own name.

But then the fluorescent-lit bustle of the *Sunrise* staff surrounded her, bearing her off to the makeup chair and breaking in with adjustments to sequence or notes on guests. Danny Rogers ambled in when Liz was almost done, submitting to his sketchy makeup with a kind of weary condescension.

"Sure glad I don't need my eyelashes curled," he noted. "At

least you don't wear falsies like that blond beanbrain they tried last."

Liz had met Rogers at several predebut press parties; she was used to his put-downs. "Brunettes don't need reinforcements there," she answered, batting her eyelashes mockingly. "I don't fade out under those lights like blondes and dishwater browns."

Danny, whose Lincolnesque looks, freckled face, and hair the color of tan shoe polish had got him named the "plain brown paper wrapper man" by the more acidic TV critics, made a face, but shut up.

Then Liz was walking out to the set, floating really, in a too-early high from too much coffee. But people kept handing her Styrofoam cups as she sat trapped in her chair and she kept drinking from them for want of something constructive to do.

Now she saw the $560,000 Plexiglas set, as new as she and worth twice as much. It was made of desk-high lengths of thick, clear plastic, topped with another glassy slab of plastic and set in a shallow X-form. She, Danny, and visiting reporters or the weather jester, Darryl McComb, sat on three sides of the X. "It'll never work," Liz had said when it was first unveiled to her like some rare architectural find. "Audiences get nervous when they see anchors' legs. It's custom, going back to the roots of television as a news medium. Nobody saw Edward R. Murrow's pins. TV newscasters have no legs."

Then she pointed out that there was a transparency problem for women in skirts that men in pants wouldn't face. Or did they expect her to wear the pants?

Nobody had considered that viewers would be able to see through the costly Plexiglas set right to Liz's knobby knees or beyond. Hoffman practically worshiped the set. It, above all, had to stay. They debated her skirt lengths for hours, having blanched universally at the mere idea of an anchorwoman in pants. In the end, they decided that colored matboard inserts on the set's seating side would shield Liz's privacy and even add a colorful note. Liz fantasized that as her epitaph—"A colorful note," like J. Fred Muggs on the early *Today* program.

Technicians scurried around her. She was early on the set, but she needed to see the show in perspective, needed to watch it stirring to life like some giant slumbering centipede of cable crawling toward its daily, ephemeral destiny.

"Pretty, isn't it?"

She turned. The man was closer than she realized, standing behind her surveying the set with the same bedazzled, distant look, and closer to her height than most men, so he was simply uncomfortably close. He smiled at her, revealing china-white teeth and drawing the black mustache on his upper lip into a narrow, ingratiating line, like a Picasso sketch.

"Think we can compete?" he quipped.

Liz looked at him, dazzled by flashing teeth, café-au-lait skin, and Colombian coffee—strong eyes. He was a Beautiful Person and knew it. She laughed with him.

"Only if I get to the makeup room before you."

He grinned in answer and stared back at the set. "It's my maiden voyage, too; I hope she's seaworthy. I'm Alfonso Delgado. I don't thing we've met, but I'll be doing the nitty-gritty while you guys hold it all together."

Liz froze. He looked different in person, close up, but that was what viewers were always telling her, though she found it hard to believe. Now she was unsure he was the man who'd bumped into her at Rosemary's New Year's Party. He was certainly the man who stood too close for custom to her now, studying the set over her shoulder with a mournful wryness reminiscent of old film on Ollie of Kukla, Fran, and Ollie fame.

He sighed, and the gesture stirred Liz's carefully fluffed hair into a somber cloud at the edge of her vision. "I'm used to the streets, man," Alfonso said abruptly, as much to himself as to her. "This live, indoor shtick gives me the willies."

Liz craned her neck to give him an amused stare. "I'm a 'live on tape' type, too. Welcome to the club."

"Hee-ey." He shook her hand, his eyes sliding molasses-slow under lowered lids to intercept hers. "Misery loves company. I liked your thing on Hepburn. You really got to that old lady."

"Not as much as I'd have liked to; she keeps a lot of herself to herself. And . . . your street people piece was excellent, too."

He finally let go of her hand, a discontented expression shifting across his mobile, almost transparent face. "Yeah. For all the good it did."

She was silent. She no longer believed that a TV reporter could point to one piece of work and say, "There, that was not only well-done, but it solved a problem or eased a pain or simply opened up somebody's mind." For an instant, Liz felt dislocated, uncertain of what she was doing here, what she would be doing here.

Delgado brought her back to reality. "Shall we go and get ousrselves strapped into this rocket-set?"

Alfonso was moving across the cable-strewn floor like a disco dancer, graceful and glib-footed. She could picture him on a spotlit floor, strutting white-suited like Travolta in *Saturday Night Fever*, a dangerously hip, self-preening force. Some technicians recognized him, paying tribute by calling out, "Hey, Fonzie. It's the

Fonz. . . ." There was something urban and hungry about the man's lean, Latin good looks, something right out of *West Side Story*.

Oh, great, thought Liz. I'm going on live with Disco Delgado and Hail-fellow-ill-met Rogers. The weatherman, Darryl, was the usual combination of glancing meteorologist and vaudeville comedian. At least, she concluded grimly, one of us is normal.

Then she was easing into the molded Plexiglas chair with the white leather cushion. The union sound man came to clip the lavalier mike to her collar. Danny had crammed his lanky form into his seat center ring and Darryl stood ready at the empty blue cyclorama, where in five minutes viewers would see him against a national weather map, thanks to the magic of television. Here in the studio, though, Darryl would gesticulate at nothing, like an emperor vacant of more than clothes. And Liz and Danny and Alfonso—terrible name, why couldn't he be a simple Ricardo or Jorge like any other self-respecting Latino?—would sit behind their transparent set, look deeply and sincerely into the camera blinking red, and begin reading the scrolling text that Artie, a thin little guy with thick glasses, fed into the TelePrompTer while sitting under a piano light and moving a roll of script as endless as toilet paper past a camera. Artie, as far as Liz was concerned, was the most important person on the set.

Now Danny was reading his relaxed welcoming lines into the camera. Liz tightened her fingers on the sheets of the script that sat before her, just for emergencies. The camera facing her blinked on in red alarm. The floor director cued Liz with a slicing forefinger. She smiled as if she'd just been surprised in her living room by extremely welcome guests, and began reading the words unrolling on the monitor.

"And later this hour, *Sunrise* will talk to a woman doctor who maintains that monthly pain needn't be taken for granted, and *Sunrise* roving reporter Alfonso Delgado"—God, pronounced it right—"will settle at our control desk long enough to introduce a special piece on the special people in the handicapped Olympics. . . ."

Done. For now. Liz's lungs collapsed from the single gargantuan breath on which she had delivered her entire spiel. Now, if she could shift pages quietly to the intro for the cramp doctor and still maintain a calm, cheerful exterior in case the cameraman went berserk and decided to focus on her when she wasn't supposed to be on camera, or to take an unscheduled, whimsical long shot that would show all three of them scratching their anklebones behind the Plexiglas set . . .

It was, she had a feeling, the beginning of a normal morning on *Sunrise*.

— Chapter 40 —

"*Liz Jordan is a crisp addition to Danny Rogers' patented* laissez-faire style, as invigorating as thinly sliced radishes that add bite to a wilted lettuce salad. She's a reporting veteran, and it shows, although early-morning viewers could use a bit less sheer competence and a dollop more of charm. For that commodity, the revamped *Sunrise* show is well served by Alfonso Delgado, who surprisingly displays an ingratiating on-set manner missing from his grimly sincere reports on the troubles of our time."

Liz looked up from the copy of the *New York Post*, which had been folded into quarters to highlight the TV column.

"Good review." Alfonso sat on the corner of Liz's large desk, looking very uptown in a gray suit and red tie.

She smiled. "Jeff Greenfield said I was 'stock newslady issue, brisk, overserious, and wooden.'"

"He said I had all the moves of a discotheque bouncer and somebody should give me my own show—announcing weekend wrestling matches."

"He loves us but doesn't want to look like he's playing favorites. Well, some good, some bad. What's new? How come Hoffman isn't bearing the good news? I hear most of the comments have been good."

Alfonso shrugged and tugged itchily at his tie. "He's busy taking bows in the executive suites. And it isn't over yet. We're still in the ratings basement. Got to get some good numbers from the Nielsen boys."

Liz extended the paper to hand it back.

"Keep it."

"Look, most of these print critics are know-nothings who wear white socks and not just to jog, although they could use it. Your hard news reports are really valuable. . . ."

Alfonso smiled a crooked smile. "Hey, you don't have to cheer me up, Liz. Anyone can cover the daily tragedies, but charm . . . that's frosting on the cake."

"Apparently I could use a little of it."

"Apparently I got plenty; why don't you coast on some of mine?"

"Because you're too good at it."

"You don't trust me."

"Not if I can help it."

He stood, arched his mobile back, and stretched. "See, that critic was right: I'm easy and you're hard. How can I complain?" Alfonso ambled through the outer office, whistling as he turned into the hall beyond.

Liz picked up the paper again. The only negative comments about her were that she was too serious, hardly a damning flaw for a newswoman. But poor Alfonso, to be dismissed as merely another pretty face or disarming presence. . . . In his shoes she would have been furious, maybe even deeply depressed. It was so unfair. As much as she distrusted his fluid, womanizing façade, he was a damn good hard-news reporter. She wished she had been able to do half the hell-raising, system-shaking stories he had done. Maybe the criticism did faze him, but he put up too good a front to show it. Latin men could be like that, all machismo and careless, laughing dismissal of anything that might cause them to lose face. Touchy as a mandarin. For the first time, she felt sympathy stir for the man. It couldn't have been easy to get where he was, even with networks bowing more gracefully to token ethnics and women these days.

Liz sighed. The critic was right. She needed to relax into the show, something Alfonso seemed to have been born knowing how to do. Or Rosemary. Thank heavens nobody so far had compared her to her predecessor. She would die if she won praise at Rosemary's expense. Criticism would be far easier to take.

She clipped a note onto the newspaper asking for a copy, destined for her father, and left it at her secretary's desk in the outer office. It felt bizarre having a secretary after years of typing her own stories, letters, and Rolodex entries. But Janice sat there waiting for work, young, as brashly "Nu Yawk" as a Macy's salesclerk, and possessed of an offhand industry that amused Liz. Presumably, Janice would soon be busy handling the thousands of letters and calls that would inundate Liz's life—communications from viewers, colleagues, and would-be sponsors of speaking engagements. She'd already been asked to serve as Grand Marshal of the Keokuk, Iowa, homecoming parade. And had accepted. Hoffman wanted his people to get out among the viewers.

Liz's eyes fell to the memo from the producers on upcoming segments in which she would partake: Liberace interview, live in studio; blind mailman, narrate field-produced film and conduct live interview in studio; and candidates for Romantic Hero of the year, three finalists—a New Jersey bricklayer, a singing waiter from Florida, and a private detective from San Francisco—live interview in studio.

Her eye spotted a newsmaking name and her pulses leaped. Rita Mae Brown, the militantly lesbian writer who was living with tennis star Martina Navratilova. Then she read the entire entry. "Rogers interview with Rita Mae Brown, live interview in studio. Jordan sit in for balance."

She'd already learned what "sit in" meant. It meant sitting on the set like a child, being seen and not heard, while Danny Rogers asked all the important questions. Then Liz finished up with her one question, designed to be suitably trivial for closing.

"Rogers hogs the interviews," Liz had exploded three weeks after she began anchoring *Sunrise*, at the first lunch date with a sympathetic ear she had found time or energy for.

Rosemary Martin continued demurely consuming her cantaloupe and cottage cheese. All the fruit that came with the lavishly mounded salad had been swept to the side. She was on a new diet, convinced that her slim salvation lay in avoiding meat, vegetables, and all but certain fruits.

"Well, he does!" Liz continued. "I have to sit there looking like some dumb dame along for the ride; the hostess—who only speaks at the beginning and end of the important stuff."

Rosemary's fork ushered a clot of cottage cheese to her mouth. She chewed with painful deliberateness, then finally spoke. "I know; I faced the same thing. After a while, the critics start saying *you're* too bland or not on top of things."

"I'm not going to sit there and take it, even if the entire staff and crew seems to be complicit in it. I'm going to start speaking out of turn!"

"Oh, don't, Liz." Rosemary's irises were as round as blueberries. "You can't. Don't you know? Didn't they spell it out for you?"

"Spell out what?"

"It's in the contract, honey chile, Danny Rogers' contract. He gets to conduct the interviews he wants solo, he gets to ask the vital questions—"

"And I get blind mailmen and a trio of all-American Neanderthals! I get to look bad!"

Rosemary shrugged and curled the last of the cantaloupe onto her spoon. "It's the way it is. If you'd done a talk show before, like I did, you'd know the male host always gets these little accommodations. He's the key person, the one they cater to and expect the rest of us to cater to."

"Is he always such a stinker?"

Rosemary laughed. "Oh, Liz, you do get directly to it, don't you? Poor child, stuck with Danny Rogers *and* the great Alfonso

Delgado. That must be like being caught between the omelet and the frying pan."

"Delgado's not so bad. Really. At least he's doing his work for reasons other than self-aggrandizement and never asks for more than he earns. It's disgusting. If Rogers were really any good as an interviewer, he wouldn't need to worry about sharing the spotlight with someone else."

"Of course he's a lousy interviewer. He's an ex–commercial announcer. Where do you think he got that melt-in-your-esophagus voice? But audiences love him. He brings in the numbers. And you're right; his contract specifically delineates what—and what you may *not*—do."

Liz had discreetly broached the matter with Vic Manzelli, the assistant producer, a fatherly little man with a bald spot on his head as round and monkishly innocent as the plump potbelly he carried above his belt.

"Then what can I do? I feel trapped."

"You're under contract for a year—nothing." Vic's cherubic smile grew shrewd. "But in a year . . . renegotiate. Put in your terms, or some of 'em."

"I'll probably be gone in a year if I'm not allowed to work on camera the way I know how to. I thought it was my impressive tapes, my sensitive celebrity interviews, that got me picked for this job in the first place. I can't shine doing the obligatory stuff, interviewing people with all the articulateness of a stump!"

Vic just shook his shiny head. "Hang in there, Liz. You're good. We all like you, professionally and personally. Maybe you'll outlast him."

Liz called her father that evening, just before slipping a frozen dinner into the built-in microwave in her new apartment. There were some advantages to success.

"Hi, Dad. You been catching the show?

"I've been craning my neck to catch a glimpse of you. For being on for two whole hours a morning, I sure don't see much of you, except when it's time to tell me a station break's coming."

"It's not that bad—but close. That anchor, Danny Rogers, he's a camera hog. And he's even got it written into his contract. I wondered how things looked from the average living room."

"You give him the old Jordan elbow, Elizabeth, if he's crowding you out. Hell, it's gotta be like two rival reporters on the same paper, trying to scoop each other blind. Get yourself an exclusive, Elizabeth, and watch him drool."

* * *

There was only one way to get an exclusive, any exclusive. Liz had to find it, court it, wed it, consummate it, and deliver it bow-wrapped to the producers. And it had to be something that appealed to their commercial little minds. She had to come up with a story they couldn't refuse.

Her first was George Hamilton, easy because he was an inveterate ladies' man of the old school, so interested in proving he could charm her that he'd do anything to gratify her. He was hot because of a pair of unexpectedly successful movies and an expectedly unsuccessful marriage followed by an avidly reported divorce. He was not a triple-play scoop, but he was a start.

"I've got George Hamilton," Liz announced one day, coming into Manzelli's office.

"Congratulations, but your private life is—"

"Not for me, dummy, for *Sunrise*. And he'll talk about Alana and his new health kick, everything—but only if he's filmed on his own ground and only to me. No live studio stuff."

Vic sat back in the high-topped leather chair that made him look like the dormouse at the Mad Hatter's tea party. "Hamilton, huh? He's an angler, likes publicity. . . ."

"But he's made quite a comeback. From playing a professional gigolo on and off the screen, he put together his Dracula and Zorro takeoffs—*Love at First Bite* wowed the critics; he's matured. That's what I'd show."

"Pretty tall order."

"I can fill it."

"All right, but you'll have to find time in your schedule to film it."

"I will!"

Manzelli shrugged. "I have a feeling I've been schnookered."

Liz winked as she left his office.

The Hamilton piece came out exactly as she predicted, only because she worked like hell to make it so. The finished piece showed the actor some considered the king of slickness relaxing in a reassuringly old-world setting—cut flowers on cloth-swatched round tables, in a Chippendale sofa backed by a Chinese screen. In fact, Hamilton had proved slippery to interview. He was too used to sliding into his charm mode and eeled away from substantive questions like a puppy from a piddle spot. Liz persisted, politely, always drawing him back to the scene of the crime—his failed marriage, his reputation for slight acting ability and surface emotional commitments to women. Finally, the real, more serious George Hamilton peeked through the perpetual deep tan like a ghost of himself. He was a civilized, likable fellow whose smooth defenses hid all-too-human insecurity caused by a world all too ready to give him a bad rap in every arena. Liz liked him better when she left; that meant she had a good interview.

Hoffman liked the tape so well he agreed with Liz that it shouldn't be cut to fit *Sunrise's* stock four- or five-minute slots. They ran it as a series, *Inside George Hamilton*, promoted it titillatingly—"Wednesday, Liz Jordan talks to George Hamilton about the women in, and out of, his life"—and drove Danny Rogers into a jealous funk.

"He's not talking to me," Liz whispered sotto voce to Alfonso when he joined them at the anchor console to introduce a filmed report on substandard conditions in nursing homes.

"Small loss," Alfonso hissed back. He was becoming a casual on-the-job ally. Certainly, he was the only one who understood her fight for a place in *Sunrise's* rising sun.

Liz's little victory was further enchanced by the idea that she was once again building her career on series, coming full circle professionally.

Then, shortly after the last of the series ran, her secretary buzzed her.

"George Hamilton calling."

Liz's throat tightened. There was always a deeply nervous moment when hearing from the subject of a piece after it ran. Did he like it, or—what really mattered—did he feel it was fair? After all, her job was to show the world what she could glean from a public figure not used to digging down to the private nitty-gritty. Not everybody could take that kind of judgment gracefully.

"Liz." The matinee idol voice was in fine baritone fettle, the tone was energetic and up. "Want to go to the Tonys with me? Dinner's included."

"I take it you liked the piece."

"Good piece. I was a bit worried about what you'd make of some of what I said, but it's okay. And I liked you, too. How about it?"

"... Uh, sure!"

With this smooth, sophisticated response, Liz made her debut as escort of a Beautiful Person. Liz went to Bergdorf's and invested in—hell, blew a sinful wad of dough on the kind of evening gown she'd always dreamed about but never had the occasion or insanity to buy: red silk chiffon made to waft around her body like a gossamer second skin, slavered with beading and cut indiscreetly low.

It was, it turned out, one of the event's more modest and subdued gowns. Liz frankly ogled the bedizened actresses who sailed regally into the theater that night, deep, doughy cleavages trembling like blancmange with their steps, as did their own layers of sequins and satin. Meryl Streep was there, wearing some odd, plain, loose gown and stepping shyly as a doe among her gawdy, glittering colleagues. Then Liz spotted Carol Channing, her head an electric blond 350-watt light bulb illuminating everything around her for a distance of fifteen feet. Liz gawked as quietly as she could, blinking in the television lights, the random explosive novas of scores of flashcubes, finding cameras pointed her way again, but unpredictably.

"You see what can happen," Hamilton murmured as they took their seats.

Liz understood. The public eye can be a hot, demanding Cyclops stare, hard to live under day in and night out. She still felt like Cinderella, and Hamilton made a typecast prince—courtly, amusing, handsome.

The next day their photos appeared in one of the gossip tabloids. It didn't reach her until Alfonso dropped by her desk, a strange new expression in his dark eyes, and dropped the two-day-old issue on it.

"Oh my gosh!" It was them all right. Liz was flinching away from the camera, and George was grinning right into it, perfect teeth front and center. The photo was captioned, "George Hamilton's new mystery lady," and the cutline identified them as "handsome George Hamilton on the town at the Tony's, with an unidentified woman in red."

"Sic transit glory," she remarked, tossing down the paper. "They not only didn't get my name *right*; they didn't even *get my name*."

"You hadn't seen it yet?"

"Are you kidding? Who do I know who reads that rag?"

"You should," he retorted, "now that you've joined the jet set."

She laughed dismissively. Alfonso strolled from her office whistling "The Lady in Red."

Liz succumbed to vanity when he was gone and studied the picture. George, of course, looked calm and handsome. Liz looked startled and slightly disarranged. The dress photographed glamorously, and the daring cleavage had been nicely erased by the poor quality of paper the photo had been reproduced on. Thank heavens for high rag content in the lowbrow tabloids.

Still, she smiled. The mysterious Lady in Red. Lyrics from the old song lilted back to her. "She's a bit gau-dy,/but law-dy,/what a per-son-al-i-ty."

A personality, that's what Liz was now, just like George Hamilton. Now that she had tasted the feeling, she understood why it was so hard to unearth the person in personality. You were *a* something—*a* performer or *a* newslady. You were beautiful or famous or important—or all three. You were a surface to be seen in the newspapers, to sell newspapers, or on television to sell yourself. Your name would become public property. Maybe the *National Snooper* hadn't pinned a name on Liz yet, but it would, and would probably pin a lot of things on her that had nothing to do with her. This week with George for real; why not next week "seen with Nick Nolte" or "visiting new love John Hinckley Jr. in prison"? It was such a small step from reality to ludicrousness— for the chroniclers of "personalities," for the personalities themselves trying to live up to their distorted billing.

What was real? Who was real? How did one become real, or when did one lose being real and live on the appearance of oneself, like the itemized image of Liz that went out over the airwaves every weekday morning into the homes of people brushing their teeth and peeing into porcelain bowls or eating their Wheaties and yelling at their spouses . . . ?

Liz hadn't expected one dip into celebrity to stir such oceanic speculations. She felt momentarily lost, sitting adrift at her big, expensive lacquered desk, sweeping around and around in her mind, asking herself a question she thought she was too old to formulate. Who am I?

Who are *you*?

She caught a glimpse of her face in the mirror by the door— the looking glass there not as a vain feminine touch but as a necessity for *a* daily television performer.

How would she really know others—her father, Rosemary, the men she dated, the people she purported to interview—if she didn't know herself?

— Chapter 41 —

"Can you keep your eyes open long enough some night to go out to dinner?"

Alfonso had braced his arms on either end of Liz's long desk and was leaning over it, his shadow covering her work, his face and body breaking the barrier the desk made.

"If I get home by nine. What's the occasion? And wouldn't lunch do?" It struck her that his body had hemmed her in not only to emphasize his invitation but to screen it from anyone in the outer office. She suspected another staff rebellion, the curse of the insecure media star.

"I like the color of your baby blues," Alfonso intoned the inappropriate cliché with mock mysteriousness. "I want to see them by candlelight."

"Oh. I had no idea this outing was so profoundly motivated."

She gave him her address, with a warning. "The apartment's a mess; I'm having it redecorated." His dark eyebrows elevated in mute question. "Yes, I know it's gauche to get a raise and run out and redo the living room, but that's exactly what Betty Rollin did when she moved up to network. I don't know what Jessica Savitch did, but probably the same thing. I guess us female TV types are on the road so much we need a well-done nest, even if it is usually empty."

"I can dig it." Alfonso straightened and dug his hands into his pants pockets. They were tight, well-tailored pants, and the pose was taut with bottled energy, despite its stillness. Liz shuffled her paperwork, and Alfonso suddenly smiled. "Six o'clock, then. Don't worry about your place; you should have seen some of the disaster areas I grew up in."

She had not exaggerated; the apartment was a disaster area. But her cleaning lady still came daily to vacuum away plaster dust and otherwise tidy up. Liz darted around the wreckage the evening that Alfonso was due, hunting for a mislaid onyx earring and finding it safe in a dusty ashtray looking like a big black cigar butt. She didn't know what Alfonso drank, so had decided on offering him wine.

By the time the doorman buzzed the apartment, she had cleared a small serving area in the jumbled living room. By the time Alfonso and the elevator soared through the twenty nine floors below her, the glasses were clean—nothing in the cupboards stayed dust-free these days—and sparkling on a coffee table tray, and the wine was on ice.

"My world and welcome to it," she announced as she opened the door to his ring.

Alfonso stepped in with that territorial hesitancy that marks the polite man—or the wary one. Why had he invited her to dinner? She toyed with the idea that it could be purely sexual—with a man like Alfonso, it could always be purely sexual—except that she had a feeling it was more than that.

He walked into the middle of the vast living room, facing the denuded panorama of twilight Manhattan with his feet apart and his hip-braced fists sweeping back the sides of his sport coat. Swashbuckling stances came as easily to Alfonso as heartfelt words. It was that the Anglo critics and competitors resented most in him, that inbred Latin panache that can be flamboyant and yet still quintessentially masculine. He whistled, an appreciative, expert wolf whistle directed exclusively at the view.

Liz, ignored in the background, smiled at her illusions.

"Some joint." He turned to study the white overmantel newly applied to the false fireplace, the off-white carpeting and seating arrangements.

"This room's almost done. There'll be white silk vertical blinds on the window-wall, and accessories, of course. And . . . you might want to see the media room—"

"*Media* room." He sounded impressed.

"It was the library, but I figured I needed a TV-stereo-VCR setup more than bookshelves." She swept the door open on her prize, a sleek, businesslike cocoon of gray flannel–upholstered walls, with a massive seating pit rising from the gray wool carpeted floor like a cave-nourished fungus. "The central island is kind of a huge, round chaise lounge, but taking these ottomans away makes it into a semicircular sofa, so I can open this room up for parties, too. If I ever have the energy to have a party," she added ruefully.

"You don't have to have a party. You're a celebrity; you can go to other people's."

"On my schedule, that's a little tough."

"They'll just have to start them earlier for you," he pronounced. "This is really something. The best equipment, too." His fingertips played a light, expert glissando over the rows of brushed chrome buttons.

"I tape the other morning shows and review them at night, just to see what the competition's up to. Sometimes I tape myself, just to see what I'm doing wrong."

"Not much." Alfonso strolled back to the living room, studying the terrain while Liz poured the wine and offered him a rich ruby glass. He took it to the ever-darkening view. Liz obligingly dimmed the lights. "That window's better than a . . . I don't know, an aquarium or a planetarium or a—"

"—tranquilizer," Liz finished wryly. She hung behind; she found herself overcautious about approaching Alfonso. Like most Latin males, his personal comfort zone was much tighter than an American woman's. He came closer sooner, touched more and more often than Liz found relaxing. She was always on edge with Alfonso yet drawn to him, as if he were a warming fire that threw off burning coals at unexpected intervals.

But finally she went to stand beside him, to relax and sip her wine and stare at the mesmerizing view. The myriad squares of lit office windows were still a mellow golden tone, looking almost painted onto one of Mondrian's aggressively geometric canvases.

With total darkness, the lights would shrink and grow brighter, twinkling relentlessly in the Black Hole that was Manhattan after dark and at a distance.

"I used to be afraid," Liz said slowly, "at living so high up. Afraid that I'd fall right off the edge of the earth, as if everything ended here at this chasm we call a city. . . ."

"It does." Alfonso stared out at the brightening lights. "This is the Big Apple, the whole cheese, the absolute center at its most extreme. In our game, if we don't make it here, we don't make it."

"There are other places . . . smaller. Maybe better."

He didn't answer, as if he hadn't heard her. And then he turned, much too soon. He was much too close. The room was too dim, the night too electric. He just looked at her, a man of five-foot-seven who didn't need to be taller, who matched her high-heel augmented height perfectly—eye to eye, mouth to mouth, hip to hip. His expressions changed as fluidly as water under the brush of wind; Liz couldn't assign them names. But he looked at her as if just discovering her, as if searching her features for some sign, and then, not finding it, superimposing it on her face anyway with the mere passage of his glance. It was an invasive, intimate examination, full of the coiled promise of the crouching jaguar.

Alfonso's hand slipped under a wave of her hair, but she felt no touch. "Nice earrings," he said. "You look great tonight. I suppose we should . . ."

All right. Right there. On the new off-white carpet, under the naked night-shaded windows. Step closer; begin the kiss, the clutch, the consummation. End the suspense, the agony, the ecstasy. . . .

". . . get going if you've got to be back by nine." His fingers tweaked the earring and he moved away.

He took her to the Algonquin Hotel, not the trendy sort of place she had imagined him to haunt. They sat first in the Blue Bar, which wasn't blue at all, on cracked brown leather banquettes, cozily isolated from the traditionally furnished lobby where post-work imbibers could sit in Queen Anne wing chairs and be served at the ring of a side table bell, like British clubmen.

The Blue Bar was small, plain, and had an overlooked air. A ruddy-faced, white-haired man with bushy side whiskers talked at the barman in a British accent. Exotic words like Tobruk and Medina drifted over his tweed-jacketed shoulder. He was, of course, talking about "the war." It amazed Liz that something that had happened before she had been born should linger on in such stock-footage form. She felt transported into a black-and-white movie. Irene Dunne and Cesar Romero in *Romance on the Hudson*, listening to Sir Wilfred Hyde-White hold forth. . . .

Alfonso ordered rum on the rocks. Liz made an instant mental note of it even as she wondered why she bothered. They sat and talked, and talked and talked, moving to the richly paneled Oak room by seven-thirty. The restaurant was crowded by then, tables set so close together that other people, if not busy shouting at one another, could easily overhear a neighbor. One got used to that at New York restaurants from the most chic bistro to the cheapest railroad-car luncheonette. By then, neither Alfonso nor Liz cared if anybody heard them.

"I had no idea Turtle Bend was so fascinating," Liz said, finishing her latest tale of life in the slow lane. Alfonso had almost grilled her on her background, her hometown, as if hungrier for crumbs of country life than for the massive New York steak on his plate.

He shrugged easily. "I've lived in cities—Havana and New York—all my life. In Cuba we had no middle-class towns; you were either a peasant or a city slum-dweller. Or a well-off landowner or wealthy urbanite."

Cuba. That filled in an embarrassingly blank dotted line in Liz's understanding; was he Puerto Rican or Spanish or Mexican? None of the above. Of course. He was Cuban. And had lived in Havana. . . .

"Havana. That must have been before—"

"Castro." The word greased his lips like castor oil, leaving them curled as if to spit the residue away. "We left then, the family. My parents, my brothers and sisters. Left everything. I was five."

"That would have been in nineteen fifty . . . ?"

"Fifty-eight. Castro officially came to power in fifty-nine, but if you weren't part of his 'Revolution' and wanted to survive it, you got out in fifty-eight. The history books don't tell you that."

"And you left everything?" Alfonso had been only five in 1958, he was four years younger than she, Liz calculated, surprised. He seemed her contemporary, and was. Still, four years was a different generation nowadays. Liz knew she was getting older when she was startled to find that younger people had achieved the same level as she.

"Everything but the clothes on our backs. We dared not stir suspicion that we were 'pillaging the people.' My father, my family, was . . . I suppose you'd say of a wealthy class. We had a beautiful house in Havana. I remember cool white shining floors—terrazzo, I think. And fanning glossy green leaves in a courtyard, the scent of some maddeningly sweet flowers. If you could have seen it, Liz, smelled it . . . And I remember my mother trailing the white floors with her long dark hems when my parents gave a party, and her looming high above me, her head framed by jewels twinkling like Technicolor stars. When I remember my mother in those days, she always seemed to be wearing velvet."

Alfonso smiled suddenly. "You know when you see a movie by Columbia Pictures and it opens with this shot of a fur-draped woman holding up a torch, and the rays of light are all fanning out? I guess it's supposed to be some hokey Hollywood representation of Columbia, the gem of the ocean, or the Statue of Liberty or whatever. But when I was first a kid in this country and got a chance to go to the movies, I thought it was my mother."

"She must have been beautiful."

"She still is. But no jewels. We left them. I never saw her like that again. Who knows, maybe I dreamed the whole thing—the house, the garden...."

"What did your family do here?"

"What do all immigrants do? Came to New York, not speaking a word of English. My mother could have done something in fashion; she was a woman of exquisite taste, but with no English ... My father was of the same useless class. So we lived in slums and they got what jobs ignorant, Spanish-speaking, impoverished immigrants could get. Dirty jobs. And we kids got jobs when we were old enough. How do you think I got to be the world's greatest street reporter? I'm from the streets, Liz."

"But you obviously learned—English and a lot more. You got an education—"

"Sure. We got it. And my parents got their own business finally. My father, he pulls down two hundred grand a year now. On a bakery. But I had to work my way through college, and those were the days my parents were working themselves white eighteen, twenty hours a day to make the business go—I should have given my money to them."

"They wanted you to go to school."

"Yeah. And besides, Vietnam was acting up. They didn't want any sons of theirs in a war; we lost too many cousins and uncles in the Revolution. But that's why I help out my younger brothers and sisters now, and any spare cousins that show up."

Liz was silent. Even the animatedly talking people around them seemed to have hushed their tones. The worst betrayal of her childhood had been the loss of a dog. Alfonso had lost a way of life, a country, a sense of security, a vision of his parents and the past that the present or the future could never live up to.

"That's why your Turtle Bend fascinates me," he mused. "It sounds like the kind of place nobody could—or would—take away from you. It sounds . . . safe. No abused kids or old folks, no street gangs, none of the sleazy stuff I cover and can't get out of covering."

"But your work, it's done a lot of good, brought all sorts of festering social problems to the public attention, helped people."

"My work has gotten me a big salary and some small fame, that's all. You think the bureaucracy that ignores the poor every day can't forget about 'em again once the TV cameras stop rolling? And face it, I got swept into my position by pure chance—I was an NYCC student activist who ended up running my mouth off in front of a camera so much that I was the only "qualified" Hispanic the local station could think of back in seventy-five when they needed one bad. And if they're going to hire an ethnic, they might as well get a liberal one, right? So they created a monster— me. Oh, I hit big, too big for them to ignore. I'm their house bleeding heart. I'm stuck in the role. If I wanted to do a piece on the Picasso exhibition—my parents were art collectors; I teethed on Matisses and Miros—they'd laugh."

"You're their answer to Geraldo Rivera on ABC," Liz mused.

"Right on. 'Sob soul brother.' Another hot tamale with a funny first name."

She sighed. "But what am I, Alfonso, except 'another' Jane or Jessica or Barbara? Granted, there are more women in broadcasting, but we're still not one of the boys. I have to fight like a tiger to do anything that feels worthwhile on *Sunrise*."

Liz looked around, suddenly paranoid. The Algonquin usually attracted the post-theater set, being located just off Broadway, or literary types nostalgic for the hotel's glory days of the "Round Table" wits. Still, one never knew when a network vice president would evidence a surprising sensitivity and show up somewhere unexpected once in a blue moon, like at the opera or a library.

"Time to get you home." Alfonso was quick to take cues, especially those delivered by body language. It made Liz nervous, and made her especially nervous that night.

Before they could do more than make the motions to leave, a woman who obviously *had* been watching them rushed over with an adolescent daughter in tow.

"Could I trouble you for your autograph, Miss Jordan?"

Liz smiled and acquiesced. It came with the territory. At least this fan had allowed her to eat first. The woman studied the notepaper she had offered after Liz signed it, glanced uncertainly to Alfonso, then thrust it his way wordlessly. He, too, smiled and signed. The woman triumphantly handed the slip to her rather uninterested daughter. The girl scanned the paper, then frowned.

"I thought you said he was Tony Orlando!" she shrilled in complaint, turning heads all along the long, narrow dining area.

Alfonso shrugged; Liz buried her face in her tablecloth-size napkin. The autograph seekers stalked off.

"At least," Liz finally sputtered, "they didn't think you were Geraldo Rivera."

"Lucky there are so few of us," he muttered. "Or they'd really get confused."

"It could be worse; she might have taken you for Desi Arnaz."

That tragicomic note ended the evening out. Of course Alfonso saw her to her apartment. Streetwise or not, he was, she realized, from very refined stock, from people forced to live far below their own standards far too long.

He paused inside her door to regard the uncurtained view again.

"Where do you live?" she asked curiously.

He shrugged disarmingly. "Condo down in the Village. One of the old railroad flats they gutted and redid. It's nice, small, suits my life-style . . . but it's not like this. Uptown's better."

Liz tried to disguise a jaw-dislocating yawn. Alfonso checked the gold watch that matched the cuff-links on his French-cuffed shirt. Cuff links—how traditional for a young turk to wear them.

"Nine-fifteen. I guess I broke your curfew."

"That's okay; it's self-imposed. But if I don't get at least seven hours of sleep tonight, I'll be corned beef hash on the set tomorrow morning."

"I'm lucky; they only make me do live duty once a week or so."

Liz yawned, openly. Alfonso laughed and stepped to her, pulling her head down on his shoulder. "Sleepy girl," he crooned, "you need to be tucked in."

She stiffened, raised her head even though the embrace was deliciously comfortable. "Alfonso, I didn't intend to have us . . . I'm not sure we should cross this line."

His face was inches away. Liz inhaled the faint scent of cologne, the stronger scent of warm flesh and blood. Alfonso's tolerant smile was already fading into an unavoidable seriousness, sensuality softening his jet-hard eyes, shaping his mouth into an open invitation. He was nuzzling her face, his lips nibbling the edge of hers. Liz felt caught in a cage of heat and breath and the soft, coaxing murmur of Alfonso's voice, so low it seemed he feared the very air would hear them, disturb them.

"Elizabeth," he said, pronouncing her name in a lilting Spanish way she had never heard it spoken before. "You're so formal; everybody calls me Al. But I like to be called Alfonso when I'm making love, so I'll call you E-liz-a-beth. Has anybody called you that, any lover? Has he, hmm? Has he?"

Ae-*Leez*-a-beth. Alfonso's lips were pressing repeatedly around the fringes of her face. Liz turned her features mindlessly to follow the bait of his mouth, to inhale the stir of his warm breath. His hands were as elusive as his lips, brushing her neck, her hair, her arms, back, waist, hip, breast, stroking her buttocks, and moving her silky dress circularly against her skin in so many places the fabric seemed to be alive and caressing her.

"Let's go into your media room and neck," he whispered, his arm around her waist drawing her in that direction.

Their momentary separation as she followed his pull broke the spell. Liz's hand pressed his jacket lapel into place, tried to push him back a bit.

"Alfonso, I don't know—I'm tired."

"Not of this?" His teasing stopped momentarily as he paused and kissed her deeply at last, pressing her body to his side until she lost her balance and lay along him, erotically swept off her feet.

Liz's breath shuddered inward in an almost climactic reaction. In seconds, she and Alfonso were mutually collapsing together on the sprawling gray flannel circular chaise lounge, Liz feeling vaguely like an actress in a James Bond movie. Alfonso's attentions, like Bond's, never flagged. They writhed and kissed together as if trying to make cinematic history.

But even the most fevered seduction couldn't overcome the potent sedative blend of nature and habit. Liz grew soporific, floating in an erotic Nivrana, responding but not reciprocating. Alfonso finally drew back to study her in the dim light.

"I'm just damn tired," she apologized languorously.

He leaned nearer, tickling her kiss-swelled lips with his fingertip, staring soulfully into her eyes until she saw what he wanted and—hesitating momentarily, weighing independence and sheer sensual magic in the balance—she took his finger into her mouth, slowly. Alfonso's pupils flared black with desire, his face was over hers, his tongue satisfyingly stroking the recesses of her mouth, his hands smoothing the skin of her inner thighs through the silky panty hose and she wished weren't there.

But she was, as she had said, simply tired. In the end he walked her to the bedroom and undressed her, nibbling lightly at her during the process. "Where's your nightgown?" he asked.

"I don't wear one," she confessed, clinging naked to him, arching to the passage of hands like a contented cat.

Alfonso smiled and escorted her into the sheets, bending to kiss her a last time and turn off the beside lamp. "*Vaya con Dios a sus seuños*, Elizabeth," he said. "Go with God to your dreams. Tomorrow you will come with me to mine."

She awoke—alone—to the brassy screech of her windup alarm. (She dared not trust Con Ed not to have a blackout.) The luminescent clock hands read three A.M. The room was dark. Liz was warm and did not want to get up, get dressed, go down to meet the limo. She hadn't even studied that day's script. She wanted to lie in bed and lose herself in some fantasy far too close to reality. She wanted Alfonso. She had never awakened so aware of having been made love to, and he had never even consummated their lovemaking. At least not while she was awake... Liz rolled her eyes at the possibilities that idea raised and finally rolled out of bed. Tomorrow, he had said, she would come with him to his dreams. Yes, she would. And tomorrow was already... today.

— Chapter 42 —

A hanging plant overhead threatened to trail its vine in Liz's taco salad. The margarita at Liz's knife tip on the highly varnished, tiled tabletop still wore its untouched halo of salt. Wendy Banks sat across from her, his familiar face looking as durable, dependable, and slightly worry-worn as denim.

He had called three days before, as soon as he had returned from a commission in the Netherlands that had taken him away for four months. He was a Midwestern gentleman; he never suggested an immediate assignation or baldly asked her to his loft. He always invited her to lunch to take her emotional temperature first. This time their reunion was held at Manhattan's first Tex-Mex establishment, Cactus Jack, in Greenwich Village. On the other hand, he never took her to lunch too far from his loft.

Since Wendy had called, Liz had made love with Alfonso twice. It unnerved her how guilty she felt.

"What's wrong, Liz?"

She looked up from the cantaloupe-size shell brimming with deliciously bad things like spiced ground beef, sour cream, and shredded cheese she hadn't had the heart to do more than disarrange.

Liz framed her answer seriously. "I always thought I was a verbal person, but..."

"I won't ask you to draw your message; you can't draw your own phone number."

The reference reminded her of skylight-lit afternoons in Wendy's design-littered loft. "At least I can spell it out. I've... met someone."

Wendy was silent, then sipped his own virgin margarita. His

lips came away from the goblet's salted rim slightly puckered. "So that's it."

"Does it show?"

He nodded. "You glow. It's . . . very attractive. Is this Mr. Right?"

"You know better than that; unfortunately, so do I. Matches are made in heaven only in grand operas."

"More of them are broken than made in operas," he muttered. "It's musical tragedy; that's why it needs all the gorgeous sets and costumes and librettos to make the message palatable." He set down the drink. "I keep wanting to ask, 'Who is he?' Nosy, aren't I?"

"No, but I shouldn't say."

"Married?" He sounded concerned.

"No, but . . . professionally it's better for us to be discreet." Liz knew she had stirred his curiosity more than slaked it. She lifted her glass. "Maybe we should get drunk."

"And go back to my place?" He backed off at the look in her eyes. "Sorry. I'm more . . . stung . . . than I thought I'd be."

"And I feel more guilty. Wendy, you're a wonderful man. I love you dearly. . . . I mean, I'm deeply fond of you. Knowing you has saved my sanity these past months; so has the little time we've managed to . . . spend together. But you've been gone four months. Surely in Europe you must have—"

"Oh, sure. If anything promising developed. And I never figured you'd remain celibate while I was gone. I know the kind of fragmented lives we both lead, with so little chance to be . . . ourselves . . . with someone else. I'll just miss you, Liz. A lot."

"We can . . . we can—" Liz laughed through sudden tears. "—still be friends."

He nodded solemnly. What a kind face he had, she thought, wanting to slide her palm along his cheek. Dear, dear Wendy. Why hadn't it ever occurred to either of them that the most adult, undemanding relationship of convenience could carry a sting in its tail—silly, sophisticated people that they had grown up to become?

Wendy's roughly delicate artist's hands slowly twirled the margarita by its graceful glass stem. "It's just that . . . decent . . . love is so hard to come by."

Liz nodded sober agreement.

"Well. Enough moping. May the better man win, and all that. And that's all I want for you, Liz, always. Decent love. It is . . . decent love?" He sounded like her father.

The blood brimmed to her cheeks; she hoped she was too old to let it show. Thinking of making love with Alfonso did not call for the adjective "decent."

"Oh, I see." Wendy took a big slug of margarita and unexpectedly grinned. "Being discreet but indecent, are we?"

"What?" Liz prodded him sheepishly. "Wendy, what are you thinking? Tell me!"

"That I feel better. Hell, I can't fight hormones. Everybody deserves a mad fling, an overwhelming 'pash,' as the British put it. Go to it; forty's looming. If you need a friend on the other end of the telephone line, or want to have lunch—"

"You make me feel like I've made a big mistake. But I'm old-fashioned." She lowered her voice so even the plant couldn't hear her. "I *cannot* make love to two men simultaneously—not in an orgy sense, but you know what I mean."

"That's what I love about you. You're honest." Wendy slid the check his way. For a moment their eyes met, and the word "love" hung heavy between them, like something they'd seen but had missed capturing.

Liz doubted that they would have lunch again, or would chat on the phone like old friends. When she was growing up, it was so hard to commit to sleeping with a man for the first time that she had never considered that deciding *not* to sleep with a man anymore could be even harder. Friends and lovers, but not either/or once the Forbidden Fruit had been sampled. Yet who could say? Anything could happen, Liz decided, with enough time. Anything in the world.

"I hear Danny Rogers is in bad odor." *Sunrise*'s rotund weatherman, Darryl McComb, leaned Liz's way over the Plexiglas expanse separating them.

Liz quailed. The union sound man already had affixed their mikes, so there was a slim chance that some overzealous mike man had dialed them up to broadcast level already. The fear was paranoid, but television shows battling for ratings produced a high-anxiety atmosphere. And more than one TV newsperson had been canned for an ill-timed off-camera remark that the sound system had turned into a nationwide public address.

"In trouble with the suits?" she whispered.

"Who else?" Darryl hissed happily back, his eyes on their beloved male anchor as Danny even now slouched his deceptively relaxed way to the anchor desk.

Several months on *Sunrise* had demonstrated to Liz just what made Danny Rogers run—ego, nerve, and backstabbing. He unhesitatingly shot constant memos to the bosses, critizing his colleagues. The first thing the victim would perceive would be a vague sense of being watched from the fringes by some vice president or another who normally never showed up on the set.

Then a conference might be scheduled to discuss why said person was "slow on the uptake" or "not pulling his or her weight."

Liz kept an extensive library of her *Sunrise* tapes in her media room at home. It cost a lot of money to tie up so many VCR cassettes, but she regarded it as cheap insurance. If Danny Rogers pointed any accusing fingers her way, she could defend herself with hard evidence on her performance. It also had occurred to her it wouldn't hurt to keep a record of her work—in case *Sunrise*'s sun set permanently and she needed to look for a new job.

Alfonso poo-poohed the very idea.

"Elizabeth! You're a star. You'll never have to look for a job; they'll find you."

"Barbara Walters *was* a 'star'; now she's doing damn good just to hang on with her specials and making a 'comeback' as coanchor on *20/20*. With all those eager young would-be network chicks coming up behind her who don't have to prove they're *news*women—hell, they wouldn't *touch* a feature story for fear of permanently tainting their hard-boiled images—she's been relegated to a passé pioneer. I'm just another trivia hound like Barbara as far as the new generation of newswomen are concerned. Let's face it; interviews with KISS are hardly socially relevant."

"But everybody was talking about yours. That's what people want to know nowadays; how unreal people live. This is the eighties; my sixties liberal shtick is losing hair and getting flabby. I'm the one that's out of step with my time, and the damn network won't let me out of my activist trap."

"I'm trapped, too," Liz pointed out. "I'm being celebritied to death."

It was true. To get her filmed segments on the air, Liz found she had to come up with subjects sensational enough to disrupt the producer's cherished schedule. To come up with interviews that overwhelming, Liz found herself pursuing the reclusive, the bizarre, the outrageous, the sexy. How many in-depth interviews could she do with brash young media egoists and flash artists?

Sometimes it seemed that her and Alfonso's career bitches remarkably paralleled conversations she'd had with Steve Harmon almost a decade before. The stage was just bigger and better lit, and the cast of characters had changed.

But Alfonso always knew what to do when career despair set in. He poked his head around her office door and lured her out to play.

"I should be setting up interviews," she'd protest at noon when Alfonso's handsome face peeped through her open door and wagged its eyebrows in a Groucho-via-Magnum gesture of ritual inquiry.

Alfonso waited. And she went. Sometimes they went to movie

theaters, sitting there in the afternoon when decent people were working, watching whatever film was on, holding hands, nuzzling in the semideserted house, finally leaving on a crackling trail of popcorn and going to her apartment or his condo.

By the time Liz had gotten around to redoing her bedroom, Alfonso was a fixture in it. Hence the decorator was instructed against "frills." What came of that and Alfonso's fondness for Liz's media room was another upholstered retreat. This time gray velvet piped in wine silk covered the walls, and the modern black-lacquered French headboard concealed lights, radio, VCR, phone—everything but, Liz said, a motorboat. Alfonso was an electronics junkie; the gadgetry decorated what Liz privately referred to as her "electric bedroom." It was also a reference to the quality of the activity that transpired there in the afternoons or early evenings before she had to get serious, study the next day's script, and get some decent sleep. *didn't she know?*

Only Rosemary Martin knew about Liz and Alfonso, and she seemed to have dropped out of media circles totally. After leaving *Sunrise*, she'd attached herself to Joel's talent agency, not doing anything more than steeping herself in the atmosphere and jargon of fast-paced, high-priced beauty. She was always wearing a new lipstick or eye shadow when she and Liz had their regular lunches. Her clotted cream complexion was now pampered with bee jelly and lamb fetus extracts. Her nails were impeccable, as always, but her hands were too "old," she said, for modeling again.

"Joel says if I can just lose thirty–five pounds, I'll be 'salable' again." Rosemary dribbled some of the special salad dressing she'd brought along atop the spartan house salad she had settled on for lunch once it had been stripped of all ornamentation but lettuce and some tomatoes.

"Thirty-five pounds! Rosie, okay, maybe fifteen or twenty, but you don't need to weigh that little. That'd be less than I weigh."

"Weight is paramount, Liz. That camera is a killer. If I'd concentrated on gettin' and keepin' my weight down before, I'd have never lost *Sunrise*."

"Oh, I doubt your weight really had anything to do with it. You were born lucky; you carry most of it below the waist, and on television, behind an anchor desk, who cares if you're packing saddlebags? You could be stark naked and no one would know."

"It shows," Rosemary insisted grimly. "All the bad things we do to our bodies show. It's not too soon for you to begin thinkin' about keepin' yourself up, Liz honey. Joel knows this wonderful doctor on Madison Avenue—all his top models go to him and they look terrific, believe it. You get goat's milk and vitamin B lamb fetus injections and you'll just feel like you never did before."

"I believe it. Yuck! How can you do that to yourself? You're looking thinner, but—"

Rosemary glowed pathetically. "I do? Look thinner? You do think so, Liz, really? And you're seein' me from just above the waist, so it must really show. . . ."

"Some," Liz conceded. "But you always looked fine to me, on camera or off."

"Joel says I'm too fat. It's a thin woman's world, Liz. If I can just lose this thirty–five pounds, I'll never let an ounce get on me again. Maybe we should stop meetin' for lunch. Maybe we could meet for tea."

"We could, but Rosemary, from the little you've eaten lately, this isn't lunch; this is abstinence."

"But I don't eat and don't eat—and nothing happens. I haven't been bad for weeks; I eat barely six hundred calories a day, and I *still* can hardly lose anything. It isn't fair!" Rosemary's eyes shone sad behind a teary veil of frustration. Liz felt momentarily impatient. There were bigger problems in the world at large, in her world, than the calories to be counted in a lettuce leaf for which one was paying $12.50.

"I know it's hard. Your metabolism is geared to hoarding calories, that's all. You can't make yourself into a sylph."

"Oh, yes, I can." Rosemary's Southern magnolia face hardened into alabaster. "I will. I'll get thin if it kills me." She tackled the naked lettuce with such resolve that will alone seemed to become something one could subsist upon as well as appetite.

"Maybe I'm too fat." Liz twisted to study her nude derriere in the bathroom door mirror. It looked like a derriere: featureless, pink, and rather unnecessary. Alfonso didn't think so.

He was behind her, the darker corona of his naked body a halo just visible beyond her own reflection. "Hmm. Let's try the pinch test."

"Alfonso!" She was laughing and dancing away, back to the tumbled bed that lay on a diagonal to a corner of his bedroom.

They ended up wrestling in the sheets and sliding to the floor, then tumbling back into the bed on its low pedestal. Alfonso's fat tests quickly became forgotten, their laughter subsided to murmurs, and the afternoon unwound yet another of their leisurely, uninhibited lovemaking sessions.

"Thank heaven for the contraceptive sponge," Liz said happily, lying on her back staring at the blank ceiling afterward. "It was such a mess before. No spontaneity at all."

"That's progress." Alfonso was trailing his fingers across her stomach. Liz admired his still-erect penis, marveling that it endured despite their best efforts to encourage it to give up the ghost.

Their lovemaking always had a fevered, frantic quality. Liz didn't know if that was something Alfonso brought to the relationship, or if it was because she was approaching her late thirties, supposedly the time of a woman's sexual peak. But that was still a few years away. She was only thirty four, after all, younger than Jessica and Diane and—maybe—even Jane. Her Turtle Bend contemporaries, the women anyway, were probably just contemplating a part-time job now that the kids were in high school. . . .

"Do you ever want kids, Alfonso?" He was only thirty, yet a man from his Latin background grew up with a powerful urge for fatherhood, if only to verify his manliness.

For once he took her seriously. "Kids." He lay back. "I don't know, Liz. Do you?"

She shook her head. "It never occurred to me. Don't laugh. I was just too busy being what I was, doing what I was. Every once in a while it occurred to me I should be thinking about having kids, but the idea never stayed on my mind. Maybe, when I was younger, if a guy I'd been . . . interested in . . . had wanted kids, I would have, or would have gone along with the idea. But here I am, still well within the age of having them, and I don't worry about it. Something must be wrong with me. What about you? I mean, hip Hispanic about town—you ever get the paternal urge?"

His face grew serious as he rolled over on his stomach. It felt oddly like they were picnicking somewhere under a spreading chestnut tree, talking about life, the universe, and everything.

"Yeah, I guess us macho types are supposed to be heavy into progeny. My own parents had six of us." He looked up, frowning. Liz had never seen Alfonso frown before. Smile, yes, almost all the time. But frown . . . "There's something in me . . . Maybe it's the way we fled Havana—night and stealth; scared, whining kids who had to be hushed up harshly. You don't forget that when you're five years old. I even seem to remember . . . blood." He sighed and looked up at her. "I just could never do it, Liz. I could never stand knowing that a kid of mine had to face losing everything like that."

"But this is America. You're secure now, famous; you make good money."

His dark head shook inexorably as she enumerated his advantages.

"You don't understand, Elizabeth. That could all vanish in a minute. What if I had a son, and I got run over by a cab, or the money got stolen? We're all just a hairsbreadth from losing it all

any minute. That's what Turtle Bend was too safe to teach you.
I couldn't do that to some little kid." *Amen*

"But even if the worst happened, it wouldn't be *you* that did
it, it wasn't your parents' fault that Cuban politics changed—"

"No, no. I know that. But *I* can't put someone in that position,
play God and make people to be tossed around like driftwood on
the waves of whatever fate might send them. No thanks. I've been
there," he finished bitterly. "I got trouble enough saving my own
skin."

Liz was silent, but reached out to caress the jet curls at his
neck. He looked so vulnerable there, like a child. But he wasn't
a child; he was a survivor, a sole survivor. He would leave no
"hostages to fortune," as Bacon once had described children. He
would live and work solo. Liz smiled behind his temptingly bare
back, realizing that her self-confessed absence of a desire for
children had freed Alfonso to admit his own terror of parenthood.
For parents had to provide security for their children, and Alfonso
had none of that to spare. *spiritual security, too!*

Her hand slowly slid from his neck down his long spine to his
buttocks. "Too fat," she pronounced, pinching. He whirled over,
atop her, she squealing, squirming, laughing. So was Alfonso.
They made love again, an act that seemed self-mocking on Alfonso's part after what he'd just said. Yet Liz began to understand
this man who thrived on being misunderstood. Those things she
was suspicious of—the easy, superficial charm, the self-indulgence,
even the smooth and practiced passion—were defenses erected to
shelter a bewildered five-year-old who had lost everything in life
before he had a grip on anything. It would not happen again.

— Chapter 43 —

"Rosie! You look positively skeletal. Come in." Liz stood aside
from the door where she'd stood too long in stupefaction and
waved her friend into the apartment.

Rosemary, beaming, minced into the room as if she were afraid
of breaking something—perhaps herself. "It shows? Already?"

"Of course it shows. You must have lost . . . twenty pounds!"

"Only twelve, but you do see it?"

"Yes, yes, yes!" Liz circled her. She hadn't seen Rosemary in
several weeks, so the weight loss seemed even more dramatic.

"That's no dirndl skirt you're wearing; that's a hip-hugging, stomach-outlining, saddle-bag showing straight skirt! And you look thin. How'd you do it?"

"Oh, that Mad Av doctor I told you about; he's a wonder-worker." Rosemary seemed embarrassed finally by the attention she'd drawn to herself. She studied the living room. "This is lovely, Liz. I'm so glad you suggested lunch here."

"Well, I haven't played hostess at all, and thought I'd better practice on you. Plus . . ."

"What is it? You have some news, don't you?"

"Not exactly news. A goody. A small goody for myself that I'd like to show you after lunch. And it's easier to do it here."

Rosemary looked around suspiciously, hunting for something spectacular but underfoot. All she saw beyond the room's usual decor was a ladies' luncheon setting for two on the coffee table.

"The salad is mostly lettuce and a touch of shrimp and crab. No mayonnaise. And you can leave the croissant if you want. It's pretty light—only lemon juice dressing—"

Rosemary perched on the off-white sofa, unfurled her red napkin with a flag-waving flourish. "Heavens, Liz. You needn't treat me like a Hindu monk or something. I can eat a croissant—or two."

"But your diet . . ."

"I can eat. That's the beautiful part of it. And I lost all this weight in just a week."

"Must be some diet."

"I owe it all to my doctor."

Liz nodded. "Well, here's a Perrier toast to diets, doctors, and—my present to myself."

"Wine would have been fine, Liz. Really, I'm not on a perennial fast anymore. All that's changed. I've discovered how to lose weight and eat, too. And that's what I'm going to do now, eat, because I'm dyin' to see what you want to show me."

Liz trotted out her mystery guest after lunch—a bag-covered hanger. While Rosemary's bleached eyebrows rose in silent comment, Liz unzipped the bulky bag.

"Voilà." She slipped eagerly into its contents, a coat, then spun back to face Rosemary. "What do you think?"

"Think? It's gorgeous. Mink?"

"Jaguar mink." Liz stroked the black-and-white fur. "It's a natural pattern, bred in."

"Designer?"

Liz preened. "Of course. Galanos."

"Oh, I've never seen anything so . . . so soft, and smashing, and—"

Liz's voice dropped an octave. "And expensive, dah-ling."

"But it's worth it."

"Well, I figured I deserved *something* to keep me warm at three A.M. as I move from the chill of the night into the limo. I was tempted by a full-length one, but street length looks good over long gowns, too, and seemed more practical, if that's quite the word to apply to this costly little pet."

"Absolutely. Street length. Turn around. Oh, it's gorgeous. Can *I* try it on?"

"*Certainement.*" Liz eased the white satin lining over Rosemary's shoulders.

Rosemary turned in the over-sofa mirror, stepping back to view her entire figure, rolling the collar up to her pale cheeks. Liz studied her while Rosemary surveyed herself. The coat with its bold black-and-white pattern overpowered a blonde, but Rosie knew that. She simply wanted to luxuriate in the coat for a bit. The cheeks that brushed the fur struck Liz as unattractively sunken, though, and Rosemary's hair had a brittle, tarnished look. The coat, like all fur coats, was bulky. It made Rosemary's weight loss less obvious. Her legs beneath the sweeping hem still looked chunky, while Liz's had been slim and shapely. Rosemary arrived at these same conclusions instants after Liz had. She turned away from the mirror, slipped gingerly out of the coat, and held it out.

"But it's your coat. Let me see it on you again."

Liz obliged. "I suppose I really shouldn't have done it, but I have so damn little *time* to spend money, and buying clothes is a chore—they all have to meet the requirements of being on camera: no busy necklines, no eye-catching patterns, no black and white. This, needless to say, isn't meant for on camera. I wouldn't wear it to Studio 54, but to the Emmys or a special dinner or something."

"Liz, have you been going to Studio 54?"

Liz rolled her eyes. "Alfonso loves that scene. I guess I can be talked into staying up late on a Friday or Saturday night now and again. Life does not begin and end with *Sunrise.*"

"No. No, it doesn't." Rosemary was subdued as she sat again to pick idly at the last beached pieces of seafood salad on her plate.

"You don't . . . miss . . . doing the show?" Liz sat quietly beside her, the coat forgotten and draped over the sofa end.

"Oh, no, I—"

"You seem . . . worried."

"About you." Rosemary turned a troubled face to Liz. "And Alfonso. Oh, Liz, maybe I'm bein' silly, or overwrought like Joel says, but I just don't think he's any good for you. Tell me it's none of my business if you want, but that's what I think."

Liz refilled their coffee cups from the thermal server on the coffee table. "What do you have against him?"

"It's just that he's so good-looking and smart and smooth and . . . and . . ." She looked at Liz, eyes half pleading, half laughing.

"Terrible qualities," Liz mocked. "It's just that he's too good to be true."

"That's it! There you go, puttin' your finger right on it as usual. He's just too good to be true. I'm worried about you, Liz. He doesn't seem your kind of guy, that's all. I never thought you'd fall for the Latin lover act."

"Aren't I human? You'd be amazed what I'd fall for, Rosemary. And what I'd put up with," Liz added under her breath. Rosemary looked more alarmed than ever. "Oh, I'm not thinking of Alfonso. I was thinking of *Sunrise* and the paranoia everyone feels. When those weekly ratings come out, everybody from the prop man to the producer goes crazy until he knows what our goddamn audience "share" for the week was. There are seven *million* or so people tuning in every day; you'd think that would be pretty respectable."

"I know what a grind *Sunrise* is. I was talking about Alfonso."

"About whom you know nothing."

"I know he's not good enough for you."

"Who is, then? After all, I've been on the cover of *People* magazine. Maybe celebrities need celebrities. I don't know." Liz sighed. "Rosie, Alfonso is more vulnerable than most people would guess. TV makes us seem so one-dimensional—a face and a voice in the living rooms and bedrooms of America that are as easy as tap water to turn on and turn off. Always there, always predictable. Alfonso's a victim of his image, too, stuck like a phonograph needle and forced to repeat one stance, one story, over and over again." Liz laughed. "Phonograph needle. Am I outdated."

"Do you feel a victim of your image?"

"Yes. Maybe I'm not trapped into fighting my own body, as you are, but my mind's divided between what I'm seen as—what I am   and what I want, or once wanted, to be."

Rosemary went white, then pink. "You think I'm obsessed about my weight." Liz was silent. "It's why I lost the show—yes, it is. You still think ability matters, that one physical handicap won't hurt. But it does; it does with women. Look at Joel's models—"

"We're not models, Rosie. We're broadcast professionals—reporters, anchorwomen, whatever you want to call us. We're paid for what's inside, not just what's outside."

"What about that woman in Kansas City who lost her anchor

slot because she was 'too old, unattractive, and not deferential enough to men'?"

"You mean Christine Craft? What is she—thirty eight? Too old! I'm glad she sued the station. That's what we have to do—refuse to be categorized that way anymore. We all know a woman has to be twice as good as a man to get half as far in journalism. We have to make the world at large see it. We have to prove our substance; then they won't constantly judge us on surface factors."

"So gain thirty pounds and watch your career go down the toilet! But you'll have made a point."

Liz shook her head. "I know a woman broadcaster can't be seriously overweight—men can't either; but Rosie, you weren't. It was mere politics, your being let go."

Rosemary shook her head mutely, a sudden tear slick turning her blue eyes as hard and shiny as marbles. Finally she spoke. "I guess it's as hard for me to accept that as for you to accept what I think about Alfonso."

"I guess."

"I love the coat, Liz," Rosemary said appealingly, as if to soften her opinion on Alfonso. "I'm glad you showed it to me."

Liz smiled. "You're the first."

Liz went back to the coat and the mirror after seeing Rosemary out. She picked up the fur and threw it on again. With her dark hair and light skin, the effect was riveting. Alfonso would love it; he didn't have her inbred Midwestern fear of flashiness. He liked to see her dressed up, to take her places where flashing photographic strobes would illuminate the frenetically charged pace of New York nightlife.

The two of them had become a noted media "couple" now. Oddly, Liz found her journalistic stock rising with the association. Alfonso's advocacy journalism reputation forced media professionals to reevaluate her level of commitment to her work. He must see *something* in her, they reasoned. The *Sunrise* job was trivializing, no matter how much they paid her, no matter how much attention she got. Now people decided that Liz had a serious mind after all. She and Alfonso were interviewed for tandem profiles in the *Parade* magazine Sunday supplement. They had replaced Marlo Thomas and Phil Donahue as America's favorite "nice" unmarried couple now that Phil and Marlo were formally wed and therefore less interesting. Nobody probed the intimate side of their relationship. They were "dating," not living together, and therefore were presumed innocent until proven guilty in the public mind.

Liz smiled at her elegant self in the mirror, remembering her father's reaction to the *Parade* piece over the long-distance line.

"Who's this Alonzo guy? He the set decorator?"

"That was Wendy," she said gently. Z.J. was past seventy five now. Though his voice got louder, his other characteristics seemed to be fading out. "And it's Alfonso."

"Mexican, huh?"

"Cuban."

A long pause. Z.J. wasn't a red-baiter, but Cuba was a four-letter word in his vocabulary.

"His family fled when Castro took over," Liz explained.

"Oh. We had some of those Marielitos kept at a camp here in Wisconsin; they were a bad lot."

"Those were last-wave refugees. Alfonso's family was among the first wave in the fifties. His family was one of the most important in Havana."

"He looks . . . slight."

"Oh, he's about your height, Dad."

"And your age, Elizabeth?"

"About."

"Is he the marrying kind?"

Liz had smiled over the phone. "Maybe."

There could be worse things than marrying Alfonso. She liked him, admired his mind, his confidence, pitied his past, his struggle to survive. She knew he had weaknesses, that he was too easily drawn to the appearance of success and fame and beauty. He had been at Joel and Rosemary's New Year's Eve party the first time she'd glimpsed him because he had frequently escorted several of Joel's models. He liked the cachet of being with that kind of woman, of being pictured in papers with that kind of woman.

Liz smoothed the coat collar up to her cheeks. Liz was close enough to that kind of woman to please his ego, and she understood him a hell of a lot better. That wasn't much, but in these cold, trickle-down days of Reaganomics, it was enough to bank on.

Hoffman called Liz into his office without warning one Tuesday right after the show had gone off the air. *Sunrise* had been doing better. Hoffman had spent a bundle redecorating his office. The desk was Napoleonic, with ormolu eagles guarding the corners. Gold bee–stamped wine leather covered the walls and the various chairs. Hoffman's swivel chair was wine leather upholstered, too, but the gilt pattern stamped in was his initials, B.H. They did not make a graceful decoration but were suitably ostentatious.

"Show's doing well," he began, then dismissed that all-important subject. "I hear you turned down a sub spot for Carson."

"It's a late-night show on another network. I'd have to do *Sunrise*, fly west, then try to get some sleep and get myself warmed up again by ten o'clock for the *Tonight* show. I'm not a robot; I'd sleepwalk through the show like Trilby under the influence of Svengali."

"Take a thermos of coffee along—or some uppers."

Liz was shocked. "You mean you want me to do it?"

"Damn right; that's valuable exposure. The *Tonight Show* is beyond networks. It's in a class by itself. If they think you're an important enough national celebrity to subhost it, go for it."

"That's just it. I'm not an entertainer; I'm an interviewer. It takes a comedian to run that spot."

"Walters has done it."

"Her father ran the Latin Quarter; she's from an entertainment family. She's at home with those people."

Hoffman's thick brows lowered. "According to *Women's Wear Daily*, so are you now, Liz."

"I take it these are marching orders."

"*Sunrise* needs it."

Liz stood. "Someday, Mr. Hoffman, that's not going to be enough reason for me."

"Look, Liz. Your contract's up soon, and you're still here. Things have been going fairly well. You've even managed to make Danny look like he's up on current events. Relax. Have fun with it. Do the Carson thing; there's people out there would kill for a chance like that."

"Then why did they pick me?"

Hoffman looked—sheepish. "It's that, uh, the networks like to put a woman on once in a while. Looks more fair. Gets a lot of media attention. So you buy yourself some sensational rag and put it on the expense account. Anything you want. Make a splash."

Liz left his office, partly excited, partly infuriated. The idea of inflicting such performance anxiety on herself under adverse circumstances—and any live nighttime work was adverse to the schedule her mind and body had adapted over the past year—scared the liver out of her. The idea of being the glamorous guest woman host sitting at television's most long-lived and famous desk tickled her down to the trivial bones in her toes. Me. Little Lizzie from Turtle Bend. Wow! Look, Pa, no hands, no nerves, no guts, no chutzpah. Look, world, I'm really not this glittering lady in midnight lace; they made me do it.

When she confessed her reservations to Alfonso, he swept her ecstatically into his arms. "The *Tonight Show*, what a coup! And you worry about your professional image? Honey, this'll *make* it!"

"You're not . . . a little bit jealous?" She waited for signs of Steve's malady.

"Jealous? Hell, no. I'll get my shot someday. In the meantime, you got it all—brains, beauty, and the front page. And I got you." He hugged her again. Alfonso was unabashedly physical, and Liz was learning to like it, despite her more restrained emotional makeup. "Do me proud," he urged, kissing her enthusiastically.

Liz wore a new emerald silk Givenchy gown that Elizabeth Taylor could have stopped elephants with in her heyday. Her hands were as cold as Rosemary's borrowed diamonds that decked her ears. In the dressing room, she studied her perfectly made-up face and found it deceptively calm. Beneath the gathers of silk that swept artfully across her bosom her heart pounded like a giant, hot, pulsing nugget of sheer adrenaline. Her cheeks were flatteringly pink, sans blusher. Her mouth and throat were dry. She sipped more of the lukewarm coffee on her dressing table. Not too much; she wasn't used to it at this hour and could get twitchy. Liz didn't know whether feeling like a jerky puppet would be an improvement over feeling like an overdecorated zombie.

Finally, she moved to the Green Room, where the evening's guests were chatting quietly to one another. An animal psychiatrist, with caged subjects. That should be an okay segment. She liked animals, and it would give her a chance to parade her gown full-length. A Las Vegas comic whose name and face were vaguely familiar and who was as hyper and brassy as most comics. Ah, the dear man—Jimmy Stewart. If she could overcome impulses to stutter and call him "Mr. Stewart" every time she addressed him, including saying "hello," that section of the show should be a dream. Everybody loved Jimmy Stewart, and Liz had researched his career from A to Z.

She waited behind the gold curtains that formed a subconscious backdrop to the memories of everyone in America, her hands clammier than ever, her throat throttled. All she had to do was walk out on cue, wait for the applause to die out—what if there wasn't any applause?—and read the stupid monologue she had written herself as it unreeled on the monitor in front of her eyes. It wasn't a comic monologue; Liz knew better than to compete on the maestro's own turf. But it was amusing, she hoped, and took some gentle jabs at the week's news, as Johnny sometimes did. Then all she had to do was sit down and ask the right questions at the right time. That's all.

When she saw the tape of the show in the wee hours of Sunday morning at home, she was half-asleep. Alfonso had braced her against him on the media room chaise and was kissing the wilted emerald silk off her shoulders. The tape unreeled in a strange fast-slow mélange. Liz looked as glamorous as she'd hoped and people laughed—actually laughed—at most of the right spots in her monologue. Jimmy was charming, the comic funny and able to rattle on without any aid from her. The animal psychologist was a bit stuffy, but the animals were endearing. Liz's gingerly court-ship of a capuchin monkey made a delightful bit, although her encounter with an unhousebroken skunk she immediately chris-tened "Flower" was even funnier.

"My dress is ruined," she told Alfonso, yawning.

"So what. The network paid for it. And anyway, you're going to be taking if off now."

"I am?"

"No, I am," Alfonso corrected, proceeding to do what he said.

They made love on the chaise while the last of the *Tonight Show* Liz performed unwatched on the TV screen. The "real" Liz was so sleepy she felt no satisfaction other than contributing to Alfonso's. It was a perfect end to what had been a dreadfully perfect day in the life of a modern media star.

— Chapter 44 —

"Who's the new boy in Hoffman's office?"

Liz seldom spoke off the set to Danny Rogers, but they were alone together in the makeup room and she was curious.

Danny scowled, causing Bessie to pause impatiently in apply-ing his TV-star tan pancake makeup. It was easy to treat makeup people like nonpersons after a while, but Danny had been gifted at that from the very beginning.

"Some hack from the *Daily News*," he finally answered.

"Con O'Connor isn't a hack," Bessie said, powdering Danny's face fiercely. "He's the best columnist this side of the Mississippi. I've been reading that man for fifteen years. Lord, I don't know how I'm going to put *makeup* on him!"

"The same way you put it on Danny Rogers, one cheek at a time." The voice was rich, self-mocking, and shy at one and the same time. Its owner stepped into the room fully, blinking a bit at the glare of the round makeup bulbs. He was a portly man in his late forties whose springy, iron-gray hair was innocent of styl-ing, whose look of professional rumplement would have shamed

Peter Falk's "Columbo," and whose blue eyes twinkled with a boy's gentle mischief.

"What do we have here, Kris Kringle?" Danny demanded scathingly.

"More like his elf, your worship," Con O'Connor returned in an exaggerated brogue. "I hope, ma'am," he soberly beseeched Bessie, "that you don't intend to baste and dust me with the contents of those jars." His observant eyes fell on Liz.

"I'm afraid she does, Mr. O'Connor," Liz said. "We all have to look pretty for the cameras, boys and girls together."

"Con," said the man, extending his pudgy hand for a token shake. His light blue eyes paid tribute. "And you should have no trouble at all with the camera. But me . . . it's a face even my mother had trouble smiling at in the cradle. All right, ma'am, I'll sit myself down and you can work your magic. Can you make me look like Mick Jagger?"

"No, thank God." Bessie was an odd little black woman in her fifties who came and went and did her job. She heard more than her share of confidences; people trapped in a chair in front of a mirror start saying oddly intimate things. But she hardly heard them, being more involved with the domestic situation of her daughter Mabel, who raised Dobermans in New Jersey, or the state of Scientology, of which Bessie was an ardent adherent.

Con O'Connor winked as he lowered himself to the chair.

"You're not . . . going on today?" Liz asked incredulously.

"I'm sort of a surprise they're introducing today. Think of me as a secret weapon, Miss Jordan. They've got to keep me heavily draped"—he elevated the blue plastic makeup cape that protected what was left unrumpled of his wardrobe—"until I go into action."

"Liz," she corrected absently. "Well, I can't say a thing about it until I see it in the TelePrompTer, so your secret is safe with me."

He beamed like a bottle-fed elf.

Manzelli cued them in at the hasty meeting convened before the show went on the air.

"I guess you've all met Con O'Connor. We're adding him as weekly color man. He'll do some essays on life, liberty, and the pursuit of conspicuous consumption, like his pieces for the *Daily News*. Think of him as our Andy Rooney."

"More like 'Jimmy the Geek,'" Danny put in loudly enough to carry.

Con spread his hands mildly. "Comic relief," he said pleasantly to Danny. "When you've got a tragedy in the making, comic relief is always welcome."

Tragedy. The word poised itself over their heads and hung there.

It was the first time Liz realized that the Powers That Be were no longer happy with *Sunrise* as it was. Con O'Connor was but a first attempt to beef up the show. Adding elements or personalities was one way to do that; subtracting existing ones was the next step.

It fell to her, as she had guessed, to read the debut introduction for O'Connor. Danny disliked last-minute script changes. Liz read the unrolling type on the monitor with the enthusiasm of a kid announcing the imminent arrival of Santa Claus. O'Connor deserved a chance. Besides, she had seen his hands tremble as he moved his script into precise position before him. A print man would be unnerved by the unfriendly circle of cameras on their imposing dollies. Liz took her uneasy eyes off O'Connor and waited to be cued. Now.

"Con O'Connor has been an addiction to New Yorkers for fifteen years. Now they reach for his *New York Daily News* column, 'Con's Space,' as automatically as they do for the corn flakes or coffee each morning. *Sunrise* wants to share the riches, so we're introducing 'Con's Place.' Three times a week, Con O'Connor will discourse on whatever strikes his fancy. We hope it will tickle yours."

O'Connor's fingers spasmed on the script, but he stared unblinkingly into the camera, like a soldier facing the cannon's deadly but inevitable eye. It was a cruel way to debut, unrehearsed except in front of the bathroom mirror, Liz would bet, and all because the producers wanted to make his appearance a complete surprise. He began reading his piece, and sounded like he was reading. On the monitor, Liz saw his lively eyes glaze. He declaimed a charming and witty essay on time-honored methods of getting up in the morning, adding a few inimitable suggestions of his own. Liz heard only the overlong breaths on which he delivered his sentences, the too-deep inhalations taken to get through the next sentence, the mispronunciations that violated network newscasting taboos.

Despite the flaws, the man's unschooled charm came through. Liz found herself smiling at the end of the segment as the camera returned to her and Danny for their closing sixty seconds of "happy chat."

"Con missed one good way to wake up—looking at the world through his eyes," she said.

"For sure," Danny agreed eagerly—after all, he was on camera and the producers evidently placed a lot of faith in O'Connor. "What do you use, an answering service?"

"A dime-store windup alarm," Liz returned. "It's never failed me. It's loud, reliable, and cheap—like a Model T."

Danny chuckled. "Now that's a news flash—Liz Jordan waking up to the crash of a Kresge's gong."

"What do you use to get yourself to the studio on time?"

"My wife," Danny retorted smugly.

On that chauvinist note, *Sunrise*'s last on-air second ticked off. Liz leaned back in the Plexiglas curve of her chair. "You mean that, Danny? Your wife really gets up at three A.M. just to see you out the door?"

"Sure. Why not?" He slid away from the anchor desk, never one to waste time chatting with his colleagues.

Con O'Connor still sat in the third chair. Liz was used to seeing Alfonso there, or Darryl. Con was looking her way, the limp script in front of him probably mirroring his inner condition.

"How'd I do?" he asked quietly as the crew bustled around them, dismantling for the day and setting up for taped interviews.

She hesitated long enough for his hopeful expression to change to a wince. "Why ask me?"

He shrugged. "You're the only one who looks honest. I guess I was right." Con turned, sweeping the script off the smooth desktop.

"Wait. Come back to my office. I haven't got a taping until eleven."

"I haven't got an office," he mentioned wryly as he followed her out of the studio and down a long carpeted hall.

Janice was waiting for something to do—and found it, bringing Liz and Con coffee in topless melamine cups with throw away plastic inserts. This was a step up from Styrofoam cups, but didn't quite match the pottery cups in the brass's offices, which their secretaries actually had to wash between uses.

Liz shut the door.

"That bad, huh?" Con was huddled over the corner of her desk and his steaming cup, like a street bum caging winter warmth from a sidewalk steam vent.

"No." She felt too professorial. "But not that good. The network ever give you any vocal training . . .?"

His salt and pepper head shook like an errant schoolboy's, deferential but impish.

"They tell you how to breathe?"

"I don't do *that* right?"

"What about giving you a pronunciation guide?"

His hands flared emptily.

"I don't know why they keep doing this—throwing people on the air with no coaching," Liz exploded. "That's what did in Sally Quinn of the *Washington Post* a decade ago. Newspaper people think they can talk on their feet, but that's not enough for television. Look, here's the network no-no list—words that have to be pronounced a certain way, like long-*lye*ved, not long-*lih*ved." Con cringed guiltily. He'd used long-*lih*ved that morning. "And there is no such place as 'Mos-cow.' It's 'Mos-co'—long *o*. These are fine points, but failing to follow them grates on the execs after a while. I'll have Janice copy this for you. If you like, get me a copy of your scripts ahead of time and I'll flag them for pronunciation and mark breath stops, so you don't sound like you have emphysema—you don't, do you?"

"I huff and puff a bit climbing the subway stairs," he admitted. "I'm in terrible shape."

Liz smiled. "Sounds like another column coming on. Your piece this morning was terrific, really. You just need a little performance polish."

O'Connor stood. "I need a lot of polish, Miss Liz. Nobody knows that more than I do. If I, uh, get Wednesday's piece done by tomorrow noon, could you and I get together, give me some pointers?"

She checked her calendar. The last thing she needed when her own career might be flagging was to baby-sit some pencil-pushing print reporter. . . . "Okay. Give me a call right after the show tomorrow."

Con paused in the doorway, his tweedy jacket still slightly askew on his shoulders, as it had been all through the broadcast. "Thanks. You're a pal."

— Chapter 45 —

Con O'Connor got an office and a special corner of the set decked with hokey newspaper-cliché props, including a stiff, high-cased old black manual Royal typewriter.

Alfonso dubbed him "*Sunrise's* answer to Gene Shalit."

"He's a good writer and a nice guy," Liz defended Con. "Besides, he's an instant hit. Hoffman is ecstatic."

"Luck!" Alfonso dismissed Con's popularity. "You were there for his debut reading; he stunk. Something got him over the stage fright fast, but if he'd kept on like that, he'd be on reruns of *Mister Rogers' Neighborhood* by now."

"Well, I'd rather have Hoffman ecstatic about something on *Sunrise* than going around glowering like he has been lately."

Hoffman wasn't the only who was glowering. Liz was at loose ends. Her apartment was totally redecorated, but she could count the number of people who had seen it on the fingers of one hand. Ever since Christine Craft had won her discrimination suit against the Kansas City TV station, Liz had found her own speaking engagements proliferating. That fall she and Craft were on the same program at a Midwestern university. During the post-speech questioning, Liz had been distressed to find herself cast as the network "pretty girl" against the "overassertive career woman" in Craft.

"We are not wicked stepsisters," Liz had defended herself and her network peers. "Nor are we glamour girls who keep our more talented sisters down on the farm because we happened to be born looking a certain way. Of course it helps to be telegenic and verbal. And who can say where the advantage of anyone's personal appearance—man or woman—versus his or her professional acuity begins and ends in such an industry? If there is an overwhelming trend to looks over journalistic skill, men suffer from it, too.

"There are no more 'weather girls'; now fat men in bow ties play clown-prognosticators on the nightly news across the country. Has the position itself been accorded any more dignity, no matter the sex of who holds it? I don't think so. Barbara Walters spent years working her way up from being cast as a cutie pie on the set to making herself a major force on the *Today* program; now newswomen who had runny noses when she wasn't allowed to talk out of turn accuse her of being 'trivial.' Jessica Savitch's career was built on never doing any work that could be construed as 'female'—and unfortunately that means empathetic stories about people. Real anchorpersons don't have hearts apparently. Look at Geraldo Rivera and Alfonso Delgado—they made their reputations doing compassionate, people-oriented stories; but ethnic men are allowed to be more 'emotional.' I think women make a terrible mistake if we scorn our heritage and instincts as women. If the world ran so well by the gospel according to St. Macho, it wouldn't be in the sorry state it is now."

She got frenzied applause, more for her closing remark than for what had gone before, Liz knew. Student audiences reacted like Pavlov's pooch to mention of world disarray.

"At least they can't accuse *me* of riding on my youth and looks," Con O'Connor chuckled one afternoon at McGillacuddy's Tavern on 48th Street. Liz had just called it a day at three P.M., and nowadays habitually met Con at one of his favorite watering holes to skim his *Sunrise* script. Liz's tutoring was the reason Con's on-camera delivery had improved overnight.

"You and Charles Kuralt," she answered, stirring her Scotch

and water with the barber pole—striped straw provided. Con glowed at the comparison.

"But I've got more hair," he finally decreed from under shaggy brows and a shaggier forelock.

"But Kuralt's is darker," Liz retorted, then laughed. "You see how ridiculous it gets? And it's much more critical for women; men are considered trustworthy if they're a bit worn around the edges."

"Worn, huh?" Con took a last, deep swallow of his whiskey. The waiter was there instantly with another one.

"You feeling worn?" Liz asked sympathetically. "Getting up in time for a seven A.M. airtime is no picnic, even if it's only three days a week, especially when you're working another full-time job."

"Hoffman wants me to go five days a week." Con celebrated finishing the sentence by downing a good half of the new drink.

"Five days a week? That's crazy."

"He says the cards, letters, and calls are pouring in. Here. This one came last week; I thought you'd get a kick out of it." He wrestled a crumpled piece of folded lined paper out of his equally crumpled pocket and tossed it to the tabletop.

"'. . . brilliant line about small-town manners . . .' Hey, that was *my* suggestion!"

Con beamed. "Yup. They don't give me time enough to credit my editor, though." He fondly fingered the paper as he jammed it back into one of the many various crumples of his sport coat. "It's nice, that kind of instant response."

"You must have gotten tons of letters from your newspaper column."

"Sure." Con's grin emphasized laugh-underlined blue eyes and whiskey-pinked cheeks and nose. "But people didn't stop me on the street and say, 'You're Con O'Connor! I saw you on TV yesterday. . . .' It's like the Second Coming, you know, when I walk down a street nowadays. Heady stuff."

"I thought you were shy." Not many people would confront Con on his reticence.

"I am, Miss Liz. But even a shy man can like a little public sunshine now and then." He drank a bit more, and then even more. "Besides, a publisher called me. Called *me*. Wants to do a book— *The Best of Con O'Connor, Live and in Print*. It'd be a combination of the *Sunrise* pieces and my old print stuff. Liz, I couldn't sell the pope's little black book before I started doing my turns on *Sunrise*."

"Is the money good?"

"Sure, but money . . . All I need is enough to keep McGillacuddy and Fahey taking annual trips back to the Auld Sod. Do you do it for the money?"

Liz leaned against the high-backed booth. There was nothing trendy about McGillacuddy's. It was a straightforward, wood-and-barglass, murky railroad car of a place—neat, reasonably quiet, and sober in its dedication to the fine art of libation.

"Money. No. . . . But I don't know why I do it anymore."

Con was quiet for a minute or two while Liz ostentatiously finished her drink and slid it aside. She couldn't stay all afternoon, and one drink was her limit.

"And why do you waste your time on an old print dray horse like myself?" he asked finally.

"It's not a waste; it's an education. Besides, it's good for the industry to have someone literate on national TV."

"Will I ever—" Con leaned back while the waiter removed his glass and replaced it with a fresh one. "—be easy in my mind about facing that camera every morning?"

"Probably not. You're not a natural performer, Con. Maybe you should stick to three days a week and not strain yourself."

He shook his head, sighing. "No. Hoffman says five—or else."

"Then can't you cut back at the paper?"

He looked very boyish glancing up at her from under a shock of wiry gray-white hair, the lowball glass cupped in his fingers like a baseball that had recently broken a window. "No, ma'am. The management can nix my appearance on 'competing media,' which includes television. I can do *Sunrise* only if I meet my seven daily column deadlines." *12 columns a week?*

His features were pleasantly blurred. Liz had spent enough time with Con to know what was coming next—the stories and rambling reminiscences, the puckish comments and funny tales. McGillacuddy's regular patrons, Con's cronies, would begin gathering around for their daily ration of regalement. The drinks were on the house—Con's, Liz's single Scotch and water, the drinks that would come later were on the house—Con was bard-in-residence at a whole string of Manhattan's Irish bars. It was where he found the subject matter for his columns, in his companions and in his alcohol-unfurled self.

"You're caught between the Devil and the deep blue sea," she commented, referring to the newspaper and the network.

He smiled. "I see a blue devil of a lecture brewing in those deep brown eyes of yours, Miss Liz. Just mind my broadcast p's and q's and keep your sermonizing to yourself."

"You of all people should know that sermonizing without a subject is no fun whatsoever." Liz winked and slid out of her seat, to be replaced by a whiskey-nosed man carrying a racing form.

On the street, she only half concentrated on hailing a cab, and ultimately found herself walking the fourteen blocks back to her apartment. Normally she avoided walking; Con was right—get a little TV fame and everybody and his first cousin once-removed stops you on the street. But today her thoughts seemed to act as a cloak of invisibility. She broadcast mental abstraction even as she subconsciously cased the pedestrians around her, always alert to personal impingement.

It was an overheated Indian summer day, ninety–two in the shade. People still walked fast, in a hurry to get—or get away from—somewhere. The street vendors' odiferous wares permeated the heavy air, blending their scents into an unholy culinary cologne that both stimulated and quelled appetite. Liz cut over to Paley Park on 57th to queue up at the brick outbuilding where the best hot dogs in New York were dispensed in crisp heated rolls. She claimed an empty white mesh metal chair near the sheet of water that perpetually pounded down the pocket-size park's concrete dead end. Sitting there, Liz let her endlessly recycled thoughts present themselves in counterpoint to the rushing, ceaselessly recycled waterfall.

Con worried her. The price he paid for his new on-camera cool was terrible. Inside, the man was still terrified, but he was hopelessly hooked on the warm wave of disembodied adulation that met the live performer's image going out over the airwaves as it came in. He had no family, no real friends. While he was an important columnist, the appreciation always came long-distance in phone calls or letters. His bosses couldn't comprehend his writing brilliance and only tolerated his quirks. So now—miraculously, unexpectedly—the television audience had embraced him, adding precious luster to a life buffed to a dull patina of gray. Liz had felt the emotional high of knowing a waiting world was watching, straining for one's voice and gestures; that instant acceptance gained merely by being there, on national TV, doing something the men who ran the networks deemed worthwhile.

"Don't you use a computer at the *Daily News*?" Liz had asked incredulously when she first saw one of his original scripts atrociously typed on limp oatmeal-colored copy paper.

"Can't do it. Those machines give me the willies. I've told the whole world about my allergy to algorithms or whatever they program the beasties with. Don't you read my column?" he finished impishly.

"I wonder anybody ever does, if it's turned in typed like this. I thought newspapers were fully computerized now—from reporter terminal to composing room."

"True. But some of us old duffers who can't adjust get to keep our typewriters. Then some smarty-pants types it into the computer and all's right with the world. Besides, I often write my column at home, at all hours."

"Get a home computer, or a portable."

The ragged head of hair shook. "You don't understand. I don't like computers. I never saw one that could fly a kite or darn a sock or sound like Rudy Vallee. I'm too old to change."

"My *father* uses a computer now!"

"I've read his stuff. He always was a flaming radical. . . ."

Liz had laughed and given up. She knew newspapers granted computer dispensations to old and valued employees who couldn't adapt to the electronic journalism age. Still, with Con it was more a question of "wouldn't" than "couldn't." The key to all his problems was a four letter word—fear.

"Fear of God, Liz," he once had roared outside the Greenwich Village bar, the last of a string of establishments they had pushed in and out of when their afternoon "drink" had become an evening of barhopping. "That's how they raised us in the old days—fear of God, Father O'Reilly, sister Philomena, and your parents in descending order. But I got my priorities mixed up. Sister Philomena used to stand behind us in choir practice swinging the long wooden rosary at her waist in a big, whiplike circle. . . . Clickety, clickety, clickety, you'd hear behind you all the time you were trying to trill 'Jesu Bambino.' Made sopranos out of a lot of us boys from sheer tension.

"They don't marry over there, on the Blessed Island. Scared to. Big men of eight-and-thirty. Celibate, you know, unless a storm blows a mermaid ashore. Bread and babies, that's all that Irish women make, and if there were pleasure in it, it'd be a sinful one. Of course, all pleasures are sinful. Take this golden goblet of whiskey I even now elevate to my lips in faithful devotion. . . ."

The people around them, and there were always people around Con, laughed appreciatively. Liz supposed there was truth in whiskey widsom, that his Irish-reared friends needed to hear their harsh faith taken irreverently to task. But there was always fear at the bottom of it, even the defiance.

"He's a loser, Liz," Alfonso persuaded when his spur-of-the-moment invitation to a movie lost out to her standing script sessions with Con. "I don't know why you waste your time on that guy. He'll be off the show one of these weeks."

"Or you will. Or I."

Alfonso's sleekly styled head shook dolorously. "You can't save the world. You should pay more attention to your own standing at *Sunrise*."

"Why?"

Alfonso shrugged. He was wearing a baby-blue sweater over a white shirt and red tie. Only Alfonso could get away with being so casual on the air.

"Have you heard something?" she prodded.

"What's to hear? That in this business you keep your mind on business or you won't be in this business? You know that, Elizabeth," he added softly, "better than any of us. Please don't forget it."

"I'll try not to," she promised, touched by the note of concern, of almost pleading, in his voice.

"Sit down, Liz."

Manzelli was being formal. He sat, too, not on the edge of his desk for once but in the chair behind it. He wore shirt-sleeves and tie, like a newspaperman.

"What's up?"

"Your contract, for one thing."

"There are four weeks to run; I thought you and my agent were working on it."

Manzelli blinked, catlike, without revealing anything. "We are, but there are some . . . gray areas."

"Oh?" Liz hated to tell him, but the notion that the network wasn't thinking of renewing her contract didn't strike terror into her heart. Numbness, yes, but not terror. Her reaction struck her as odd, but she needed time to dissect it.

Manzelli leaned forward confidentially. "We're asking for an extension, same terms. Now, before you blow a gasket—" Liz had been contemplating doing nothing of the kind. "—calm down. This is top-secret stuff. Danny Rogers is leaving the show. We'll need a replacement."

"Danny's been—"

"He's leaving; that's all we're gonna say about it. But, um, you're in the running for his spot."

"Oh, come on, Vic. Since when is the network going to name a woman anything but second banana?"

"Maybe since you. There just aren't that many top personalities around for a show of our kind. Most of the candidates are either too soft or too hard, too cold or too hot. A Jessica Savitch type just wouldn't be right for *Sunrise*."

"She's dead," Liz pointed out, and Manzelli winced. What made Liz wince was how quickly TV executives had begun referring to a "Jessica Savitch type," as if she had been merely one pattern from a great big cookie cutter in the sky. She had written the book on "Anchorwoman," but she hadn't lived it long.

Everyone in the business knew that Savitch's so-called meteoric rise had been trailed by train of personal disaster—first her physician-bridegroom's suicide, then rumors of her verbal stumbles on the nightly newsbreak and possible drug use. Now, finally, she'd died on a dark highway in a mysterious car accident and no one had Jessica to envy or gossip about or secretly pity anymore. Judy Woodruff, another blond network correspondent, had slipped into Jessica's prime anchor spot on public TV's *Frontline*. In weeks, viewers had forgotten whether Judy looked like Jessica or Jessica like Judy. . . . Sic transit meteors.

"You know what I mean," Manzelli was saying. "We need someone with enough stature but also enough warmth to carry a show like *Sunrise*, which goes into people's homes during the most intimate hours of the day. You're a candidate. And some men as well. We'll still go with—"

"Boy, girl."

"Right, but we might make the girl the lead anchor. Who knows?"

"And in the meantime, you want me to hang on, sans contract, sans raise, while you make up your minds?"

"Bluntly put," Manzelli said, but he didn't add any softeners.

"If my agent agrees—"

Manzelli stood. "We're set, then. This could be a big career move for you, Liz. Sure, it wouldn't look much different to the folks out in the countryside, but we'd plan some specials for you, maybe even some sort of spot on the nightly news."

Liz left his office, puzzled. "Some sort of spot on the nightly news." There was no such thing. On the nightly news, it was either all or nothing, as Barbara Walters had found out so bitterly. Liz tried to analyze it, suspecting the network of trying to sucker her along on vague promises without offering anything substantive while *Sunrise* adjusted to the loss of Danny Rogers. And it would be a loss, at least outwardly. Danny made *Sunrise* run.

She couldn't wait to break the news to Alfonso, so invited him over for a candlelit microwave dinner.

"What's the occasion?" Alfonso wondered, nibbling her neck while she watched the microwave turntable spin its expensive burden of catered squab.

"I wanted to debut my new dining room," Liz explained, wafting the squab and spinach soufflé and Caesar salads to the lacquered parsons table in the mirror-lined dining alcove.

Alfonso did something tricky and difficult with the cork puller, and a chilled bottle of French champagne reclined on ice in the chrome wine stand that normally served as a plant stand for an ivy.

They sat on the velvet-upholstered side chairs, with time only for a quick toast before Liz got nervous about the food staying hot and ordered Alfonso to "dive in."

"To you, Elizabeth," he said, his eyes sparkling like black champagne in the richly reflected candlelight.

"To . . . *Sunrise*," she answered cryptically, then explained over dinner. "So, by the time I left Manzelli's office, all I knew for certain was that Danny Rogers is as good as gone."

"I know."

"You do?"

"Hoffman called me in to give me the same song and dance he gave you. Nice work, kid, hang on. Trust me; you might get a big chance."

"*Hoffman* called you in." Hoffman was Manzelli's boss; ergo, Alfonso was a more vital employee. . . .

"Yeah, Hoffman. Not bad for an immigrant kid, huh? But you're right. The network will never go with a woman up front— or an ethnic. They'll dangle the bait in front of us for a while for looks, then import some white guy."

"Hispanics are white."

"You know what I mean. Some snow-white guy. Some WASP, or at least some actor who changed his name to sound WASP-ish. Or maybe . . . maybe they'll go with a woman, like Mondale did."

"I hear she might get a million dollars to write a book whether she makes it or not."

Alfonso grinned and tackled the chocolate silk pie, courtesy, like the rest of the meal, of Moveable Feast on 58th. "Maybe you will, too."

Rosemary and Joel held a fancy dress halloween party that year, or maybe Rosemary did. She invited everybody from *Sunrise*—the producers, Danny Rogers, the cameramen, Liz, Alfonso, even Con O'Connor.

Of course, all of Joel's willowy clients were there wearing the most glitzy, revealing costumes that money could rent. And so did Rosemary. Most of the models had searched the array of people to come as and came up playing glamorous females in clinging costume. And so did Rosemary. A number of Morticias slunk around in slit-to-the-thigh black velvet that showed a lot of sheer-stockinged leg. And so did Rosemary.

"Rosie!" Liz hardly recognized her friend, and held her by the elbows so she had to be still a moment. "That *is* you?"

Rosemary took a shallow puff on the long rhinestone-jeweled ebony cigarette holder in her bracelet-swagged hand.

"What have you done to yourself?" Liz wondered.

"It's Halloween, darling," Rosemary purred, running a palm

lightly over the blond marcel waves that clung to her head. "Can't you tell?"

"But who are you supposed to be?"

Rosemary simpered mysteriously, but Alfonso, done up as the Scarlet Pimpernel in white wig behind Liz, answered for her.

"Jean Harlow, right?"

Rosie nodded happily, posed with a hand on one slim hip, then darted back into the crowd.

Liz turned to Alfonso. "I can't believe it."

"She does look like Harlow. I never noticed that."

"Not that! Her weight. She must have lost . . . thirty pounds."

"Thirty-*five*!" Rosemary announced behind them, rushing to greet more unrecognizably attired guests.

Liz shook her head in a daze. Rosemary, outglittering the copious rhinestones that bedizened her sleek 1930s gown, flitted away like a jeweled Art Noveau dragonfly. Liz herself had thrown caution to the winds at the costumers and had come as Scarlett O'Hara in the family drapes, complete with hoopskirt. The outfit had its impractical side, but when the photographers from *People* magazine came, Liz merited a solo shot sitting amid her cartwheel of green velvet skirt looking up the spiral staircase while the photographer shot down.

"Nice move," approved Alfonso when Liz had been released back to the mainstream of the party. "You should look like Vivien Leigh."

"It never occurred to me," Liz retorted, tossing the black sausage curls massed at her neck and shoulders, thankfully just a hairpiece. Being a Southern belle required toting around a lot of weight and putting forth enough effort to drive a ditchdigger, she concluded, wondering how much of the iron butterfly mentality had been impressed on Rosemary growing up in the South.

Con O'Connor was there, surprisingly, in cowled brown serge robes.

"Miss Liz," he greeted her.

"Well, fiddle-dee-dee, if it isn't Friar Tuck!" Liz guessed back.

Con eyed her gently swaying skirt, then the ample curve of his rope-tied belly. "It looks as if this is as close as we can get to exchanging courtesies this evening, and the bar is even harder to cozy up to."

But he managed to do it religiously, Liz noted out of the corner of her eye that evening, her guarding gaze torn between watching the frantic Rosemary dip in and out of the crowd and Con's solid figure, which always hovered near the portable bar with its lineup of bottles of all strengths and descriptions.

Alfonso did not partner her exclusively that night. Partly it was the blamed skirt, which kept beaux at arm's length. Partly it was Liz's anxious abstraction.

"I can't tell if you're looking for someone more important to talk to or—" he complained once.

Liz fluttered her prop fan nervously. "It's Rosemary; she's so different, so animated and thin and brittle."

"She's showing off her new figure." Alfonso peered over the tightly-packed heads around them to target Rosemary. "And worth showing off, I'd say. She looks all right now. Better watch out for your *Sunrise* spot."

Liz ignored him. "And Con, Con looks . . . I don't know. Pasty and desperate. Driven."

"Driven to the bar. What's new? You're not your brother's or your sister's keeper. Why don't you forget them for once, and concentrate on me?"

She did as he suggested, whirling suddenly and batting her eyelashes in time to her fan. "Why, Sir Percy, I had *no* idea you were feelin' lonesome. You must come to Tara sometime and let me show you the premises. . . ."

"Premises, premises," he quipped. "Why don't you just start with your modest New York apartment, Miss Scarlett? I think the Civil War is over."

The cabdriver had great fun at the expense of Liz's skirts. She was glad as she stuffed the yards of green velvet onto the grimy cab floor that her rented gown would be cleaned by someone else.

Alfonso, despite looking like an overcivilized bullfighter in his late eighteenth-century courtier's outfit, was as happy as she to slip out of their outmoded garb. They left a trail of waistcoat and petticoat and stock and stocking in the pale living room and down the hall to the bedroom.

There, they regarded each other breathlessly, standing naked on either side of the pedestaled bed until Alfonso put a knee down on the comforter and reached out a hand; Liz met him in the middle.

Maybe it was the make-believe quality to the party, their artificial costumed roles, the champagne that had flowed like sea foam, but there was a giddy, playful edge to their lovemaking that night. Their hands and faces reached for each other, clung, slid along the accustomed shape and texture of their respective bodies as if searching out the costume behind the discarded costume.

Alfonso lay passive for once under her ministrations, the soft sojourn of her lips across his skin, her ceaselessly caressing hands. He was still even when she mounted him and rode him rhythmically, faster and faster, until they seemed to be racing each other to some unseeable goal.

Liz tumbled off and let him resume the lead again, watched his dark eyes glimmering above her like negative stars, watched them fall to earth, to her, as he bent near to merge his mouth and breath with hers, always his fingers stroking within her and she moving with them until they were suddenly joined, genitals to genitals, and she didn't know how or when or if it would stop.

Motions, calculated, unbidden. Moments wild and docile. Moving, moving, within, without; making love. Knowing old touches that incite, discovering new ones that offer even more . . . and always, unspoken, the common, divided goal. For him, for her. Release, ceaseless motion, ceaseless release . . . and then, yes, yes, yes—this time! Together, the Everest scaled from opposite sides, the air wire-thin and metal-cold harder to breathe. Panting, panting, panting and now . . . him, her—oxygen exploding into stars, reeling backward down the visionless slopes, back to base camp, back to metabolic baseline, down, down, down into blank collapse.

"Did you come?" Alfonso asked, rolling away from her into the endless white of rumpled sheets.

"Are you kidding? Was that a simultaneous—"

"You bet." He laughed and lightly slapped her rump as she rolled over on her stomach and braced her chin with a doubled-over pillow. "You want something from the fridge? A beer or something?"

He was already silently walking away, over the thick carpet as if through snow. She had a sudden flashing vision of Alfonso, his Latin face haloed by artic fur, a small figure in the endless ice and snow, growing smaller, smaller and colder by the second. She didn't know why she thought that, when her body felt so warm and well-worn and he seemed so near. Somewhere, sled dogs howled.

"Want something?" He was at the door, naked, waiting, impatient.

"Yes," Liz said, then paused. "Surprise me."

— Chapter 46 —

"You ever hear of ERA?"

Liz raised her eyebrows. It wasn't like Con O'Connor to make an overobvious joke, even in a bar, especially at McGillacuddy's, where he had a certain reputation as raconteur to uphold.

"You ever hear of the Declaration of Independence?" she asked back.

Con frowned, troubled. "I don't mean the Equal Rights Amendment—or the realty company. It has something to do with television." Liz still looked blank. "Anyway, the ERA report says I get good vibes from typical television viewers; that's what Hoffman told me."

"Oh, *that* ERA. It stands for Entertainment Response Analysis. Some outfit makes bundles wiring average citizens to electronics, playing them popular songs or showing them TV personalities, then recording their unconscious reactions. It's called 'psychographing.' There was some dustup a few years ago about the morality of using it. I mean, people have lost their jobs because of the silly system. It drives the civil libertarians crazy. Big Brother blues, and all that stuff. So you got a high ERA rating; that doesn't surprise me. I could have told them that for free."

"Yeah." Con knocked back another slug of whiskey. "And Alfonso scored high, too."

"Alfonso always scores high."

Con gave her a sharp look, then took a second swallow of whiskey instead of saying anything more. Alfonso hadn't been coming around in the last two weeks. Liz was beginning to taste a slightly bitter sense of abandonment she knew better than to let show. Maybe Alfonso was just overworking.

Con cleared his throat. "So this ERA thing can get people fired?"

"Or demoted or consigned to the lower levels of Hades. I'm surprised Hoffman is using that kind of witch-doctory research. Serious newsmagazine producers shouldn't depend on measuring how many nerve cells jump when a familiar face appears on TV. And it can boomerang. Supposedly Howard Cosell and Barbara Walters are *dis*liked, yet they stir such a strong response that people *like* to watch them anyway. Are you going to do a column on ERA? If so, get the bastards. They don't have any stake in the ethics of TV journalism, believe me."

Con clutched his drink more tightly than usual. "Liz . . . I heard— They say *you* didn't register well on the ERA." He tilted his glass bottoms up and anxiously looked for the waiter.

"They would do me, too, wouldn't they?" Liz mused. " It's kind of a backward compliment, isn't it, considering what I think of ERA? Or maybe I was just having sour grapes in advance."

"But what does it mean?"

"Who told you?"

"Manzelli told me about my, er, score, and mentioned that Alfonso and me were the highest. I heard about you . . . through an open door. Hoffman came in after me, and I hadn't left the outer office yet."

Liz sat back. "That means more than the stupid ERA report—that nobody's told me. Even TV producers don't like to bear bad news. So little Lizzie didn't get a passing grade. . . ."

The waiter deposited Con's fresh drink with his usual flourish. Con waggled his eyebrows in the direction of Liz's glass and the waiter retreated to get another. Liz didn't object.

"Maybe you should talk to Manzelli about it," Con suggested.

"I could. But he'd just dance around the subject. With Danny about to ride off into the sunset, everything—everybody—is up in the air. Apparently Alfonso and I were competing for the head anchor spot. Guess this puts Alfonso in the lead now."

"He's a slick one."

"Yes." Slick and sorely missed, she thought.

She went back to her apartment and made two phone calls. First she tried Alfonso's loft, but his answering machine suavely reported that Alfonso "can't come to the phone right now" and asked her to leave her name and number. She didn't bother.

Then she tried her agent. Jerry Silver had worked with her since she came to New York, booking innumerable lucrative speaking engagements, smoothing out the details of her magazine interviews, negotiating her all-important network contracts.

His secretary suggested she call back, but Liz insisted her business was urgent.

"Liz. What's happening?"

"That's what I was calling to ask you. Any progress on my contract?"

"They're stalling."

"I knew that. Supposedly because they don't know what they're going to do with the show. But how long can they stall?"

"As long as they like, if you want to keep working. Look, Liz, I'll call you if anything changes. Until then . . . what's to say?"

"Okay. Thanks, Jerry."

Liz hung up feeling she'd been given the brush-off, feeling that nobody wanted to look her in the eye or tell her the truth.

Workdays were apparently calm. Danny played out the last days of his reign in character—aloof, condescending, unruffled. Alfonso only came to the studio for his live introductory segments, dashing out as soon as he finished. Once Liz managed to catch him in the makeup room with only Bessie in attendance, and struck.

"Alfonso! *Dune* is debuting for the Christmas trade. I thought we might see it."

"*Dune*, huh? Great book. Uh, say, Liz . . ." Alfonso divested himself of his blue plastic makeup cape. (Girls got pink, although Liz often appropriated the blue just to be difficult.) He edged Liz into the hallway where Bessie couldn't hear, and leaned what would have been uncomfortably near, except Liz had become accustomed to his physically crowding presence.

"Look, Liz," he said, seeming to forget that he almost never called her "Liz." The name sounded harsh and alien from his lips. She realized she liked being called "Elizabeth" and should have taken the longer form of her name for her TV byline, except that it was too impossibly late for that now, too impossibly late for perhaps a lot of things now.

"Maybe it's best," he went on, reminding her of someone long ago who'd once told her what the best, most sensible thing to do was, only she couldn't remember who or what or just when . . .

"Maybe it's best that we cool it for a while. There's a lot of change coming for the show. We should back off and let events take their natural course, you know? Reevaluate later. Besides . . ." He took her icy wrist and shook it encouragingly, the way some doctors will when they've just told you bad news. ". . . maybe we've been seeing too much of each other, been getting too inbred. You know what I mean? We should widen our horizons, see new people—"

Liz tore her wrist out of his lax, warm grasp. "I assume you've already taken your own advice. Is that why your phone is always on automatic answer?"

"Liz," he reproached, not really answering her. "You're a big girl; you know things change." Big girl. All grown-up, grown-up, grown-up.

"Funny. I don't think you ever have." And she was striding down the hall, her anger pulsing through her veins in time to the pound of her heels on the flat industrial carpeting. Thump-thump, thump-thump. Left, right; left, right. Left ventricle, right ventricle. A heart didn't break; a heart got aggravated to death.

Con O'Connor caught up with her on the set, where she'd fled for—ironically—some peace, quiet, and distance. On the set, she was a different person, a serious professional whose first priority was to function smoothly.

"Lizzie."

Why did he call her that? She hated it.

"McGillacuddy's today? Got a fresh script." He patted his breast pocket, which crackled.

Liz leaned back while the union sound man clipped her tiny mike to her neckline. "Can't today, Con," she said in light, taut tones. "I've got too much to do."

She'd never turned him down, a sign of her weakness, not his. He looked like a little boy she'd just told to play by himself and it was raining outside and there was nobody else or anything interesting left to do. He crumpled, like his clothes, looking pale and gray and empty.

"I'm sorry, Con, but—" My God, her voice was going to break, as if Alfonso Delgado was actually worth crying over, for Christ's sake. "I can't, Con." Sharp, final, like a parent saying no. At last. Liz speaking like a parent, not looking back. Firm and final. It's for the best.

Con slid into his chair without another word. Liz was busy paging through her script one last time, wondering why a group of anonymous test subjects had disliked her so much, wondering why she disliked herself so much more than she disliked Alfonso at the moment. But then, he hadn't been a fool and he didn't stand to lose anything he cared about—like a job, a certain self-pride, a good lover.

The show went through its scripted paces, and Liz moved with it, amazed by the superficial level of concentration it took to keep her functioning apparently smoothly.

She went home right after the show, even though Janice raised her eyebrows when Liz sailed out without even a glance at the usual white-bond mountain of correspondence. "Dear Miss Jordan. I really like what you said about (fill in the blank). My high school class is investigating careers, and I wonder if you would tell me what it's like to be a famous woman on TV. Does it take much training? Did you have to go to graduate school? Does Teen Board modeling at your local department store help? (et cetera, et cetera, et cetera)"

In her apartment, Liz found herself wondering where Kitty was, and if she was happy with Stephanie. She wondered, for that matter, where Stephanie was—it had been a long time since they'd contacted each other—and Steve. Where was he? Probably not in Philadelphia. She went to her closet and unzipped the heavy plastic bag, pulling out a supple black-and-white furred sleeve.

Mink did not make a very comforting pet. She zipped up the bag again and wandered into the dim media room. For kicks she rewound the tape of that morning's show and sat in the darkness watching it, watching herself. She looked and sounded perfectly normal, but that was off-putting to TV-watching America, according to ERA. Not good enough. And *that* was off-putting to Alfonso Delgado, friend to the famous, lover to the successful, ex-everything to the weak link.

She spent the weekend sulking in her apartment, thinking about calling home, about Rosemary or Con. In the end, she called

Alfonso, at midnight Saturday. When his recorded voice said he couldn't come to the phone right now, she hung up with relief. If he had answered in person, she would have hung up anyway. She didn't know what to say to him—perhaps she never had.

Manzelli called her at two o'clock Sunday morning, an hour before her trusty alarm went off, his voice barking with city-editor urgency. She felt oddly transported to some other bed and time, to being on call like a news reporter again.

"Have you heard?" he demanded gruffly.

"No. I haven't been near the TV or read any papers this weekend."

"Some weekend," he commented. "Con O'Connor died yesterday. Heart. A drinking buddy found him collapsed at his typewriter at home. I guess we all knew he drank heavily. I've already pulled all the tape on him we have and we're editing it now. The limo'll come by for you in half an hour. We want you to write and deliver the obit from the show for him. You seemed to know him best."

She did it. She pulled herself together, dressed in something, got to the studio, and worked wildly until airtime to interweave the film on Con, the facts of his life the producers had researched, her own numbed grief, into one compact "package" for *Sunrise*.

Everyone on the set gathered around her after the show was over, as if she were the focal point for their own sense of shocked loss. Great job, Liz, they said in chorus, looking sympathetic. Great job. That's what it all was. A job. For Alfonso. For Con. For herself. She remembered Con's gradual graying look as he tried to juggle both newspaper and television tensions and over-commitments, his habitual overweight, his legendary drinking. He was the very model of a modern newsman, doomed to meet the reporter's massive coronary at forty three or fifty one. According to the record, Con had been forty eight. No one could have stopped him; he was Casey Jones and the iron-wheeled train was set in its arterial tracks.

For not the first time, Liz wondered about a profession that accepted the martyrdom of its men and the disposability of its women.

Liz mulled over her career, what to do about her negative ERA rating, how to give Alfonso a run for his money on *Sunrise*. She had a very personal stake now in showing him he had underestimated her. She couldn't get off the show to attend Con's funeral on Tuesday. By then the mail had started coming in. Through some unforeseeable fluke, her obituary for Con had stirred the viewers. Liz herself hardly knew what she had written or said, except that it had come from the honestly stricken heart. She had recorded it on her VCR but couldn't bear to play it back. For her, the living, to bask in glory for her last publicly private words to the dead seemed macabre. *ah, yes, all at once.*

Then, Friday afternoon of that same dreadful week, Myrtle called. Liz's father had suffered a massive stroke. He died before she got there Saturday night. On a gray November Tuesday a week after Ronald Reagan had been elected president for a second term, ✓ Liz stood in the icy, relentless wind amid the melancholy rattle of tumbling leaves and watched Zachariah Jordan's body lowered into the cold autumn earth of Turtle Bend. *1908 – 1986*

— *Chapter 47* —

Christmas was coming. Nineteen eighty-four, *the Orwell year* of doom, had come and almost gone with only the usual landmarks—death and taxes. Ansel Adams had died, and Truman Capote, Richard Burton, Ethel Merman, Lillian Hellman, and Peter Lawford. Women had achieved new, dubious landmarks of equality in the political arena: Geraldine Ferraro became the first woman vice presidential candidate of a major political party— and lost the election; Margaret Thatcher survived an attempted assassination; Indian leader Indira Gandhi didn't. In 1984 Ronald Reagan was reelected president, to no one's surprise, and Minnesota's pride at providing native sons for national office faded with Walter Mondale's resounding defeat. Taxes had been the issue that had fueled the seemingly endless campaign, that and the federal deficit, which also seemed endlessly self-propagating.

The *Sunrise* editors were readying tape of all these events for a year-end roundup. Sound tracks of "The Way We Were," "Memories," and "Happy Days Are Here Again" leaked from assorted editing rooms, bathing the *Sunrise* staff in premature nostalgia.

For there was still Christmas to celebrate. The *Sunrise* set was decked in cherry red from the banks of poinsettias behind the anchor desk to the artificial hearth-glow warming the Christmas interview set.

Liz had settled into numb but dogged routine, waiting for the ax by running for the winner's circle. There was no reason to take time off to go home for Christmas. With her father dead and Myrtle resuming contact with her own, remote relatives, Turtle Bend was finally and firmly in Liz's past. So she held down the

Sunrise fort, intending to fight to the last woman, herself. Her coanchors these days were a revolving sequence of razor haircut—topped young men from around the country, all vying for a permanent spot on the show. Life was chaotic with new greenhorns at her right hand day after day, but nothing could disturb Liz's balance. She handled the confusion with cheerful stability. Even Alfonso cast her puzzled glances when he sat and fiddled with his scripts the moments before he went on camera. She ignored him. Maybe the *Sunrise* anchor job was the most poetic form of justice for Alfonso, she had decided. Maybe she didn't want it.

So what did she want? Liz didn't know. And then one afternoon she went home, back to her cold, quiet apartment. It was a mess. She was having the expensive upholstered gray velvet bedroom walls torn out, expunging the most intimate traces of Alfonso. Plain paint and wallpaper would suit a girl from Turtle Bend well enough in the future, she had concluded.

There, among the square white envelopes of social invitation and long, business-size envelopes of solicitation, was a large manila envelope with the return address of a Turtle Bend attorney.

Liz sat right down to open it, expecting—and finding—her father's will. There was no letter from Myrtle, just a copy of the will, its legal length folded a grandoise four times. She read it, not surprised to find the house had been left to Myrtle. She'd always known Myrtle would outlive her father, and so, apparently, had he.

There wasn't much for assets. A small life insurance policy would go to her, and any mementos she cared for from the house or newspaper. And the newspaper. The *Turtle Bend Sentinel*. Liz's hands shook a bit as she read the interminably long paragraph pertaining to it.

Neil Wetland had gotten it, all of it, lock, stock, and copy desk. Liz had expected him to be awarded some share in the paper, some interest, a percentage. She had seen that handwriting on the wall long ago. But *all* of it—Her entire body was shaking now. Liz realized that at the back of her mind lately she'd been nursing a vision of herself returning to Turtle Bend, of continuing the Jordan tradition of donning the hat of lady editor. It was an obvious, graceful exit from the present career cul-de-sac, a way to leave an already-lost *Sunrise* without losing face. Now even that escape route had closed.

Her eyes followed the serified type one more time.

> Because my only child, Elizabeth, has done so well
> in the world, both financially and in establishing a career
> in New York City, I am leaving my life's work, the

Sentinel, to one I know will have the desire to continue the tradition I started. Neil Wetland has worked beside me for many years, earning my gratitude in the past and present. My hope is that he will continue to enhance the paper's honor in the future.

It wasn't the money; a small-town newspaper is worth its editor's keep and his pride, but that's about it. It was to be so totally left out, merely because she'd been successful, as if to have been dependent or disappointing merited more regard from a parent. Liz let the will fall from her limp hand to the floor. She pressed her fanned fingers to her eyes. Sitting there on the expensive little hallway bench that was so preciously decorative no one had sat on it before. Miraculously, it held her weight.

Something was coming together, rapidly, like tape sped through a monitor on fast rewind; fragments of the past and present, jagged as mirror-silver dagger, painful to see, flashed blinding insight deep into her brain. It was all coming together, or coming apart. Love and approval, loyalty or betrayal . . . The hall was fashionably dim. If Liz peeked through her fingers, it seemed filled with more than was really there. A small brown-and-white figure sat by her feet, endlessly watching, endlessly wagging. A man stood by the mirror, softened by weight and age, watching her sadly over one slumped shoulder. Was it Con? Z.J.? In the mirror itself, a slim, dark young man with a Mephistopheles mustache smirked slyly over the old man's shoulder.

Liz spoke to them, really to only one of them. "You . . . used . . . me. That's all I was to you, something you needed for a while, something you saw you would lose the use of. So you replaced me. You *replaced* me! Daddy . . ." She was crying aloud now. Everything she had done to make her father proud of her, her achievements, had been a waste. He would have liked a well-baked cherry pie better. He really hadn't expected more than that from her, and, getting more than he had expected, he ignored it. Love and approval. No wonder the loss of Whizzy had been so wrenching. With him had gone Liz's childish sense of security. No wonder she had overlooked Alfonso's cynical outlook; he had seemed to approve of her, and her success, as Steve had not. As her father had not, ever. How sad—she had been trying to live up to an image of herself she thought her father held, and the more she strove for it, the farther she moved from the very person she sought to get closer to.

Liz picked up the will, refolded it carefully, and put it back in its manila envelope. "Maybe I don't need approval as badly as anyone thinks I do," she said, taking satisfaction in the slight echo the hall made of her words.

— Chapter 48 —

The Rolodex on Liz's lacquered bedroom desk flipped open to the B's. She impatiently riffled through to the M's, found the entry, and dialed. It had been so long since she had called Rosemary that she had forgotten the number. Guilt twanged like an out-of-tune guitar string in her gut. She remembered Con's face the last time she had seen it—lost and pulling away. But he had been lost long before he'd found her.

There was no answer. Liz hung up, frustrated. She finally wanted to talk, about herself, about what really mattered, and there was no one to talk to. She tried Rosemary's number at impatient intervals all afternoon and evening, and still got no answer.

Then her abominably early bedtime intervened. She went to sleep hungry and unsatisfied in every other possible way as well. As soon as she was back in her network office after the next day's show, she flipped open her work Rolodex, her spirits rising, planning a spur-of-the-moment lunch at . . . at the Rainbow Room; why not? Of course Rosemary would go; she really didn't have anything else pressing to do, and if she didn't want to eat, they could go look at the giant Christmas tree in Rockefeller Center, snigger at Liz's competition at NBC, and settle for a light snack at the Russian Tea Room. . . .

No answer. Liz put down the receiver reluctantly, aware of how badly she need to talk to somebody by the anguished, angry writhe of her stomach. Then, suddenly galvanized, she flipped open the Manhattan phone book—no light task—and found Joel Martin's business listing. "Model People." Liz smiled at the appropriateness of the phrase to Rosemary and Joel's photo-spread lives as well as his talent agency. She dialed and was put through immediately.

"Liz. Happy holidays. What can I do for my most glamorous anchor lady?"

"Same to you, Joel. I was afraid you and Rosemary were out

of town for the holidays—" There was no comeback murmur, so she went on. "I haven't been able to reach her at the co-op; maybe I didn't call at the right times."

"I really can't say, Liz. We're not together anymore."

"Not together?" She didn't quite understand.

"I haven't lived at the co-op for a month. We're splitting. Maybe she's visiting her family or a fat farm. I just don't know."

"Oh. Well, I'm sorry." That didn't seem the right thing to say; Joel didn't sound in need of consolation, just brisk and bored with the entire subject. "Do you know anyone who might know where she is?"

"I never kept up with Rosie's friends. I don't know that she had any, besides you. Sorry I can't help you, Liz. If you need a nice-looking escort for some semipublic New Year's bash, though—"

"Thanks—but no. I'm keeping my own company these days."

They exchanged brief good-byes; all the while Liz's imagination twisted itself into a sick knot of anxiety. She sat for a long while with her palm still on the receiver, reluctant to unhand the illusion of communication and control.

She rose and put on her red wool coat—some people never learn, she thought ruefully, remembering the unfashionable precursor of this coat she had worn more than a decade ago in Minneapolis. Liz was abstracted in the long elevator ride to the main floor. Christmas was coming, and the elevators were jammed with people going to and fro on shopping expeditions. Cabs were commandeered for the same purposes. Liz stood on the cold curb and waved until she finally attracted one. Maybe red coats weren't so dumb.

At Rosemary's co-op, she had the doorman ring and ring, long after it was obvious there was no one there.

"I'm just worried," she explained. "I can't reach her, and no one knows for sure that she's out of town."

"It's Christmas, Miss," he explained in turn. "Lots of people leave town."

"I know, but . . ."

A passing man paused, standing in his impeccable chesterfield, looking mildly helpful. "Are you looking for the woman who was taken away in the ambulance, perhaps?

"When?"

"A couple of evenings ago."

The doorman nodded consideringly. "Not my shift."

"Was she blond?"

"Very blond," the man answered. "Very pale. She looked sick. I think a neighbor found her and called the ambulance."

"Do you know the neighbor, the hospital?"

He shook his head and moved on, having put his penny of goodwill into the Christmas pot. Liz looked beseechingly at the doorman, but he shook his head also.

"This is too big a building, Miss, to find out. Why don't you try the hospitals?"

Liz let him hail her a cab, went back to her apartment, and with fingers colder and stiffer than they'd been since she left Minnesota, sat in her coat by the phone and paged through the Manhattan yellow pages to H.

"The hospitals." There were so many in Manhattan, and all overbooked for Christmas. Most of the voices on the other end of the line were harried, curt. They had no time to search out patients who only "might" be there.

"No, no Rosemary Martin here. *Albert* Martin. Have you tried a maiden name, ma'am? Sometimes people get rattled when they're sick."

"I don't know it. . . . Thanks." And she dialed the next hospital, and the next.

"Her name is Martin. Mrs. Joel. Or she could be listed just as Rosemary Martin." How fleeting was fame. No one reacted to the name that had once beamed into their morning lives every day of the week. Rosemary Martin. Liz could have been inquiring about Mary Smith.

Finally, a slim reaction.

"Martin." *Tsk.* "Well, yes, we list an R. Martin. Emergency two nights ago. Strange, I don't see a room assigned. Perhaps they simply released her or sent her somewhere else. We're extremely hard up for beds right now."

"I'm sure that's her," said Liz, who wasn't. "There must be some record. . . ."

"Oh, yes! We did keep her, but not in the regular rooms or wards. There simply is no room at the inn this time of year. She's here. Try ER."

"ER?"

"Emergency room."

"She's still there?"

"That's what the records say."

Thanking the nurse effusively, Liz hung up, grabbed her purse, and headed onto the street again to trawl for another taxi. It was getting dusky; Christmas lights twinkled in shop windows or laced sidewalk trees in tiny golden strings. Liz barely noticed them, watching the street signs crawl by in the bumper-to-bumper traffic, twisting her cold, gloved hands around her purse strap.

St. Bartholomew Hospital was rambling, old, and overcrowded, like most inner-city hospitals, and Manhattan was all inner-city. Liz battled the hubbub and the mobs of waiting people, all apparently as anxious as she, until she found the emergency room.

"Rosemary Martin?" she inquired, wondering if another death was to be added to 1984's grisly public and personal toll.

"Martin . . ." The nurse, once crisp, was now as wilted as used Christmas wrapping paper. "Oh, yes." She sighed. "You a relative?"

"Friend."

The nurse's lips tightened. "Sad case. We had to keep her here in emergency; there were no free beds anywhere, and the damage has been done. She hasn't been able to name a personal physician, so—"

"Can I see her?"

"Of course." The woman led Liz through a frenzied interweaving of whining children, wailing women, and street-shocked men, past winos and bedraggled ethnics and white-clothed harried nurses and doctors bespattered here and there with Christmas red. In a green-tiled room along with three strangers, Rosemary lay on a gurney, a makeshift curtain veiling her from the others.

"Rosie!" Liz, after a headstrong fight to find her, found herself approaching the bed gingerly. "What's wrong with her?" she asked the nurse confidentially.

"Stroke," the woman pronounced, reading the chart dangling from the gurney's foot. "Some paralysis on the left side of her face and arm. Looks like it could have been a lot worse."

The nurse bustled back to the busy hallway; Liz edged closer. "Rosemary?"

She still looked thin, marvelously flat under the hospital sheets, and pale, typecast for the role of *Camille*. But her face was empty, Liz thought, just empty. Vacant of emotion, expression, recognition.

"Rosie . . .?"

The blue eyes glittered suddenly. Tears.

"Liz," Rosemary said. Only it came out "Lhish," almost as if she were mimicking Foster Brooks playing a lush.

"I couldn't find you, Rosie. No one knows you're here."

Rosemary's eyes turned to the ceiling while tears welled in her lower lids and overflowed slowly down her cheeks to her ears. "It'sh jusht as well."

At first Liz thought Rosemary was sedated, and eyed the IV dripping slow sustenance into her arm. And then she understood. Paralysis of the face and left arm, the nurse had said. Liz saw the mouth pulled low on one side, the flaccid, thin cheek, the drooping eyelid. Rosemary's face was a schizophrenic Greek mask of comedy and tragedy in the flesh—one side up, one side dragged remorselessly down.

"How are you feeling?" She put her hand on Rosemary's arm, the right one.

Rosemary's head shook slightly. Her hospital-flattened hair was lusterless. "Not good. I—" She laughed bitterly. "I'm a mesh, Liz." She laughed again, weakly hysterical. "An em-ee-essh-essh. It waz thoze damn injectionz. Lizzen to me. I z-z-zound drunghk."

Liz could barely understand her, and didn't know how to hide it.

"That damn quack." Rosemary swallowed, with difficulty, and took a deep breath for more air to speak with—Rosemary, who could once deliver a fifty word sentence on one breath if she had to. "Those shots. The doctor here was . . . livid." Rosemary gasped. "Livid ish better than 'furioush.' I have to pick what I shay now." The right side of her mouth quirked. "You okay, Liz?"

"Fine, fine." Liz was beginning to follow her slurred speech. "Does Joel know?"

"No. I don't want him to."

"When I called him, he said you were separated."

She nodded, painfully. "New actressh. Twenty-five. Fits his 'lifestyle' bedder, he says." Rosemary moved her head to survey herself downward with some difficulty. "I guess."

"But you need someone to help you with doctor bills. . . ."

Rosemary's head shook wearily. "No problem, Liz. Good alimony. Joel is generoush. That way."

"What about a decent doctor? Have you got a personal physician?"

There was a long pause while Rosemary's face twitched as she tried to manage an expression too complicated for her frozen musculature now. She sighed.

"Physhishun. Jusht that quack on Madison Avenue. . . . Who needs doctorz when you're bound for glory?"

"Maybe you can sue him."

"Shigned a paper. Can't. Can't do anything."

Liz sighed in her turn and wiped the tear tracks from Rosemary's face with the sheet edge. There was no visitor's chair; there was nothing to do but stand and lean over Rosemary like a doctor or a worried mother.

"I'm coming back, Liz," Rosemary articulated with determination. "I am coming back. I'm going to fight this. I'll be back and working. I will."

"Of course you will." Liz squeezed her right wrist, the good one. Rosemary's left arm lay crooked against her chest, like a broken bird wing. "Of course you will."

When Liz got back to her dark apartment, she sat down by the phone and started to call in a few favors. By the time his service had reached him at home, the eminent plastic surgeon Liz had once interviewed for the show was probably looking forward to rest and relaxation, not emergencies from remote acquaintances. But he recommended the best doctor in Manhattan to supervise Rosemary's recovery.

"It sounds like she'll do all right, if she has the spirit for it."

"She says she does, but doctor, it's such a long way back. Facial paralysis and speech impediment are real handicaps for a media woman, much worse than a few excess pounds that don't even show on camera. Why do women do such silly, self-destructive things?"

The surgeon sighed. Liz imagined he had a warm, home-cooked meal awaiting him, as well as the wife who made it, children, and a real, scent-dispensing pine tree decorated for the holidays.

"I've seen women want any number of silly, self-destructive things done, simply to look better in their own eyes, or that of the world. It's a superficial society out there, Miss Jordan, especially the performing world, and some of us buy the image. At any cost."

Image. Liz hung up. Hung up on image. Women did it; men did it; nowadays, even children did it. Packaging. Designer everything, from jeans to expensive smells. Looking good, feeling good, even if it kills you. You can't pinch an inch on a skeleton. Losing jobs, losing self-esteem, merely because of how one looked. Too old, too fat, too tough—and out. Boys and girls together, but mostly girls, born to be girls until senility.

Liz wasn't a maniac, success-obsessed imitation of a person, trendy to her toenails. Yet she, too, had been caught in the trap. Why? How was Liz Jordan hooked? What was her emotional drug of choice. What did she really need, and who? There weren't many people left to depend on, she knew. Except one, one person she'd always underestimated. Herself.

— *Chapter 49* —

It was the week before Christmas and all through the network not an executive was stirring, expecting some respite from the usual grim struggle for survival.

Liz hit Hoffman's secretary for a ten A.M. appointment right after the *Sunrise* sign-off.

"What can I do for you?" Hoffman asked when she came in and sat down.

"Not nail down my contract, apparently."

"I thought Vic Manzelli explained the delay is to your advantage."

"Only if I get the lead anchor job."

He was silent.

"So." Liz went on, "I've decided we might as well let the contract lapse."

"You want to leave *Sunrise*?" Hoffman sat up. He was used to tossing staff members overboard; he wasn't accustomed to them jumping off voluntarily.

"It's been a year; Danny's gone."

"You've, uh, done well."

"But the electrodes don't like me."

"I'm sorry you heard about that, Liz; it was a minor downturn in reaction. Nothing to seriously worry about. You're still a top candidate for the anchor spot."

"I'm still hanging on the line, out to dry, while you boys in the suits make up your mind. Sometimes I don't know how you even decide which color Guccis to buy—brown or black."

"Now, listen here. No need to get smart." Hoffman's dapper face frowned in sudden insight. "Does your agent know about this?"

"No, but you do. Maybe that's enough."

"Are you saying you're quitting *Sunrise* and the network?"

"No, but I'm close to it."

"What would make you stay?"

"Interesting work, that's all."

Hoffman was stumped. "Let me think about it, get back to you."

"Certainly." Liz smiled. Her heart was no longer doing a rat-a-tat fast enough to keep time with the Rockettes' chorus line. She felt calm, objective, together. "We can always talk about it."

That was on Monday. Tuesday she had lunch with Jay McGovern, who looked dumpier, more grizzled, and drank more than ever.

"You miss the money more than you think you would," he groused over his pasta. "And the politics in public television, sheesh!"

"You're still there."

"Yeah. Too old and too bald to change jobs now. It's not so bad. But Liz, you don't have a—how can I put it?—a hard-news profile. They usually look for academic types or more—"

"—serious—"

"—people. Yeah. Some might think you're just another pretty face."

"Well, I'm not bald, Jay, and I'm only thirty-four—only!—but I am serious about a career change, and I am a woman, which someone once pointed out to me long ago is an advantage in a profession that still confines women mostly to the clerical pool. Surely something could be worked out."

"If you're serious." He looked up sharply, his mouth trailing pale fangs of spaghetti.

Liz smiled. She'd been making a regular habit of it lately. "I have never," she told Jay, "been more serious in my life."

"How can you do this to us? To me, to Barry, to the network!"

Manzelli was playing bad cop to the absent Hoffman's good cop, who would be called into play later. "We invested a lot in you; we made you, Liz! If another network is making a competing offer, you owe it to us to let us match it."

"I haven't talked to another network."

"I know how things work." Manzelli sat on his desk, looking harried. "A word passed along, an 'understanding' reached at lunch. You don't have to go into formal negotiations to flirt with other networks. I thought better of you, Liz."

Guilt rolled off her back like confetti. "What if I told you it wasn't a network, Vic?"

"Not a network? What are you up to? Jerry Silver doesn't even know."

"Talking behind my back? *Tsk, tsk.*"

"Come on, we've always kept in touch, been concerned about your career."

"My career. My career is me, Vic. Have you and Jerry ever considered that? That I might want to be a happy person, someone who likes her work and takes pride in it and who just doesn't have some knee-jerk instinct to go for the higher salary or the more visible job or the easier way out?"

"Liz, you're talking wild here. You can't just walk out like the network was some podunk station. Cool down. Think it over. We're always here to talk to, me and Barry. We're not ready to revamp *Sunrise* completely—"

"Oh, if I left it might throw things into a bit of a mess. Is that it? You need me to tide you over while you play with the male cast, then you replace me."

"Not true, not true, Liz. You know better."

But she didn't, she thought as she left his office? Alfonso was coming down the hall toward her, toward Manzelli's office. She could always duck into Darryl McComb's office, but decided not to. They passed, like leery ships in the night. When he was behind her and couldn't see her face, Liz tried a smile. It stuck. She wondered if Alfonso was smiling now.

Jay McGovern called her that night.

"They're interested. They've got some big plans to expand in the news and public service division. They want a woman of experience and stature. They hadn't thought of you—"

Liz laughed knowingly.

"—but they're interested. Can you get a day off for a powwow?"

"Saturday or Sunday."

"Not good."

"Noon to nine, then."

"Better. I'll set it up." Jay paused. "Liz, you really want to do this? Public TV can be a graveyard for a network journalist. Shows get unfunded fast; big plans shrink to nothing. It's chancy."

"Sounds right up my alley," she returned cockily. "You know what the network is doing now that I hinted I'm quitting? They want me. They're scared somebody else is after me with a big offer and they want me. They only trust their own judgment when it's confirmed by someone else's, preferably a competitor."

"You're in a sweet position, then. Why don't you milk it? This is a real swing out over a mile-high chasm."

"I used to have fun swinging," she answered. "Besides, somebody big *is* trying to lure me away from the network."

"You're kidding? Who?"

"Me, buster. Me."

Eight hours into Liz's grueling boardroom luncheon-into-evening grilling session, Larry Carver leaned back and fanned open the sheaf of her résumé.

Carver was a public television power, but not a household word the way Bill Paley or Roone Arledge was. His wife didn't make the photographic pages of *W*, and his annual salary didn't make *Fortune* magazine.

He leaned forward and looked at Liz. "I had no idea you'd done so many groundbreaking stories in the good old days at WBGO."

"Jay insisted I reveal every nook and cranny in my career. We all have to cut our journalistic teeth somewhere."

"You still got them?"

"I've brushed up on the news daily and floss regularly with the First Amendment."

The other executives around the mile-long conference table, one of whom—my God—was a woman, smiled.

Carver wasn't satisfied with a quick, cute reply.

"I must admit I had never thought of you as one of our more heavyweight journalists. . . . Prove me wrong. If you had carte blanche to cover an hour-long in-depth piece for a public television news special, what would be your topic?"

Trick question. Liz's mind rapidly replayed a decade's worth of major issues—Vietnam, the economy, starvation, AIDS, popped into her mind, then something controversial from the past.

"The abortion clinic bombings." Carver's face was carved from teakwood. "It's fascinating," Liz argued, "this domestic terrorism by people dedicated to preserving life; the way modern scientific developments in fetal research are challenging social perceptions of conception and pregnancy; the right to life and death and who has it. I dealt with it once. This time, I'd go back and do it right— for now."

"That's a pretty . . . touchy . . . subject." The lone woman delicately articulated what they all were thinking.

"You didn't ask me what was easy to cover, but what was important to cover. This is public TV, isn't it?" Liz asked in her turn. "Whose network is it, anyway?"

This time their smiles were wry, but she read agreement in them.

She called Jay McGovern at ten when what was left of her got home.

"This is the wreck of the Hesperus. I got the job."

"They told you already?" He sounded incredulous.

"Of course not. I just know I did. I stuck my neck out and they hung a W-2 form on it, so to speak. I don't even care that I'll hardly get any money."

Jay *harumph*ed into the telephone. "It's better nowadays, thanks mainly to my loud bitching. You should get a couple hundred thousand or so. They try to come at you with any less, you holler for Uncle Jay."

"Gee, maybe I can afford to keep my place. And my hair-dresser. Thanks, Jay; I mean it. I couldn't be happier."

It was one o'clock in the morning, two hours before she had to get up. The room was dark except for the phosphorescent clock face and the fancy seashell night-light plugged in near the bathroom door.

Liz was scared. She was an orphan of the dark. She had no father, no mother, no lover, no one but herself. Not even a dog or a cat. She was scared. She knew she wouldn't sleep again. She was telling Hoffman and Manzelli she was quitting tomorrow, she was going to do something with public TV. She might write a book. Oh, they'd go white over that one. She was leaving.

And she had been left. So she was alone now, and didn't like it. Rosemary was no help; Rosemary needed help, needed Liz to be strong. Liz was alone and she would make it, but maybe, maybe, she deserved one kind word from somewhere.

Liz picked up the phone and turned on the bedside lamp. Her Rolodex was across the room on the desk and she didn't want her feet to get any colder than they were. Cold feet. She chuckled. How perfectly Freudian of herself.

But she remembered the number. Remarkable, she thought as she dialed. What if she got a butcher in Queens? That was impossible. The exchange at least had been for Manhattan. Maybe there are some things that are impossible to forget.

It was vile manners to call someone this late, someone you hadn't talked to in too long, someone who might not even be there, or not be there alone, like you. Then she would say she was sorry and hang up. And later find somebody else, somewhere, to dial at one in the morning. Damn *Sunrise* job, didn't even allow her the latitude of waking up worried at three in the morning like everybody else. No, it had to be one. . . . It had to be you, it had to be—Ring. I looked around and finally found—Ring.

Tense suddenly, Liz froze to the phone, as paralyzed as Rosemary. Hang up, get off before you make an idiot of yourself. What would she say?

"Hello."

God, he was there. Maybe. Was it him, or a wrong number? Hang up. Ask. "Wendy?"

"Liz. How *are* you." He still sounded sleepy, but he had the name right.

"Oh, pretty . . . decent."

"Good to hear. I've been . . . wondering . . . about you."

"Me, too. I mean, I've wondered what you were doing, if you were in town."

"What's wrong, Liz?"

"Wrong? I'm just calling a little late, that's all."

"A lot late."

"Too late for friends?

"No . . . but something's happened. Has he—"

"Gone. And so is Daddy, and so is my network job. It's all gone, Wendy, every last bit of it. It makes me want to laugh, and it makes me want to cry, but most of all, it makes me want to talk to . . . someone."

"I said you could call. Why didn't you?"

"I feel . . . dumb."

"Yes?"

"I might cry!"

"That's what phones are for."

"You sound really awake now. I did it, didn't I?"

"Yup. Might as well talk; I'm not going back to sleep either."

"How did you know?"

"I've done it."

"Have you thrown it all away? Seen it just go, until there's nothing but you left?"

"Liz, that's life."

"And death. But that's the way it is. I feel like everything in my life has boiled down dry, to nothing, that there's nothing left that I believe in but me—"

"Funny, that's the part I always like best."

Liz clutched the phone. Her knees were drawn up under the sheet and she realized her feet were finally warm. Wendy was waiting on the other end of the line, calm, maybe a bit amused, very patient, for her answer.

"The part you always liked best." Liz thought, then smiled in the dark. She was getting damn good at it again. "Me, too."

About the Author

Carole Nelson Douglas is the author of the historical LADY ROGUE and the recent Del Rey fantasy EXILES OF THE RYNTH. She has retired from a newspaper career in Minneapolis/St. Paul to write fiction full time and now lives in Fort Worth, Texas, with her husband.